TELLING A THUMPER

Paul M. Fleming

Backbone Books LLC

ISBN-13: 9798333842527

Cover artwork and design by: Aaron Kim
Library of Congress Control Number: 2018675309
Printed in the United States of America

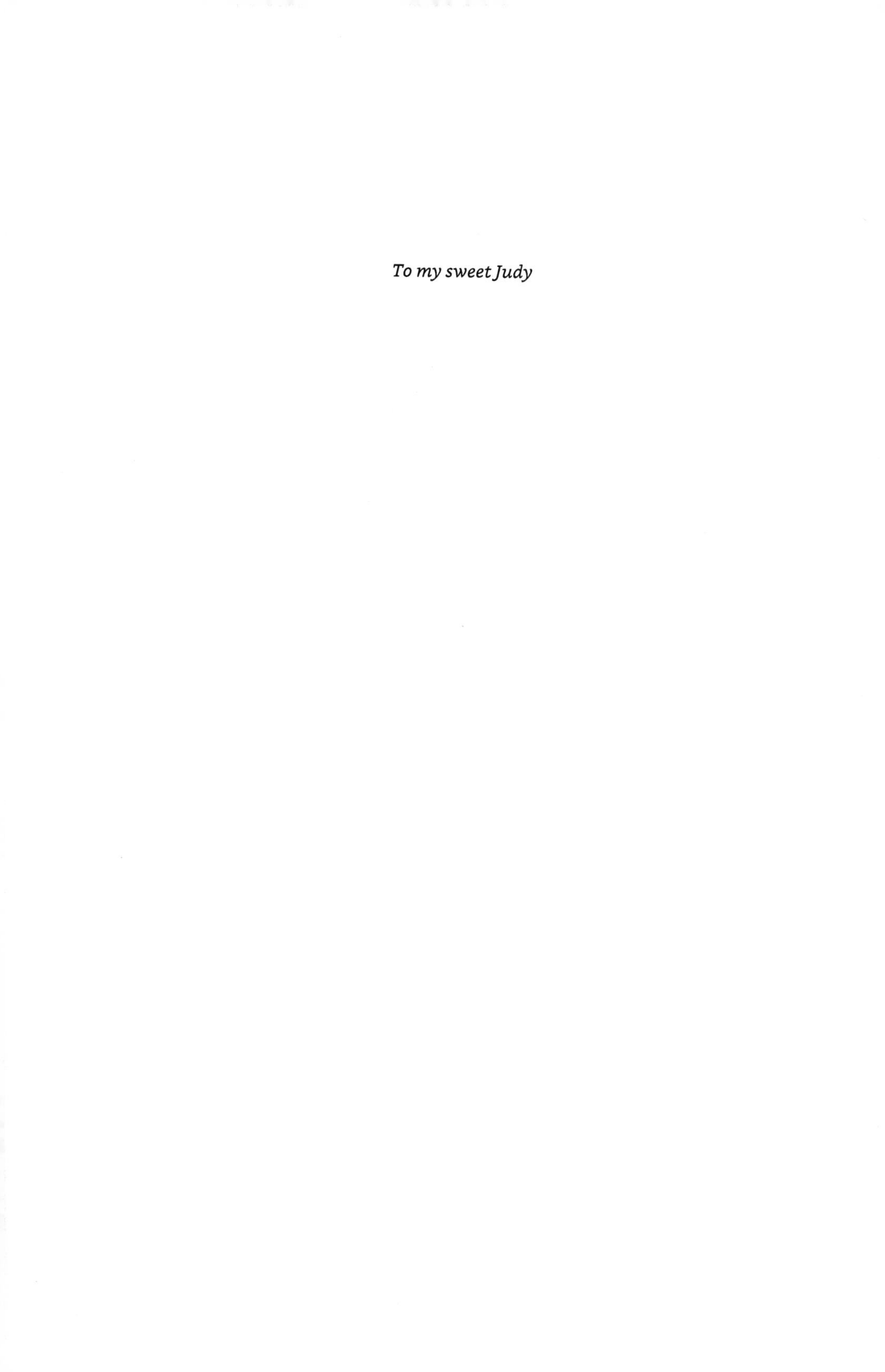

To my sweet Judy

Now I know what a ghost is.
Unfinished business, that's what.

- Salman Rushdie, 'The Satanic Verses'

Revenge is an act of passion; vengeance of justice.
Injuries are revenged; crimes are avenged.

- Samuel Johnson

Blind don't mean you can't, you know, listen.

- Stevie Wonder

A NOTE TO READERS

Justice versus vengeance. It's a tug of war that's always intrigued me. The former of course relies on righting a wrong through our legal system. But what if that system – for whatever reason – doesn't deliver the closure we desire? What if personal justice (revenge, vendetta, payback...) comes into play? That moment when the avenger becomes a perpetrator. From afar, many of us might be satisfied that the newest victim "had it coming to them." But what if it's more personal? Perhaps there's real pleasure experienced even when someone else suffers -- because closure has finally been delivered. Slippery slope.

Welcome to *Telling a Thumper.* A multi-generational family saga told entirely through the experience of a young blind protagonist. What he hears, feels, smells, and senses – as he seeks the truth, and ultimately justice. As his story unfolds, you'll encounter plenty of dark secrets – supplied in large part by a quirky ghost with a horrifying past.

Telling a Thumper paints a seamless 1970s backdrop with rich historical tidbits (music, politics, war, and culture clashes), adding depth to a blind teenager's perception of a tumultuous era. Combined with the steady unraveling of our spirit's story (including a tragic 1896 mining disaster) you'll be transported to an historical event that may very well leave you gasping for air.

I hope you enjoy *Telling a Thumper* -- a sweeping family mystery with a paranormal twist that unfurls entirely through a sightless protagonist. From his righteous quest for truth to a jarring conclusion that blurs the line between justice and retribution. Or is it simply *just revenge*?

Maybe it's better you decide that for yourself.

Paul M. Fleming

August 10, 2024

CONTENTS

CHAPTER 1

Fireworks and Flowers

Wednesday June 17, 1970 -- 8:00 AM

Colin lazily searches the bed for his pillow before pulling it gently to his bruised face. The cool touch of cotton soothes the prickly brush burn blanketing his forehead.

"Wake up. They're fighting again." The words are flat, emotionless. *"Maybe we should go down there."* Colin buries his face deeper into numbing tranquility.

The pillow peels away and slips from his fingers as that matter-of-fact tone questions, *"you hear that, right?"*

"Hear what, Pete?" Colin yawns, then retreats under the covers. He smells Pete's presence more intensely than usual. Charcoal. Like the sweet, smoky aroma from briquettes that his stepfather pours into the kettle grill perched on the back porch of their suburban Philadelphia home.

"Seriously, aren't you supposed to have extraordinary hearing?"

Colin tilts his head toward the sound of Pete's voice. He feels agitated. "They're having an adult argument. That's what adults do."

"Sometimes I think you enjoy their quarrels."

"Piss off, Pete."

"That was unnecessary."

Colin doesn't respond. He lacks the stamina to challenge Pete, especially when he's right…again.

"We should calm things down."

"We? What are *we* going to do?" Colin rolls to the side of the bed and reaches for the floor, his fingers groping through shag carpet. "Where are my socks? Did you take my socks?"

"My feet were cold. You know I get cold when I'm nervous."

Colin sighs, surrenders, and in one movement arches upward, swivels left and takes three measured steps to the dresser. His left-hand lands naturally on the knob of his sock drawer. Yanking it open, he grabs the first pair he touches, then launches backward onto the bed. "God, I hate walking on this carpet in bare feet. It feels like worms."

Pete suppresses a laugh.

Colin surrenders and chuckles too. "What's so funny?"

"Your socks don't match."

"Really? Well then... while I visit the lion's den why don't you hang out here for a while and rearrange my sock drawer."

"I should come. You might need me."

Colin responds sharply. "For what? They can't see or hear you."

"I'm doing the best I can, Colin. I don't even know why I'm here."

"Sorry Pete. It's all cool," he says sincerely. Colin slides to the foot of his bed. "I've got this." He reaches for his cane. Not there. Sweeps the carpet with his right foot. Nothing. "Pete?" Silence.

He mutters, "okay, we're playing this game again."

With the layout of this 100-year-old home lodged in his brain, Colin doesn't hesitate. Twelve steps from the edge of his bed to the doorway then straight into the hallway, where his feet escape the dreaded shag and embrace smooth hardwood. He veers slightly to the right then slows his pace as the timeworn floor sags and squeaks. Slender, agile fingers barely brush the wainscoting as if skimming precious piano keys with a legato touch. He approaches the master bedroom and pauses. The heavy oak double doors must be open. Sunlight pokes through, offering a slight contrast to the muted shadows that typically define his vision. From the bedroom, a gentle swish of curtains announces the arrival of a cool summer breeze. It carries the scent of sweet viburnum. Inhaling deeply, he leans against the roughly plastered wall. He savors smells from his mom's garden, one of the few sensory pleasures he gets from this house. A striking contrast to the odd collection of odors that sought any open window of their 4-unit apartment building in the Grays Ferry section of Philadelphia. Six years. That's how long It's been. Six years since he used to identify those colliding aromas flowing from scores of row homes on Gerrit Street. Six years...since the eviction from his childhood home.

He's 18 now. Moved here about a year ago when his mom, Hannah, married Ben, whose thriving family counseling practice provides a lifestyle and stability that Colin never knew growing up. Colin feels his mom took the convenient way out and settled for someone she doesn't love. And he's quick to correct people who refer to Ben as his father. "He's my stepfather, not my real father." There's a hole in Colin's life and he wants to fill it with the truth about Tommy Byrne – his real dad. In a few weeks it will be the Fourth of July, marking four years since his father disappeared. It's the worst time of the year for Colin. Like the hollow feeling he gets when the heavy percussion of fireworks reminds him of the way his dad used to "describe" their sounds by tracing the shape of each burst on his back. For some reason, this recent holiday has awakened Colin's desperate loss more deeply. Maybe it's because he's opening a new chapter in his life, still rejecting the possibility his dad abandoned him. Maybe it's because his mom has been able to move on.

His reflections are interrupted by Ben's muffled words, drifting up the stairs. "Keep your voice down. He'll hear you."

Colin approaches the narrow staircase six long strides away. His mother's whispered response is vague. He squats on the first step, presses his face into the spindles of the banister and listens attentively for her voice, but only hears Ben reassuring her, "he's ready. You'll see."

"That is a bummer. She really doesn't want you to go." Pete's flat voice nearly launches Colin through the spindles. Colin whispers through clenched teeth, "how many times have I

asked you not to sneak up on me like that?"

"Just trying to help."

"Well, I don't need help." On his feet, Colin guides mismatched socks down the stairs. Right foot, left foot, all the way down. Just like his dad taught him. Pete's voice comes from below.

"Land mine down here. There's a vacuum cleaner sitting in the foyer so move to the right unless you want to get impaled."

Colin refuses to answer but still follows Pete's instructions. He pivots sharply at the bottom of the steps, but nearly trips on the electric cord.

"Easy Colin. Smooth sailing now."

Colin breezes his way to the swinging kitchen door. He leans in. The door briefly snags against the threshold before surrendering to the weight of the high school graduate who has added ten pounds of pure muscle this summer. Stubborn hinges announce his arrival, but he is met with silence. The heavy scent of charcoal punctuates Pete's presence. *"It's okay Colin, they're hugging each other now."*

The next voice Colin hears belongs to Hannah. "Colin, sweetheart, did we wake you up?"

"Well, sort of...yeah, you did. What's going on with you two?"

His stepfather joins the conversation. "Sorry Colin, your mom's just a little nervous about you going off to college..."

"Mom, we talked about this. Swarthmore is a mile away. I'll be fine."

"Maybe boarding is not such a good idea. I mean, you could live here. I could drive you..."

"I...need...this. How am I supposed to take advantage of their music program when I'm living here? It's not that far and you can visit any time you want. You and dad always encouraged me to do this. No excuses, right?" he asks forcefully.

Born premature, Colin received high levels of oxygen for his underdeveloped lungs. By the time he was removed from the incubator the die had been cast. In Colin's case, excessive damage to the retina had triggered severe vision loss. Retinopathy of Prematurity was the official explanation for the mistake. Colin's parents took little consolation learning there were other "ROP" babies like him. None of the medical excuses mattered. Their baby was blind.

Still, as soon as he was old enough to understand and ask questions, his parents' message was relentless. *NEVER USE THIS AS AN EXCUSE.* Blaming any setback on his blindness was forbidden. It was a sentiment that made him grow strong and confident. By the time he was ten, he cherished their faith in him. He heard other kids complain about their parents and he couldn't relate. He was the lucky one.

Until the drinking.

Colin takes a slow, deep breath, runs his hands through his shoulder length hair and exhales.

"Honey are you okay?"

Pete's voice is further away. He's probably pacing behind Hannah and Ben now. *"No, you're not okay. Get it off your chest. Tell them you'd be a lot happier if Ben was out of her life."*

"I'm fine, really mom. Just need you to give me a little room here...like you used to do."

"A lot of room. Away from him...away from me."

"Listen," Ben interjects. "I want to have a proper conversation about this, but you know how crazy my Wednesdays get. I've got a ton of paperwork and dictation to catch up on and I still need to organize my office."

Colin cackles, "is it as sloppy as everything else around here?" His mother's muffled groan satisfies him. Ben firmly slaps his stepson on the back and says blandly, "I promise we'll talk."

Ben's even-tempered tone annoys Colin. As his stepfather's footsteps shuffle past him, Colin nastily mutters, "I don't need your counseling. Save it for your clients." He hears the familiar clack of Ben's shoes hitting rough clay tiles, then abruptly stopping.

"Your mom is giving him the evil eye...wagging her finger...and off he goes."

Ben's footsteps echo down the narrow side hallway that leads to his office. Colin hears the office door shut softly. He feels Hannah closing in. Braces for the hug. "I'm sorry we upset you, Colin. We're doing our best."

She feels more fragile to him. He softens his tone. "I don't care about him, but you just need to let go. Stop trying to fix everything."

She hugs him closer. "With all you've been through, sometimes I feel like you can't wait to get away from here." She lowers her voice. "Away from Ben. It's obvious. We both feel it."

"How many times can I say this, mom? Just because you've been able to move on doesn't mean I'm ready. But I still love *you*. I still need *you*." Teasingly, he says, "I'm counting on you to help me with my laundry and meals."

Hannah sighs, then also manages a more playful tone. "So, this is how it's going to be. What happened to that independent college freshman, huh?"

"You're making her cry. You're not helping the situation here."

"Mom, are you crying?"

"Good God, Colin you really do have a sixth sense." She gently pats his bruised forehead. "You're leaving this house just in time. You can't even stand up straight in that creepy basement. You need to be more careful when you're working out down there. And please, please, please take care of these." Her hands squeeze his fingers. "You treat them like your head, and you can kiss that music scholarship goodbye." Colin finds her shoulders and hugs his mother. She twirls a handful of his hair. "I'll be fine Colin, really. Even better when you get a haircut. You sure have your father's hair. Even more red if that's possible."

They are interrupted as Ben shuffles back into the kitchen, then pushes the swinging door forward toward the front of the house. The door remains open. "Hannah, did you put the vacuum cleaner away? We weren't finished...."

"No, no, I definitely left it out." Her voice trails off as she follows Ben out of the kitchen, the door swinging behind them. "I'm going crazy, where the hell is it?"

The kitchen is silent. Colin walks to the sink, feels for the strainer and grabs a clean glass. He slowly turns on the water, letting it run over his index finger until it turns cooler. He fills his glass, then drinks slowly. Colin lowers the empty glass and taps it gently on the countertop. Softly, he speaks. "Pete?" No answer. Still hushed, but more emphatic this time. "Pete!"

"I just tidied up a bit. Come on, you know I can't live with clutter. Besides there's no need to vacuum that hopeless mess of an office."

Colin drains the glass and places it in the sink. "She's freaking out enough as it is. I don't need you putting her over the edge." He walks effortlessly toward the kitchen door, far from surprised when he hears Pete rinsing the glass and placing it quietly back in the strainer as he responds, *"I apologize. I'll be more careful, I promise."*

Tilting his head toward the sound of the vacuum cleaner coming alive, Colin wearily adds, "...and I'm not leaving for college because I want to get away from you. Understood?"

"Fine. But perhaps there's something you need to comprehend as well."

"What is that supposed to mean?"

"Maybe it's <u>your</u> attitude that's 'putting her over the edge'. And that anger you allow to fester inside of you? Forgive my selfishness, but It leaves no space...for me."

Colin straddles the threshold and slumps against the door jamb. The window above the kitchen sink opens with that familiar squeak. The scent of sweet viburnum drenches the air.

CHAPTER 2

Black Hole

Wednesday -- 10:00 AM

Hours later, Colin follows his typical Wednesday routine. He slides onto the padded seat of one of four metal-framed chairs surrounding the round, wobbly kitchen table. Uneven layers of tattered tape and liquified adhesive stick to his gym shorts, refusing to release as he bends to tie the laces of his high-top Converse sneakers. Down the side hallway, he hears the muffled banter of Ben's monotonous dictation. Outside he listens to his mom's 1965 Mustang backing down the steep driveway, scraping the front bumper as it dips into the street. Colin cringes as metal grinds concrete. Despite needing a new front suspension, his mom still insists her Mustang is "the coolest car I'll ever drive." Every Wednesday or Thursday she volunteers at a food bank in the city and seldom returns until late afternoon.

This is Colin's time. First, a workout, then piano practice. He misses his friends and the demands of school, but his summer routine keeps him plenty busy. He stands up and stretches his nearly six-foot frame. His right hand holds the slender cane that just reaches his armpit. With the tip still touching the floor he slides it forward. He switches hands, just like he practiced with his dad until it was pure instinct. His left index finger rests on the flat grip. Sweeping side to side within the boundary of his broad, muscular shoulders, he advances toward the basement door. He wraps his hand around the intricate detail of the hollow bronze doorknob, then jiggles and twists until the door finally releases. He mutters quietly, "fix something around here Ben, anything." Next... the light switch. While it barely makes a difference, a soft white light casts enough of a shadow to frame the open portal. Cautiously he feels for the top of the doorway, lets the cane slowly drop to the next step, then gently lowers his head as he begins his descent. Damp air escapes the basement and clings to his body. He grabs a handful of his freshly laundered t-shirt and inhales deeply.

"Trying to get away from me?"

Colin stops on the second step and steadies himself, gripping the splintered railing. "Nope, he says without concern. Just getting a workout in, that's all. You know you're welcome to join me, Pete."

"And you know I'll have a panic attack if I go down that black hole."

Colin shakes his head. "Welcome to my world. Every day is a black hole. "Hey man, I'll be right here with you. Just try to..."

"We've been through this. I can't. I don't know why but I can't. Just like I don't know why I ended up in this house. Or why I can't go into Ben's office."

"Easy Pete. We're cool. We've got the rest of the summer to figure this out."

"And then you'll forget about me. I'll be alone in this sloppy house. I'll never find peace."

There's despair in Pete's voice. Something Colin hasn't heard before. Selfishly, he says, "so now you and my mom are both making me feel guilty."

"That wasn't my intention. I'm sorry...maybe we can listen to the Phillies game later?"

Colin effortlessly reaches the basement floor and raises his voice slightly, knowing Pete remains frozen at the top of the stairs. "Sure, but don't forget I still need to tickle the ivories after my workout."

Pete ignores his reminder about piano practice. His voice is hollow now, barely a whisper. *"It's a doubleheader. A twi-*

nighter.”

Colin quietly whines, “great, twice the torture.” He remembers to remind Pete to keep the door open but it’s too late. First a solid thud then the patter above of his special friend’s footsteps moving briskly down the hallway – choppy steps only Colin can detect.

Pete. His troubled spirit or friendly ghost -- Colin really isn’t sure what to call him or what keeps him stuck here. There’s no reason for his presence in Ben’s home. No history with the house. No previous knowledge of Colin. His memory as murky as his new friend’s eyesight.

Their relationship began the very first day Colin moved into this house, nestled in the middle of a quiet street in Swarthmore, a small college town 20 miles southwest of Philadelphia. It was early last Summer. He was 17, adjusting poorly to life with his new family. His mom and stepfather were giving him space, letting him explore the house, encouraging his independence. By his third night, he was pounding on the double doors of the master bedroom, telling Ben there was an animal in his room. The next evening his screams brought them to his bedroom where they assured him that the whispered voice and the tugging pillow were part of a nightmare. In the days that followed, Colin was afraid to spend time in his room. He slept on the couch downstairs, struggling to explain the “feeling” that no matter where he went in his new home he was not alone. Until that day he sat trapped in Ben’s office, barely listening to his stepfather counsel him. Ben is a renowned psychologist and successful family counselor. So, who better to guide him through this “perfectly normal transition?” During their conversation Colin definitely felt different. Not because he was connecting to Ben’s rambling advice. No, things just felt less peculiar sitting there. The “presence” he experienced elsewhere in the house was gone. Completely. He left the office more curious than confused. He needed to find out if he was going crazy or getting closer to an explanation. The answer came two days later -- another

Wednesday, about three weeks into their arrival. His mom was starting her first day at the food bank. Ben offered to drive her into Philly. That was rare. He hated driving into the city. Colin, gathering strength to confront this secret, had assured them he would be okay. After they left, he decided to find another place in the house where he could sense a weaker presence, just like he felt in Ben's office. The one place he had not explored was the basement. His mom, who visited the space to do laundry, told him it was off limits until she could clear things out and make it safe for him. Ben also warned him about the faulty door. "On top of my list to fix," he assured him. On that monumental morning, Colin carefully worked his way down the basement steps, promising himself he would go no further than the bottom of the staircase. He began his journey to the answer. With every step he felt a stronger detachment from that feeling. He was calm. He was alone. And then his cane landed directly in a laundry basket, tipping its contents and Colin toward the basement. He instinctively grabbed his head and curled his body just before landing on the concrete floor. He was bruised for sure but felt okay. Nothing seemed broken. Then, the misplaced aroma of charcoal. And his first conversation with Pete.

A weak voice from a young man -- maybe in his twenties. *"Colin, are you okay?"*

Colin stuttered, "who are you?"

The response to Colin's nervous query was flat, uninteresting, and peppered with curious, odd expressions. *"I should have warned you. I'm sorry. You're not crazy. I'm glad to finally say hello. This is some pumpkins for me."*

Colin remembers getting to his feet, finding the railing, wanting to get closer to the voice that came from the basement doorway above him. He remembers feeling curious, not afraid.

That curiosity has never waned, but he's still no closer to a revelation of Pete's purpose in his life. He has learned the meaning of many of Pete's unusual expressions. Apparently, "some pumpkins" means "a big deal." Pete uses that one a lot.

In turn, Colin has taught him the meaning of "groovy" and "bummer" and -- one of Pete's favorites – "far out." It's amusing to hear Pete work today's slang into a vocabulary borne from another era. Still, he has no sense of time or connection to his past. He's lost, for sure. Very lost. Pete has said it himself. *"I'm terribly misplaced Colin. That's a bottom fact."* Which means *the undisputed truth.*

Colin has also come to accept a strange complexity to Pete's grasp of the present. This misplaced spirit belongs elsewhere yet arrived in Colin's life with a working knowledge of modern technology and an odd interest in the Philadelphia Phillies baseball team. After 12 months together, there is so much Colin still struggles to grasp about Pete's identity. There's even a disagreeable bent to Pete's disposition that Colin rarely experiences. He justifies it as Pete's protective side. Maybe possessive is a better description. He hears the distant hum of a lawnmower, and it reminds him of one of those moments. Last summer, soon after they met, Colin was planting some flowers for his mom. Siting on the rear porch, surrounded by bags of potting soil and flats of impatiens, he carefully worked with large clay pots that felt cool to the touch in the morning shade. A new landscaping crew was working nearby. A mix of young voices, from kids probably his age, turned to snickers and stifled laughter. Colin, seasoned enough to know he was now the blind kid being ridiculed by a bunch of morons, just ignored the mockery. As a lawn mower came to life, he could feel the grass clippings blowing his way. It was excessive. It was deliberate. Shielding his face from the yard debris, Colin heard annoying giggles as the mower moved away from the porch. Then, a shrill scream. The mower stopped. But the anguished sound of someone in pain was relentless. Nobody was laughing anymore. Turned out that one of the kids broke his ankle, probably by stepping into a hole in the lawn. The injury was grotesque, a freak accident they said. But the victim insisted something struck him from behind. His buddies didn't see anything. It was just them and the blind kid on the porch. It was strange. So was Pete's reaction when Colin asked him about it. *"I found his treatment of you unforgiveable so perhaps he had it coming to him."* There were other times when Colin sensed a vengeful stance from Pete, whose quirky hot and cold personality can be exhausting. Just another reason why Colin needs an occasional break from his shadowy companion. Like right now -- his quiet time. He paws the air to his left until he feels the gap between a makeshift canyon of boxes, furniture, and discarded clothes – "no man's land" his mom calls it. This jagged path to the rear of the basement is where she and Ben shoved every moveable item so Colin could have that promised safe area now occupied by his weights and punching bag. He turns right, leans his cane against a special notch in the railing and moves independently towards his safe zone. Instinctively he slouches beneath massive ductwork coming from the ancient furnace. Still hunched forward he clears the last hurdle, a thick wooden beam that runs the width of the house. The beam is supported by several load-bearing posts anchored in a relatively new concrete floor. Beyond the beam he can stand upright and make his way to the center of the room. He finds the low-hanging light chord. Pulling it produces enough light to outline the area where his bench and free weights are located. His foot finds the carpet remnant he uses for floor exercises. He lowers himself, crawls to the center of the carpet and begins warming up.

Upstairs, he hears the gruff buzzing of the private doorbell. Odd. This is usually when Ben grabs lunch and catches up on paperwork. Again, the buzzer is pressed. It means a visitor for Ben. His clients enter the property from the street using a special driveway that runs along the north side of the house, opposite from Colin's position. They slip into a carport sheltered year-round by a tall stand of arborvitae that block any view from the street and the neighboring property. Visitors press the special buzzer and are admitted directly into Ben's secluded office. It's a normal routine. But never on a Wednesday. Colin should know. His life is shaped by routines and habits. He jumps up from the carpet, adjusts his gym shorts, approaches his weight bench, and finds his boxing gloves. They were a recent graduation gift from his cousin Katie, his real dad's niece. She got them for Colin because he refused to give up his boxing routine despite his mother's heated objections. He needed to blow off steam, he confided to his cousin. He shares everything with her…everything except Pete. So, she gave the gloves to Colin saying, "If you're going to bash a bag pretending it's Ben, you're not going to bust those fingers. These are the best – Joe Frazier trains with them!" He loosens the laces and slides his hands into the gloves. Moves freely around the uncluttered basement, slicing the air with a series of jabs and uppercuts, pounding the gloves together between warmup punches. He works his way to the far end of the basement until he brushes against the heavy leather punching bag that hangs from the master beam. He steadies the bag and steps back, far enough so he must rotate his hips to hit the target. Anticipating his first thrust, Colin digs his big toe into the floor when his routine is interrupted by shouting. Brief, but intense. It's not Ben's voice. He steps away from the bag and listens. His arms are still in position to throw another punch. Now he hears Ben, his voice rising but controlled. Another shout, more intense this time. Colin drops his hands and pulls the gloves away. He quickly moves toward the steps, gliding freely through the uncluttered space until his forehead collides with the support beam.

"Shit!" He drops to the floor, bare knees meeting cold concrete. He wants to yell but holds back. Touching his forehead, he feels new blood exiting old wounds. "You stupid shit." Instinctively he pulls his t-shirt up to dab his forehead, making it sting. More shouting…like an argument. Once again, he is on his feet, remembering this time to crouch safely under the duct work. Closer to the steps he can make out a female's voice. From the top of the step, he hears a question asked so calmly it could have been inquiring about the time of day. *"Colin did you hear that, can you hear me? What should I do?"*

Colin hesitates. instead of choosing the steps he turns and finds the gap into no-man's land. Plunges toward the unknown, further from Pete's dull request. The deeper he goes, the closer he gets to the space directly under Ben's office. His head brushes up against more ductwork. Reaching up, he wraps both hands around the flimsy circular tube and guides himself closer to the basement's edge. His progress is interrupted by stacked boxes that easily move. His hands separate the flimsy crates, creating an opening wide enough for him to squirm through. He can still feel the ductwork above as dust settles on his head and clings to his sweaty face. Now he hears whimpering, directly on top of him. Colin can smell the basement's dry-laid structural stone – he is at the edge of the foundation wall. To his right he brushes against a piece of furniture, maybe a desk. It's low enough for Colin to climb on top. Leaning against the rough-hewn wall to maintain his bearings, he keeps moving his hands until he finds the end of the ductwork. It sways easily away from the exposed ceiling. He hears voices drifting through the floor vent of Ben's office. A swath of poorly installed insulation drops on Colin's head. He silently curses another of Ben's partial projects and pushes the handful of resilient fiber away from his face. Tilting his ear toward the ceiling, Colin hears his stepfather speaking in quiet, measured tones.

"None of that makes any sense. Don't you see? You've imagined this before..."

The woman starts to speak but Ben hushes her. "Shhh...keep your voice down. Colin strains to hear her whispered response, "Please, don't even go there. I know what I saw."

This isn't a stranger. No...the voice is familiar.

Ben replies in a steady tone. "Or, what you wanted to see. Listen, I need you to calm down. If it happens again...if you think..."

Colin can hear his own heavy breathing as he focuses intently on her hushed reply, "I don't think...I know."

IT'S HER. OH MY GOD...

"Okay, so *when* it happens again, I want you to call me... understand? But don't come to the house blurting things out without any evidence. It's too risky. Hannah can't know about this..."

Colin flinches at the sound of his mother's name. His heart is pounding so fiercely it feels like his eardrums will burst. He stumbles back and falls into a pile of discarded dry cleaning and winter coats. He is swimming in moth balls, suffocating in confusion and fear of...what? WHY IS SHE HERE...WHAT DID SHE SEE? He rolls toward the gap in the boxes and falls to the basement floor. Still on all fours, he crawls towards the steps, finally gaining his footing, knocking down anything in his path. Panting heavily, he finds the first step, trying to move faster than his body will allow. He hears his cane rattle to the concrete and roll away. Grabbing the railing he moves more confidently until he reaches the closed door. Turns the knob left and right. Jiggles it violently. The latch does not cooperate. He curses Pete for shutting it. Curses this house.

He smells Pete's presence before he hears him. *"Colin? Is that you?"*

"Jesus, Pete, who do you think it is? Let me out!"

"It won't budge. You should have left it open. Wait, did I shut it? I did. This is my fault. What should I do?"

Colin suppresses his frustration, takes a deep breath instead and tries to reason with Pete. He presses his palms against the door and leans forward. "It's okay, but I need your help. Listen carefully because we don't have much time."

"I'm listening."

"That patient you heard, did you see her?"

"I didn't see anything. His door was closed."

Colin grimaces. "Doesn't matter, Pete. She probably left his office already by the private door. Go outside and see if you can get a glimpse of her."

The only response is Pete fiercely shaking the doorknob.

"Please, you're wasting time. Go! Try to get a good look."

"I'm going."

Colin slides to the second step and rests his head between his legs. Everything aches. And nothing makes sense. His bewildered breathing steadies and he exhales through the confusion. Above his head the doorknob turns very slowly. Colin hears the latch click and release. He is on his feet immediately as the door creaks open. "Did you see her?"

"Colin, are you okay? What are you talking about? Your head. You're bleeding again."

Ben squats down and leans into the open doorway. "Colin, who were you talking to?"

"Nobody."

"It sure didn't sound like nobody. You said, 'did you see her.' Who were you talking about?"

"Look, Ben, I hit my head, lost my bearings, and panicked a little. Now, I'm drawing a blank. I'm not even sure how I got to the top of the steps."

"Let's get some ice on that forehead. You might have a mild concussion."

"I'll be fine, really." Colin gets to his feet. Feels Ben's hand guiding him. "You've got two steps here, be careful." Colin feels the tension in Ben's unsteady grip – rivaling his unsettled voice. "Okay, let's get you up to your room. Try to rest a little and I'll check on you before Hannah gets home. Oh man, your mother is not going to be happy about this. You know she's going to blame me."

Colin steps into the kitchen. "I need to sit down."

"Sure, sure."

Ben guides him to the kitchen chair. The tacky tape fastens Colin to the seat. "Let me get you that ice." Colin hears Ben pouring cubes, more of them hitting the counter than finding the bag. Several drop to the floor and ricochet past Colin's high-tops. Ben screws the top on the bag as he approaches Colin. Silently he presses the bag against Colin's forehead.

"My cane. I lost it at the bottom of the steps."

"Right, okay."

Colin hears several of the cubes rattling over the steps.

Squeaky footsteps pause half-way down for a few seconds then resume. Ben's return to the kitchen is much faster. Colin imagines his stepfather escaping the basement two steps at a time.

"Colin, it's a mess down there. What happened? What were you doing?"

As Ben's shadow intensifies, Colin reaches for his cane. "Like I said, I got confused. Panicked. Lost my bearings I guess."

"Uh huh," Ben says unconvincingly. "Well, it looks like we've got even more to explain to your mom than just the new dent in your head."

Colin begins tapping his cane on the floor. "Fair enough. But I've got a lot of questions too."

Ben is standing directly in front of Colin, crowding him as he responds, "what kind of questions?"

"Don't be nervous Ben."

"I'm not nervous," he says forcefully. Just curious, that's all."

Ben' smugness unnerves Colin, who responds meekly, "sure, Ben. Well, seems to me we've both got a lot of explaining to do."

Ben pants deeply. Colin can sense his stifled anger. He feels it so deeply he trembles.

CHAPTER 3

Big Picture

Wednesday -- Noon

Colin, lying flat on his bed, slides the pleated ice bag off his forehead and tosses it in the direction of Pete's voice. "That's the best you can do? A black car? Do you know how many black cars there are....?"

"It was down the street by the time I got outside. I'm not even sure it came from this house. Actually, it might have been...dark green? But shiny, very shiny. It looked new."

A window opens. Colin hears Pete unscrew the cap of the ice bag and pour water into the yard below. The sputtering of a lawnmower fills the room. "Pete, keep that window open, will you?

"You always enjoy the smell of fresh-cut grass."

He feels the mattress tilt. They don't physically contact each other. Never have. But Colin feels a connection to the blurred image.

He softens his tone. "Listen I'm sorry. I've got a headache and I'm a little pissed off."

"Yes, you are. Now let's get past it and consider all the possibilities. It's time to focus on the big picture here."

Colin is on his feet. "Ah, the logical Pete has returned." He finds the bean bag in the far corner of his room and plops down. "I can't believe I backed down with Ben. I know Katie's voice. It was her. I'm sure of it. I'm such a wimp."

"Maybe there's a reason you held back. Why would your cousin be secretly visiting Ben?"

"Whatever the reason, they're hiding something from my mom," he says accusingly.

"Perhaps you were half-listening?"

"Pete, please don't ..."

I heard Ben suggest that this person, whoever she is, was imagining something, so...perhaps she truly is a disturbed patient..."

Colin laughs defiantly. "Katie? Seriously? No, she's not a patient." Colin's finger stabs the air. "For as long as I've lived here that man has never disrupted his Wednesday routine. No! Katie came uninvited – just to tell Ben about something he doesn't want my mom to know about. I knew I couldn't trust him. This proves it."

"Colin, it proves nothing. Besides, your cousin drives a white vehicle. I've seen it enough times. It's a white..."

"Thunderbird," Colin says begrudgingly.

"Ahh," Pete whispers, *"that's it...Thunderbird. Delightful name for a vehicle."*

"Cool it with the sarcasm, okay?"

"Very well. But it would help greatly if you paid attention to the facts, not your feelings. Now, we both know Ben is going to be up here soon. Clearly, you made him nervous. He wants to find out how much you know. So, how about this approach..."

Colin pounces from the bean bag, his bravado stirred. "Sorry, I don't care about your big picture. This time I'm getting answers. I'm not backing down."

Pete calmly responds. *"Please take a deep breath and listen."*

Colin's pulse quickens. "I have a right to know."

"Okay, so why not ask the person you trust most -- Katie...why not wait and just ask her? Just be patient...play along for now and see what you can learn. Don't let your anger control you, Colin."

Resentfully, Colin responds. "I am *not* angry. I'm, I'm..."

"Confused. That's all. Perfectly understandable. Remember, big picture. What have you got to lose?"

"My mom's trust." Colins sags onto his bed.

"All the more reason you want to get this right. If you really

want Ben out of her life, isn't it smarter to get all the facts instead of making accusations you can't support. Don't be like Thompson's Colt..."

"Thompson's Colt," Colin repeats in a biting tone. Really? What does that mean?"

"My apologies. It's just an expression. It means 'Don't do something unnecessary,' Colin. Something that could put her over the edge, right?"

Another jab at Colin's role in pushing his mother to the brink unleashes his biting reply. "Sure Pete. After all, we have a huge head start. Let's see...we know this mystery woman drives a black or possibly green shiny new car."

"Enough Colin." Without a hint of anger, Pete ends the conversation, *"I've had enough of your sarcasm. I need some space."* The bedroom door opens and shuts with authority. Alone, Colin mutters, "sorry Pete." Even if his misplaced companion stuck around for the apology, Colin knows he went too far. Pete's search for solitude could be for one hour or it could be for days. The longest he ever went was three weeks when Colin made the mistake of calling Pete a "walking contradiction." Pete made Colin pay for it – starting with his bedroom. Colin is a slob, yet everything is perfectly in place, only because of Pete's meticulous housekeeping. His mom has joked that "a teenager's room should not look this organized." It wasn't tidy during those three weeks while Colin paid the price for his insult. He finally apologized after his underwear disappeared.

Now, Colin runs his hand across the top of his dresser. Everything is exactly where it's supposed to be. He opens his sock drawer. Already organized. Colin shakes his head. His room may be shipshape, but Pete can't manage to tidy up the details about that car. He's so focused on the "big picture." Walking contradiction for sure. The lawnmower belches and briefly stabs the silence. He sits on the edge of his bed, lays back and slides slowly down towards the shag carpet. WHY WOULD KATIE BE TALKING TO BEN? WE DON'T HAVE SECRETS. SHE'S

THE ONLY ONE I TRUST. SHE GETS ME.

Through paper-thin walls of their Gerrit Street apartment, Colin recalls his mom's despairing plea to "call your niece." It was routine – like the produce man shouting from his pushcart or the clinking of milk bottles settling in wrought iron baskets welded to rusted railings. "It's time to call Katie." For his young ears it just meant something was going to get fixed. As he got older it meant more. A debt covered. A bill paid. A disorderly conduct charge dropped. Katie knew lots of people and it seems like they all owed her a favor. Maybe it was because of all the people she met in her travels. She was a jet-setting stewardess for TWA. Gone frequently -- often a few weeks at a time -- but then she would swoop back in and re-enter Colin's life with a passion. Always there for him.

Colin's tangled memories are interrupted by a slow knock on his bedroom door. There is very little light remaining on this side of the house by midday. He opens the door to a muted indistinguishable shadow. From the hallway Ben says, "Listen Colin, I've been thinking. It's not a good idea to hide what happened in the basement from your mother. She needs to know."

"Sure, but what about what happened in your office?"

"What about it?"

"There was a woman in there shouting at you."

"Colin, were you eavesdropping? Is that why the basement is such a mess?"

"She was shouting."

"She's a client." There's less restraint in Ben's tone. "A lot of my clients get distraught." Ben still lingers in the hall.

"Okay, but...."

"But, what?" Ben asks with a grinding edge.

Colin holds back. "I just heard shouting and got worried."

"Okay, but you know I can't disclose my private discussion with a client, right?"

TO HELL WITH THE BIG PICTURE. "What if it wasn't a client?"

Ben stammers, "I, I..."

"Are you lying to my mom?"

Colin's already limited vision of Ben grows smaller, as if his stepfather is shrinking down the hallway. Colin pursues him. With every step his voice rises. "Was that my cousin...was it Katie you were talking to?"

"Alright, this must stop. You're not making any sense."

Colin is so close to Ben he can hear nervous breathing. "You're not denying it. Tell me the truth or I tell my mother."

Again, Ben matches Colin's intensity. He's not backing down. "Sure, okay...after we tell her about...those imaginary conversations. I heard you talking through the door."

"I told you I was dazed," Colin stammers. He rubs his forehead.

"We'll discuss it more when your mother gets home."

"You're changing the subject."

"I'm trying to be a parent."

"Well, you need a lot more practice. Besides, you are not my father."

Ben weakly says, "I know Collin, you remind me all the time." He shakes something and Colin realizes he is holding another ice bag. "Here get this on your head. Maybe we can minimize the damage. And don't tell her you didn't practice."

"You want me to lie?"

"Just take the ice bag."

Colin cups his hands. Ben forcefully plops the bag into his open palms. Colin squeezes the cubes, but nothing can cool his rage. He stomps back to his room, and slams the door shut.

He feels achingly alone.

CHAPTER 4

Mrs. Judson

Wednesday – 4:00 PM

Ben's cramped office, tucked in the rear of the house, sits a dozen steps from the kitchen. With renovations scheduled soon, everything is out of place. Colin is sitting next to his mom, hip to hip, on a sagging love seat that has been moved within arm's length of Ben's cheap desk – a Sears purchase from his bachelor days. His bare feet rest on a large, rolled up carpet that monopolizes any remaining leg room between the love seat and the desk. Colin's toes flex into the carpet's jute backing. Ben's distant voice comes from the kitchen. He's on the phone with Mr. Humphrey, the neighborhood handyman. "Don't forget the schedule I gave you Tim. It's important you start on Saturday, right...and remember you'll need some help moving things out of the way..."

Ben's office is one of the rooms in this house that appeals to Colin's senses. A century ago, it was the original kitchen. It smells musty, feels like it's holding secrets, but mostly reminds him of their tiny kitchen back on Gerrit Street.

His mom squeezes his hand, but Colin is elsewhere, back to that small space in Grays Ferry. He remembers colliding and laughing with her as she taught him the Twist, his stocking-feet snagging cracks in the thin linoleum floor. Listening to Chubby Checker, Elvis Presley, and Ray Charles on the radio. Keeping beat with a wooden salad spoon while music poured from the kitchen and filled their apartment.

His thoughts are interrupted by the question his mother squeezes into every conversation. "Are you practicing?"

"Mom, seriously?"

"You're going to be competing with the best..."

"It's not a competition. I already got the scholarship."

"Nonsense. There's always competition, Colin. Even Mrs. Judson would tell you that. Oh, she would be so proud of you. To see how far you've come."

Colin swallows hard. He clears his throat. "I know. I think of her every time I play her piano. It keeps me motivated."

His relationship with that piano started innocently enough in 1962, just a few weeks before Christmas. Colin was tagging along with his father, who was struggling with Mrs. Judson's stubborn radiator. Until that day Colin's image of their Gerrit Street tenant was the childless middle-aged widow who gave piano lessons in the apartment above. When she played, Colin would turn off the radio just to listen to the purest melodies fill their building. She could sing too, crooning softly as she moved around her apartment. Colin and his mom loved her soothing voice.

He remembers how chilly it felt when he entered her apartment for the first time. Her hands were even colder as she pinched his cheeks and commented on how big he was getting. The smell of her hand cream made him queasy. His father set to work and told his son to sit on the sofa and not touch anything. Mrs. Judson's sweet voice interrupted.

"Oh, Colin. I wish I had some things for you to play with."

"It's okay Margaret, he'll be fine."

"Well, the least I can do is get him some cookies. Would you like that Colin?"

"Yes Mrs. Judson, thank you."

Colin heard the tin being opened. "I just made these for my students, so they're nice and fresh."

"My friend Mary. Mary Dugan. She comes here sometimes."

"Mary, sure. She's a good student. Always practices between lessons."

"She has her own piano?"

Colin heard his father sigh, not sure if the radiator or his questions were annoying him.

"Actually Colin, most of the students at St. Gabe's are permitted to use the piano in the music room to practice, since very few have one at home. The sisters are really kind about that." She guided the cookie plate into his hands. "You go to St. Gabe's, don't you?"

His father, retrieving a tool from his toolbox, answered, "Colin splits his time between there and St. Lucy's over in West Philly. They've got a special school they started for the blind, but the transportation is kind of tough, so his mother worked out a nice program with Mother Alma at St. Gabe's to…."

"Can I try it? The piano I mean. Can you show me?"

"Margaret, I'm sorry. He's got a lot of energy this morning."

"What ten-year old doesn't a few weeks before Christmas?" Mrs. Judson's cool hands immediately guided him from the sofa. "Of course, dear. Watch the coffee table and let's just swing around here. Excuse us Tom."

"Margaret, that's not necessary."

"It most certainly is. You worry about that radiator while me and Colin tickle the ivories."

Colin laughed. "What does that mean?"

"Well, piano keys are made from ivory and now your fingers are going to tickle them..."

Before she even seated him on the padded bench, Mrs. Judson placed his hands on the solid walnut console. He was surprised. It felt like any piece of furniture. Still, he just wanted to play it. She let him touch the woven caned panels on the front. Patiently he waited, knowing his father would not tolerate anything less. She wrapped his fingers around one of its front tapered legs, finally speaking almost reverently, "this is not just a musical instrument Colin, it is a work of art." Satisfied he had been patient long enough, he offered, "wow... do you think I can play it now?" He felt for the bench and seated himself.

Leaning over his shoulder, she placed the thumb of his right hand on a key. He shivered. "Okay, this is called the middle C of the piano. For now, this is going to be your starting point."

"Can I play something?"

She tussled his hair. "Ready to jump right in, are you? Well, let's see. It's Christmas so...."

"Jingle Bells. Let's play that."

His father chuckled.

"Okay now let's relax your wrists. You need to be calm, channel your energy into the music." She softly sang the words as she guided his fingers. "Jin-gle bells." They tapped the same keys again. "Jin-gle bells. Now you try it. Just those three notes. Relax those..."

"Can I play the whole song. I think I can do it."

With a little guidance from his teacher, he actually did. He relied more on the sound each key produced. Instinctively tapping the same key to create that sound again. If he made a mistake, he rarely repeated it. More Christmas songs followed. At some point he remembers his dad stopped using his tools. The only sound came from Colin tickling those ivories. Mrs. Judson called it "playing by ear."

Colin can't remember if his dad fixed the radiator, but his conversation with Mrs. Judson is a vivid memory. "He has a gift Tom, there's no question. At this age, without reading music, he is already hearing and understanding sounds. It's almost automatic and it is rare. But..."

His father interrupted, "we can't afford to buy a piano, Margaret."

"Let's not get ahead of ourselves. There are still learnable music skills that can take him far, but he doesn't need his own piano for that. We have one right here, don't we?"

"Margaret, even lessons are just not...I don't think we can swing it." His dad shook the nearly empty cake tin. I need to pay you for all the cookies he just ate!"

Mrs. Judson's laughter, almost a squeal, remains with Colin. So did her solution.

"Tell you what. I've got a lot of tarnished silverware that needs polishing. Why don't you bring Colin over here on Friday evenings, after his homework and chores are done? He can polish for thirty minutes, strengthen those fingers up, and then I'll give him a thirty-minute lesson. How does that sound?"

"I don't know how great that silver is going to look."

"Dad, I can do it."

"Tom, if he polishes half as good as he plays, I think I'm getting the better part of this deal."

His dad's calloused fingers rubbed Colin's scalp. "Son, what do you say?"

"Do you think it would be okay with mom?"

"Something tells me she is going to love it."

Mrs. Judson squealed. Colin remembers racing ahead of his father, clinging closely to the banister until it safely delivered him downstairs to share news that would change his life.

Now, Ben's voice brings him back from Gerrit Street to the reality of this cramped office and the conversation he wants to avoid. "Sorry about that. Just tying up loose ends with Tim Humphrey." His mom squeezes his hand tightly. Colin knows it's a silent plea to stay calm. She needn't worry. He's *not* going to challenge Ben again. He's *not* going to mention Katie's name. He's *not* going to put his mom over the edge. He's going to spare her and grudgingly lean on Pete's gentle guidance -- *the person you trust most is Katie...why not wait and just ask her?* He squeezes her hand even harder.

Colin hears Ben's plodding footsteps from his left. His toes scratch the carpet's rough backing. His stomach tightens. He doesn't hear the door shut, so he immediately imagines Pete hovering by the threshold, ready to forgive Colin but still afraid to enter the room. Pete calls Ben the "Michelin Man." Colin's own sightless version of the plump tire man helps him relax. He grins slightly.

"Colin, you seem rather content," Ben says surprisingly as the swivel chair squeaks loudly, surrendering to his stepfather's husky frame.

"Oh, I'm just glad that, you know, we are getting a chance to talk. About today, I mean…"

His mom rubs his shoulder. "We are too, honey. I'm sorry I wasn't here."

Ben adds, "are you feeling, okay? Your head I mean."

"Yeah, yeah. Probably looks worse than I feel," he says calmly. "Really, it's fine."

The chair squeaks again and Ben erupts, "damn this thing. Sorry, it just started doing this. It's probably driving my clients crazy. Hannah, I think it's time to replace it."

"Well now's the time Ben. You're remodeling anyway, so why not? You deserve to be comfortable."

"And my clients don't deserve this." The chair releases its load as Ben stands and leans back against the shallow sill of the bay window framing the back yard. Colin can sense the change in the remaining daylight that once filled the window. "Okay, well…office renovations are not the subject here," he says timidly. "So…Colin, I told your mom everything…"

Collin hesitates. "Um… all of it?"

"Yes, Colin everything. You heard my client shout..."

"A woman. It was a woman," Colin says calmly, more of a reminder than a reproach.

Hannah gently rubs his shoulder. "Colin, honey, I know it was a woman." He squirms away and leans -- almost kneels -- on the rolled-up carpet. "Was she a new client?"

"I can't answer that. It's confidential."

"So, she's never been in your office before?"

From the hallway…" *Thompson's colt…Thompson's colt."*

Colin throws up his hands. "Sorry, sorry. That was unnecessary." He slumps backward in the love seat and feels a spring threatening to poke through the cushion. He sits straight up and squirms.

His mom gently touches his forehead. "Colin... you sure you're, okay? You did bang your head pretty hard."

"Again," Ben emphasizes with a biting tone.

The pause in the conversation is a hint to Colin that his mom is probably glaring at Ben. She softly says, "Colin, is it true that you were eavesdropping? You can't be doing that, you know that, right?"

Colin's toes dig deeply into the jute. He's reluctant to lie but does it anyway. "I wasn't. I mean…I just wanted to make sure everything was okay. The door was locked, I couldn't get out and I just panicked."

"Ben, that awful door." Colin feels her weight tilt forward on the love seat. "Maybe when Tim Humphrey gets here, we can ask him to fix it. Please?"

"Okay, let's not change the subject." Ben shifts from the window, inviting light back into the room. As his moving image splinters the daylight, Colin hears his foot catch the rolled-up carpet. Colin instinctively puts his arms up, anticipating a stumble. Ben mutters, "damn this room!"

"Hey, listen guys we can always talk later, maybe when it's back to normal in here."

"Nice try. But not a chance, Colin. We're together so let's talk. Listen…."

His mom swiftly interrupts, "you were talking to someone again. An imaginary someone."

"No. I was having a conversation with myself," Colin say calmly but confidently.

"Ben says you were having a full-blown conversation with someone about his client."

"Full-blown? What does that even mean? That's crazy, mom. I was just talking out loud. It's nothing new. I've done it before."

"Sure son…."

"Please Ben." Colin waits forever to continue. "Don't call me that. I'm not your son."

"Hey, I didn't mean it that way. It's just an expression."

Colin rubs his hands through his hair and drops his head toward the carpet. "I'm sorry Ben. I know. I shouldn't have said that."

"Uh, okay...that's fine," Ben replies. He sounds befuddled by Colin's apology.

"Honey, you know Ben cares very much..."

"Hannah, it's okay, really. I respect how Colin feels. My bigger concern is him going to Swarthmore in the Fall and having conversations – with *himself*. Not a good first impression."

"Embarrassed the word will get around town, Ben?" His voice swells. "Ruin your reputation?"

Pete's plaintive groan overlaps Ben's response, "now *that* wasn't fair, Colin."

"Come on Ben. Have you ever heard a teacher, ever, tell you that I was talking to imaginary people at school? Be honest. Both of you."

In harmony, they respond, "no."

From the hallway: *"That's because you forbid me from going to your school."*

"Okay, then can we please drop this? I'm fine. And if Ben thinks that I'm some sort of freak because I talk to myself at home, then I'll stop, okay."

Further down the hallway: *"You can't stop. We need each other."*

"Colin, your mom, and I are proud of you. You're a great kid. Never been in trouble. A brilliant musician who's going to be the next Ray Charles..."

Now, from the kitchen, almost yelling: *"He's really laying it on thick, don't you think?"*

"...we just want the best for you, that's all."

Colin stands up. "So then trust me, okay?" His voice trails off, "The way dad used to...that's all I'm asking."

His mom grabs his shoulders, guiding him past the carpet and through the clutter. "We will honey, we will."

Ben's silence is dubious. As Colin contemplates his stepfather's mood, the room's stillness is interrupted by the front doorbell, then the door opening quickly, followed by Katie's unmistakable voice. "Hello, people, I've got grub!"

Colin's mom pauses as they reach the narrow hallway. "I

invited her for dinner. Plus, I wanted to see her new car."

Colin hears the kitchen door swiveling open and the rustle of grocery bags.

Colin's throat tightens. He can't swallow. He almost whispers, "Katie got a new car?"

"I'll say. An Olds 442. She's going to let me drive it!"

"What...what...color is it?"

Colin's cousin responds incredulously from the kitchen. "What kind of question is that? When have you ever cared about the color of a car?"

Colin fakes a laugh as she enters the hallway and reaches him in just a few skips. She hugs him and adds dramatically, "what the hell happened to your head?"

Hannah interjects, "oh he just whacked it downstairs working out."

Ben follows, "hey Katie, thanks for bringing dinner."

"Not so fast Ben. I brought the food. But you and Colin are going to cook it."

"Fair enough, I'll fire up the grill."

Hannah interrupts, "hey, hey, hey, not so fast. Not until we drive that car."

Katie empties the bags while teasing Hannah. "Think you can handle it? She's got a lot more muscle than your puny little Mustang."

Hannah is giggling as she and Katie both grab an elbow and push Colin towards the front door. He can't think straight. Needs time to sort this out. "Wait, I need to put my shoes on."

"No way, live dangerously my boy." Normally he laughs a lot when his cousin is around. Right now, he's just numb. They reach the front door and Colin feels the last rays of afternoon sun wash his face. Sensitive to the direct, bright light, he instinctively slips on the always available sunglasses from his pants pocket. The cool grass welcomes his bare feet as they race across the lawn towards the street.

His mom shrieks, "oh my God it's gorgeous. You really did it. I love it!

"I know, isn't it great? I had to wait a few extra weeks, but it was totally worth it."

Katie is still cradling Colin's arm. Hannah is in the street, her voice beckoning her son to join her. "Colin, come feel its lines... it even feels fast. And you know what honey? The color really is gorgeous. What is it?"

They are close to the street now. "It's called Sherwood green, isn't it slick?"

Colin's bare feet reach the warm asphalt. He senses the sun escaping behind the houses across the street.

"I don't know Katie, as soon as the sun disappears it almost looks black. Oh, hell – black or green, who cares. It sure is shiny!"

Colin swallows hard.

Nearby, Pete gasps.

CHAPTER 5

It's Complicated

Wednesday – 7:00 PM

Colin briskly drags an aluminum-framed armchair thirty feet or so to the back of the yard. It's familiar territory. His hand reaches out until it touches a massive pin oak that marks the last clearing in the yard before dense woods skirt the property line. The trunk is so large that Colin can barely wrap his arms around it. A similar sized tree rests thirty paces to his right. Ben calls the two trees "the twin towers" as a reference to the two skyscrapers under construction at the World Trade Center in Manhattan. Between these two pillars hangs a threadbare hammock, Ben's special place to relax. Colin brushes the hammock, passes the second tree, and plops his chair on a patch of clay and pebbles. The frame wobbles as Colin settles into the nylon webbing. Agitated, he wants to be as far away from the house as possible – detached from the animated conversation of three adults on the porch. He hasn't heard from Pete for hours. From the woods behind him he hears the gentle meandering of Little Crum Creek. The trickle of its soft current usually calms him. Not this evening. Gnats fill his nose. Another mosquito bites his neck. The chair's frayed webbing pinches his thigh. His forehead burns. The scant daylight this Wednesday still offers is useless to him. He is in a much darker place. Katie's laughter drifts down from the porch. Until today, listening to her would make him smile. It meant excitement and adventure. In the toughest times it embodied escape.

Now, the creek's whisper surrenders as her bubbly voice breaks the silence. "What are you doing hiding down here?"

"Just trying to chill." He hears the chinking of bottles, getting louder as she approaches.

"With all these skeeters and gnats? Not my idea of chilling."

She stands right in front of him, but Colin sees nothing. The air is cooler now. It rustles the trees. He feels a cold bottle tapping his thigh. "Here, college boy, don't tell your housemates."

He grabs the bottle's neck, his thumb searching for the cap. It's already open. Colin takes a long swig.

"Easy does it now. That's all I brought to your party."

He holds the soothing, sweating bottle against his forehead, but says nothing.

"Okay if I join you?"

Normally, that would be a welcome request. "After this beer, how can I say no?" His response is flat.

"Well, that's all you get, so sip it." He hears her ease gently into an empty lawn chair. It barely squeaks. She always smells nice. Sweet but subtle. "So, cousin, you wanna tell me what's going on?"

"What time is it?"

"Um, almost 8:00." She jiggles his chair. "Don't change the subject."

"No, no. I was supposed to listen to the Phillies. I forgot..."

"Supposed to? You hate baseball. Was Ben making you listen?"

He sips his beer and gently burps. "No, no...never mind, it's not important."

Her voice is sterner, now. "Colin, what's going on?"

There's an unusual silence. Broken by Hannah's voice from the house.

"Everything okay down there?"

"We're fine Hannah, thanks!"

"Fine," Colin scoffs.

"She's worried about you. We're all worried about you. You

barely said a word in the car today. And your parents..."

"He's not my parent," he crackles. "You should know better than anyone."

"Colin, buddy, it was just an innocent expression. It's a lot easier than saying 'your mom and Ben.' That's all. Nothing more." The wind shifts. Warmer now, blowing down from the house but driving the mosquitoes back toward Little Crum Creek. "Besides, that's not what's bothering you, is it?"

"I've got a lot on my mind."

"Colin, you can talk to me. We've been through a lot together. You can trust me."

He lets the empty bottle slip from his fingers onto the lawn. "Can I?"

"Ouch. That doesn't sound good. Is it me? Did I do something?"

"Will you always tell me the truth?"

"So, it is about me. Oh my God, Colin," she implores. "Tell me what's going on."

His stomach stirs. "Answer my question, Katie."

Her bottle rolls and clinks against his. She is holding his hands now. "I've never lied to you."

"Were you in Ben's office this afternoon?"

"Shit."

"That *was* you." He pulls his hands away. She tries to touch him, and he swipes at her arm.

She lowers her voice. "Colin, Colin, Colin. It's complicated."

"Why are you whispering? What are you and Ben hiding from my mom?"

"Oh my God. You heard everything." Her voice sounds nervous. "I'm so sorry."

Colin unleashes a torrent of agitated questions. "Tell me right now. What were you doing in his office? Who did you see that you are hiding from my mom? This is your only chance, I swear..."

"Your father. I saw Uncle Tommy."

Completely blindsided, Colin stutters, "what do you mean,

my dad? You saw him? Where...why didn't you...."

"I've seen him before..."

Colin swipes the darkness but finds her bare leg. He can feel his cousin recoil. He moves his hand quickly until it grazes her chair's plastic armrest. He squeezes hard and twists so violently it throws her to the ground. His voice is hushed but harsh. "You've seen him before, and you never told me? Never told *us*?"

She is on her feet. Her scent is closer. The smell of beer mingling with her plea, "don't be angry. Let me explain."

"Take me to him," he demands.

She gently pulls the empty bottle from his hand. "I don't know where he is."

Colin tugs his hair with both hands, shakes his head. "You just said you saw him. You're not making any sense. Katie, are you drunk? How many beers did you have? Are you taking drugs? Why, don't you..."

"Shut the hell up."

Her words startle Colin. She is no longer pleading for forgiveness. "Stop talking and give me a chance to explain... okay?"

Colin sags into his chair, realizing he is sweating and breathless. He doesn't argue. He doesn't say anything.

She whispers, "listen I'm just going back to the house to tell Hannah and Ben that you and I are going for another ride, okay?"

"I told Ben. I...I confronted him. He knows I know."

Katie sputters in reply. "Fabulous." Flatly, she asks, "what did he say?"

"He lied, of course."

"I'll be right back."

Colin's heavy breathing is his only response.

He hears the back door open to the kitchen. Ben starts to speak but Katie quickly interrupts as the slamming door blocks the rest of their conversation.

"So, you've had quite a day already."

Colin, drained of adrenalin, says, "I was wondering when you were going to show up. Where have you been? Did you hear all that?"

"I heard enough, and I can't wait to hear the rest."

"Pete, you don't think she's pulling a fast one, do you? Like she's not coming back down here. I'm half-expecting her to burn rubber down the street."

"You mean in her new, shiny green car?"

"Alright, I owe you an apology, okay? Please don't pout. I need your help," he says glumly.

Pete's voice trails away. *"Apology accepted. I'm going back to the house to peek in on things. Make sure she's coming back."*

"She better. I'm going out of my mind down here..."

Almost immediately, the back door opens, and Ben's hushed voice carries down the yard. Colin strains unsuccessfully to listen. Finally, Katie arrives alone. "Come on Colin. Let's go for that ride."

"Why? Where are we going?"

She's already pulling him up from his chair. "I want to share something with you, but not here. He already thinks I'm crazy."

"Ben?"

"Yes, Ben. Like I told you it's complicated."

Colin is on his feet already heading up toward the house. "Did he tell you I knew?"

"Yup. Just now. It's the first chance he had without your mom around." Katie pants as she catches up to Colin. Breathlessly, she says, "he also asked me if you said anything to me."

Imagining Ben staring down at them, Colin quickens his pace. "And?"

From behind, Katie says, "I flat out lied. I told him no, okay? Slow down...what's your hurry?"

"He probably doesn't believe you. Where did you tell him we were going?"

"For ice cream. Hey, Colin, slow down. Don't fall. Wait for

me." She muffles a giggle.

He turns and waits impatiently for her to catch up. Incredulously, he asks, "what's so funny?"

"Come on. It's pitch black out here. And you're leading the way. It's like...."

"Don't say it, Katie. I'm not in the mood..."

"Like the blind leading the blind. Sorry I couldn't resist."

"Still not funny."

They walk to the left, arm in arm, around the porch and towards the edge of the house. Then, down the side path, approaching the private carport and the street beyond. From the open kitchen window, they hear "Aquarius" by the Fifth Dimension. Hannah is singing along, dishes clanking in the sink. *"Let the sunshine. Let the sunshine in, the sunshine in..."*

"Colin, I promise to tell you everything. And then we'll fix things with Ben."

He remains silent. They reach the lawn and head to the curb and car.

She stops and hugs him tightly. "I promise." She gently pushes him away. "But I don't know if I want you in my new car smelling like that."

"Like what?"

"It must be on your clothes."

Colin smells his shirt.

"From when you were cooking with Ben. Charcoal. Can't you smell it?"

"Katie, we didn't cook outside, remember? We were out of charcoal, so Ben used the oven."

"Right. Okay, well then one of your neighbors is cooking right now. You smell it right?"

Colin's mouth is suddenly dry. "I can...yes, I smell it."

"It's pretty intense. My nose is burning."

CHAPTER 6

Wallingford

Wednesday – 7:30 PM

Colin refuses to stop for ice cream. He wants answers. "Fine," Katie says. "But you'll have to be patient for about 15 minutes. Don't make me tell you again." She has that "Katie edge" to her voice so Colin knows better than to challenge her. They drive in silence. Even the radio is quiet. Colin briefly considers venturing into Pete territory, but Katie's bombshell about his dad overwhelms him. NO WAY. NOT NOW.

Finally, she announces, "okay we're in Wallingford." She has rented an apartment here for several months, although Colin has never even visited. The car creeps along for a bit, turns sharply right and then veers quickly left before stopping.

"Colin promptly asks, "are we at your apartment?"

"Nope. This is the Wallingford Train Station. We're at the rear of the west-bound platform."

Rapidly, he asks, "why are we here…is this where you saw him?" He opens the door and steps out. The air is still and surprisingly quiet.

Katie joins him. She is calm and deliberate.

"Okay, I can legitimately tell your mom and Ben that I shared the station's location with you. It's close to my apartment. In case you ever want to pop over from school."

"Really?"

"Yeah, for real. Now, let's keep walking."

Colin is curious but considerate. "Thanks for doing this,

Katie. For confiding in me. You know you're like a big sister to me."

"Are you kidding? I'm sorry it took so long. Sorry you had to ask me, but I was starting to think I was going crazy. I'm not joking." They reach the pavement outside the station, and she guides him down the street, explaining, "when your dad left, I wanted to believe so badly that he would come back..."

Colin's voice rises in agreement. "Right, me too."

"So, at first, I thought maybe I saw what I *wanted* to see. Not what was *really* there."

"Katie...please...what did you see?"

"Okay, okay," she says with restraint. "So, we just passed my apartment. That's how close I am to the station. Now, up ahead is an intersection." She grabs Colin's elbow and turns him to the left. "Directly across the street is a real estate office. That's where I recently saw him...standing under the awning. Looking in the window...pacing...and then he was gone."

"That's why you went to see Ben?"

"Right...my meltdown."

"But it wasn't the first time?"

"Hell no. I saved the first for last." She yanks his shirt sleeve and pulls him back down the sidewalk. "Okay, we're going this way." The polite beep-beep of a car horn halts them both. Colin feels his feet slipping off the curb, but Katie pulls him back. "Sorry buddy, I got you. All clear...we're crossing the street." She picks up her pace. Colin's pulse quickens.

"Where are you taking me?"

Right here...a little coffee shop where it all started."

Katie takes a deep breath, mutters, "I didn't eat for weeks after this," and then she spares no detail. Colin never interrupts as she explains what began outside the coffee shop on a Monday afternoon in early May. It was the day of the Kent State shooting, and everyone was absorbed by the tragic events. The dark gray sky matched the mood of the day. A group of customers next to her had a portable radio perched on their table. *ANTI-WAR PROTEST...FOUR STUDENTS*

DEAD...NATIONAL GUARD SOLDIERS FIRED THE SHOTS. As Katie listened, she noticed a crowd across the street, gathered in front of Burke's Appliances. Probably watching the news unfold on the color television in the front window. Then she saw Uncle Tommy, separated from the crowd, moving briskly down the street.

"It was the red hair I noticed first. How many people, except you two, have a mop like that? His chin was buried in an olive-green jacket. When our eyes met. I nearly shit myself."

She tossed a five-dollar bill on the table and bolted down her side of the street until she was matching him, stride for stride. He seemed to be floating, never slowed by other pedestrians, never stopping at intersections nor checking for cross traffic. She was sweating, shedding her yellow wool sweater, but never losing sight of that red hair. A gentle rain began pelting awnings of the shops that lined the slippery pavement. She moved to the curb, anxious to cross the street. To her left a Red Arrow bus bounced towards her and slowed to a stop. She realized she was standing in a pick-up zone. Frantically, she waved the driver on, but the doors were already open. Her clenched hand pounded the side of the bus, encouraging its departure.

Gas fumes filled her nostrils. When the dense exhaust cleared, his back was turned to her -- facing the parking lot of Wallingford Auto, a used car dealer that consumed half of the block. Stenciled on the back of his jacket were the words, O'MALLEY'S MINING SUPPLIES. Larger drops of rain smacked the asphalt. As soon as she stepped into the street, he began to move – as if they were tethered to each other. Still with his back to her, he glided deeper into the lot. "Uncle Tommy, wait. Uncle Tommy, it's Katie, wait for me!" He never turned or looked her way. The rain picked up as she reached his side of the street. A steady spring torrent drove people off the sidewalk until only she remained. There...that walk, his walk, at the rear of the lot. Rain slapped a steel corrugated garage where he was standing, teasing her to come his way. She pounded through puddles.

"Uncle Tommy!" He never turned around.

Finally, Colin – overwhelmed – eagerly asks, "did you go after him?"

The edge is back. "Of course, I did…let me finish, okay?" A bus idles nearby. The hissing of its air brakes drown out Colin's tepid response. "I just miss him."

"Colin, I don't have a miracle ending to this story, you know that, right?"

"I just want to be with him again."

"Me too, buddy. Me too." Sternly, she adds, "I'm just trying to be honest with you. That's what you wanted, right?"

"Keep going," Colin says with resignation.

"Remember, I saw him enter the garage. I was soaked from the rain when I finally got to the door that Uncle Tommy…uh, sorry…that your dad entered. It was locked. I kept pounding and pounding until somebody finally opened. The guy was pretty pissed off. Told me I couldn't come in. Then I just burst into tears. Said I needed to talk to the man who just went inside…the man in the green jacket."

"What did he say?"

"I think he felt sorry for me. Let me in…but insisted nobody came through that door. He pointed to the mechanics behind him and said they were the only ones allowed in the garage. The only public access to the building was from the front where there was a customer waiting room. I remember he was shouting over all the noise. I was half-listening… looking around the garage to see if Uncle Tommy was there. That's when I saw the jacket. I could see the name… O'Malley's Mining Supplies."

Colin's heart races, matching the energy in Katie's voice as she presses on.

"It was slung over one of those tool chests on wheels. I screamed 'there it is!' I must have been loud because I swear everybody in that place stopped working. People were looking at me and this dude grabbed my arm to hold me back from going into the garage. I shook him off and ran to the jacket.

"Maybe it belonged to one of the mechanics?"

"Not a chance, Colin. Nobody owned it. This guy checked, believe me. He wanted me out of there. Then, this older guy comes over and tells me he recognizes the jacket.

"So, it was his?"

"I just told you nobody owned it. Let me finish for God's sake."

Colin groans impatiently. "You're taking a really long time to get to the point."

"Right...so this old guy tells me he remembers seeing the jacket all the time when he was growing up. But he's not from around here. He's from northeastern Pennsylvania. Past Scranton. He said O'Malley's was the only game in town, and everybody wore their stuff. You know, hats, t-shirts, promotional shit. If you were connected to mining, you knew about O'Malley's. Anyway, they escorted me out of the place. They were polite enough, but I think they had enough of me."

"Do you have the jacket?"

"Finally, a meaningful question."

"So, you have it?"

"No, no, no. I realized I left the jacket behind, so they let me go back to grab it and it was gone. Vanished. Nobody else but the three of us were in that room. I think it was a sign from Uncle Tommy. He's leading us somewhere, Colin."

"Listen, I'm not saying I don't believe you..."

Katie cuts him off. "And one other thing. The old guy who recognized the jacket said he was originally from Scranton. That's coal country."

"So?"

"I think our family has a way-back connection to coal mining. I'm just so disconnected to the past I don't remember what it is. So, I've got some homework to do."

"I want to help," Colin says excitedly. "What can I do?"

"Right now, you can move your butt double-time. We need to get back to the car and get you home."

As they move briskly down the street, Katie suddenly slows

and comments on a vehicle inside the used car lot. “God, that might be the ugliest color I’ve ever seen on a truck. Gotta be an Earl Scheib special.”

Colin pays no attention.

CHAPTER 7

Adrift

Wednesday – 10:00 PM

The gentle rumbling of Katie's new car has a tranquilizing effect on Colin.

"Last chance for ice cream," she says insincerely.

"No way," Colin replies. "Any chance we could drive forever?"

"Sorry, my new toy guzzles gas. Have you thought about what you're going to say to Ben, now that you know what he knows?"

"There's a big difference, Katie. He thinks your nuts. I believe you." The 442 idles at a traffic light. Colin sinks deeper into the lumbering chassis. Every bone in his body believes her. They share a bond forged out of the love, sacrifice, and devotion of one person – his father.

Katie never knew her own father. From the cradle, her home was with their grandmother, Nana Bee, and her unmarried son Tommy. His sister, Bridget (Katie's mom), only showed up when she needed money from Nana Bee, who hid every penny she could from her careless daughter. Uncle Tommy loved Katie as if she were his own child. When World War II tore him away, Katie became housekeeper and caretaker for an ailing Nana Bee. Katie knew cancer would take her long before Uncle Tommy made it home. She was two weeks short of her eleventh birthday when her grandmother went into the hospital for the last time. Her mother disappeared for good once she realized Katie would not let her close to Nana Bee's secret stash. Katie was alone for almost six months until her uncle returned from Europe.

Colin hears Katie softly humming an obscure tune. NO WONDER SHE'S SO TOUGH.

"Hey, you got pretty quiet. Everything okay?"

He laughs. "Do I really need to answer that?"

In an upbeat tone she says, "well *I* feel better. At least I'm not hiding anything from you. We'll figure this out together. But for now...you my friend are on your own." The car makes a series of familiar turns into his neighborhood. Katie finally pulls into the driveway.

"What time is it?"

"A lot later than it takes to get some ice cream. We need to get our story straight, including what you're telling – or not telling – Ben."

Colin feels overwhelmed. "Katie, there's stuff I need to share with you, too. Stuff I've been dealing with for...for...almost a year."

"Oh man, Colin, seriously? Well, spill it buddy."

Colin senses a halo of light from the right.

Katie growls. "The lamp post just went on...and here comes Ben. Crap! Okay, I'll do the talking."

Colin's chest flutters. "What are you going to..."

Sharply, she says, "roll your window down. He's coming."

Colin fumbles for the handle and finally gets the window moving. He hears Ben's breathing and heavy feet hitting the driveway.

"Where'd you go for ice cream? New Jersey?"

Colin whiffs the strawberry scent in Katie's hair as she leans across the console. "Nah, change of plans. Just a little road trip to Wallingford. Wanted to give Colin the lay of the land."

"Odd time for that."

Colin's palms are sweating.

"Not really. Remember, I'm taking him to his orientation next Monday while you're away, so... wanted him to get familiar with the train station. In case he ever visits my apartment."

"Uh, huh."

Colin feels Katie's breath quickening. Ben's silence is excruciating. Colin's neck is pounding. Finally, Ben says, "couldn't you just wait until orientation day?"

Katie is out of gas. She's not responding.

Colin releases the breath he's been holding for the last 30 seconds and blurts, "she told me."

Warily, Ben says, "she told you what?"

Colin stiff-arms Katie before she can speak and continues. "Everything. About my dad. Seeing him in Wallingford... I think she's nuts."

He feels Katie's body relax as Ben replies in a surprising tone, "really?"

"Yeah, that's crazy. If my dad was here, why wouldn't he just come to see me?" He shifts toward his cousin. "I know I already told you this Katie, but it makes no sense. And my mom doesn't need to hear this. You'll put her over the edge. Sorry, that's how I feel."

"You're right. You're both right," Katie say timidly. "I'm sorry I upset you and I won't say anything to Hannah. I promise." Colin senses relief in Katie's voice.

Ben opens the door slowly. Colin crouches slightly and swings his rubbery legs toward the driveway. He clears the door and Ben closes it gently. His stepfather's voice is muffled and distant. He must be leaning inside the car window. His words to Katie are unintelligible. Finally, Ben offers his elbow. They move easily toward the house. Katie fires the ignition. Ben says approvingly, "you did the right thing Colin." As her car rumbles away, Ben says hesitantly, "listen, if your mom asks, let's just stick with the ice cream story."

"Another lie you want me to tell her?"

"You're kidding me, right?"

Colin considers a futile response but surrenders. "Fine."

"Good. And no phone privileges until the weekend. I just told Katie not to call you and I don't want you calling her, understand? Consider it the punishment for breaking curfew."

Colin pulls away from his stepfather. He briefly stumbles as he scoffs, “curfew? I don’t have a curfew. I’m going to college, remember?”

Ben’s voice feels closer. “Okay, then you’re grounded without phone privileges for eavesdropping on a client conversation.”

Colin slides further down the walkway. His ankles touch the prickly edges of the yews he helped to plant last summer. He shuffles left. Ben firmly grabs his wrist.

“Colin, please? You mom is waiting inside. She’s been frantic since you and Katie took off for your little three-hour adventure. We already agreed with your cousin that we’re not going to say anything about her crazy story, so can we just give this night some closure?” He offers his elbow and Colin yields.

They are connected again as they reach the front door, but Colin feels desperately adrift.

CHAPTER 8

Grounded

Thursday June 18, 1970 – 1:00 AM

Colin gently touches the embossed dots and rigid clock hands of his braille watch. It's past midnight but slumber eludes him. He wrestles with the unresolved issues robbing him of sleep. WHY WOULDN'T MY DAD JUST COME TO ME? WHAT'S THE MINING CONNECTION? WHEN WILL I GET THE CHANCE TO TELL KATIE ABOUT PETE?

He'll see his cousin on Sunday when Katie will be staying overnight while Ben and his mom attend a conference in New York. In their absence, she'll be responsible for getting Colin to his freshman orientation on Monday. That's four forever days away. It reminds him of all the times his mom would comfort him when his dad was traveling. "It's only a few days, Colin. Your dad will be home soon." Tommy Byrne's job as a truck driver meant crisscrossing Pennsylvania, New Jersey, and Delaware roadways more often than being with his family. Until his return Colin would lean on lingering memories. Listening to the Eagles on the radio while his dad carefully explained every aspect of a game that Colin could never see nor ever play. Sharing time together was all that mattered.

By Colin's ninth birthday, it was beer and bourbon that mattered more. Soon, his dad's rare times at home meant squandering a paycheck at Murray's, the local pub that was just a five-minute stagger from their apartment.

To feed his habit, his father picked up odd jobs from their

landlord, doing maintenance, shoveling snow, and plunging toilets. He also hooked up with Gino Moretti, the boastful tenant across the hall. Moretti was also a trucker, but his aspirations seemed bigger. He drove his own dump truck. It was a 1958 medium-duty Chevy with lots of wear and tear, but he owned it free and clear. He repainted it a bright lime green. Said he wanted people to see his truck and remember that "Gino Moretti is in town and open for business." Too massive to park on their skinny street, he kept it in a parking lot next to one of the slaughterhouses that rimmed the Schuylkill River

Colin's mom didn't trust Moretti. He always had a different girlfriend and didn't hide his love of gambling either. Once, Colin heard his mom complaining to his dad, "all he's good for are bimbos and bookies." Colin thought his neighbor had an odd scent. Once, he told his mom that he smelled like a doctor's office. She laughed and told him it was Vitalis, a hair tonic that Mr. Moretti used abundantly. He was part of the first wave at Normandy and would talk about his infantry experience constantly. Once, he let Colin hold a souvenir he brought back from Europe, a Luger pistol he claimed he took off a dead German in France. First, Colin touched the cold metal, let his fingers linger on the barrel.

Moretti pulled it away, then sounded agitated as he struggled with something mechanical. "Damn magazine," he muttered. "This hasn't worked right since I got it." Colin stepped back in fear and Moretti laughed. "Don't worry kid. I got it, I got it. This thing needs a good cleaning, that's all."

"What's that smell?"

"What...this?" Without warning he brushed a rag under Colin's nose. It smelled sweet and mildly pungent...kind of like the licorice Mrs. Judson gave him when he completed a lesson.

"This is Ballistol. I use it to clean my gun. Best stuff you can buy," he bragged.

Colin heard the smooth sound of metal on metal. "There we go. Here, now open your hand."

Colin nervously held out his palm and felt a small metal

object roll across his fingers. One end had a smooth tapered tip. Colin kept pinching it. "Is this a bullet?"

"Well, my boy, it's called a cartridge. It's the real deal. A 9-millimeter Parabellum cartridge."

"It's not a bullet?"

"Yeah, that's the bullet at the tip but it also includes the powder and primer."

"I don't get it."

"Jeezus, it's just an unfired round of ammo, okay? You put them in the magazine and shove the magazine into the butt of the pistol." Moretti slipped the gun into Colin's small hand whispering, "pretty heavy, isn't it?" And then forcefully, "listen, don't tell your folks about this." His neighbor's stern warning was accompanied by the blended aroma of Vitalis and Ballistol. It made Colin nauseous.

A few times Colin's dad borrowed Mr. Moretti's truck for local runs and would let Colin ride along. The window on the passenger side only opened a crack but still allowed the sweet and sour smells of their neighborhood to fill the cab. From the aroma of the Bond Bread bakery to the stench of raw sewage pouring into the Schuylkill River from the Dupont paint plant. He could feel the texture of the streets as the V8 engine dragged 16,000 pounds of metal over cobblestone and trolley tracks. Once, his dad even drove into West Philadelphia, through the University of Pennsylvania and past Franklin Field, where the Eagles played. He made sure Colin heard about every detail of the horseshoe-shaped stadium that his son couldn't see for himself. That trip lasted less than an hour, but it was wonderful. He felt complete.

Now the cacophony of this empty night fills his room. High-pitched chirps of crickets beneath his window. The long horn blast of a distant locomotive carving its way through Delaware County. Ben's harsh chainsaw snoring growing louder and louder. Colin presses his pillow against his eyes, smothering tears.

Grounded.

CHAPTER 9

Kryptonite

Saturday June 20, 1970 – 8:00 AM

Ben is running errands. His mom is already in the garden. Colin shuffles down the hallway to Ben's office. He stops and jiggles the doorknob. Locked. ONE MORE DAY. He makes his way back through the kitchen, brushing his hand across the spot where the phone usually hung from the wall. It's barren now, except for a few thin wires that tease his fingertips. KATIE WILL BE HERE TOMORROW. Colin instinctively extends his arm and gently shoves the swinging door forward then veers right. Before he hears the hinges release, Colin is already in the living room -- a location he visits purely to play his piano. He's grateful for this routine. It helps pass the time. Pete is usually here to listen -- but not today. Colin's been spending less time with his friend. It's subtle but noticeable. He pushes that aside and orients himself to the room. Trusting his internal radar, he shifts slightly to his right, confident that he's facing Mrs. Judson's piano, which barely fits between two narrow, floor-length windows facing the street.

For the next hour he concentrates on a handful of demanding scales and arpeggios. His mom is right about practice. As he considers a piece to play, his routine is interrupted by workers arriving to tackle Ben's office renovations. Soon, animated banter competes with their rock and roll music bouncing off the walls of the narrow hallway outside their workspace. He slides off the bench and fleetingly considers asking them to be quiet. Instead, he closes the lid of the piano that Mrs. Judson left to him in her meager will. He gently rubs her prized work of art. He was surprised by her generous gesture, especially because of the way it all ended. Still, he misses her.

By mid-morning Mr. Humphrey arrives. He turns the music down, then chats with Colin, who graduated high school with his son. The transplanted Texan's slow, easy-going drawl soothes Colin. He could listen to him all day. They are standing in the kitchen, where Hannah has left a fresh pot of coffee for the workers. Colin hears the sugar spoon settle on the countertop followed by a long, slow, slurp. "So, Colin, you taking advantage of these summer days before getting serious about college? You are taking it seriously, right?"

"Oh, sure Mr. Humphrey. This scholarship is a big deal. I don't want to let my family down."

"Hell, son, don't let *yourself* down. You worked hard for this. Deserve it for sure."

"Thanks sir. I'll take it seriously, don't worry."

"Good, good. Don't be wasting your time protesting this damned war and skipping class now…you hear me?"

Before he can answer Colin is interrupted by Pete's monotone voice down the hallway. *"I can't get back to the kitchen. I'm stuck Colin."*

"Colin, you're not thinking of joining those protests, are you?"

"Oh no, no sir. I won't…"

"Colin, I need your help." Pete's plea distracts Colin from Mr. Humphrey's opinion about anti-war demonstrations.

"Son, are you okay? Did I upset you? It's just that with my Bobby enlisting, it seems a shame his friends are looking the other way, not that I'm suggesting you are."

"No, no, I get it, Mr. Humphrey, I do. I just remembered that my mom wanted to talk to you about a couple things. She's out back pruning roses and told me to make sure I sent you out there. I almost forgot, that's all."

His coffee cup slides on the counter. "Good. Taking responsibility. Listening to your parents. That's good. Not enough of that these days."

The radio volume surges as Led Zeppelin rattles the walls. "Damn those kids and their blasted music. That's probably why your mom wants to talk to me."

"I doubt that Mr. Humphrey. She'd be the first one to crank it up."

He rinses his cup in the sink. "That so. I didn't figure her for one of those radical types."

"Oh no sir. She just likes..."

"Colin, are you going to help me?"

"Hey Mr. Humphrey, I'm heading down the hall to the garage. Is there anything in the way, you know...blocking my path?"

He chuckles. "No, no. I listen real good to your mom. She told us to make sure we keep things clear for you." He pauses. "Wait now. There's that damned stove in the hallway that your father insists on keeping."

Colin doesn't have the energy for another "he's not my father" conversation. He recalls the small stove tucked in the corner of Ben's office. His stepfather called it a "conversation piece." Said it gave the room "character." He moves toward the hallway. "So, the stove is out there?"

"For the rest of the day, probably. Come on, I'll walk you down if you want, just to be safe?"

"No that's okay. It's easier for you to go out the back door right here. I'll be fine. Just hand me my cane over by the basement door if you don't mind."

"Sure thing." The contractor gently slides the cane into Colin's hand.

"Thanks Mr. Humphrey." Colin turns toward the door, mentally mapping where the old stove must be, and how to get to Pete. Wait. He turns back, keeps his voice casual. "Hey, I'm curious. Ben's stove, how old is it?"

"Well, it may not have been the first coal stove from the very first kitchen but it's plenty old. I told your father if he wanted to preserve it, we could just move it to the basement, get it out of the way. But he insists on keeping it there." Colin hears him opening the rear kitchen door.

"So, this house had coal delivered, right?"

"That's right. A couple other houses on this block were built the same. In fact, right about where you mom is gardening was the location of the coal chute. Went straight into the basement. Kicked up a hell of a lot of dust that's for sure. Maybe I'm not supposed to be telling you this, but there's still a temporary door covering that opening. Your parents should really think about covering it up permanently. Makes me nervous. Okay, enough. I better get going before I forget to talk to your mom. Then, we'll both be in trouble."

"Thanks for the history lesson, Mr. Humphrey." The door rattles shut. Colin hears muffled voices below the kitchen window. Adrenaline pushes him down the hallway, his cane sweeping broadly until it taps solid metal. Pete's voice shouts above the blaring radio, *"it's the stove, Colin. That's why I can't get through."*

Colin says nothing, keeps moving until he reaches the entrance to the garage. He opens the door, instinctively placing his cane on the first of two shallow steps. He reaches the floor and waits for the door to close behind him. The quaky tone of Jimi Hendrix' Stratocaster subsides, leaving Colin's eardrums vibrating. The blended aroma of gasoline and lawn fertilizer fills his nostrils. A simple breeze carries the pleasing smell of cut grass and tells him that at least one of the two double garage doors is open.

Pete is still shouting above the now-muffled music. *"It's the stove. That's why I can't go in..."*

Colin interrupts, whispering, "hey, I heard you the first time, okay? Stop and please listen to me. It's the coal that keeps you away from the office...and from the basement."

"What coal?"

Colin leans against the tapered front grill of his mom's

Mustang. "Mr. Humphrey told me that coal used to be stored in the basement. That's why you can't go down there, Pete. For some reason, coal is your kryptonite."

"My what?"

"Seriously? Where did you come from? It's the material that weakens Superman. He can't go near it."

"Superman. Yeah, I've seen those stories in your bedroom. Maybe I should start reading…"

"And your smell!" Colin's voice is still hushed but excited.

"What are you talking about?"

"You smell Pete. Sorry, but you smell. There's this odor when you're around." Colin is almost giddy now.

"And you never told me about this? Why didn't your mom or Ben complain about it?"

"Because...well, because they can't see you so I guess they can't smell you. I never said anything because I know how sensitive you are, but you've always had this distinct odor."

"Coal?"

Colin moves briskly around the car, his fingers barely touching its cool body. "Yeah exactly. And guess what?"

Pete is silent.

"I don't think I'm alone. The other night, before we went out for our drive, Katie smelled you too. It was intense. Pete, I think she can sense your presence. I'm not alone. I'm not crazy."

Still no answer from Pete.

"Where are you? Don't be pissed off. We're on to something." Colin is no longer sure where Pete is standing. He moves to the rear of the car, feels the fresh breeze sweeping up the driveway. "Pete, please?" Colin is no longer whispering. "Hey, remember, big picture, right? Come on, talk to me." Colin recoils when his mother's voice responds. "Colin, who are you talking to?"

He doesn't respond.

"Colin, there's nobody here." Hannah continues to probe, her concern escalating. But Colin is unreceptive. He feels undone by the startling sound of Pete's anguished sobs echoing off the garage walls.

CHAPTER 10

Father's Day

Sunday June 21, 1970 – 7:00 AM

Colin sits in the rear passenger side of his mom's two-door coupe. Colin is squeezed behind the Mustang's Pony Edition bucket seat, occupied by Katie. His mom is driving. They are headed to the airport after attending the 6:00 AM Mass at Saint John's in Wallingford. That was part of his mom's deal with Katie. She would drive to the airport if they went to Mass first. It doesn't help that today is Father's Day. It was a brutal reminder for Colin as he listened to the priest bless the dads in the pews. He recalls walking to church with his parents in West Philly, squeezing both their hands – comforted by his dad's laughter. He lingers on that feeling, barely acknowledging the banter upfront until Katie cranks up the radio. Her voice rises as she thanks his mom for the ride. "Always appreciate this, Hannah. This Philly to Pittsburgh route is a grind. I know it's only a day but I'm still worried about parking my new baby in a remote lot."

"No problem. Happy to do it. Aren't you getting tired of this?"

"Just milking this gig for as long as I can. I know I'm living on borrowed time. At 35 I'm a dinosaur. Used to be you were out at 32 but they need me right now and the younger girls lean on me. So, we'll see. In the meantime, I appreciate the lift. Never take it for granted."

"Just don't forget you'll be returning the favor, right?"

"Absolutely. I'll be cutting it close, but I'll be there tonigh.t" The music lowers as Katie directs her next comment to Colin. "Big day on campus tomorrow, right Colin?"

Colin doesn't respond, too preoccupied with all the things he needs to say to Katie.

"Colin, hey mister, did you hear Katie?"

"What? Sorry. What did you say?"

The car brakes as his mom approaches a traffic light. "Geez Colin, Katie is taking you to your orientation. Remember, Ben and I are going away? You did remember, right?"

"Are we still in Wallingford?"

Hannah's voice is irritated now. She jams the floor-mounted stick shift into second gear. "Are you even listening to me? Snap out of it."

"It's okay Han, he's probably suffocating back there. Roll your window down, Colin."

"Mom, can you tell me when we pass the used car lot?"

"What? Why the sudden interest in Wallingford?"

Katie's insincere voice spins a convenient lie. "Oh, Colin and I were talking about maybe visiting some time while he's at school. You know...taking the R3 since the station is right in front of the school."

"Taking the train? On his own? We need to talk about that."

"Sure, sure. I thought we'd hop on the train after his orientation this weekend. I mean, It's only one stop from my apartment. And one of the landmarks is the used car lot. So, I was just helping him get familiar with the area, that's all."

"Sounds like you already have this figured out, but we still need to talk about it, okay?" The radio's pushbutton is pressed, interrupting a TastyKake jingle.

Colin can't hear his cousin's response but feels more air rushing into the car as she rolls down her window. The chatter subsides as the Mustang picks up speed, heading south towards the airport. Elvis Presley fills the void with *The Wonder of You*. His dad loved Elvis.

He recalls the lyrics of *Return to Sender* spilling from the transistor radio his dad gave him for his tenth birthday, a rare celebration when his father was home and struggling to stay sober. They were walking to the Gerrit Street deli for a double scoop of Breyers vanilla ice cream. As they negotiated the broken pavement, holding hands, Colin–could feel him trembling. Approaching the deli, Colin was less interested in getting his ice cream and more pre-occupied with the question that made his own body quiver. "Dad, can I ask you something?"

"Depends on the something, I guess."

Colin stopped and turned off his radio. It was a brilliant summer day, and he could see his father's unmistakable shape crouch down and lean in. "Dad....um. Do...." He choked his words.

"It's okay son, what is it?"

"Do you drink because I'm blind?"

His father swallowed him. "No, no, no. Oh Colin, never think that. Never."

They were still planted in the middle of the sidewalk, neighbors skirting around them. His father moved him gently to the side, until they were seated on the curb between two parked cars. Colin heard the pinging of a cooling engine.

"Colin, this may be hard to understand but let me try to explain, okay?"

The lump in Colin's throat prevented him from answering. He nodded vigorously, tears dripping down onto his small hand that still squeezed a dollar bill for ice cream.

"Oh my God look at you. You are so brave."

"I'm not brave. You're the hero."

His father managed a laugh. "You need to stop listening to Mr. Stiles, and listen to me, okay?" His father handed him a clean handkerchief. "Don't blow your nose in that. I'm going to need it too."

"Okay dad."

"Good. Now listen. So, you have a condition, right? You're blind and you can't see. Well, I've got a condition too. I think I was born with it – just like you. But my condition is different. Some people – like your mom. They can have one drink and stop."

"You never have just one."

His father exhaled deeply. "Exactly, son. That's my condition. And the only way I can get rid of it is not to drink at all. I can't even have one."

"So, can't you drink something else, like soda? You should try ginger ale, I love it."

"That sounds delicious. Let's go get that ice cream and I'll get a ginger ale, okay? And one more thing, I want you to know something important. I'm proud of you. Colin, you are my hero, and never forget it." His father tried to suppress a sob and snorted. They both laughed.

Colin thrust the handkerchief toward him. "Thanks. You can blow your nose now. I'm okay."

His father guided Colin to his feet and positioned him toward the deli. He placed Colin's hand on the mailbox just a few feet away from where they were sitting. "Okay son let's see if you can get to the front of the deli on your own. There's an ice cream cone waiting for you with your name on it."

"Colin, hey Colin, are you taking a nap?" Katie's voice snaps him back to the present. He hears the familiar sounds of the airport. He wants to tell her she can't leave. Not now. Not until he gets to tell her about Pete. "Why don't you jump up front for the ride home, stretch those legs." She pulls him out of the car, grunting. "God, you gotta stop growing."

His mom answers first. "Tell me about it. I buy enough groceries for a family of four."

Katie is already hugging him, whispering softly, "just a few hours and I'll be back, right?"

Colin squeezes her tightly. "Please hurry."

"Hannah, I'll call you if my schedule changes. Otherwise, I'll be back by 5:00."

"Great. You're coming straight to our house, right?"

Katie pounds the top of the car and carefully closes the

door on Colin's side. "Don't worry, I'm already packed for my overnight. Bye!"

Colin rolls up the window as the shrill blast of a police whistle directs the Mustang away from the curb. His mom mumbles, "this traffic just keeps getting worse. I hate this place. And I'm not too happy with your attitude either, mister. You barely said a word and when you did you were making no sense. Are you smoking pot? You can tell me you know."

"No, I tell you that every time you ask, which is about twice a week."

"Damn, it's so confusing getting out of this place...okay this is it. We're good. Did you ever think the reason I keep asking is because you're freaking me out? Talking to imaginary friends. Making Ben's life miserable."

"He grounded me!"

"You were eavesdropping on his conversation with a patient, Colin. Don't you get it?"

"He disconnected the kitchen phone, mom."

"No...we're getting a new phone during the renovations. He was just getting a head start."

"Do you hear yourself? Ben? Mr. Handyman? What if I need to make an emergency call?"

"Well...you can use the phone outside our bedroom."

"That phone hasn't worked properly since the moon landing. Maybe Ben could get a head start on that before we land on Mars."

The only response is a defeated sigh from his mother. Suddenly, the car leaps forward. Colin grabs both sides of the bucket seat. His shoulders stiffen at the sound of his mother slamming the gearshift. His feet press the floorboard as the Mustang responds to another twitch of the pilot's throttle. Realizing he's been holding his breath far too long, Colin exhales sharply.

Calmly, with a commanding undertone, Hannah finally asks, "Did something happen between you and Katie?"

"What do you mean?" Colin pants. He slides the bucket seat

back as far as it will go.

"You've been acting strange since she came over on Wednesday night."

"We just went out for ice cream."

"That was a pretty long time for ice cream."

"We were just talking about...dad."

"What about dad? What were you discussing?"

"Lots of stuff." He hesitates. Then, reclaiming his bravado, he says sharply, "Katie gets me." The Mustang slowly settles. He regrets his remark instantly, even before the hurt in his mother's voice pierces him.

"Okay, um...well I'm used to that crabby attitude but your cousin, the person who 'gets you,' kept trying to talk to you and you basically ignored her today...and me of course. Asking crazy questions about parking lots." She takes a deep breath. "Just...please don't piss her off. She's doing us a big favor tomorrow. She's been so good to us."

Colin tries to be more soothing. "You think I don't know that? You think I don't remember? After the eviction, Katie saved our lives," he says passively.

His mom sounds exasperated. "You don't have to remind me Colin."

Colin matches her frustration. "But that's just the point, I can't remind you because you never want to talk about it. Especially Ben. All he wants to do is bury the past. Move on. Make a new beginning. Blah, blah, blah."

She rubs his shoulder. "Well maybe he's right. Maybe the healthy thing for all of us, including your cousin, is to remember the good times and build a better life for ourselves. Starting with your time with Katie this weekend, okay?"

"Sure. Maybe I'll just introduce her to my imaginary friend."

His mother growls and spits her response. "Why don't you clam up and take a nap? I'm in no mood for your sarcasm." Colin slides down in his seat and arches his head back. *THAT WAS THE LEAST SARCASTIC COMMENT I MADE THIS MORNING.*

CHAPTER 11

Peace Offering
Sunday – 1:00 PM

Colin washes his hands at the kitchen sink. He splashes cool water on his face, flips his head back and runs wet fingers through his hair. He spent the last hour digging in the garden with his mom. She's going strong, but Colin's had enough. Still, another hour closer to Katie's arrival. Mr. Humphrey's cackling crew reminds him they are putting the finishing touches on Ben's office. His mom is a little uncomfortable they're working on a Sunday, but Ben wanted everything finished before leaving for New York. Colin rips a clammy t-shirt over his head, sniffs his armpits, and flinches. Ben's office door opens. The racket intensifies, pouring down the hallway and into the kitchen. Colin flips his soggy shirt over his shoulder and spins around at the sound of the refrigerator door opening, followed by the snap of a pull tab. In between gulps Ben offers, "you want a Tab?"

"No thanks. I'm gonna clean up."

"Aw, come on. You look like you need it." A kitchen chair scrapes the linoleum. "Come on, sit." Ben's tone is inviting, not stern.

"Fine."

Colin sits on the edge of the chair, purposely avoiding the sticky vinyl against his bare torso. Ben plunks a can in front of Colin and groans as he squeezes into his seat. Colin 's index finger teases the pull tab but doesn't open the can. He hates sugar-free soda. Another thing Ben should already know. *HE'S*

BEING NICE. GIVE HIM A BREAK. "Thanks."

"Consider it a peace offering."

Colin taps the soda can on the table.

Ben lowers his voice. "Lighten up, Colin. Listen, we've given your mom plenty to fret about over the last week. Starting with me. I could have been less defensive, more open with you. We should have been working together on this. Doing the best thing for your mom. Instead, I pushed you away. Not exactly an honorable choice in my profession. So, kudos to you for coming around on that thing with Katie. Not upsetting your mom with stories about your dad."

Colin smirks. "*Crazy* stories," he teases.

"Um, let's just say confused," Ben offers guardedly. "Anyway, here's my final peace offering." Ben slides a long narrow carton the size of a shoe box across the kitchen table. Colin feels its weight, smells the newness of its contents.

"Go ahead, open it."

Colin is already tucking his fingers under the corrugated side flap and pushing back the lid.

"Do you know what it is?"

His fingers touch familiar buttons and knobs. "It's a cassette player, right?"

"Yup, but it's the latest technology. Uses these newer Scotch cassettes." Ben gets up from the table and comes around to Colin's side. He places a box of cassettes in front of him. "Higher frequency, better quality. I have no idea what that means but the sound is supposed to be improved. I figured if you're going to be writing songs, you might as well have something portable you could use to record all those lyrics -- instead of going around talking to yourself."

"Um, thanks. That's nice," he says begrudgingly.

"You really were just shouting out lyrics yesterday, right?"

"Yeah, I had this song in my head...I went to the garage to be alone and figure out the words. I was just tossing out lyrics that were in my head when mom arrived and declared me insane."

"Hey, it's okay. She's doing the best she can. You're lucky to have a mom like her." He hesitates. "We're both lucky."

Colin doesn't respond. He plays with the buttons of his new cassette recorder. Ben pierces the awkwardness. "Oh, I almost forgot." He turns Colin's left wrist and drops a microphone into his open palm. "This is better than the one I use for dictation. Plugs right into your recorder and will give you great sound quality along with these fancy tapes."

"You're really laying it on thick."

Ben chuckles.

"What's so funny?"

"It's about to get thicker." Colin hears a phone being removed from its cradle. The wall phone! "Brand new push-button phone as promised. It's yellow, not that it matters to you, but that's what your mom wanted. He steps away. "And finally... hear that?"

Colin leans forward and frowns. "No, not really."

"Exactly," Ben says excitedly. "That, Colin, is the quiet new latch for the basement door. The guys finished up on this stuff while you were out in the yard. I wanted it to be a surprise."

Colin allows a smile and nods approvingly. "Mom knows about this?"

"Of course, we planned it together. In fact, she has a little something to go with your cassette recorder, but I won't steal her thunder. For now, you better get that shower. I've got to pay these guys and get ready for our trip. So, we're good?"

"Yeah, we're good," Colin says grudgingly.

Ben's steps are already fading. Colin fully expects some commentary from Pete, but the room is silent. The emptiness is unsettling. Colin rises from the table, leaving all of Ben's peace offerings behind. He opens the refrigerator and returns the unopened can. As he leaves the kitchen, his fingers brush the handset of the new phone. *KATIE WILL BE HERE IN FOUR HOURS.*

CHAPTER 12

Mr. Stiles

Sunday – 4:30 PM

After a long, hot shower Colin sprawls sideways across his bed, hoping sleep might fill the void until Katie arrives. He feels pressure on the edge of the bed. The lingering scent of Pete creeps into the bedspread. He rises to his elbows. "Hey, stranger." The bed lightens and Colin hears things being spread out on the floor.

"What are all those boxes and gadgets?"

"Hey, don't mix that stuff up, okay? They're peace offerings from Ben, plus a bunch of cassettes from my mom about preparing blind students for college. She came up here about an hour ago. I sort of forgot to take the gifts from Ben up to my room."

"On purpose?"

"You get right to the point, don't you?"

"You're the one who mentioned it. And what did you mean by 'peace offerings?'"

Colin swings over to the side of the bed, stretches his legs and rubs his thighs "Ben's words...not mine. You know, maybe if you were around more...I wouldn't have to do so much explaining. Are you okay? You seem to be absent...a lot."

"it's not on purpose. I can't explain it. I can't control it. I'm...I'm slipping away."

"Slipping away?" he repeats nervously. He stands and his legs feel rubbery. "Is it me? Did I do something?"

There's a faint knock on his closed bedroom door. As he

walks shakily towards the middle of the room his feet scatter the cassettes. His head swivels slowly towards the knocking. “Come on in,” he says weakly. The door opens and Ben whistles in surprise. “Wow, you really are getting into this. His mom’s eager voice follows. “This makes me so happy. Maybe you and Katie can listen together.”

Colin collects his thoughts while Pete interrupts.

“Tell them the truth. You don’t have time for this. You’re worried about your visitor from the dead...standing next to them.”

There are three blurs in front of Colin.

Hannah continues. “Speaking of Katie, I forgot to tell you her flight was delayed just a bit. She’ll be an hour or so late.”

Colin hides his disappointment. “That’s okay mom. I’ve got plenty to keep me busy.”

He casually takes in the random patterns of shadows throughout his bedroom. A partially drawn shade allows enough sunlight to reveal Pete’s presence by the window.

“Well, just remember what this weekend is about,” she says eagerly. “I hope you’re looking forward to this Colin. It’s a big step.”

“Yeah, sure mom. I mean, I’m not super stoked or anything like that, but yeah, I guess.”

“You guess? Honey, this is a big deal. Meeting faculty and kids you’re going to be spending a lot of time with. Listen to those tapes, okay. It might help.”

Ben laughs as Hannah playfully hits Colin with a pillow.

“Okay good...Hannah we’ve got to get moving.”

“I know, I know. Remember to call the hotel and leave a message after you get back from orientation, okay?”

“I won’t forget.”

“Good. Now, give me a hug.” Colin extends his arms. She leans in and smothers him.

“I just put lasagna in the oven. It’s not completely thawed so you’ll need a little more time. It should be ready by six o’clock. And maybe you could clean up this room a little.”

Colin’s playful response is not intended for his mother.

"You're right. It feels sloppy in here."

The window shade releases, snapping loudly.

Hannah shrieks while Colin suppresses a smile.

"Ben, things are falling apart around here. You might as well add that to the list."

"Hey, I'll have you know my list is getting shorter."

Teasingly, Hannah badgers Ben. "Not for long, I also asked Tim to seal up that access to the coal chute…"

"Oh, I already know. He told me when I *thought* I was writing his final check."

"Yeah, sorry. This one's not negotiable. I'm afraid of squirrels getting down there."

Ben whistles lightheartedly. "Okay, let's go."

Within minutes the front door closes after one final goodbye carries up the staircase.

"Sloppy?"

"It was a joke, Pete. And what's with the shade? You scared my mom."

"I was angry."

"Ironic…a wise man once told me that you shouldn't let your anger control you."

"Well, You've got a few hours until your cousin gets here so, feel free to figure that wise man out." Sadly, he adds, *"something he hasn't been able to do for himself."*

Colin senses the spirit's departure. His compassion for his misplaced companion is real. With all the sincerity he can muster he says loudly, "I haven't forgotten you. I promise."

As soon as the heartfelt pledge leaves his lips, the front door opens downstairs. Colin hears heavy panting and footsteps pounding the stairs. From the hallway Ben's breathless voice surprises him. "Hey Colin." He enters the room. "Sorry, I almost forgot. I left the Wallace's phone number down on the kitchen counter for Katie. Just in case you need it." His voice is already disappearing down the hallway. "I know you won't use it, but it makes your mom feel better…leaving for real this time." The front door slams shut.

Colin scoffs. "The Wallace family," he mutters mockingly. He hasn't spoken to them or any neighbor for almost, well almost forever. There's nobody on this street he can rely on. Nobody like Mr. Stiles.

By far, Leonard Stiles was Colin's favorite Gerrit Street neighbor. In his mid-sixties, Stiles was a First World War amputee who lived with his sister in the ground floor apartment. Colin barely remembers the sister. But he vividly recalls the gruff old veteran and their time together. Every day, weather permitting, he and Mr. Stiles would sit on a squeaky metal glider that took up most of the narrow porch fronting the street. Mr. Stiles -- always muttering, belching, or farting -- would bring a pillow and slide it behind Colin, protecting him from the glider's rigid, basket-weave design that left impressions on his back.

The neighborhood was their blank canvas, and his elderly friend painted it for him.

Colin especially enjoyed his colorful descriptions of Buddy May, the neighborhood bully. "Oh, here he comes Colin. Our friend Mayo strutting like a big man. Swear to God, I've never seen a boy walk like him. Pretty sure he just shit his pants." Colin would laugh and Mr. Stiles would rub his hair. They talked about everything. Football, of course. Mr. Stiles loved the Eagles, just like his dad. And the old man always teased him about the nuns at St. Gabriel, Colin's parish school located a block away. "You ever get in trouble with any of them sisters, you come straight to me, you hear?" Colin politely agreed, knowing he would never take him up on the offer. Mr. Stiles was the closest thing he had to a grandfather. His mom's parents, who lived in New Jersey, rarely visited. If they did, it was only when they were sure Colin's dad wasn't around. His mom kept telling Colin they were "very private people." But Colin understood. He pieced together enough of his grandfather's cold, hushed comments to his mom during fleeting visits in their cramped apartment. He did all the talking. His mom never responded. Her silence tore a hole in

Colin's soul.

TOMMY BYRNE WAS NEVER GOOD ENOUGH FOR YOU HANNAH.

WE WARNED YOU.

WHAT WERE YOU THINKING MARRYING A DRIFTER TEN YEARS OLDER THAN YOU?

THAT BLIND CHILD IS YOUR PUNISHMENT FOR GETTING MARRIED TO A DRUNKEN MICK.

That's all Colin is to his only living grandfather. *THAT BLIND CHILD*. Regardless of his mom's excuses, Colin knows the truth – her parents don't care about their grandson. As for Colin's dad, his parents have been dead for decades. Colin's paternal grandfather fought in the First World War just like Mr. Stiles but was killed in action just days before the conflict ended. Colin's dad was only three years old, too young to salvage any memories of a young soldier who never came home. Colin never met his paternal grandmother, who died while his dad was serving in Europe during World War II. So, while most of the kids at school and in the neighborhood had grandparents, Colin had Mr. Stiles.

Once in early Spring 1961, on one of the first days warm enough to sit outside, Colin worked up the courage to ask Mr. Stiles about his missing leg. He was nine years old, and the old man let him feel his stump. Colin recoiled. "That's okay son, that's okay. You hear all of them morons out there in the street playing war and firing their toy guns. That's not war." He guided Colin's hand back to his amputated leg. "This is war Colin and it ain't fun. Remember that." Colin told Mr. Stiles that his father would not talk to him about fighting in Europe. His porch mate leaned closer. His breath smelled just like his dad's. He whispered, "God bless Tommy Byrne. Your father is a good man Colin, a good man indeed. I hear him upstairs crying at night. I know you do too. But just remember this, Colin. Your daddy is a hero. Never forget it, okay?"

That's when Colin realized that his father's nightmares were not a family secret. Everyone in their thin-walled apartment building heard what he experienced most nights. His mom would always come to his room and softly reassure him, “daddy is just having bad dreams about the war.” The nightmares never stopped. Neither did Mr. Stiles undying admiration for Colin’s dad.

Colin stands up and smiles. He misses Mr. Stiles. Longs for another porch conversation that always left him feeling proud of his father. The only person who makes him feel that way today is Katie. He smells the lasagna and remembers -- she’ll be here soon.

CHAPTER 13

Don't Be Afraid

Sunday – 6:45 PM

Katie's warm embrace at the front door renews Colin's hope for answers about his father. She steps into the foyer. Well-traveled luggage gruffly pounds the carpet.

"Fog in Pittsburgh. Gets me every time. Sorry I missed your mom and Ben. I'm sure she'll call later to check in."

"Definitely. Just to make sure you didn't abandon me."

Going through the motions, he gropes for her luggage.

"Leave it smart-ass. Let's eat first. Jesus, something smells good. Are you cooking?"

"Lasagna in the oven. Mom put it in before they left."

Katie wraps her arm around him and steers him towards the kitchen. "So, I'm two hours late and now you're feeding me. What's wrong with this picture?" They enter the kitchen. Colin leans against the counter while his cousin opens the oven door. Suddenly he's hungry.

"Okay, it's starting to bubble. Hannah timed this perfectly. And of course, she already has the table set."

Colin chuckles. "Actually, I did that. How does it look?"

Perfect, my man, perfect. Hungry?"

"A little."

"Well, I'm famished." The rattle of her shoes hitting the linoleum startles Colin. "Can't believe they make us wear these blasted things all day." She gently nudges Colin aside and reaches behind him. "Excuse me buddy." She turns on the radio. A familiar song fills the kitchen then quickly vanishes as she twirls the AM dial and stops. "Oh, love this one, ever hear this?"

"Katie, they play it every ten minutes."

She shouts over the music. "Yeah, I heard it three times coming from the airport. I kept telling the cab driver to turn it up. Can't get enough of it. I even love the group's name, Five Stairsteps." She pushes the volume so high Colin can feel the countertop vibrating.

Ooh child…things are gonna get easier…

He smiles, moves away from the radio and plants himself in his usual chair at the kitchen table. His cousin is singing loudly.

Colin taps the table, matching the song's tempo, feeling the promise of this weekend.

"I see you, Colin. Come on you know the words." She grabs his hand and pulls him to his feet. They glide freely across the floor – just like he used to do with his mom on Gerrit Street. He sings too, determined to match his cousin's intensity.

We'll put it together and we'll get it undone.

They both laugh. His cousin gives him a bear hug and kisses his forehead. "That's my Colin."

The music is so loud they barely hear the phone ringing. Katie says, "I'll get it. Probably your mom." She shouts into the phone as Colin scrambles to turn off the radio.

"No, no…just listening to some music while your lasagna finishes…I will…let it cool five minutes, got it…don't worry I'll get him there on time…okay enjoy your trip and drive safely… Hannah, I got it…okay, okay…bye!"

"Got all your instructions?"

"Oh man, that lady needs to relax." The handset lands back on its cradle.

"I don't want to go," he says breathlessly.

"What are you talking about?"

"Tomorrow, I don't want to waste a whole day."

"It's your orientation, Colin. You're going."

"I'm frustrated, Katie. We don't have time."

"We'll make time, mister. Can you imagine telling them you didn't go?"

"We'll fake it."

"Right, until the school calls to find out why you didn't show up. Are you sure you're smart enough to get a scholarship?" She playfully jabs him.

"I can't even sleep. You told me all that stuff about seeing my dad and now I'm supposed to just show up on campus tomorrow like everything is normal?"

As she removes the lasagna from the oven, she says, "relax Colin, okay? We can figure this out. Now, sit down."

Reluctantly, he slides back into his seat.

"We'll let this cool..."

Colin is startled by her unexpected gasp, followed by the impact of the baking dish hitting the floor. He jumps up, recoiling from the scalding food that whips his face sideways.

Katie's trembling words confuse him. Her voice is empty of all the happiness that moments ago sang a favorite song. "Who are you? Why... where's my uncle!" Colin steps towards her, realizing immediately what is happening. His eyes focus on Katie's subdued shape cast against the harsh kitchen light.

She is joined by another familiar form.

The air no longer carries the pleasing aroma of tonight's dinner. Instead, it smells dusty. Feels clammy.

"Don't be afraid. I'm Pete."

Katie's blurred image separates from the spirit and disappears. Colin cringes as her body strikes the floor.

"She fainted Colin."

"Is she bleeding, is she okay?" Colin is on the floor, swiping away her discarded shoes, scrambling to her side as chunks of broken glass burrow into his knees.

"Her butt hit the floor first. She's not bleeding."

"Katie, can you hear me? Are you okay?"

She groans and sits up. "Where is he? That man. He looks like Uncle Tommy."

"Pete? He looks like my dad?"

She squeezes Colin's arm tightly. "You know him?" They both stand as Colin steadies her. Perplexed, she repeats, "you know him?"

Colin sweetly reminds her, "I wanted to talk to you about this the other night, but Ben interrupted, remember?"

Over Colin's shoulder, Pete's matter of fact voice declares, *"I'm right here."*

"Move away Colin. Move! Oh, Christ. He's wearing the jacket. That same jacket. Where did you get that?"

"I have no idea why I'm wearing these clothes."

Colin interrupts. "What do you mean he looks like my father? "Is that my father? Is that who you saw in Wallingford?"

"There's a definite resemblance, but no...up close...no, it's not Uncle Tommy."

Colin's confusion grows -- his senses are as messy as the slop on the floor.

Katie is breathing rapidly. "Oh, God. I'm gonna barf."

Colin can feel the energy of Pete's body sliding by, approaching his cousin. *"Oh, please don't do that. Take a deep breath, okay? I won't hurt you."*

Katie response is muffled. Her hands must be shielding her face. "His lips aren't moving. I can hear his voice, but holy crap his mouth is shut."

Colin shudders.

Katie's confused voice continues, "is he alive?"

Colin matches her intensity. "No, of course not!"

Pete calmly responds, *"please stop shouting over each other. You both have a lot of questions, so we all need to settle down... maybe start over?"*

Less fearful, Katie's slightly shaking voice probes again, "was it you I saw near my apartment?"

Colin watches Pete's image edge closer to his cousin. *"I don't know. I'm sorry."*

"Come on, did I? You were floating all over town, remember?"

"No. I have trouble sorting things out, Katie. Maybe we can help each other. But first..."

"What, tell me what?" She sounds more composed. Eager for answers.

"We should clean up this mess. And maybe you should tidy yourself up, too."

Colin chuckles as he plucks dried cheese from his long hair. "Trust me. You won't get another word out of him until this kitchen is spotless."

She manages a giggle, "Oh my God, you're a mess too. You need a shower more than me, Colin." She turns more serious. "And your knees are bleeding. Are you hurt?"

"Nah, I'm used to punishing my body. But I need that shower." He nods in Pete's direction.

"Well then why don't both of you get yourself cleaned up. I'll manage this catastrophe."

She utters his name for the first time. "Thank you...Peter. You don't mind?"

"Katie, he *wants* us to get out of his way."

Pete adds, *"watch your feet. There's glass on the floor."*

Colin glides his palm along the kitchen wall until he finds the phone. He lifts the handset and brings it to his ear. His sticky index finger searches the rotary dial, then responds instinctively to the feel of Ben's a new push-button replacement. He quickly punches the first digit.

"Who are you calling?"

Colin doesn't respond to her, focusing intently on the next number.

Pete whispers, *"he's ordering pizza. Pepperoni and mushrooms."*

Colin smiles and places his hand over the mouthpiece. "I need to eat before we get started. We've got a lot of catching up to do."

Some day, yeah. We'll put it together and we'll get it undone.

CHAPTER 14

The Medallion

Sunday – 11:00 PM

Colin sits cross-legged on thick-piled carpet in the middle of the living room. Mrs. Judson's piano rests just six feet behind him. He feels her presence more than ever. To his left is Katie, nursing a beer and complaining about her sore ass. To his right is Pete, humming quietly and saying very little. His cousin speaks softly to the spirit.

"You're actually pretty good looking for a dead guy whose mouth doesn't move."

Colin smiles. Finally, someone else understands. Despite the utter confusion and disorder, he appreciates one rock-solid truth – he's not crazy. And neither is Katie. Each carries a burden that Colin believes is a bit lighter tonight because they no longer bear it alone. For some reason they have been linked to someone beyond this world. Beyond normal. He yawns heavily.

Katie chuckles. "Are we boring you Colin?"

Fatigue shrouds Colin. It feels great. "It's weird. I'm exhausted, but in a good way."

"That's the way I feel about this beer…it's kicking my butt."

Pete chuckles. *"I'm glad we met, Katie."*

Colin stands slowly and moves toward the piano bench. Tenderly, he says, "Pete, even though we've been together for a year, I feel like I'm *just* meeting you. Tonight, I learned for the first time that you look like my dad. Katie, can you describe him to me?"

"Me? Hey, you know him better than anybody."

"No, I mean physically. Describe his features to me."

"Oh, sure, sure. But you can't see so what does it matter?"

"It means everything. God, I just found out his mouth doesn't move. What else is there?"

Katie doesn't hesitate. "A scar. Yup, on the left side of his face...a big one. From his cheek to his chin. That's why...when I saw him up close earlier...I knew it couldn't be your dad. So, Peter...what's the story with the scar? Care to share?"

"I'm afraid I have no recollection."

"Really?" Katie says skeptically. "Hard to believe that doesn't conjure up something nasty."

Colin calmly interrupts. "Okay, a mysterious scar. What else? One eye in the middle of his forehead?"

She sighs. "Oh no. Two beautiful blue eyes, just like your dad. In fact, a lot of features that remind me of Uncle Tommy. The red hair of course, and his chin is kind of round." She pokes Colin's chin. "Like this." She tweaks his nose. "And this upturned nose. That's a dead giveaway."

Pete chuckles. *"Dead giveaway?"*

Katie laughs too. "And he likes puns. Now if you could only remember seeing me earlier..."

"But I don't remember seeing you. I don't remember anything."

Katie yawns and mumbles, "that's right. He's got amnesia too."

"Don't stop trying Katie," Pete pleads. *"Help me remember."*

Katie doesn't respond. Colin senses her drifting off. He plops sideways on the bench. His fingers brush the piano's familiar walnut surface. He swears he can smell Mrs. Judson's hand cream. To his left, Pete's image is barely visible by the dim light of a lamp perched on top of the piano. The room is hushed. Colin feels tranquil. Katie abruptly snorts and breathes heavily. Colin and Pete giggle in harmony. The ghost moves past Colin and disappears toward the sound of his sleeping cousin.

"What are you doing?"

"Just putting this blanket on your cousin. She looks so peaceful

for a change."

Colin smiles. "Not used to having that much energy around here are you Pete, or do you prefer Peter?"

"She can call me whatever she wants as long as this goes somewhere."

"This had to be a pretty weird night for you."

"Actually, Colin, I feel different. Hopeful, I guess. For both of you but maybe for me too. You look exhausted."

"What time is it?"

Pete responds flatly, *"Almost midnight."*

"Okay, that's enough. I think I can sleep."

"No!" Katie's voice jolts Colin. He springs from the bench. "Peter, Peter," she squeals. She is fully engaged. "Peter, have you ever seen a picture of my uncle...Colin's father?

"No, never, I..."

Colin hears her pattering through carpet, then rustling through her bag. Her voice is animated. "You're kidding. You've been hanging around for a year...doing your friendly ghost thing... and you've never seen one goddamn picture?"

Colin hears the snap of her purse or wallet, her fingers fumbling. Defensively, he snaps, "I don't have any pictures to show him. What would I do with a piece of paper that I can't see? It's not Pete's fault. Give him a break, okay?" He slumps onto the piano bench. His cousin slides next to him. The solidly built bench barely moves.

"Colin, if you could see me now, I would be taking my foot out of my mouth. Sorry. That was pretty stupid. Sometimes I just forget. You're just a normal kid to me."

"Forget it. Really...we're all exhausted."

Pete, standing inches from them, says *"I'm not tired. "I don't sleep, Katie."*

"You don't sleep. Well then, why don't you use all that extra time on your hands and try to remember if you recognize my uncle, how about that? Go on take it." There is a long pause. "What's wrong? He won't take the picture."

Colin explains. "He can't touch it as long as you are holding it." He stands up and moves away from the bench. He nods toward his vacant seat. "Put it down."

His cousin gasps slightly. "Okay, that's creepy. Sorry, but that's just creepy."

"What's going on? What's he doing?"

"He's floating Colin. His feet are six inches off the floor...and his eyes are closed."

Colin's brain revisits small slices of the past twelve months. It jolts him to consider all the physical things about Pete he never witnessed. He always thought of him as just another person he couldn't see. He assumed it all. That his mouth moved. That his feet were always on the floor. He imagined Pete the way he approached the image of any person teasing his damaged optical nerves. Pete – despite his quirks -- was still very much a human presence. Until tonight.

"Okay now he's turning really slow. Wow, this is kind of crazy. He can do all this crazy shit and he's still trapped here. I'm starting to feel sorry for the guy."

"This might go on for a while Katie."

"Well now is not the time for him to go all Twilight Zone on us. Peter! Hey! Get back here! Can't you talk some sense into him?"

"Katie, please be quiet. Seriously. Shut up."

Her silence tells Colin she is probably shocked by his response. He sits on the piano bench and speaks calmly -- in a way he never would have spoken to Pete in the past.

"Pete, we really want to hear what you are thinking, but only when you're ready, okay. We're going to call it a night. Take as long as you need."

"Colin, we don't have a lot of time. What if he takes days to come back to you?"

"Then he takes days. He can't be rushed. Good night, Katie. We'll talk in a few hours."

Colin's bruised and wobbly legs carry him to the sofa. He lands hard on the silk brocade fabric and curls his body onto his stomach. His left-hand drops to the floor and touches the glossy texture of a wallet-sized piece of paper. He imagines it is the photograph of his father. He pinches its edges and clings to those times when his dad made him feel important. He pulls the photo close to him and tucks it under his chest.

He closes his eyes and remembers the Spring of 1966. That's when his dad began taking Colin to Little Crum Creek Park -- the tiny patch of woods and wetlands that quickly become their favorite destination. Usually, they would sit on a small wooden footbridge that arched over the creek. Colin would swing his legs over the side. Feel the water's coolness as his toes pointed closer to the current. His dad would toss stones into the creek right under his feet until water leapt up on Colin – laughing when a sizeable splash would reach his face. And he would describe everything to his son.

"That rustling you hear is a deer walking on the right bank."

"There's a frog sunning itself on a smooth boulder right below your feet."

"Tilt your head back. The sun is slicing through the trees and lighting up the bridge. "Feel it?"

He did. He felt it all. Safe and loved.

As spring inched closer to summer, Colin could feel the difference in the park. The air was warmer. The smells were richer. Birds chattered from every direction. Each day -- further removed from Gerrit Street -- revealed a difference in his dad, too. On Memorial Day they made a special visit to the park. As they approached the footbridge, his dad suddenly stopped.

"Hey, pal, I've got something for you. Listen, I know I haven't given you much to connect with my family. That's not on purpose. I just don't have the memories or the relatives who can make sense of the past. But I do have this, and I want to give it to you." He gently took Colin's right hand, then turned his palm up. He placed a small felt bag into his hand. "Open it."

Colin fumbled with the bag. His dad retrieved it from his fingers and offered to help. "Here, now open your hand again." Colin felt his father place a small metal object in his palm.

"What is it dad?"

"It's the closest thing you're going to get to a family heirloom. It's a medal."

"Yours? From the war?"

His father chuckled, "No, even better. It belonged to my father. Remember his name was Colin, too. You were named after him."

"But you said he died in World War I...you never knew him."

"That's right. It was returned to my mom. Then she gave it to me before I shipped out for Europe in 1942. I was 25 years old, Colin"

Colin carefully touched every indentation of the small round object. He let it roll through his fingertips. "It was his?"

"Yup. Here let me show you."

He took Colin's finger and guided it across the surface. "It's called the Order of Saint Barbara Medallion. Feel that? It's a likeness of Saint Barbara standing in front of a tower."

"Who's Saint Barbara?"

Before he could answer there was a barrage of footsteps on the narrow bridge. His father instinctively paused to fill in the blanks for Colin. "Just a bunch of kids with fishing rods heading down to the creek." Then he continued, "She's the patron saint of artillerymen. My dad was in the artillery." He flipped the medal in his son's hand. "Here, feel that? It's a cannon."

"Why did he get a medal?"

"I don't have a lot of details. The medal is given to men who are part of the Order of Saint Barbara. There used to be a ribbon attached to it, but that's long gone. Anyway, it was given to artillerymen who showed the highest level of integrity and moral character."

"So, he was really important, right?"

His father wrapped his arm around his son's shoulder and pulled him tighter. "I don't know if he was important in terms of rank, but it meant he was a really good person. He lived his life well and was a good example to the men he served with.

So, yes...come to think of it he was important. That's why I'm proud you're named after him."

They continued to the footbridge. In six paces Colin knew they had reached the apex of the wooden structure.

"Dad, why are you giving this to me? Don't you want to keep it?"

"Well, here's what I'm thinking. I never knew my dad. And you know I lost my mom before I came back home from the war. Your poor cousin Katie had to deal with most of that. She was only ten years old, but my sister was useless...so Katie had to grow up fast." His dad seemed to wander. The churning creek and the squeals of the kids fishing filled the void. Colin waited patiently. "I guess what I'm trying to say is that family is important. I don't want somebody else to put this in your hands after I'm gone. I want to be the one to do it. To give you some small connection to your past that comes directly from me, not some tin can or scrap book. Make sense?"

"Yeah, it does.

"Good, 'cause I've been babbling way too long." He handed Colin the felt bag. "Let's put this away, okay?"

Colin placed the medal safely in the threadbare bag and pulled gently on its strings. Realizing that his sweatpants didn't have any pockets, he clutched the family treasure tightly in his fist. His father touched his elbow and guided him forward. "Come on, let's take a walk." He guided Colin to the bottom of the bridge and steered him left, upstream from where the kids were fishing. "You know, Colin this tiny little stream makes its way through Delaware County, joins up with Crum Creek and then eventually dumps into the Delaware River down by the Boeing Plant. Think about it. A few trickles here that turn into a raging river.

"Mr. Stiles says the Delaware smells like dead fish and shit."

His dad chuckled, murmuring, "Leave it to Mr. Stiles to ruin a special moment. Okay, never mind about that. The Little Crum doesn't have raw sewage pouring into it. It's clean and fresh and we're going to enjoy it."

"You want me to drink it?"

"Oh God no, Colin. We're going to walk through it. Sit down here and take off your shoes and socks." He felt his dad plop down beside him to do the same. Colin still squeezed his keepsake in his hand as he removed his footwear. They both stood up together.

"Careful now we only have a few steps down the bank." The grass and mud felt much colder than Colin had imagined. His dad locked one hand behind Colin's elbow while grabbing his other hand to guide him into the creek.

"You're still holding your medal."

"I don't have any pockets."

"Okay, give it to me."

Colin shifted his weight and, in an instant, slipped on moss-covered stones that sent him tumbling backward. His father grabbed him as Colin shouted, "my medal. I dropped it!"

His dad quickly moved Colin towards the fringe of the creek bed, letting go of his son in the shallow water. It was frigid but Colin only had one thought as he groped mostly stones and mud. He panicked and shouted, "where is it? Can you see it?" His father didn't answer. Colin just heard him frantically splashing, then the slap, slap, slap of his bare feet on the hardened path as he raced toward the footbridge.

"Stay here!"

Colin, still on all fours, climbed out of the creek. He was shivering. Strangely, he thought about the grandfather he never knew. About the family heirloom his widow entrusted to their son. How, for a few precious moments it was Colin's father's gift to him. Now, it was gone. Lost by his blind son, his wife's *PUNISHMENT FOR GETTING MARRIED TO THAT DRUNKEN MICK.* Colin's mud-stained fingers pinched his eyes, and he began to cry. He wasn't feeling sorry for himself. His tears were meant for his father.

Then he heard their voices. The kids who were fishing downstream. "Hey mister...is this what you're looking for?" A miracle and a second chance. Colin swore he would never lose the medal again. Back at Katie's apartment he tucked it away in a Sucrets tin placed carefully under the mattress jammed into his makeshift bedroom. He checked for it every night, shaking the tin first then opening it to rub his fingers over the medallion. His confidence returned and he would check less often. He discovered it was gone on the Fourth of July, just days after his father disappeared. His mom said that maybe his father needed it more than him and would return it when he came back.

Four years later, he's still waiting -- dreaming of a breakthrough from this unlikely collaboration with Pete and Katie. He lingers on that hope, praying that his newfound patience with Pete will pay off. Finally, sleep arrives.

CHAPTER 15

The Riddle

Monday June 22, 1970 –8:00 AM

Colin sweeps into the kitchen, bathed in the aroma of freshly brewed coffee. Its nutty, smoky and tickles his senses. Katie's cheerful voice greets him. "Hey, ready for some java?"

"Yes! I hope it tastes as good as it smells."

"Not to brag but I make a mean cup of coffee. You still take yours black and boring?"

"Is there any other way?" He heads toward the counter and pivots slightly to his right – drawn to a rare pattern of morning light that washes the rear of the house. He can feel the warmth on his hair as the sun's rays filter through the window above the sink. He's grateful for the perspective it brings to the start of his day.

The coffee pot clanks on the stove as Katie says, "thanks again for my wake-up call. I'd still be comatose."

"You can thank Pete for that. He got me going first. All I did was pound on your door…for…five minutes I guess."

"Sorry, I was wasted after our pizza party. That one beer kicked my butt. Let's see, the last thing I remember is my favorite cousin telling me to shut up." She presses the warm mug into his hands.

Grinning widely, Colin buries his nose in his mug and savors the smell. He takes that treasured first sip and gags.

She giggles, slyly. "What's the matter?"

"You put sugar in this."

"You bet. Two heaping teaspoons. One for each time you told me to shut up."

"I can't drink this, no way."

She jiggles the mug from his grip. "Good," she says smugly. "That means more for me. By the way, Peter really is a perfectionist. This kitchen looks immaculate." She pours another cup and slides it along the counter. "Here, just the way you like it."

"Thanks." Meekly, Colin asks, "so, any chance I can talk you out of orientation?"

"Next question," she says firmly.

"Hey, it was worth a shot. Alright, then what are we going to tell Ben when he gets back?"

"We? That's a joke," she chides him. "You already threw me under the bus remember…you told Ben I was nuts?"

"Yeah, I did...sorry."

"Although I must admit that turned out to be a brilliant move, scoring some points…"

He slurps his coffee deliberately. "Wow, that means a lot… coming from a fabulous fibber like you." So, what are *you* going to say to Ben now that you've met Pete?"

Katie's exaggerated reply is sarcastic. "Sorry, Ben…you were right… that wasn't my uncle I've been seeing. It's actually a ghost whose been hanging out here with Colin for the last year. So, your stepson is nuts too. Oh…and don't tell Hannah, but the ghost bears a remarkable resemblance to her missing husband."

Colin is drowning again. He imagines his mom and Ben at the conference. Enjoying themselves. MOVING ON. "The thought of us sharing any of this with my mom is going to freak him out."

"Do you blame him? Hannah finally has the normal life she deserves. Putting the past behind her and along comes her missing husband's wacky niece…and her cranky kid with this startling news. What would you do if you were Ben?"

"Protect her," I guess.

"You guess? Colin, that's what Ben has been doing for years. You were too young to understand or appreciate just how supportive he was -- of your dad too by the way. Don't forget, I was the one who introduced Ben to your parents."

How could Colin forget. November 22nd of 1963. His father was on a road trip with Mr. Moretti. It was a Friday. Colin had a head cold with a light fever, enough to sway his mom to keep him home from school and give him the weekend to feel better. At lunch time she made his favorite, Campbell's chicken noodle soup with plenty of Saltines. She took his temperature, which was normal. That's when she told him.

She and his dad were sorry they had been fighting so much. His cousin Katie introduced them to her friend from Delaware County who was a marriage counselor. She referred to him as "Doctor Ben." He was going to help his parents be friends again. They would have to take the train out to visit him every week, but he was doing this as a favor for Katie. He remembers asking his mother, "will he be able to help dad with his nightmares?" And his surprise at the numb response his mother provided. "I don't know sweetheart, maybe he can help your father take more responsibility around here." Colin felt guilty. He was only eleven, but he understood that his mom was experiencing her own recurring nightmare. She was struggling too. Most of the details of that morning have faded. But the afternoon hours are burnished in his brain forever.

The pounding on the apartment door. Mrs. Judson telling his mom to turn on the television. "President Kennedy has been shot." Within thirty minutes the fatal news was delivered. He was gone. Colin could hear murmurs on the street, neighbors collecting to share the shock and grief of this paralyzing moment. His mom grabbed his hand and guided him down the steps to the front porch. The weather was unseasonably warm, almost 70 degrees. There was a hush that seemed out of place for this bustling street where so many people gathered. Mr. Stiles took his hand and encouraged his mom to talk to the neighbors. "This is not the time to be alone Hannah." His voice sounded shattered. His breath full of cheap whiskey. The old man reminded Colin about their trip to Independence Hall two summers earlier. It was the Fourth of July and President Kennedy made a speech. His dad and Mr. Stiles talked about it forever. Now, this terrible moment would linger far longer.

The national grief was slowly overshadowed by a return to the arguments, nightmares, and drinking. His parents did visit Doctor Ben. Colin even accompanied them a couple times when Mrs. Judson was unable to watch him. He remembers sitting in the waiting room, listening very quietly to his transistor radio, while raised voices would be tempered by Ben's calm commentary. He dreaded those train rides home. His parents barely spoke.

In late Spring 1964 they were evicted from their Grays Ferry apartment after Mrs. Judson accused his father of stealing from her. His mom went through the motions – saying all the things you'd expect from a supportive spouse but still sounding lost and deflated. Katie's career was in full flight. Her stewardess assignments kept her away for weeks. Back then, she lived in a spacious Swarthmore apartment, close to the college. Her roommate had just moved out, so she offered to take Colin's family in temporarily while they got settled. That's why they moved to Delaware County. Not to be closer to their marriage counselor, but simply because of Katie's generosity. The plan was to continue their counseling sessions, take the summer months to find Colin a suitable school, and eventually locate a place of their own. Within weeks a lot of different men showed up at the apartment, always looking for his father. They were happy, polite, and sober. Their visits were brief, and usually ended with his dad informing his mom that he was going to a meeting. Whatever they did at those meetings seemed to be making a difference in his father's behavior. He still hit the road for stretches but when he returned, he appeared healthier and happier. Colin was old enough to realize how hard his father was working on his sobriety. That's what made his disappearance so puzzling.

Colin's patchwork memories are interrupted by the squeak of the kitchen door as it swivels slightly then stops abruptly. The scent of charcoal overwhelms him.

"Peter, my new friend, we were just discussing you."

"I really need to talk to both of you...before you leave."

Colin's stomach stirs. "What is it?"

"I lived before Tommy."

Before Colin can respond, Katie says, "not following you, Peter. What does that mean...you lived before Uncle Tommy?"

Silence lingers, as Colin and his cousin wait for a response. Colin presses his fingers against his pounding temples. Finally, Pete begins to speak with an odd inflection in his voice that sounds bewildered.

"What I mean is...I left this world way before Tommy arrived. So, I never knew him. But we have a connection. I have a strong feeling about it."

Pete's image moves closer to Colin who responds, "okay, it's a start. I don't know where we go with it...but it's a start." The rare angle of the morning light is intense. It penetrates the kitchen and reveals an image that leaves Colin breathless. He sees more of Pete than he can ever remember. Details, not shadows. A face with some structure, still beyond recognition. But enough of a difference to deepen the words that Pete utters next.

"But...I met him."

Colin, confused, is still holding fast on the image before him. He doesn't want to look away. Katie asks the very question still tumbling in Colin's brain.

"Wait a minute. You just said you never knew him. That you came before him?"

Colin finally speaks. "Pete, if that's true then it's impossible for you to have met him, right?"

"I recognized the picture that Katie gave me. I've seen him before. I feel it. I know it."

Katie grips Colin's arm. Her energy spreads throughout his body.

He squeezes her hand. "Okay, now what are we supposed to do with that?"

"Hey ease up Colin. Didn't you say we needed to give Peter some space? And didn't he deliver? He gave us a riddle to solve. 'I lived before Tommy, whom I never knew... but I met him.' That's what we heard, right Pete?"

"I believe that's accurate."

Colin is dubious. "Really? I was hoping for something a little less confusing. I mean... what do we do now?"

"*You* are going to your orientation. I'm going to do some digging."

"For what?"

Colin hears liquid swirling down the drain. Waits for her answer.

"Remember, before Ben grounded you and cut us off, I was going to do some homework?"

Colin perks up. "Around our family's connection to mining?"

"Right. Well, I think I might be on to something, especially now...after meeting Pete. But first I need to make a phone call."

"Who are you calling?"

Katie sighs hesitantly. Before Colin can pester her further, Pete interrupts.

"Katie, there's more. I remember the auto dealer. I don't remember seeing you. In fact, I don't remember many of the details you shared. But I was in that town...on that street."

Colin hears Katie's fingers nervously tapping an empty mug. She asks, "do you remember hanging around the real estate office, on that same street...just a couple days ago?"

Colin waits for a response as the sound of the empty coffee pot and clinking mugs echo from the deep sink. "Pete?"

Katie responds. "He's not here. He's gone." She rustles his hair. "He's remembering, Colin."

"What about that riddle? Makes no sense."

"Well college boy, that's because you're thinking like a mere mortal. These last 24 hours have changed things for me. There's a supernatural solution staring right at us. And slow-poke Peter is hopefully leading us there."

"What's that supposed to mean?"

The promising light of the early morning abruptly dissolves. Gentle raindrops peck briefly at the window.

"It's getting nasty out there."

Within seconds a howling wind announces the arrival of a soaking rain. It feels like a fire hose is blasting the house. Colin's world is dark again. For the first time he is afraid of where this search is leading them. Maybe memories are enough. Maybe he doesn't need the truth.

"Colin, we have to go. Now!"

CHAPTER 16

Charlie

Monday – 9:30 AM

Colin stands beside a registration table where he was deposited by his cousin. His cane instinctively sweeps forward and gently taps the foot or leg of someone who is clearly annoyed.

"Hey, watch it..."

THE PAUSE. AND HERE IT COMES...THE APOLOGY.

"Hey, man...sorry...I didn't see you."

Colin doesn't respond. Doesn't smile. Let's his dark side take over. He gets to be pissed off at people too. Starting with Katie. She barely made sure he was checked in for orientation, offered shallow words of encouragement and was on her way – shouting last-minute instructions as her voice disappeared. Now, he's alone in the middle of this chaos while she goes off to do her digging, whatever that means. His damp dungarees cling to his legs. He pulls the zipper down on his jacket, breathes deeply and exhales. As much as he grudgingly admits he needs to be here, he'd rather be helping her solve the riddle.

I LIVED BEFORE TOMMY.

Instead, he is jammed into a damp room full of soggy students who will be spending the next few hours getting to know stuff they'll probably forget by the time school starts. He doesn't need this. He needs answers.

BUT...I MET HIM.

"Hey, are you Colin?"

A throaty voice interrupts his confused thoughts. "You're

Colin, right?"

"Um, yeah, how did you know?"

"This is probably going to shock you but you're the only blind guy with a white cane in this whole room."

He laughs. It feels good to laugh. But it's that voice. Colin has never heard a woman's voice sound like this. "Who are you?"

"Oh, sorry. I'm Charlene. Charlene Taylor, but just call me Charlie, okay?"

"Sure Charlie, thanks." Suddenly the damp air smells fresher. "Are you a music student?"

Her raspy response is firm and confident. "Sure am. Just finished my second year. So, I understand the sour look on your face. It rained when I had my orientation too. Plus, half the campus was protesting so it was pretty lame."

"Now I don't feel so bad."

"Good. That's my job...make sure you feel welcome. All kidding aside, it's an incredible program and today you get to hang out with me instead of getting trampled by all these kids tripping over themselves."

He lowers his head and whispers, "that's great...how long do I have to stay?"

"For the duration, mister. So, what's the best way to guide you? Not sure how this works."

Colin smiles. "It's cool. Um, if I can just grab your elbow, I'll follow... if that's okay."

"That's it?"

"Pretty much. Or I could use my cane and whack half the incoming class on their ankles."

He hands her the cane.

"Right, let's go with Plan A."

He squeezes her elbow and Colin melts. *MAYBE THIS WON'T BE SO BAD AFTER ALL.*

CHAPTER 17

Trust Me

Monday – 4:00 PM

Colin feels encased by steam rising from the sidewalk as the sun burns off the morning's rain. Charlie discusses the concert schedule for incoming freshmen while she guides him down the main path to the train station and public parking. Colin is half-listening as Charlie warns him about an approaching set of steps.

"Hey Charlie, what time is it?"

"A little past 4:00, we're almost there."

"Sorry, but my cousin doesn't like to be stood up."

She sounds disappointed. "Too bad. They just broke ground on the new music building, and I was going to...okay, I think this might be your cousin coming towards us. She's not smiling...almost running...seems frazzled."

"Yup, that's probably her."

Before Charlie can respond, Katie's rising voice interrupts. "You're late. I told you I would be waiting for you at 4:00. Instead, I had to park the car."

"Katie..."

"I was worried about you. Geez, I don't need this right now." She grabs a handful of his jacket. "We need to go..."

"Hey Katie, hold on just a second. This is Charlie."

"Hi. Come on Colin, we're wasting time."

Charlie taps him with his cane. "Hey, don't forget this."

"Thanks for all your help today, Charlie. I really had a good time."

"My pleasure. Don't be a stranger around here, okay? There's more stuff before the semester starts."

"Okay, give him a little peck on the cheek so we can go."

Colin is surprised by Charlie's laughter. She gently squeezes his hand. Her scent reminds him of his mom's roses.

"Oh, Christ almighty, let's go. It's like an oven out here."

They move swiftly down the path, his cousin encouraging Colin to move faster. "Sorry to take you away from your escort." She pulls him close but doesn't slow down. "She's cute. You did okay, Colin."

"Yeah? I really liked her voice."

"So, she's cute *and* has a nice voice. Sounds like you hit the jackpot."

"Yeah, well...you kind of left her in the dust back there."

Katie picks up the pace. She yanks him across a street, veering left down a fractured sidewalk. "Watch your step... where the hell did I park? Oh, crap I'm looking for my car not the Mustang." She stops suddenly and jerks him back towards her. "Okay, get in."

As soon as Katie turns the key in the ignition, Stevie Wonder blasts *Signed, Sealed, Delivered.* Colin shouts above the music, "So, you're obviously jacked up about something. Are you going to tell me what's going on?"

Katie lowers the volume. "Colin, do you trust me?"

"Do I what?"

"Trust me. Do you trust, me?"

"Of course. What kind of question is that?"

The Mustang accelerates then stops abruptly.

"Damn these traffic lights."

"Why are you in such a hurry? Where are we going?"

"To the airport."

Colin fumbles for the radio and turns it off. "What for? What's going on?"

"We're taking a little road trip."

He turns sideways in his seat and grabs his head in disbelief. Says nothing.

The hard click of the turn signal bounces off the dashboard. The Mustang veers sharply left.

"Colin, you said you trusted me, right? Well, I've got a pilot friend who owes me a favor. He owns a small plane and he agreed to take us on a short flight…"

"How short?"

"Near Scranton. Maybe an hour."

"Why?"

"I'll explain all of that when we get on the plane, okay? I promised we would meet him by 5:00 so let me concentrate on that right now, please. We're getting on 95 so I can finally make up some time."

"Katie, I'm not getting on any plane, especially a small one, without some explanation. Does my mom even know about this?"

The only response is the Mustang's rapid acceleration.

"So, she doesn't know. She thinks you're hanging out with me in Swarthmore. Instead, you're driving her car to the airport and flying me to Scranton with some pilot friend of yours…"

"His name is Doug. You'll love him. And don't worry. We'll be home way before tomorrow night when Hannah and Ben get back."

"Now we're staying overnight?"

"In the back seat…I packed a bag for you, bought some things at Kmart. Played it safe and got you boxers...and some snacks for the flight." The car slows down. "Good, we're actually a little early." The car's tires bite into loose gravel while Colin's stomach churns.

"I'm not getting out of this car unless you tell me what's going on."

The Mustang slows to a halt. Colin's hears the clunk of the shifter on the console as his cousin reverses the car and gently brakes. She turns off the ignition.

"There's a lot to talk about. A lot. You said you trusted me."

"That when I thought you were taking me out for a

cheesesteak."

"Let's get going. I'll explain everything."

Colin stubbornly folds his arms and leans his head on the backrest.

"Colin?"

He slides further down the seat. Hears her exhale in frustration as car keys jingle. She quickly opens the door. Her feet settle into gravel. The buzzing of small planes makes all of this suddenly real. Quick steps on loose stones signal her path to the rear of the car where she pops the trunk. It closes quickly. Her pace slows as she returns to the open door. Her voice is the calmest it's been since they left Charlie. "Colin, I'm getting on that plane with or without you. So, grab your bag if you're coming." He hears the door's hinges squeak slightly then stop. "Oh, I forgot to mention…I'm pretty sure that our friend Peter is our great grandfather."

Thump.

CHAPTER 18

Entombed

Monday – 5:30 PM

Katie was right. Doug is cool. He sits next to Colin in the cockpit of a Cessna Skyhawk, working through his pre-flight checklist. Colin feels the fuselage above and to his right. His hand presses against the wide window. Doug gently takes Colin's free hand and guides it over the controls, patiently explaining every detail of his newly purchased plane. His hands feel sturdy and confident. Colin relaxes. Katie sits in the rear, shuffling papers. Doug leans in and whispers, "okay, feel this button here? It's super important. If Katie starts to annoy us, just push down real hard and she'll be ejected from the plane."

Colin smiles while Katie interrupts, "I hear everything you're saying Douglas, so maybe you should just concentrate on getting us out of here."

"So, Colin, this button works while we're still on the ground. Should we go for it?"

Colin tilts his head toward the rear seat. "No, she's my only ride home."

Katie snorts, but Colin knows she wants to laugh. "So how do you two know each other?"

"I'll let her answer that question. Katie, what version of our story are you telling Colin?"

"Just the truth. Doug is a pilot for TWA, so we've been on quite a few flights together over the years. That's it."

"That's boring."

"Sometimes the truth is boring Colin."

"But you said Doug owed you a favor."

The pilot interrupts. "Oh, really, that makes me very curious. Katie, we've got a few more minutes before the tower clears us. Why don't you tell Colin why I owe you a favor?"

"Okay so both of you can shut up. In fact, Colin it's time to come back here and sit with me. Douglas, mind your own business, and get us out of here. Colin and I need to catch up."

He guides Colin out of his seat. "You are leaving our tiny little cockpit and all privileges that come with being my co-pilot. Maybe on the way back you can sit up here, how's that sound?"

"Cool. Thanks man."

The banter ends. Doug's focus is flying his plane. Within minutes they are moving at a steady pace along the runway. Katie reaches over and buckles Colin in. He hears her seatbelt snap into place. "Katie, I've never flown before."

"Just relax. I'll be with you all the way." The plane accelerates and so does Colin's pulse. He can sense the plane leaving the ground.

"This is not how I imagined taking my first flight."

"Well maybe for now you can keep this to yourself, okay?"

Colin can't respond. He's holding his breath. Within minutes he senses the plane veering slightly to the right and gaining altitude. The whirring of the propeller soothes him. He turns to his cousin. "Tell me everything."

She takes a deep breath and hugs him. As she pulls away, she says, "there's a lot to take in so be patient. And don't interrupt."

"I'll try," he says sincerely.

"While you were flirting with Charlie I went back to my apartment and found a box buried in my closet. I'm not exaggerating when I tell you the last time I opened it, Nana Bee was alive."

"So, it's been decades."

"Twenty-five years. Well before you were born Colin. That's for sure...and you're off to a bad start with the interrupting."

Colin chuckles. "Right. Keep going."

"She gave me the box before she went into the hospital for the last time. It wasn't much but it was the only connection she could offer me to the past. I don't remember much of our conversation. But I do remember this." She places a musty object on Colin's lap. "Be careful…it's falling apart."

Colin gently probes the surface as he imagines an 11-year-old Katie trying to be strong for her grandmother. His throat aches.

"I'll describe it for you," Katie says, reverently. "It's a cheap photo album. Really, it's nothing more than a couple pieces of hand-cut cardboard. The spine is held together by a braided gold rope pushed through random holes. As homemade as it gets."

Colin tries to open the album, but Katie gently stops him. "Careful, Colin. It's flimsy. Of course, these pictures are old. Some go back to the Civil War. Nobody smiles. Lots of grim faces. Kind of sad, really. Everything looks the same, except for this photograph." She teases his fingers with a curled piece of paper. Colin pinches it and asks, "who is it?"

"A face that made me look twice. She carefully describes the photo for Colin." It's a grainy picture of three young men wearing work overalls and standing near a wagon. I was drawn to the one in the middle. He's wearing a jacket over his work clothes. A familiar jacket."

Colin gasps quietly but says nothing.

Katie continues. "I found a magnifying glass in my junk drawer and saw something immediately."

"Something?"

"The guy in the middle of the group has a visible scar on the left side of his face." Colin's hand, still cradling the photograph is trembling. Katie gently holds his wrist and slips the picture from his hand. She explains, "the name on the wagon is hard to read but it says *NEWTON COAL COMPANY…*and on the back is some smeared printing that says: *1895…FIRST DAY… PITTSTON…NEWTON*"

Colin's mouth is bone dry. "Sorry for interrupting, but what does that mean?"

Tenderly, she says, "It's okay buddy. I had the same question. Then I found this."

Colin holds out his hand expecting to touch something, but Katie explains, "It's very brittle so I'm going to hold it because there's something I need to read to you, okay?"

"Um, okay...what is it?"

"It's the front page of the *Scranton Tribune*. The date is Monday, June 29th, 1896." Katie clears her throat. Her trembling voice struggles to read:

EIGHTY MINERS ENTOMBED

Now, 10,000 feet in the air, Colin listens intently as Katie reads the newspaper account. Her voice has lost all its spunk and sarcasm. There is only grief, as if she were reading an obituary.

BETWEEN SEVENTY AND EIGHTY HUMAN LIVES WERE BLOTTED OUT EARLY YESTERDAY MORNING IN THE TWIN SHAFT AT PITTSTON BY A CAVE-IN...

SO GREAT IS THE LOSS OF LIFE AND SO FRIGHTFUL THE SUDDENNESS WITH WHICH THE HARDY MINE WORKERS WERE CUT OFF THAT IT IS HARD EVEN FOR THE PEOPLE OF PITTSTON WHOSE DEAR ONES ARE IN THE ILL-FATED MINE TO REALIZE THE FULL FORCE OF THE TERRIBLE DISASTER...

IT IS SAFE TO SAY THAT NONE OF THE MEN ENTOMBED IN THE MINE WILL EVER COME OUT ALIVE.

Katie pauses. "And then there's this."

Colin waits, his heart throbbing in his throat.

"It says, *NAMES OF THE MEN WHO ARE ENTOMBED IN THE MINE.* It lists most of them."

He already knows the answer to his question but chokes it out anyway. "Pete?"

"Half-way down the column..."

PETER BYRNE, ASSISTANT FIRE BOSS,
MARRIED, TWO CHILDREN.

"That poor man," Katie whispers.

"Katie, he was buried alive. He suffocated to death in a mine shaft. That's his tomb..."

The plane's drop in altitude matches the sinking feeling in Colin's stomach. Doug's distant voice barely penetrates the grief. "On our approach, buckle up."

With her free hand, Katie instinctively tugs at Colin's belt, while squeezing his other hand.

Colin continues, "Katie, that's why we're the only ones who can smell the coal. We're his only living relatives."

"That's not true Colin."

"What do you mean?"

He hears the rustling papers before his cousin repeats the news report, "Peter Byrne, assistant fire boss, married, two children.... so, if Peter is our great grandfather, then one of those children is our grandfather, right?"

"Yup, Colin Byrne. I was named after him."

The plane dips sharply to the left, wobbles briefly and continues its descent. Colin's ears pop. There is greater clarity in his cousin's voice now.

"And he had a sister. Our great aunt...her name is Coleen."

"She's alive?"

"Oh, very much so. She's 78."

"How do you know?"

"Because while you were at school, I was busting my ass looking for answers...alright, heads up we're touching down."

Colin sits up straight. He feels the plane dropping rapidly while swaying liberally. Before he can respond, the wheels chirp as they bounce briefly off the tarmac and settle back down. Katie holds his shoulder firmly as the Cessna decelerates.

She continues. "It all came back to me as I was digging through our family stuff. I remembered Aunt Coleen from Nana Bee's funeral. Twenty-five years ago. That's the last time I saw her."

"You didn't answer my question...how do you know she's

still alive?"

"I talked to her."

"Today?"

"Why do you think we're here?"

"I have no idea why we're here, Katie. I was just supposed to trust you, remember?"

She reaches across his chest to unbuckle his seat belt. "Well then what are we waiting for? We're about to meet Peter's daughter."

CHAPTER 19

Stolen Silver

Monday – 7:00 PM

Katie is already complaining as she climbs into the rental car. "They must have rented this piece of crap to a chain smoker. God, Colin, how can you even eat the way it stinks in here?"

"I'm starving. You never fed me, remember?" He shoves an entire Tastykake Butterscotch Krimpet into his mouth but manages to keep talking. "These are my favorite...want a bite?"

"No, I just want some fresh air." Her window opens, inviting a medley of noise from the Wilkes-Barre Scranton Airport. "Can you believe the reception on this radio? It's useless."

Colin licks butterscotch off the crumpled Krimpet wrapper before tossing it to the floor. "Here, Katie. Let me try."

The car creeps slowly as she mutters, "they should have more than one line letting people out of here." Colin leans into the dashboard, gently teasing the tuner.

A sudden blast of the horn sends him reeling backward.

"What are you doing?" he shrieks.

She laughs. "At least something in this car works." They finally roll to a stop. Colin slinks deeper into his seat as Katie informs the rental agent about everything that's wrong with her vehicle. He appreciates the agent's soothing voice, providing careful directions to Interstate 81 North. The car pulls sharply away. "Okay, I think I know where I'm going. Should take us about 30 minutes. Doug wrote directions so hopefully we won't get too lost."

Colin digs through his bag and finds another Krimpet. He tears the wrapping with his teeth.

"Colin, I remember when those were hand-wrapped in wax paper."

He shrugs and begins licking the icing. "Nice guy, Doug."

"Yes, he is and don't go fishing for anything more than that."

"Okay, okay. Well, we've got at least a half hour to kill so let's talk about Ben instead."

"You need to give that a break too...I don't know what you want me to say."

He tosses his bag onto the rear seat and wipes his hands on his pants. "I've been thinking about what you said before. I've been tough on the guy," he says sincerely.

"That's an understatement. He's been patient and kind with you and your mom..."

"And?"

"And you've been anything *but* understanding."

"Maybe. I guess. It's just that I can't help thinking he drove my mom away from my dad. I mean one minute he's their marriage counselor and then suddenly my dad disappears, and he starts courting her."

Katie rolls up the window. "Well, your version may sound more sensational but it's also not the way it went down."

"What do you mean? I was there."

"You saw what you wanted to see."

"I can't see...remember?"

"Geez, can you please give the *'I can't see'* line a break? Alright, then you *felt* what you wanted to *feel*. It didn't matter what Ben did for your parents, he wasn't going to please you."

"Why do you stick up for him so much?"

"Because he's a good friend. He helped me through some tough times – and don't think about going there either. Listen, he cares about his work, about helping people. And he was helping your parents...a lot."

"Then why did my dad leave?"

Her hand grips his shoulder and tightens. "I don't know

Colin. It crushed me too...you know that. But it doesn't mean we get to blame Ben."

"I'm not blaming. I'm just angry I guess."

"Okay so be angry but give the guy a break. I don't have any idea what he talked about with your parents. That's confidential and it's none of my business. But that's the kind of respect Ben has for his clients. He would never betray their confidence."

Colin pauses. Bites his lip. Finally says it. "Did *you* ever talk to my mom about it?"

"About what?"

"Anything...what happened to my dad?"

"Sure, it's no secret she was pretty jammed up when he left."

"Katie, he didn't *leave,* he *disappeared.*

"You're right. Bad choice of words. I mean...your dad was working his AA program. Hanging out with the right people. Everything was good."

"But it wasn't always good."

"No, there were problems of course."

"My dad stole from Mrs. Judson."

"Nobody ever proved that, Colin."

"And nobody ever explained anything to me. Maybe I was too young. Maybe my parents were just trying to protect me. I get it. But I'm going to college in the Fall. I deserve to know."

Katie's silence lingers like the stale cigarette odor.

"Katie, tell me...please?"

"Okay Colin, but you must swear that you won't tell your mom. She confided in me. Told me it would make it worse if you knew the whole story. I agreed with her then. I understood her intentions. I still do. You always came first, and she was going to protect you no matter what, but..."

"But...what?"

"They may have had their differences, but they still wanted the best for you. It just got complicated, out of control."

"So, explain it to me...please?"

"Okay, okay. So, the plan was to get out of Philly, put the

incident behind them, continue the counseling with Ben, and rebuild their lives. That's why I offered my apartment to your parents. I wanted to help too...and protect you."

"From what? What happened?"

"Well, first you need to understand where I was in my life. So that was...1964. I was finally breaking away from that early grind of tough routes on small planes. It was big time for me. Major cities. Popular destinations. I was single of course."

He snickers. "I remember a lot of boyfriends... a lot."

She taps him playfully. "There were a few, cause...all bets were off if a stewardess got married. So, I had to play the game, but that was okay. I had Uncle Tommy and his cool younger wife who was closer in age to me. Best of all, you were a big part of my life. The travel made it tough but any chance I got I would spend with you guys."

"I remember," Colin says fondly.

More somberly she says, "yeah, well time away from you also made the changes in Uncle Tommy more dramatic whenever I came back. He was struggling big time. Your mom was heroic, but I saw the cracks. She was feeling hopeless and worried about you. Then...she began confiding in me."

"That must have been weird."

"Definitely tough for me – being a confidant to the woman who was married to my uncle. I needed to get out of the middle, so I introduced the prospect of marriage counseling."

"To my mom?"

"No, to both. Surprisingly, Uncle Tommy agreed right away to meet Ben. He said he would do whatever it took to make it work. Your mom was the cynic. I guess she was broken by too many years of lies and shattered hopes. Still, she tried, I guess. And then one Spring night, she called me. It was late on a Friday evening. I remember because I was in the middle of *The Twilight Zone*. I can still hear her hushed voice. You were asleep and Uncle Tommy was on a short run to...I think it was Atlantic City...not that it matters."

"Friday night was piano lessons with Mrs. Judson."

"Yes. So, you do remember."

"Sure. Dinner followed by homework then up to her apartment for a half-hour of polishing silver…and then my lesson."

"And that's where your mom's story started. She told me something was *off* that night. She was whispering and sobbing that she could hear the music from the apartment above, but the routine laughter and chatter were conspicuously absent. It made her uneasy."

Colin's faded memory opens a bit. He has a lump in his throat. "I remember. It felt like Mrs. Judson didn't want me there."

"When she brought you back to the apartment, she asked if she could speak to your mom upstairs to review your schedule. Hannah thought that was odd, but she told you to get ready for bed and went upstairs."

"I remember that part, too. They always did the schedule right in front of me. Always."

"Well…here's why that night was different. When they got to her apartment, Mrs. Judson said she needed to show your mom something. Or, more accurately, to show her what was missing. Her silver. A piece here and a piece there but enough that she knew they had not been misplaced. They were stolen. And the only person who handled her silver was you. Only you knew where it was stored…"

"In her bedroom closet," he recalls somberly. "I remember I polished fewer pieces that night. It threw me off, but I didn't think anything of it."

"Well, your neighbor strongly suggested that you might have been tempted to take a few things. Of course, Hannah protested. She told me she angrily scolded Mrs. Judson for even thinking that. Mrs. Judson reminded her that sometimes you would come to the apartment alone to practice."

"She was right. We had a spare key."

"As soon as she got back to their apartment, your mom looked for the key. She said Uncle Tommy had tapped a small nail on the kitchen window frame to hold the key. The nail was bare. Still, she believed in you. She didn't trust your father. Inside your hall closet she found his toolbox. She opened the lid. Inside was a bundle of silver, Mrs. Judson's apartment key, and the final blow -- a small purple bag that she recognized. It contained family jewelry that her mother reluctantly gave to her on her wedding day."

"My poor mom."

"I felt the same way, Colin. I remember how I couldn't hold the phone because of my trembling hands – trying to console your mom while fighting the grief I felt over the mess Uncle Tommy had created." As she shares these bruised memories with Colin, he can sense her profound sadness even now. He feels it too. But he's also confused.

"What about my dad? Did he admit it? Did he come clean?"

"Well, he took the blame for it, Colin. The evidence was pretty overwhelming, but he claimed his innocence with a passion."

"Then why did he...take the blame?"

"Mostly to protect you. He and your mom both agreed that you shouldn't be dragged into it. Mrs. Judson went along with it after they returned most of her stuff."

"Most?"

"Yeah, apparently there was a piece of her jewelry missing too. A diamond brooch shaped like a piano."

"Yeah, I remember it. She used to let me touch it for good luck after each lesson. Said it was a gift from a past student who ended up touring in Europe. She told me someday I would be even more successful, and she expected a bigger piece of jewelry from me. Honestly. I barely paid attention to it."

"Well, it was a big deal for her. It really pissed her off that it was never returned, and I guess it kind of stuck in her craw. Anyway, she insisted that your family move out. So, the original plan was just to quietly leave, but you know how that goes down in a neighborhood like yours. Almost overnight the gossipers labeled your father a thief and the eviction rumors spread fast. It was hard for your mom and dad to save face."

"Maybe Mrs. Judson started the rumors."

"It's possible. Who knows? Maybe it made her feel more righteous, since she probably felt shitty that she fingered you. Still, getting out of Philly seemed like a brilliant move at the time. Everything felt like it was heading in the right direction and – just for the record – Ben was a big help in that transition."

"Okay, I got it."

Katie pulls the car into a gas station as Colin hears the ding-ding-dinging of the air bell that announces their arrival. He rolls down the window and inhales deeply. He loves the sweet smell of gasoline.

She asks the attendant to fill the tank and playfully taps Colin on his nose. "You okay?"

"Yeah, I guess. Thanks for revisiting tough times. I really appreciate it."

"Good. Well, I'm not sure we solved anything, but we sure killed a lot of time sorting stuff out. And we are officially in Carbondale."

"You know, there's one thing doesn't make sense to me."

"Colin it was six years ago, I could have messed up some of the details."

"About the key hanging by the window?"

"No, that's a pretty vivid detail. Hannah told me that's where it was kept. Why?"

"My dad used that key as a lesson about responsibility. He told me if Mrs. Judson trusted me to use the key, then I had a responsibility to keep it safe. And I did."

"So, where did you keep it?"

"Not by the window, that's for sure. I kept it in my Sucrets tin. Under my bed."

CHAPTER 20

Aunt Coleen

Monday – 8:00 PM

It's early evening by the time Katie finds the street where Aunt Coleen has lived for the last four decades. The rental slows car as it drifts to the right. Colin cringes when the front-tire rim scrapes the curb and grinds to a stop. "Okay, welcome to Carbondale. This is the place. Geez, it's pretty beat up." She pauses. "Not much better than most of the houses on this street. Actually, it's kind of cute if you can get past the missing shutters and a yard full of weeds."

They open their doors simultaneously. As he steps out of the car Colin feels the same humid air that gripped the Swarthmore campus just a few hours earlier. He has that same skittish sensation that often grips him when meeting someone for the first time. Except for Charlie. That was unusual.

Katie escorts him along the sidewalk. "My God, she's a tiny little thing."

"You see her?"

"Yup. Already standing on the porch. Hair white as snow. She's got Pete's sad eyes too. She's wearing a turtleneck sweater that looks as ragged as this house. How can she be wearing that thing in this heat?"

Katie stops and struggles to open a gate.

A deep gravelly voice instructs, "just jiggle the latch darling. It'll cooperate."

Under her breath, Katie complains, "can't budge this thing."

"No, no...you're way too gentle with that."

Colin hears squeaking steps. Their aunt coughs loosely as she approaches them. Colin smells a sickly combination of stale cigarettes and cheap perfume. "Well, well. Katie, last time we met you were little more than a ten-year old squirt, saying goodbye to your grandmother... and you must be Colin."

"Hello Aunt Coleen," he says timidly. "it's nice to meet you."

She shakes the latch so violently it makes the sidewalk shiver. "Well, so polite and the mirror image of your grandfather, God rest his soul." The gate groans as she forces it open. Cigarette odors envelop Colin. He holds his breath, but the perfume cocktail is already attacking his brain.

"Colin, your cousin tells me you're going to college to play the piano...maybe you'll get famous just like that blind, colored fella. Good for you. I bet that Helen Keller lady would be real proud of you too. Maybe you'll get to meet her."

Colin can't help replying, "Um she died a couple years ago."

"That a fact? Well, she's still proud of you, I'm sure."

There is an awkward pause in the conversation, until Katie finally adds, "well thanks for seeing us on such short notice. That was very kind of you Aunt Coleen."

"Well, you caught me on a good day. Not often I pick up the phone...too many crackpots calling these days. Didn't expect you to be here this fast though. Must be important. Come inside and we can talk. And watch your step on the porch. A couple boards are soft."

Once inside, Colin smells the clutter – the way a deer senses danger. They form a single line with Aunt Coleen leading the way. Katie reaches back for his hand and squeezes it firmly. She pulls him through a labyrinth of boxes and damp newspapers that line a narrow hallway. The air inside is rancid. Like musty old gym socks that he forgot to give his mom to wash.

Finally, they settle in an area that Aunt Coleen refers to as her "deliberating den." She turns on a single lamp that barely alters Colin's dim perspective of the room. She invites them to sit but Katie holds Colin back as she removes several items from an overstuffed sofa.

Suddenly, Katie shrieks, "Holy Christ." Colin leaps backward and stumbles into a side table close to Aunt Coleen, whose raspy laugh fills the cluttered room. "Oh, that's just Pitch. He's harmless. You interrupted his nap." Katie offers a weak laugh and comments, "that's one of the biggest cats I've ever seen. Seriously ever."

"Been with me twenty years or so."

Colin finds the sofa, touches a sticky cushion, and remains standing. He asks, "why do you call him Pitch?"

"Pitch black. Like anthracite coal. Now don't just stand there, sweetheart. Sit down." She laughs heartily again. "Katie, the look on your face, I'll chuckle about that for weeks."

Colin reluctantly sits as Katie interrupts, "well, I'm glad you got a kick out of it. He's had all his shots, right?"

Aunt Coleen's tone changes dramatically. "Tell me why you're here. And don't bullshit me."

Katie's startled voice loses its confidence. "Well, like I told you on the phone, I'm trying to put together a family tree. I started doing some digging, found an old photo album and read some information about your father. That would be Peter Byrne, correct?"

"Go on."

"And well, I thought it would be helpful to...you know...fill in the blanks. Get a better picture of our family..."

"Let me get this straight. You call me this morning. A few hours later you've traveled over a hundred miles...what did you do, anyway, fly up here?"

Colin mumbles, "actually we did. In an airplane."

She giggles. "Well, that's usually how people fly Colin. But at least somebody's telling the truth. So, you fly up here and then drive that piece of crap Jap car to visit someone you could care less about just to, to...what did you say, 'fill in the blanks,' right? Well, honey, your story lacks the shine of truth. Now, you want to try again?"

Katie is silent. Colin hears the clink of a cigarette lighter.

Smells butane as the liquified gas lingers briefly. He slides to the edge of the sofa and leans forward. It feels like any surviving oxygen is being sucked out of the room. He can smell his own armpits. His damp clothes are sticking to his skin. The perfume is intense.

He gulps back nausea and says, “Aunt Coleen, I know this is going to sound crazy. I can’t explain it, but I feel like I have a special connection to your father. It’s a feeling I can’t shake. And I want to learn as much as I can about him.”

Their great aunt doesn’t respond. Colin hears her wheezing, each labored breath making him more uncomfortable. He feels Katie stand, her flat voice lingering above him. “We’ll leave. We shouldn’t have come.”

“Is he haunting you Colin?”

His chest is pounding but he can’t answer.

“Are you the one he’s confusing now with that mysterious personality of his?”

Katie tries to speak.

“Hush. You had your chance to tell the truth. Colin, when did you first meet him?”

“About a year ago.”

“Well, that’s about right. That’s when he quit spending time here. Hated this place. Always said it was too cluttered. Then one day…gone.”

Katie hesitates, then almost whispers, “how long was he here?” Colin is relieved to hear Aunt Coleen respond.

“Let’s see. He showed up in 1966, a couple days before the Fourth of July. I remember. It was a Saturday because I spent the morning hanging flags in town…getting ready for the parade on Monday. Back then we didn’t work on Sundays around here.

“So, July 2nd?”

Last time I checked a calendar, that’s a couple days before the Fourth of July.”

When I got home here, he was plopped down right there where Colin is sitting. Talking to me but his mouth was shut.

Scared the shit out of me...then I recognized his face. From pictures my mom gave me. Strangest thing. He didn't know why he was here. He didn't even know he was my father. He was lost, really. I'm the one who told him that he was my daddy. Wore that miner's jacket and didn't even know why. How strange is that? I mean, ain't a ghost supposed to have a reason to haunt you?"

Colin responds first. "Actually, he did the same thing with me, Aunt Coleen. But I didn't know who he was. I couldn't see him. I could just..."

"Smell him. I smelled it too."

Katie adds, "like coal?"

"The smell of coal is hard to describe. If it's wet, it might be musty and if it's dry...Lord you pick your own word to describe it. For me dry coal just smells like gravel...earthy you know? But burning coal? That's what I smelled when I was around my daddy. That's intense. It can stop you in your tracks. It makes me think about that day he died. Who knows what was going on down there. Did he suffocate or burn to death? Don't even want to think about it."

Katie begins the question, "can you tell us what happened that day?"

Colin's trembling voice adds, "the day he died."

"Well, I was only four, so I really don't remember anything. But my mamma talked about it all the time. We lived really close to the Twin Shaft. The collapse of the mine was so explosive it threw her out of bed. A lot of the wives ran to the mine, hysterical of course. They didn't even have a list of the men who were down there. Well, they did but the list was buried too. My mom said she knew as soon as she got there that my father was gone."

Colin interrupts. "Buried alive."

"Four hundred feet below the ground. Almost 200 acres caved in. They never had a chance. And they never recovered the bodies. Lots of widows that day."

Katie responds, "I'm so sorry. Was there an investigation?"

"Worthless, really. Some complained two weeks earlier that the walls could crumble but they were ignored. After the investigation, there were safety recommendations that were pretty much ignored too."

As the mood darkens so does Colin's eyesight. His only visual target is a spastic halo of light bouncing off Aunt Coleen's white hair from the single lamp flickering behind her. To his right, out of the darkness, Katie's voice sounds more confident. Without a hint of anxiety she says, "You know I met Peter, um your father, too. Just a few days ago for the first time. After talking with you, it seems he only appears to relatives...you, me, and Colin...and yet he shows up in our lives with no idea why."

"He's an odd bird, for sure. Mamma always talked about his different ways. Then I saw it for myself. Annoyed the piss out of me always wanting to clean this place up. I told him, 'I keep my house neat and tidy just fine without you.' He was getting under my skin."

Katie is on her feet, brushing past Colin, her voice more animated. "Aunt Coleen. I forgot to ask; did he ever live in this house?"

"Never. My mom moved here at least ten years after the accident. When she died from the Spanish Flu I just stayed put. Been here all my life. But my father has no connection to this house."

"And he has no connection to Colin's house, yet he showed up in both places with no sense of purpose. Why?"

"Okay, miss smart-ass, you've been leading your blind cousin and me around far too long. I'm giving you one more chance to come clean. Tell me why you're here or this conversation is over. I have to feed my cat."

"Tell her Katie. Tell her or I will."

"Okay, okay. It's not like we...*I* was trying to deceive you. We just have a lot of shit happening so maybe you can stop judging us and listen, okay?"

The only sound is their aunt wheezing.

"And can we turn on some lights in here? I can barely see the front of my hand."

Aunt Coleen's response is as flat as if she were asked the time of day. "I like the lighting soft in here. I can see you just fine. Go on."

Colin hears Katie take a deep breath and exhale slowly. Calmly, his cousin recounts her recent sightings of Pete. Finally, she describes their confusing conversation with Pete this morning and the riddle that prompted their excursion to Carbondale.

I lived before Tommy...but I met him.

When Katie finishes, Aunt Coleen coughs roughly and speaks directly to Colin.

"Your cousin telling the truth Colin?"

"Every word."

"You got anything to add, sweetheart?"

"I just want to know what happened to my dad. Like Katie told you...about this morning... Pete said, 'I lived before Tommy...but I met him.' Well, half of that makes sense. He came before him because he was his grandfather, that's obvious now. But he also said, 'I met him.' How could that be? He died over twenty years before my dad was born."

"Well first Katie did the right thing showing him that picture of your dad. He needs those triggers to keep him focused. He's all about the big picture you know."

Colin smiles and Katie affirms, "oh, we know."

"Right, so keep feeding him the facts. It's the best chance you have of getting to the answers you're looking for. But Colin honey?"

He takes a deep breath and responds warily, "yes, Aunt Coleen?"

"You need to be prepared for some tough answers, hear me boy?"

Colin gets chills as he feels Pitch dart behind his legs.

"Answer me, Colin."

"Yes...I hear you."

"Good, cause if your cousin got all her facts right, it seems the last time I saw *your* daddy was right about the time *my* daddy plopped his rear end right there on my sofa."

Katie's confused response is already on Colin's lips. "Hold on now. Right here in Carbondale? You saw him?"

"I said that's the *last* time I saw him. Been around here plenty of times before that."

Irritated, Colin asks, "Why didn't you tell us?"

"I did just tell you. You never asked about your daddy before, now did you? You just invade my home. Cousin Katie here strutting her stuff and telling a thumper, instead of just coming out with it. Fact is, I had to drag it out of you, isn't that right?"

The cat leaps on to Colin's lap. He forcefully swats him away.

"Easy now Colin you don't want to get on the wrong side of Pitch, or me for that matter."

Colin slumps forward. "Please, please stop all this. Just tell us what you know, I can't...

"You familiar with the term bootleg mining?"

Katie slides alongside Colin and rubs his back. "No, I'm sure we're not."

"Not real common around here anymore. Used to be everywhere back in the thirties, during the Depression. Hard times meant illegal mining. Families working at night to dig for enough coal to heat their homes with maybe enough left to sell to other families in the area. There were thousands of bootleggers back then."

Katie asks, "and today?"

"Pretty much all the mines are closed around here now so there's just a handful of men with the right equipment and the guts to find some veins where they can still dig the stuff up and sell it to the highest bidder. All depends on how risky they want to be."

Colin's curiosity is stirred. "What kind of risk?"

"Well, they go into the abandoned mines and take their chances. Excuse me if I'm insulting your intelligence here but we're talking about anthracite coal…"

"Meaning what?" asks Katie.

"Oh Lordy, girl. Anthracite is rare. Eastern Pennsylvania is one of the only places in the world you're going to find it. And it's difficult to mine – you have to blast it out of the earth. So dynamite is common.

Colin's shaky voice delivers the next question "Is it legal?"

Aunt Coleen giggles and teases Colin. "Well! I suppose if you follow all the rules. But then you can't make any money, so what's the point? Pretty soon the government will regulate bootleggers right out of business."

"Are you saying my dad was illegally mining coal up here?"

"No, no, no."

Frustrated, Katie says, "Okay now I'm confused. What's your point?"

"He wasn't digging it up, darling. He was delivering it!" Every few weeks or so he would pass through, pick up a load and deliver it, mostly to Philly but a few times to New York. Don't ask me to who or for how much. I have no idea. He just told me he was doing it temporarily, trying to pay off some debts he owed."

Colin holds back, allowing Katie to ask, "how often did Uncle Tommy stop by?"

"Whenever he passed through, I guess. You sound surprised."

"It's just that he never mentioned it to me…or Colin."

"Maybe he just cared about his family more than you do. After all, I was his father's only living relative. He cared plenty. Used to brag about Colin all the time. I think he may have even mentioned that you were flying around in planes all the time. Said you were spunky -- I think that's the word he used. Yeah… spunky. Left out the part about you being a smart-ass, though."

Katie ignores her jab. "I'm sure his visits meant a lot to you Aunt Coleen. I still find it odd that he never mentioned it to us."

"Well, truth be told I guess I was helping him out a bit. Been in Carbondale my entire life so I have connections."

"What kind of connections?"

Colin perceives a glowing dot of white as she briefly lights another cigarette. "I can pretty much tell you every family that still bootlegs these mines. So, I made connections for them, and they gave me cigarettes in return..."

Colin's neck tingles. He interrupts. "They?"

Katie presses. "You said *they* gave you cigarettes. Was Uncle Tommy with somebody else?"

"Sure was. Never came in the house with him though. Wait...I take that back. Maybe once or twice in the beginning. Good looking dago. Gave me a couple cartons of cigarettes that he stole up in New York. Well, he said he bought them cheap, didn't pay any taxes...so in my mind he stole them. In the beginning I think he was just checking me out, wanted to make sure my connections were legit. After all he and Tommy were up to no good. Transporting bootlegged coal in that big bright God-awful green truck of his. What a terrible thing to do to such a beautiful machine."

Colin jumps from the sofa and nearly stumbles. "What was his name, the other guy?"

"The dago?"

"Yes, yes...do you remember his name?"

"How could I forget? Just the like radio commercial." She hums an unintelligible tune.

"Aunt Coleen, I don't know what that means."

She suddenly erupts into song, "Everybody goes to Gino's... cause Gino's is the place to go."

Colin' stomach tenses. "Mr. Moretti."

Katie leans into her cousin. "Colin, who is that? Moretti?"

"He, he was our neighbor on Gerrit Street. You remember. He lived across the hall from us."

"The flirt?"

"Um, yeah, I guess. Dad used his truck sometimes...even after we moved in with you."

Aunt Coleen weighs in. "I don't think Tommy liked him very much. He always made apologies for him. Said he wasn't a friend, just a business partner."

Colin takes over. "What else did he say, my dad, about Mr. Moretti. Anything?"

"No darling. Same old routine every time. Until that summer in 1966. They did their usual run and never came back. That's the last time I saw your father. Come to think of it I saw that truck a few more times around here but that was the end of Gino and my cigarettes."

"So, I want to be sure. you said the last time you saw my dad was the morning of July 2nd?"

"That's a bottom fact."

"Later that same day Pete...um your dad...showed up here, right?

"Whammo! I remember I was listening to Frank Sinatra... Strangers in the Night. Ironic huh?" Softly, she croons, "dooby-doooby-do. Doob-dooob-doob-dee-daa..."

Colin cringes. Aunt Coleen starts to wheeze and cough. He asks, "are you okay? Do you want some water?"

"No, sweetness. I'm just fine. Anyway, daddy showed up here all confused...trying to tidy up the place. Of course, I tried to smarten him up a bit. He was fascinated by all the trucks and cars passing by. I know a thing or two about that, so I schooled him up pretty good. Taught him all about baseball, too."

Colin gulps. "The Phillies?"

"That's right! That dreadful excuse for a baseball team. But he loved listening on the radio, especially. Rarely missed a game."

Colin grips the edge of the sofa. His shoulders ache from the tension. "So, Pete was here for about three years...until... 1969..."

"Colin, that's about the time you and Hannah moved in with Ben."

"Slow down you two." Aunt Coleen's hacking cough follows. "How do you know Ben?"

"God damn it woman, when were you going to mention..."

Colin holds up his hand. “Katie, please…Aunt Coleen, you met Ben?”

“Never met him a day in my life.”

“But?”

“But that private investigator who was snooping around let his name slip once or twice.”

CHAPTER 21

Clever Lies

Monday – 11:00 PM

Colin steps onto the unsteady porch, leaving Aunt Coleen and her cluttered, musty home behind them. He ignores his fatigue and confusion and...breathes. Fresh air. Humid and thick, yet less defiled than anything his lungs have felt in nearly three hours. He washes in an unexpected light that his eyes don't usually experience late on a summer night. Katie's comment reveals the reason. "Colin, you cannot believe the full moon. It is absolutely brilliant."

"I can feel it, Katie. Hey, can we promise each other something?"

She squeezes Colin through the stubborn gate. "What's that?"

"We'll never come back to this house, ever."

She barely manages to laugh. The twisted conversation with Aunt Coleen consumes them both as they walk in silence to the car.

Driving away from the dilapidated house, Katie is the first to speak. "Listen, change of plans. First, I need to get to a 7-Eleven for the biggest cup of coffee they have. Then, I'll call Doug. We're not flying out of here tomorrow morning."

"We're driving home now, aren't we?"

"At this time of the night, it's only a couple hours. Our car is at the airport anyway, so I'll return the rental there and then we'll get home."

"To Pete."

"Poor Pete. We've got a lot to sort out, but first let's make that pit stop."

After several wrong turns tagged by colorful commentary, Katie finally locates a convenience store that is still open. "Okay Colin, I'm going to grab a coffee then make that call. Do you need anything?"

"What I need to do is take a piss. I'm coming in with you."

"I thought you went at Aunt Coleen's – right before we left."

"I couldn't. It smelled so gross and I'm pretty sure the plumbing wasn't working."

"God, everything about her and that place creeped me out. Are you as confused as me?"

Colin opens the door. "I can't talk anymore. Nature calls."

"I'm right with you. All this peeing talk... I need to go too. Might as well do it now, we've got a long drive ahead."

Within 15 minutes they are on their way. Katie advises Colin, "Listen I know we have a lot to talk about, but I need to find the turnpike first, then we can catch up."

Colin closes his eyes without resistance. He is asleep in minutes. Unsure of how long his nap lasted he is startled by Katie jostling his shoulder. "Colin, Colin. We're just passing the signs for Pittston, remember...that's where Pete was buried alive..."

Katie's commentary barely registers as Colin returns from his deep slumber. "How long have I been out?"

"Not sure how long you've been asleep, but you've been snoring for at least 30 miles."

"Sorry, I didn't realize how tired I was. Do you want me to drive?"

She shoves him playfully. "Very funny, but no thanks. Besides, the coffee is kicking in and we're getting close to the Northeast Extension. But I do have one question before we get into the serious stuff."

Colin tilts his head in curiosity. "Go ahead."

"Back at the house. Aunt Coleen jumped all over me about not mentioning your dad. Said I was strutting my stuff and telling a thumper. What does that mean – telling a thumper?"

"It means lying. She said you were lying."

"How do you know that?"

"Oh, from Pete. He's uses that expression too. She probably picked it up from him when he visited her. It makes sense now. A lot of his strange expressions are probably from the turn of the century. Common slang. I've heard them all, believe me."

"So, he uses 'telling a thumper' with you?"

"Oh yeah. The way Pete explained it to me...a thumper isn't just a fib. It's more like a well-thought-out, clever lie. Like telling Aunt Coleen that you were researching family history."

"So, I should be flattered? Aunt Coleen thought I was clever."

"I wouldn't go that far. I think you pretty much annoyed her."

Katie laughs. "Hey, join the club auntie...God she was creepy."

She rolls down her window, inviting highway sounds and damp air to tweak Colin's senses. The car crawls to a stop. The kind voice of a toll-taker wishes her good morning. It's Tuesday.

The car quickly accelerates.

"Okay Colin, enough about thumpers. Where do you want to start?"

Colin doesn't hesitate. "Mr. Moretti."

"Yeah, I wasn't expecting that one. All I remember is a flirty guy who was usually having a party whenever I visited you guys."

"My mom hated him. Said he was a ladies' man and a heavy gambler. Told me to stay away from him. One time I heard her screaming at him."

"About what?"

"I don't remember. I came home early from school one day and I heard them arguing in the hallway. I guess they saw me and clammed up. He was trying to be all buddy, buddy with me while my mom was pushing me towards our apartment. The hallway reeked of Vitalis. She shut the door, hugged me, and warned me again not to go near him. And then she made me promise not to tell my father."

"Did you?"

"I told Mr. Stiles."

"Why him?"

"I could talk to him about anything. I told him about Mr. Moretti before and he said he wanted to know anything else the guy did that made me uncomfortable."

Colin feels the car slow considerably.

"Are you pulling over?"

"Rest stop. But we're not finished talking about this." Colin is surprised how long Katie drifts through the parking lot before finally turning sharply and stopping the car. She presses Colin for more. "What happened earlier that made you go to Mr. Stiles?"

"It was stupid."

"Tell me."

"Can we stretch our legs?"

She guides Colin from the car and offers her elbow as they negotiate a narrow gravel path that seems dangerously close to the turnpike traffic. He slows his pace and hesitates. Tractor trailers feel like they are coming right at him.

Colin tightens his grip as Katie assures him, "don't worry, it's safe. We're just on the edge of the parking lot. Now tell me, what happened with Moretti?"

Colin shares the incident he had with Moretti when he slipped the German Luger into his hand. He describes how that same afternoon, he innocently told Mr. Stiles while they sat on the porch. Colin recalls the conversation for Katie, starting with Mr. Stiles' reaction.

"He did what?"

"He let me hold a Luger. Said he got it off a dead German in France."

"That smacked ass. What was he thinking?"

"Please don't tell my dad, please?"

"Colin, if I told your father, he would wipe up the sidewalk with that jerk, you understand? I don't need to cause any more trouble for Tommy. Just promise me you won't go near that gun, you understand?'

"Is it dangerous?"

He rustled Colin's hair. "Jesus, boy. It's a gun. Of course, it's dangerous. And he's crazy enough to keep bullets in that thing. Listen, during the war captured Lugers were a big deal for hotshots like Moretti. Sometimes the Krauts would use them to lure souvenir hunters and the gun would end up being rigged to a land mine or a booby trap. Happened a lot."

"Do you think he really got it off a dead German?"

"It's possible but knowing Moretti he probably won it in a rigged card game. Listen, here's the other thing…this Luger had a real touchy safety mechanism that most Americans were unfamiliar with. So, guys would be carrying one around in their pocket and it would accidentally discharge, blowing their balls off."

Colin started to laugh but Mr. Stiles cut him off. "I'm not kidding Colin. No more guns with Moretti, do you hear me? Or I *will* go to your father, and we'll all regret that."

Colin promised. That's when Mr. Stiles also instructed him to come to him if Mr. Moretti did anything else that felt uncomfortable.

Katie interrupted. "So that's why you told him about the argument in the hallway."

"Right."

"What did he say?"

"He said it was a good thing that my mom was giving that prick a piece of her mind. Those were his exact words…God, I miss him."

"Yeah, sounds like somebody I could hang around with. And it sounds like Moretti was not exactly everybody's favorite."

"I guess not. I think my dad just tolerated him so he could borrow his truck…or they would go together if it was a two-man job."

"Well, obviously, they were lugging illegal coal around the

East Coast. Funny, whenever I visited, I never saw that truck. Guess I just wasn't paying attention."

"Oh no. It was too big to park on the street. He kept it down by the river." If you saw it, you'd have a hard time forgetting."

The turnpike traffic feels more distant now. There is a flurry of sounds from disconnected travelers beneath a sudden halo of bright lights. Colin stops and tilts his head. "Where are we?"

"On the other side of the parking lot, right in front of the rest stop. I'm going to grab one more coffee. Do you need anything.?"

Colin declines so Katie leads him to an unoccupied picnic table. "Be right back."

Rather than sit on the narrow bench Colin slides onto the top of the table and dangles his legs over the side. He grips its roughly hewn edge. Takes a deep breath. Moretti's truck. Memories linger. Like the times he joined his dad when he borrowed the truck for short local runs. People would always kid his father about its unique green color. He recalls the time they picked up a load of watermelons out in Bucks County. By the time they headed back to Philly his dad was laughing, trying to describe for his son how hilarious it looked driving a big green blob. He smiles. Looks up to a lifeless sky full of stars he cannot see. WHERE ARE YOU DAD?

He hears Katie panting, squeezing his name out between gulps of air. She's running – he can feel her feet slapping the surface of the parking lot. "Colin, Colin...Oh my God...the truck...in the parking lot..."

Confused, he says excitedly, "here...the truck is here?"

Catching her breath, Katie half-laughs, then barks, "no, no, no. Moretti's truck was in the parking lot in Wallingford. The night I took you there. Remember?"

"Oh, yeah...the Earl Scheib special? Are you sure?"

"How many ugly lime green trucks can there be? Besides, that's too much of a coincidence. I was meant to see that truck."

"Why?"

"How the hell do I know? But we better figure it out. Okay partner let's go."

He slides off the table. As Katie swiftly guides him toward the parking lot, she slurps her coffee and mutters, "Moretti, Moretti, what's his story?"

Colin stumbles. They are moving too fast. He pleads, "Katie…please…slow down.

"Sorry, I'm a little revved up." She slows to a normal pace.

Still huffing, Colin says, "Aunt Coleen said my dad was paying off some debts. Do you think Mr. Moretti had something to do with that?"

"It's possible. You know, it might be worthwhile reaching out to Mr. Stiles just to see if he can shed any light on things. He might know something that could help."

"God, yes. It would be awesome just to sit on the porch with him one more time."

"Does he still live on Gerrit Street?"

"Yeah. My mom still calls him occasionally."

"Okay, let's add him to the list."

Katie stops, announcing they've reached the car. She opens Colin's door. "Another important thing we haven't discussed -- the private investigator."

"Right, what's up with that?" Was Ben spying on my dad?"

"Or searching for him?"

"What do you mean?"

"Well, if our goofy aunt has her dates correct, it sounds like that PI started showing up in Carbondale *after* your dad went missing."

Colin runs his hands slowly through his long hair and squeezes his straggling locks tightly. "She also said the PI told her he was working on behalf of the family. Ben wasn't family. So, who sent him?"

"Well, I'm just going to have to ask him myself."

"Who?"

He hears her rummaging through her bag.

"Let's see…Sterling Honeycutt, private investigator."

"What are you reading?"

"His business card…I *borrowed* it."

"From Aunt Coleen!?"

"Hey Colin, like she's ever going to miss this. When we were leaving, I saw it on the floor next to her chair. I think you knocked it off the table when that fat cat freaked you out. So… I took it."

"You're crazy…you know that, right?"

"Thank you. I'll take that as a compliment. Get in."

Colin slides his tall frame into the front seat. "We keep adding all these little pieces, but nothing is coming together yet."

Katie is already turning the ignition. "Colin, sooner or later, we have to talk to Ben and your mom." Silence fills the car as they consider their options. Katie takes the leap. "I think it has to be Ben first."

Colin counters quickly. "No. I need to be honest with my mom."

She squeezes his bicep. "We could arm wrestle, but I think I might lose."

"Never mind Katie, we both know there's somebody who comes before them." He closes his eyes as the rental car stubbornly gains speed. He waits for Katie's answer.

"Peter of course."

CHAPTER 22

Papa Pete

Tuesday June 23 – 1:30 AM

The full moon casts a handsome glow upon Colin's neighborhood. It's a rare sensation for him. Katie accelerates down the street and turns the Mustang sharply into the driveway. Colin opens his door before the car comes to a full stop. The dome light barely illuminates his cousin as she slams the shifter into park and disappears from view. Colin moves around the front of the car, its warm hood supporting the palm of his hand as he guides himself towards the house. Katie nudges him briskly to the front door, neither one saying a word about their shared goal.

They don't have to wait very long.

Colin immediately feels Pete's presence as the door opens. Katie turns on the light and exclaims, "Peter, we missed you. We've got a lot of catching up to do." Before Colin can join the reunion. Katie delivers another unexpected observation. "God, Peter, you look like death warmed over."

Pete quietly chuckles as Katie continues, "well of course you do, you're already dead, but you just look really tired. "

"I didn't expect you back so early, but I'm glad you're here. I missed you both."

Colin finally speaks. "Are you okay?"

"I, I feel...drained. I'm having trouble concentrating."

Colin struggles to focus on Pete's scrambled image. "Katie, can you turn on more lights?"

"Sure thing. Let's go to the kitchen."

Colin hears the swinging door open and confidently paces off the same steps he's been negotiating for the past twelve months. He enters the room and feels its welcome illumination. The brightest light, the one directly over the kitchen table, provides Colin his first fragmented glimpse of Pete -- his great grandfather. His voice sounds terribly worn.

"Can you see me, Colin?"

"Hey, Pete. I missed you big time." Colin feels Katie's reassuring arm around his shoulder as she tenderly adds, "and we've got a lot to share with you."

Her arm slides from his shoulder. "I'm going to show him the picture."

She passes in front of Colin, briefly blocking the kitchen light as she places the photograph on the table. "Do you recognize this?"

Colin feels his heart flutter as Pete's image slides softly to the left and disappears completely. He waits patiently for Pete's reaction to the photograph.

His response is cathartic. *"That's me…in the middle. With the Reilly brothers. Sean…and…and Danny. My best friends. We went wake snakes plenty of time."*

Katie taps the table tenderly. "Wait, I'm sorry. What is 'wakes snakes'?"

Colin explains, "it means getting into trouble, you know, mischief."

Pete continues somberly. *"I lost them -- both of them. It was my fault they died. My fault they didn't get out."*

Colin feels his eyes welling up. He swallows hard. "So…you remember?"

Katie moves a chair towards Colin, urging him to sit. She shifts another chair slightly and plops down next to him. Her voice – surprisingly patient -- encourages Pete. "Why don't you tell us everything you remember about that day?"

Colin hesitates, then gently interrupts. "Hey, do you mind if I record this? Pete, is that okay?"

"He's nodding his head 'yes' Colin. But hurry up, okay?"

Katie's voice is slightly less passive.

"Colin squirms. "Um, you'll have to go up to my room. I left everything on my bed."

Katie groans. Pushes her chair away.

Pete calmly interrupts. *"Wait. Everything is there on the counter. I tidied up a bit. Thought you and Katie might want to listen to your tapes together."*

"Peter saved your ass, Colin."

Colin exhales slowly. "Big time. Thank you, Pete. Katie, make sure you put in a fresh tape."

Katie returns swiftly and places the equipment in front of Colin. "You're set. Let's go."

"Good, thanks." He plugs in the microphone, placing it on the table. Instinctively he finds the RECORD button. "Katie, after tonight, nobody is going to question our sanity. He reaches forward and clicks the RECORD button on the cassette machine.

"Pete, say something."

"What do you want me to say?"

"That's good enough." Colin stops the machine and clicks REWIND. The tape quickly snaps back to the beginning. "Shhh. Listen."

Their brief conversation is replayed. Colin's voice is sharp. Ben wasn't kidding. And then...

what do you want me to say?

Pete's words are barely audible, as if his mouth were full of cotton.

"Is that what I sound like?"

Katie responds. "No Peter, we hear you loud and clear."

"That's right Pete. We do. You might sound a little garbled on this machine, but these high frequency tapes still manage to pick up your voice." Colin leans in and presses REWIND. "Hold on just a second." It whirs to a stop. His fingers feel heavy as he presses RECORD. He makes his decree through trembling lips. "Let's tell the world."

They are transported to Sunday morning, June 28th, 1896. In his matter-of-fact tone, Pete recollects the tragic incident that took his life nearly 75 years ago.

"It was a little after midnight. Our shift had just begun. The men were a little nervous. Especially the ones who had been hearing the squeezing of pillars."

Colin interrupts. "Sorry. A pillar, you mean like a wooden post?"

"No, no, it's the coal itself. You can't extract all the coal or the soil and rock above you would cave in, so you leave some of the coal in place. That's called a pillar."

"So...you leave coal behind?"

Katie's irritated voice breaks in. "Jesus Colin, just let him talk."

"That's okay. Colin is just trying to get the big picture. I can explain. We called it room and pillar mining. As you move along horizontally, rooms of ore are dug out while pillars of untouched material are left for support. The wider the pillar..."

Colin jumps in. "the less coal the company is excavating."

"Correct. Their width varies, but they can be anywhere from six to twelve feet. I've seen them even bigger and unfortunately much smaller too. At Pittston, there were complaints."

"In the year we've known each other, you never came close to remembering this?"

"It's all coming back for me Colin. Everything."

"Well, that's good Peter. Now, maybe if Colin could shut up with his questions you can continue to remember."

Ignoring his cousin Colin presses on. "Okay, now I get it. So, go ahead... the men heard the squeezing?"

"At least two weeks earlier. Sean and Danny...they both heard it. Somebody, I don't recall who, told our supervisors but of course nothing was done about it. I mean, people complained about things like that all the time. Most of us were more concerned about explosions...lots of trapped gas down there. Anyway, that morning I was part of the first group that was working in the sixth vein

– the very bottom. The Reilly boys were right with me. We were inseparable. Almost immediately I heard the squeeze. I got nervous because I could see chipping of the pillars...from the pressure. Thing is, it never stopped. It got worse. Some of the boys wanted to leave. I remember Eddie Hughes defied our boss and left early in his shift. Finally, word was sent that they were adding props for additional support. Honestly, I think they told us just so we would calm down and start working. Sean was nervous, but I had already convinced his brother to stay so he stayed too. He wasn't going to leave Danny behind. We all knew what it meant to lose a day's wage. It didn't matter..."

Pete goes silent. The cousins, almost in reverence, choose silence too. Colin sees Pete's image moving below the kitchen light. He imagines the grief on his face. The pain in his eyes. He waits for Katie's irritated voice to urge Pete forward. But all he discerns is her restless breathing. The house is so quiet, Colin can detect the faint trickling of Little Crum Creek – extinguished finally by Pete's continued reflection.

"I don't know where the first wall collapsed but after that it was like a deck of cards. The thing I remember most was the noise, the thunder. I've never heard anything like it. Odd that I remember this, but my shoes were blown off. I recall Danny calling for his brother. They died because they trusted me. I told them it was going to be alright. The Reilly boys never saw their families again because they listened to me."

Again, silence.

Pete softly repeats, *"they never saw their families again. That's all I remember, I'm sorry."*

Colin is tongue-tied. He reaches out for Katie, who takes his hand and speaks first. This time her inquisitive tone is gentle. "What about *your* family?"

Colin quickly asks, "do you remember who you left behind?"

"Fannie, my love...and our children. Coleen. She was four. And my little boy, his name... was Colin too."

Colin grins. Heart thumping, he leans forward.

"That's right. And do you remember..."

"My name?"

Colin and Katie reply simultaneously "Yes."

Katie adds, "who are you?"

"My name is Peter Byrne. But my friends call me Pete."

Colin presses the STOP button on the recorder.

Katie's confused voice inquires, "why are you stopping? We're not finished."

"We have the facts now. We don't need this anymore. The rest is just for us…for our family."

Pete's image fades from Colin's view. Soon his voice, now soothing, is closer than ever. *"I want to talk about my family."* He is standing behind the cousins, between the two people who have done the most to get him to this place.

Colin turns toward Pete's voice, desperately wishing he could see him. Overwhelmed by the reality of the moment, he barely manages to ask, "do you understand who we are?"

"I know your father's name is Thomas Byrne. Is he, my grandson?"

"That's right and Katie's mom, Bridget – she was your granddaughter."

Katie adds, "listen boys we have plenty of time later to draw a family tree. Peter, what Colin is taking a long time to say is that you are our great grandfather."

"Imagine that. I'm talking to my great grandchildren. It's beginning to make sense."

Katie presses for more. "At least your presence here – your connection to me and to Colin…that makes sense because we're family. That much is clear. But the rest…still doesn't add up to anything. Why are you here? And what happened to my Uncle Tommy…your grandson."

Pete adds, *"… Colin's father."*

Colin stands and calmly says, "there must be a deeper connection that brought you here." He is drawn to the window where light from the brilliant moon splatters the lower windowsill and bounces off the white porcelain sink. Colin fiddles with the faucet. On. Off. On. The odor of chlorinated water fills his nostrils. Fully focused, he presses Pete. "Remember, you said you met him so help us understand how that's possible? You died in 1896 but your grandson – my dad – wasn't born until 1917."

"I don't know Colin. I need more time. I need help remembering."

Colin quickly turns off the faucet. "Okay, we'll keep working on it."

Katie groans impatiently. Colin hushes her with equal vigor. "Shh...we need to give him time, space...just like before Katie. We're here to help."

Pete's chilled voice breaks the tension.

"Katie, there are two things that I think might be helpful."

"That's more like it. Go on Peter. Let's hear them."

"Well, first, I don't think it's very polite for you to speak to Colin the way you do. Your impatience is beginning to irritate me."

"Oh, really, I can't wait to hear your second observation Peter."

"Well actually, the way you just addressed me is what I wanted to discuss. I would appreciate if you stopped calling me Peter. It's about time you started treating your great grandfather with a little more respect than that."

Colin cringes, but Katie giggles. "Colin just so you know he just winked at me when he said that. So, what would you like us to start calling you...grandpop?"

"No actually, I think I prefer Papa Pete."

Colin laughs. "Papa Pete, you sure?"

"Yes, that works just fine. In the meantime, maybe you can stop complaining and look for more things to share with me. How does that sound Katie?

"Fine."

"Fine, what?"

"Um, fine...Papa Pete."

"Very nice, but the next time you say it please don't roll your eyes."

Katie buries her head on Colin's shoulder. "He's smiling Colin. It's freaking me out, but his mouth is moving. I can see a

God-awful set of crooked teeth."

Pete adds, *"I think I remember having a tooth pulled a week before the cave-in."*

Colin claps his hands and erupts in laughter. Katie joins him but still manages the last word, "Hey Papa Pete, I liked you better with your trap shut."

A peculiar silence follows, triggering the familiar emptiness Colin experiences whenever Pete leaves his presence.

"He's gone Colin. We never got to tell him about meeting Aunt Coleen. Maybe that's for the best. We really got a lot out of him, don't you think? Hey, you okay?"

Colin moves back to the table and sinks deeply into his chair, surrendering to the sheer exhaustion of the last 24 hours. His arms feel like the dumbbells down the basement that he abandoned over a week ago. His weary brain struggles to make sense about his great grandfather's fate near the turn of the century.

"We're losing him, Katie."

"What are you talking about. You said he's always disappearing."

"Trust me. This is different. He's fading away. I can't even see him, and I know it. I can hear it in his voice. I feel helpless." He manages a gentle grin. "I could use a hug."

She embraces him. "Hey, we're going to figure this out. Look how far we've come in the last week. "She raises his chin. "You know, Papa Pete didn't show up here just to remember he was buried alive in a mining accident. He came here for more. He came here to help us learn what happened to his grandson. He just doesn't know it yet."

Colin sighs. "He came here for us."

Katie leans in, nose to nose. "Two crazy cousins who can't tell anyone what they know."

"You have massive coffee breath."

She pushes him away. "Well, you reek of cigarettes."

"Thanks to you and your little Scranton adventure."

Laughing, she teasingly asks, "Do you miss Aunt Coleen?"

Mimicking her gravelly voice, Colin says, "okay, miss smart-ass, you've been leading your blind cousin and me around far too long."

Katie howls and hugs Colin again.

Their laughter is disrupted by muffled voices and the twisting of a key in the kitchen door.

CHAPTER 23

Madness

Tuesday – 3:00 AM

Hannah's frantic voice skewers Colin's conscience. "My God, you're okay!"

Katie is silent as she steps away from Colin, allowing Hannah to sweep in and embrace her son tightly. The kitchen door shuts forcefully as Ben, sounding drained, interrupts. "We've been trying to reach you since 6:00 last night, Colin. You were supposed to call after you got back from your orientation, remember? Your mom has been freaking out."

Hannah grabs Colin's hair firmly. "Are you okay…and why do you smell like you a pack of cigarettes? Have you been smoking? Katie, did you let him smoke?"

"No, of course not."

Hannah's grip on Colin's hair tightens. "Why are you both standing in this kitchen at 3:00 in the morning. What's going on? Where were you?" Her nails dig into his scalp. "And why were you smoking?"

"Mom, I wasn't smoking." Colin stops speaking, hoping his cousin will deliver an alibi. Finally, he waves his arms wildly and breaks the awkward silence. "Katie's been smoking since she got here on Sunday night. I couldn't take it. After the orientation she wanted me to stay overnight at her apartment, but it reeked of cigarettes. I tried to make it through the night, but I couldn't. I just wanted to come home."

Flustered by his fabricated tale, Colin peels his mother's

fingers from his face as Katie spins her own thumper. "It's my fault, all my fault. The storms were bad yesterday, the...uh... power was on and off around here, so I decided to let Colin stay at my place after his orientation. And I completely forgot about calling you. He told me he needed to call but I ignored him. I'm so sorry we...I made you worry. I'm really, really sorry. We were just having a good time. From the moment I got here we haven't had a boring moment. By the way, your lasagna was delicious."

Colin snickers and Hannah pounces. "What's so funny big shot? Hmmm? It was your responsibility to call, not Katie's. Ben had to leave his conference because of you...and we got a speeding ticket...once again because of you. I am so pissed off right now."

Ben's calmer voice cuts in as he moves past Colin towards the kitchen table. "What are you working on here?"

Colin's heart leaps. He stammers, "just listening..."

"He's obsessed," Katie says accusingly.

Colin is initially confused, not sure if Katie is spinning fact or fiction. Then, he gets it...of course. Deliberately, he chooses a defensive tone. "Hey...where did that come from?"

"Colin is obsessed with all these tapes and these...these tips for blind people going to college. He won't shut up about it. Frankly, he's been nothing but annoying this weekend."

"Hold on," Hannah quibbles. "You just told us you were having a good time. 'Not a boring moment,' isn't that what you just said?"

"Well, I lied, okay? Colin pleaded with me not to tell you. I tried to get him to stay at my apartment to distract him from this stuff. But he wanted to come back and make me listen to these tapes and all this bullshit. I'm sorry, I know you got him this stuff. But it's a rip-off, really. And that's why we're still up at 3:00 in the morning. I can't take it anymore. Sorry, but it's true."

Colin hears Ben fiddling with the tapes. The recording with Pete is still in the machine. The sound of the tape rewinding launches him instantly toward the kitchen table. He misjudges the distance, and his arms feel nothing but air. Off balance, he careens unsteadily into the table. Hannah gasps as tapes scatter, some hitting the floor. Colin yells, "that's bullshit, Katie. You're just pissed off because I made you clean out the ashtray in the Mustang."

Now Hannah pivots her anger toward Katie. "You were smoking in my car?"

"No, God no. I know better than that. Colin is confused. He hasn't been himself since he met his cute little girlfriend at the orientation."

For the first time Hannah's voice sounds good-natured. "Oh, Colin honey, you have a girlfriend."

"Mom, please. I just met her."

"What's her name?"

Colin scratches his head and folds back into a chair, panting. "Charlene, but her friends call her Charlie."

"Believe me Hannah, I saw the way she looked at him. She is smitten. Even invited him back to visit, right Colin?"

"Mom, can we talk about this tomorrow...or later today I mean. I just want to take a shower and get some sleep, okay?"

Ben adds, "I'm all for that. Let's call it a day or night or whatever the hell we're calling this."

Colin pushes his weary body up from the chair, his hands sticking to the annoying tape that crisscrosses the seat. Then Katie speaks.

"Hey Ben, I know this is an inconvenience – considering everything I put both of you through, but would you mind driving me home?"

Colin shrinks reluctantly back into the stickiness.

Hannah, clearly irritated asks, "now?"

Ben follows. "Really, why now, Katie?"

"Because once everybody crashes, I'm stuck here until somebody rises from the dead and who knows what time that will be. I just want to be home. I've got a lot to do."

"It's okay, Hannah, I'll take her. It's only 15 minutes. It's not a problem."

"Well, it's a problem for me. She can wait. Besides, now that we're home early *because* of you, I decided to work at the food shelter later today. So, I can drop you off at your apartment before I head into the city."

Katie reluctantly asks, "what time is that?"

"I don't know. 11:00? Noon? Does it really matter?"

"I'd rather go home now."

Ben's offers again, "I don't mind. Grab your stuff."

Colin gets to his feet, fighting his fatigue. "I'll go too. I'll keep you company."

Hannah shrieks in disbelief. "Fine, I've had enough of all of you." She pounds the kitchen door. It swings stubbornly for a few seconds then muffles her trailing voice. "And no smoking in my car Katie!"

"Do you get the feeling she's a little annoyed with me?"

Ben's keys jangle as he replies, "it's been a long day for all of us. Let's get you home. We can take my car."

Nothing is said as the three make their way to the garage. Ben grunts as the heavy garage door lurches upward and grinds to a stop. Colin finds the rear door handle of Ben's 1962 Ford Fairlane. His mom calls it the "most boring car in the family." Colin likes the Fairlane though. Maybe because it reminds him of his father. He can remember his dad telling him that the car's name was derived from Henry Ford's Michigan estate, Fair Lane. Reminiscing about his father is a timely reminder why he's in the back of this car right now and not buried in bed. Before Ben is even out of the driveway, Colin leans forward and taps him on the shoulder. "Listen, we need to talk to you."

"Really, from the way you two were going at each other back there, I'm surprised you're even willing to be in the car together. I've got to hand it to you, though. I lost count of how many times you changed the subject. And no offense but both of you smell like a locker room."

Colin gives Ben some space. He flops back in his seat and

turns sideways, leaning almost against the door. "Go ahead Katie."

"Colin and me, we're fine. Never been tighter. We just really need to talk to you."

"So much for a quiet ride to Wallingford."

They turn right out of the neighborhood. Colin knows every inch of these roadways he's never seen. No maps. No mile posts. Just instinct.

WE'RE ON SWARTHMORE AVENUE.

"Okay, you two, what's up?"

Katie pounces. "For starters, don't challenge our sources or ask any questions, okay? Just tell us the truth."

"Unfair but go ahead."

"Did you hire a private investigator to find Uncle Tommy?"

"How did you..."

"Yes, or no?"

"Yes, but how did you know about him?"

"Hey, remember no questions."

The Fairlane brakes erratically then turns left.

THIS IS YALE AVENUE. ON THE RIGHT SHOULD BE LITTLE CRUM CREEK PARK...THE FOOTBRIDGE...THE MEDALLION... BETTER TIMES. WE'LL BE ON THIS ROAD FOR THE NEXT FIVE OR SIX MINUTES.

"You're really catching me off guard here. I mean, there's so much to explain."

"So, start explaining," Colin says coolly.

Ben's reluctant account begins in the Fall of 1966, a couple months after Colin's dad disappeared. "It was my idea to hire Sterling Honeycutt. I knew Hannah couldn't afford it, but I felt an obligation to her and Tommy."

"What kind of obligation? Why," Colin asks rudely.

"We had become more than clients. I had allowed them to become my friends. Is that a satisfactory answer for you?" he replies sarcastically.

Neither of the cousins respond.

"Honeycutt was a meticulous investigator, but his work was

slow and tedious with limited results. Still, I continued to pay a monthly retainer, hoping for a breakthrough. It came almost a year later.

"Care to share," Katie says politely.

"He connected a trail of evidence that pointed to Tommy's presence in the Scranton area around the time of his disappearance. But Honeycutt warned me not to expect a happy ending. The evidence, he said, may never lead to closure for the family."

Colin interrupts in a civil tone. "What did he mean? Was he saying my father was dead?"

"I'm not sure Colin. He may have known more than what he was letting on. He never wanted to play guessing games with us. He would only share facts, not theories. That's the way he worked." Ben taps the brakes. The car veers in a prolonged 45-degree turn to the right before finally straightening out.

WE MUST BE PASSING UMOJA PARK. A FEW MORE MINUTES TO KATIE'S PLACE.

Ben's tone gets more somber as he continues. "Unfortunately, he never got a chance to finish the case."

"You fired him?" Katie asks incredulously.

"No. He was killed. Murdered actually...right before Christmas 1967. At a rest stop on the Northeast Extension. Coming back from Scranton one night. Shot in the back of the head, mafia style."

Katie gasps. "Oh Jesus Ben. That's a little freaky don't you think?"

"It was pretty unnerving, yeah."

Colin hangs over the front seat. "So that was it? You stopped looking?"

"We got all of Honeycutt's files from his widow, Tracey. It was a little daunting, but I wanted to keep going. Your mom was more reluctant. She wanted to protect you, Colin. Settle down and move on. She was on the fence about what to do next and then..."

"Then what?" Colin squeezes Ben's shoulder.

"Listen, I'm a little uncomfortable talking about this. Your mom should really be part of this conversation."

Katie's hand grips Colin's wrist and squeezes hard. "You can tell Hannah whatever you want, but we need to know everything Ben."

"Are you still seeing things?"

"Don't change the subject. Something happened that cooled your heels on finding Uncle Tommy. What happened?"

The car abruptly slows, swerves right, and stops. No one speaks. The only sound is the tap, tap, tapping of the Fairlane's poorly tuned engine. It matches the pounding of Colin's temples.

I'M SO LOST. I DON'T KNOW WHERE WE ARE.

"Ben," Colin pleads. "Please tell us."

"I'm walking a fine line here, ethically."

"Oh, screw your ethics. We're talking about family not some strange client. We need to know. At the very least, Colin needs to know. He's 18 for Christ's sake..."

"Your mom got a letter from your dad."

Colin, breathless, stutters, "he's alive? Where is he?"

"It's not that simple. A few months after Honeycutt died...so 1968...March maybe...she got a letter from your father. It was postmarked Las Vegas."

Colin's head is spinning. "What did he say?"

"This is the tough part, Colin. He said he was moving on...don't try to find me...Colin needs a father he can count on."

The engine taps louder as Colin sinks deeper. "He wouldn't do that. He would never abandon me. Never."

"He sent something with the letter. A medal he took when he left. Said it belonged to you and he wanted to return it."

Colin's mouth is dry. He fumbles for the door and pushes it open. He's met by thick humid air mixed with burning oil and smoke that feels as dark as his soul. He stumbles out of the car and into the waiting arms of Katie who holds him tightly. They are both sobbing but she still manages to whisper, "Something's not right here."

The engine shuts off. They are joined by Ben who keeps his distance, saying only, "this is not how I wanted you to find out."

"When were you going to tell me?"

"That was your mom's call, not mine. She saw how well you were doing, and she didn't want to upset you."

"And it gave you the excuse you were looking for to marry her, right? That letter was the best thing that ever happened to you!"

"You're angry right now and rightfully so, but you've got it all wrong Colin. All wrong."

Colin lunges wildly but Katie intercepts him. "Easy Colin, easy. I'm pissed off too but let's give Ben a little breathing room here, okay? He shared a lot of stuff he didn't have to tell us."

"Oh great, now it's two against one."

She presses him back against the car. He doesn't resist. His shoulders sag.

Ben cautiously interrupts. "I should tell you that your mom doesn't actually have the letter and medallion."

Colin groans loudly then mutters through clenched teeth, "who does?"

"She...she gave it to her parents' attorney for safekeeping. That's all I know, I swear..."

Colin cringes.

THAT BLIND CHILD IS YOUR PUNISHMENT FOR GETTING MARRIED TO A DRUNKEN MICK.

"Oh great, my loser grandparents are involved."

"Also, her father is dying...pancreatic cancer. She hasn't told anybody."

"Humph. That's one secret I could care less about. I just want the letter and medal, that's all. I don't want anybody else touching them." Colin digs his fingers into his palm where his father placed the medallion at the top of the footbridge in Little Crum Creek Park.

DAD, WHY ARE YOU GIVING THIS TO ME? DON'T YOU WANT TO KEEP IT?

He feels Katie's thumbs brushing tears from his cheeks. Colin sighs. Little Crum Creek is miles away. Ben's voice brings him fully back to reality.

"Look, I did what you asked me to do. I told you the truth. Now, give me some time. Let me talk to Hannah first. She's my wife and I deserve that chance before the two of you create another crisis I can't control."

Colin stiffens but Katie presses him back against the car.

Ben continues. "That's all I ask. Then the three of us will sit down and sort this out, okay?"

Colin shakes his head. "No. The *four* of us. Katie, too."

Katie releases her grip on Colin. "Hey, promise me you won't do anything stupid. Get some sleep. I'll do the same and later, after Ben has a chance to talk to Hannah, we'll get together."

"I want my medal. I want that letter."

"Jesus, were you not listening to what I just said? Take it easy, okay?"

"Colin, Katie's right. Just give me a little time with your mom. The sun's coming up in a few hours. Let's get some rest and deal with this like adults. Okay?"

"Okay, but you better talk to her soon or I will."

Katie hugs him. "Okay, big shot. And Ben…those record from Honeycutt. You have them?"

"Yeah. I haven't looked at them for a while, but they are extremely organized, believe me."

"We need to take a look at them, okay?"

"Sure." He opens both passenger-side doors. "Now, let's get you home, please?"

Colin hears Katie slide into the front seat while Ben guides him into the rear, then shuts both doors. As he walks around to the driver's side Katie whispers, "hey I mean it. No funny stuff."

The door opens and Ben groans as he settles into the driver's seat. "So, I have one request and it's pretty fair, considering all I've shared with you. How did you find out about the private investigator? Nobody knew about that but Hannah and me. Nobody."

Silence.

"You owe me this much."

With resignation, Colins says flatly, "just tell him."

Katie spits out, "Aunt Coleen."

"Coleen from Carbondale?"

"The one and only."

"How? I mean when? No, that's absurd."

"That's all you're getting Ben. Sorry, that's enough."

"No. You don't get to tell me something like that and then just drop it," Ben says emphatically.

Colin feels unsettled as Katie responds with increasing curiosity, "Okay, go ahead."

"When did you speak with her? Katie, when did you speak..."

"I heard you the first time. Yesterday. Colin and I met with her yesterday."

"You *met* with her. Where?"

"No more questions Ben."

"Fine, but the two of you have a major problem."

Colin's chest is fluttering. "Why?"

"Because Aunt Coleen has been dead for at least a year."

CHAPTER 24

Hurry

Tuesday – 11:30 AM

"Colin, we've got a situation."

Pete's words barely penetrate the barrier of sleep between madness and reality.

"Wake, up please."

The first thing Colin senses is the smell. A terrible concoction of odors. His own. He realizes he is fully clothed. "I never took a shower."

"Although quite obvious, it's not important right now."

Colin rubs his face and smells remnants of the airport, rental car, and Aunt Coleen clinging to his grimy fingers. Ben's incredulous words break through his fog. "Aunt Coleen has been dead for at least a year."

He shudders and sits up slowly. Smelling his left armpit, he grimaces and moves to the side of the bed. "What time is it?"

"Almost noon. And the day is not off to a good start."

"What's the matter, did the Phillies lose again last night?"

"I never got that far. I was shinning around this morning, looking for Ben's sports page in the kitchen. That's when I realized the tapes were missing."

Colin is fully awake. With dread, he asks, "where…where are they?"

"Ben has them. He's listening to them right now."

Colin moves too fast, his instincts betraying him as he misjudges the doorway. His toe slams into the edge of the open door and twists awkwardly. He screams loudly, a mix of pain and anguish over the consequences of his laziness.

"Colin, are you okay, are you hurt?"

"Why did you take so long to tell me? Maybe you should have been spending less time 'shinning around,' whatever that means. Pete, why weren't you paying attention?"

The absurdity of his question is obvious, but Colin bottles it up for now. He limps down the hallway, pawing the wall as he moves to the steps. The spirit's flat distant voice offers a gentle suggestion. *"Remember to call me Papa Pete."*

This is not how he wanted Ben to discover Pete. Not after the news about Aunt Coleen. Colin recalls Katie's weary voice as they sat in Ben's car before the sun announced another unsettled day. "Ben, we can't both be crazy."

And now *this*. He reaches the staircase and negotiates twelve excruciating steps down to the landing. Then, several more paralyzing paces to the closed door of Ben's remodeled office. He pants heavily, the sweat resurrecting his stale body odor. His toe throbs in unison with his pounding heart. Colin places his hand on the closed door as cool air escapes from the office and swirls around his bare feet. It carries the sound of a muffled voice. His own voice.

Colin: Do you remember who you left behind?

He considers opening the door. Hesitates. Fingers the doorknob.

Pete: "Fannie, my love...and our children. Coleen. She was four. And my little boy, his name... was Colin too."

Colin: That's right. And do you remember...

Pete: "My name?"

Colin opens the door as Katie's voice join his own.

Colin and Katie: Yes.

Katie: Who are you?

Ben's chair squeaks. Colin's stomach drops.

My name is Peter Byrne. But my friends call me Pete.

The tape ends. Ben's breathing sounds anxious.

"All this time, you were never talking to yourself, were you Colin?"

Colin leans against the door jamb, orienting himself to the direction of Ben's befuddled voice. "Never. It's always been him since the day we moved in."

"Why didn't you say something? I could have helped...I think...Oh God I don't know what I think. This can't be real, can't be happening."

"That's why I didn't say anything. You just would have thought I was crazy. Sent me for tests. Put me on drugs. Explained it away as some sort of trauma about missing my dad."

Colin is not expecting Ben's sudden movement towards him. His stepfather grabs his shoulders tenderly and pulls him in. He hugs Colin briefly then steps back. "I'm so sorry that you lived with this alone..."

"Until Sunday. Until Katie met him."

"Ben chuckles lightly. "Of course, Katie's in on this."

Colin grabs for Ben's arm. "Can we sit down? My foot is throbbing."

"No wonder. It's bleeding." He guides Colin to a different loveseat placed in a familiar spot. It smells brand new. "Are you okay? What happened?"

"Papa Pete told me you were listening to the tapes. I stubbed it trying to get down here."

"I wasn't prying Colin. I thought I was just listening to the tapes your mom gave you. Didn't realize these were yours. It was an accident."

"Why are you apologizing? I'm sorry you had to find out this way. I swear we were going to tell you today. I swear." He pauses and tries to lighten the moment. "Hey, you weren't kidding about those high-frequency tapes. They work. At least they prove we're not crazy."

Ben settles into the loveseat. He grips Colin's knee firmly, saying, "I want to believe you Colin. I want to believe both of you. But I'm still catching up here. He said his last name is Byrne. He talked about Coleen. So...Papa Pete, that's what you called him...he's your grandfather?"

"No, our great grandfather. That's why Katie and I think we can see him because he's related to us."

"Right, right. That makes him your dad's grandfather."

"Exactly. You figured that out faster than I did." Colin leans back and allows himself to regroup. "Sorry, what day is it?"

"Tuesday."

Colin rubs his face. "Why aren't you seeing clients."

"I didn't schedule any. Remember, we were supposed to be coming back today."

"Right, right. Where's my mom?"

"She left early for the food bank, still steaming. And now this. She needs to know."

"There's a whole lot more than this she needs to know."

"So, Katie never saw Tommy?"

"No. It was Papa Pete all along. Katie realized that when she finally met him the other night. And Papa Pete didn't just show up here. He also visited Aunt Coleen's place, too..."

Ben sighs. "Aunt Coleen." The tape recorder hums. "it's all a bit unsettling."

Colin flexes his throbbing toes. "Yeah, I'm still trying to process that one. It sounds like Papa Pete showed up at her place around the time my dad went missing."

"Okay well she was still alive then for sure. It was later... sometime last summer...they found her dead in her home. She had a lot of breathing problems. Emphysema, I guess. We didn't even go to the funeral which looking back now was kind of shitty. We had a lot going on then."

"And that was summer of '69, right?"

"Definitely. In fact, it was July. I remember because it was right around the moon landing."

"That's when Papa Pete arrived here."

"You're sure."

"Positive. Ben...Papa Pete is in our home for a reason."

"Is he here right now? Is he watching us?"

"Well, obviously I can't see him, but I can always sense his presence."

That's when Colin feels Pete's closeness. Not in the hallway… or at the threshold…but here, inside the office. He knows Ben is pressing, but Colin doesn't have the stamina. "He's not here right now."

"Well, sooner or later I'll need a sign, Colin. Something."

Colin laughs, feels himself relaxing for the first time this morning.

"What's so funny?"

"There have been signs every day, but you just never realized. Like your missing sports page. Or the vacuum cleaner disappearing." He laughs again as he says, "or my tidy room!"

"He cleans your room?"

"Every single day. You don't think I'm that neat, do you?"

"That was always a mystery to me."

"Well, mystery solved. Papa Pete hates clutter."

The room gets brighter as the afternoon sun fills the office. Ben stands up and passes in front of Colin. He plops himself down in his new chair. It barely squeaks. "So, how the hell did you have time to visit Scranton? What did you do, fly?"

"As a matter of fact, we did, but that's an even longer story. I still can't believe we spent hours with that woman, and I didn't know she was…"

"Dead?"

"Yeah. I mean, I've had a little bit of experience hanging out with dead people. You'd think I would have picked up on it. Her house even smelled like a crypt."

"Well, I need to know everything about your visit with her. Everything."

Colin squirms in his seat. "Can you call Katie and ask her over? We can explain it together."

"I don't have time for that. It could be hours before she shows up. I need to know everything, before I tell your mother."

"I thought we could do that together, too."

Ben is back on his feet, popping in and out of Colin's limited view. Distracted, Colin drops his head and just listens.

"Well, you thought wrong, Colin. I'm going into Philly to speak with her."

"You hate driving into the city."

"I'm not driving. I'll take the train, grab a cab to the food bank and..."

"You really don't have a plan, do you?"

"I'll figure it out. Maybe take her out for lunch. Explain everything I know. Prepare her for whatever happens next. That's why you must be honest with me. I can't hurt her. She's been through too much."

Colin's mood softens. "You really do love her, don't you?"

Ben's image moves rapidly toward Colin, his voice rising with every step. "What kind of foolish question is that? Of course, I love her. I love both of you. All I've ever done is try to protect both of you. Especially you, Colin. I gave you space to heal. Tried to respect how you were feeling. But at some point, you must separate feelings from facts."

"What's that supposed to mean?"

"What happened between us -- your mom and me -- was a natural thing. It took years to evolve. She and your dad were my friends. Remember, I was the one who hired Honeycutt. Why would I have done that if I was trying to steal her away?"

Colin fidgets. Moves to the edge of the rigid cushion. Rubs his knees anxiously. "But I didn't know any of that. I just saw you getting closer the longer he was away."

"We *were* getting closer. Like I said, it happened naturally. After Honeycutt died, and then the letter from your dad arrived...you mom said 'enough...we have to move on.' That was her choice, not mine. She put an end to it because she thought it was unhealthy for you..."

"Does she love you?"

Ben's voice never sounded more sincere. "Colin, I don't think your mom will ever love me the way she loved your dad. That's not my expectation. I just wanted to settle down, create a loving home, and enjoy our best shot at a normal life. So, we started talking about getting married. Jumped through a lot of legal hoops and then finally reached that day where we all got to start a different journey. It was the happiest day of my life."

For the first time in forever, Colin feels ashamed. "All I did was make it miserable for you."

"It was tough. And then your cousin threw fuel on the fire."

"You mean thinking she saw my dad around town."

"Wasn't expecting that one. Put yourself in my shoes. We finally put the past behind us. Married and ready for a new start and then Katie starts telling me Tommy's in town. It complicated everything. In fact, I was ready to encourage your mom to talk to you about the letter from your dad. I figured you were eighteen and it was time to come clean. But I dropped that idea when I thought your dad might be back. And I couldn't tell Hannah what Katie saw..."

"Why not?"

"No way. Not without some proof that he was here. I mean, I love your cousin but that's not how I operate. I wasn't telling your mom anything without physical proof."

"Turns out you were right. So, what are you going to tell my mom now? I mean, seriously...a few hours ago you were planning to tell her that I knew about the private investigator and my dad's letter. Now, you're going to show up unannounced at the food bank, take her to lunch and then casually mention that Katie and I have been hanging out with a family ghost?"

"I was thinking about leaving that part out...for now."

"Ahh, that sounds more like Ben, the procrastinator."

"No, I'm thinking about your mom's state of mind. I want to give her time to process the truth. It's a better plan than getting blindsided by you and Katie."

"That's feels kind of unfair."

"Facts, not feelings, Colin. Just being honest with you. Your mom does not react well to surprises...most of us don't. So let me lay the groundwork with her. Based on how that goes, we can decide when to share these with her." He fiddles with the tapes still resting on his desk.

Rattled, Colin replies, "you want her to hear those?"

"Of course. And I have to tell her about Aunt Coleen, too. No more secrets, right?"

"Right."

"Good. So, tell me about your visit with Coleen. Don't spare any details."

Colin unravels the story, painting a detailed picture for Ben. When he first mentions Moretti, Ben interrupts him. "Never liked that guy...and I know he gave Hannah the creeps. She hated that Moretti and your dad were still working together after you left Grays Ferry. I just can't believe Tommy got tied up in this bootleg mining. And what about those debts Tommy owed? Did Coleen say anything more about that?"

"Nope. Just what I already told you...that the bootlegging job was temporary...just to pay off some debts."

"To whom?"

"Don't know."

Ben moves out of Colin's line of vision and quickly opens a nearby door. Must be the closet. He grunts as he slides something onto the newly refinished hardwood floor. More noises from the closet and then he returns to Colin's side. He places something next to the loveseat.

"Here." His voice trails off again as he says, "there's one more."

The closet door closes, and Ben returns, commenting, "I forgot how heavy these were." A second object thuds onto the floor.

"What's this?"

"Homework. For you and Katie. She asked about Honeycutt's files. Here they are. By the time we got these back from his wife, Tracey, we were moving on. Looking for closure. Hannah made me promise to let it go. Okay, I need to get moving. Not familiar with the train schedule."

Colin's field of vision shrinks as Ben draws the curtains behind his desk.

"What about my dad's letter...and the medal?"

"Colin senses Ben's brisk movement then hears the office door open. "One step at a time, okay? Please call Katie and get her butt moving."

The door gently shuts. Colin anticipates the sound of the heavy garage door opening. Seconds later, the Fairlane's ignition struggles briefly then succeeds. The rhythmic tapping of the motor echoes lightly down the hallway, disappearing as the garage door slams shut. The office walls briefly rattle. Colin reaches to his left and rubs the surface of a box...homework. Papa Pete joins him on the loveseat.

"I believe him, Colin. In fact, he's starting to grow on me."

Colin slowly applauds. "So, you *were* listening." He lifts his right arm and sweeps it in a circular motion around the room. "What do you think of the office renovation?"

"Not my taste, but that's growing on me too."

"And the coal stove?"

There is a distinct pause before Pete responds. His inflection changes. *"Yes, it's... here."*

"But so are *you*. In a room where you never set foot before. This is a big deal. Wonder what it means?"

His great grandfather's hopeful voice weakly responds, *"maybe we're getting closer to the truth...but I'm afraid Colin."*

"Of what?"

"Time. My time. Every moment I feel closer to the truth, I also feel my stamina dripping away. Like just now, when I heard you and Ben talking about Coleen."

Colin cringes. "Oh man, I'm so sorry we didn't tell you this morning. You disappeared on us."

"No need to apologize. Especially for something out of your control. For what it's worth, I indeed remember living with Coleen. But I cannot recall my purpose. I don't know why I had to endure that pig sty."

Colin's heart sinks. "Maybe you weren't supposed to know then. You've come so far. We're closer than ever. Hang in there, Papa Pete."

"Please, hurry Colin."

CHAPTER 25

Evidence

Tuesday – 12:30 PM

Katie arrives thirty minutes after Ben's departure. A fresh pot of coffee is already brewing in the kitchen. Colin first warns her about Papa Pete's state of mind. He can sense her helplessness. He feels it too. Then he fills her in on his chat with Ben.

She takes a long slurp of her coffee. "Wow, I give him a lot of credit, Colin. I hope he knows what he's doing."

"I know. I keep imagining their conversation. I wish I was there to support my mom. Tell her it's going to be okay."

"You'll have plenty of time for that. If we get busy here, maybe we'll have more to share with both of them. It's almost noon. Let's get moving."

Colin sighs heavily and plods down the hall towards Ben's office.

"Whoa, hold on there. What's with the grumpy face?"

"I feel useless."

Katie nudges his chest playfully. "What are you talking about? We're a team."

"No. You lead, and I follow. Everywhere. Like right now. You're the only one who can read those files. You're the only one who can organize them. What do you need me for?"

"Ah, I get it. We're going to have a pity party. Let's invite poor Pete and Mr. Honeycutt's widow...and I know...here's a good one...let's invite your friend Charlie. She can listen to you whine and whimper."

"Katie, you can stop."

"Not until you let me talk to your old pal…Mr. Stiles…yeah, give me his phone number. I mean, he should be here, too. I wonder what advice he would give you, hmm?"

Colin slumps against the wall and laughs. "He would tell me I had more brains than a dozen of those nitwits in the neighborhood put together."

Katie abandons her sarcasm. "Colin, I don't need your eyes. I need your brain. So, get your brailler while I organize these files. Help me make sense of this shit."

He bumps into her, apologizing as he scurries towards the kitchen. His sore toe reminds him to slow down and pay attention to his path upstairs. Within minutes he returns with the case containing his writing machine. He clears a spot on Ben's desk and opens the case. He remembers Mr. Stiles giving it to him on the last summer night of 1963. Colin was starting third grade the next day, still splitting time between St. Gabe's and St. Lucy's. He recalls the bitter lemonade he was sipping while Mr. Stiles excused himself from his usual perch on the steel glider. When he returned, he placed the case beside Colin, who was fidgeting restlessly.

"Listen I know you use one of these over at St. Lucy's. Seems like an important thing for a kid like you. So…figured I would get you one for home. Help with your homework and things like that."

"Where did you get it? I mean, thank you but how did you know?"

"Them nuns owe me plenty of favors, okay? Let's just leave it at that. Now, don't let me down. This better not be collecting dust under your bed, hear me fella?"

"Yes, sir, loud and clear."

"Good, good. And for Christ's sake Colin. Stop drinking that stuff. It tastes like piss."

Colin shakes his head and smiles. To his right, he hears Katie's rapid breathing as she moves boxes and rustles files.

"Colin, this guy was beyond organized. He's done a lot of our work for us."

"Thank you, Mr. Honeycutt," Colin chirps as he inserts a sheet of paper and presses the line feed key. "Okay, where do we start?"

Over the next few hours, they stitch together a timeline defined by receipts, phone records, photographs, interviews, maps, eyewitness accounts, and even maintenance records for Moretti's truck. The embossing head inside the machine keeps pace as Colin rapidly strikes the six keys – one for each dot in a braille cell. Each sheet of paper turns Honeycutt's research into calendar events that reveal a common thread. The private investigator was not just tracking Colin's father. He was pursuing Moretti's whereabouts. The deeper Katie digs into Honeycutt's records, the more detail is added to the timeline. Aside from bathroom breaks and coffee refills the cousins are glued to their task. It's an innocent observation from Katie that finally breaks Colin's concentration.

"I miss Papa Pete's annoying questions."

Suddenly, Papa Pete's absence is profound. Until now, it usually meant he was off brooding about something Colin did to hurt his feelings. Until now he was just *temporarily* missing. Now...Colin is *losing* him. He tries to share his feelings with his cousin.

Her hardheaded response is unexpected but needed. "Well, never mind... back to work. We're making progress."

Around 3:30, Katie announces they've exhausted all of Honeycutt's findings. Colin pulls the last piece of braille-encoded paper from the braillewriter. He rolls his neck and flexes his shoulders. He's been typing for hours. Running his fingers across the raised dots he asks, "you sure there's nothing else? It feels a little thin towards the end."

"Things were a little less organized around the time he died. That's understandable. He probably never got the chance to make sense of some of that stuff. Still, we've got a lot to think about." She sighs with resignation. "Let's hear what you've got."

"Katie, we both know what I've got." He grabs the stack of thick braille paper to stop his hands from trembling. "I don't have to read this. It's not going to change anything."

"Unless we missed something," she offers feebly.

His composure weakens. "But we didn't. It doesn't sound good for my dad. His fingers deftly touch the letters on his first page of notes. His father's disappearance haunts him as he recaps his timeline for Katie.

WEDNESDAY JUNE 29, 1966

- *Attends AA meeting. Sponsor said he was in good spirits*
- *Home for dinner with family. Everything normal*

Kate stops him. "I know it's just a coincidence but isn't it weird that date is right around the time of the Twin Shafts disaster?" Colin waits while Katie rustles through some papers. She continues. "Yup, that newspaper article I read to you was printed on June 29, 1896...the day after the collapse." A brief silence is followed by the sound of her pen clicking and intense breathing as she scrawls something. "Like I said...probably a coincidence. Keep going." Colin revisits his timeline.

THURSDAY JUNE 30, 1966

- *The day he disappeared*
- *Left apartment to go to morning AA meeting -- Never showed up*
- *Eyewitnesses saw him at a coffee shop near Swarthmore campus with an unidentified woman.*

Colin stops abruptly. "Okay that's weird. Who was he meeting with? He was supposed to be with his AA buddies and instead he's talking to a strange woman. Do you think he was having an affair?"

"No. He wasn't having an affair. Trust me."

"Why...what do you know...what does that mean? 'Trust me.' You said, 'trust me.'"

"Yeah, I know what I just said. Your dad was not having an affair. He...was..."

Colin screams, "He was what? Why are you doing this? Tell

me what you know."

"Okay, but don't interrupt me. Or I swear I'll shove that braille machine where the sun doesn't shine."

"Okay, okay...so tell me."

"He didn't share much, only that he had been meeting with a realtor. He wanted to move out of my apartment and give you and Hannah a place of your own. Don't know much, just that they met a few times near the college. This woman had a kid going there so it was convenient for her. Your dad seemed to like her. Said they had a lot in common. That's all I got."

"Did my mom know about her?"

"I seriously doubt it. He wanted to surprise her, remember?"

Colin sits up and tilts his head toward Katie's voice. "Wait, wait, wait. When you saw Papa Pete in Wallingford...he was staring in the window of a real estate office. Right?"

"He was. But that doesn't mean anything."

"Or it means everything. That why we put ourselves through this agony. At the very least we're going to check it out, okay?"

"Absolutely. You're right." There's a bit of energy in her voice as Colin hears her scribbling. "Okay, got it. Keep going."

Colin revisits his document. His fingers scan the characters.

"Well one thing we can agree on. My dad and Moretti left town together. That's for sure. And coal country was the destination." He returns to the indisputable evidence.

FRIDAY JULY 1, 1966

- *Eyewitnesses place him at a service stop on PA Turnpike (Northeast Extension heading toward Scranton) in bright green truck. Leaking oil heavily. With another man (dark hair, muscular, olive-skinned, talkative)*
- *Records from Howard Johnson's motel near Carbondale confirm two men (using aliases) stayed one night. Clerk confirmed he provided transportation to and from local repair shop for their truck.*
- *Ellerson's Truck Repair confirmed that 1958 medium-*

duty Chevrolet truck registered to Giovanni Moretti was repaired. Picked up by customer and another male companion. Carbondale police sources also confirm sighting of truck ("hard to miss") but nothing suspicious.

Colin pauses and Katie jumps in. "Well, Aunt Coleen wasn't making things up, that's for sure. He doesn't respond; just keeps reading his notes. His voice is quivering.

SATURDAY JULY 2, 1966

- *Late afternoon. Anonymous source in Pittston confirmed bright green truck with a load of coal getting gas. Not the first time he saw the truck but usually there were two men. This time the quiet red-headed guy wasn't around. Just the "obnoxious wop" who said he was hauling the load to a customer in New York City.*
- *Eyewitnesses confirm sighting of green Chevrolet truck at two different gas stations on 84 East. Single male driver matches description of Moretti.*

Colin's voice falters. "So, after Pittston Moretti is by himself."

The only response from Katie is the furious scratching of her pen against paper. Then the agitated tapping of her pen on Colin's stack of notes. He feels the energy in his own fingers. "What are you writing?"

"This and that. Keep going."

The following sheets unveil more details of Moretti's journey, without a mention of Colin's father. His pace quickens as the timeline continues to reflect Honeycutt's pursuit of the truth, but a lack of clues to his father's disappearance. Colin mumbles his way through the repetition. Trips to the Scranton area. More to New York. Once to Baltimore. Back to Philly.

Katie interrupts. "Okay that's enough. We're missing something. We've got a private investigator who was pretty good at his job. He didn't spend another whole year just bouncing around Pennsylvania and New York. He knew something. Was following something. There's got to be more."

"Ben said this was all he got from Tracey. Do you think he's holding back? Hiding something?"

"Absolutely not. I believe everything Ben has told us."

"So does Pete...I mean Papa Pete. Says Ben is growing on him."

"Well, there you go. Let's give Ben the benefit of the doubt here. He's going to be back soon with Hannah so let's wrap this up."

"What were you writing?"

"So glad you asked. Now, just hear me out, okay?" Flipping pages tickle Colin's curiosity. "Now, let's set aside coincidences and agree that we're dealing with some supernatural shit here. And if we do that, well...we have some dots to connect."

Colin squirms anxiously but says nothing.

"Okay, `here we go. First there's the timing of your dad's disappearance. It's very close to the date that Papa Pete died..."

"Well, give or take a day."

"Close enough, Colin. Second, Pittston is jumping off the page at me. It's where both Papa Pete and your dad disappeared for very different reasons. Third, you're right about the realtor. We've got to follow through on that. How can we ignore the connection between Papa Pete leading me to that office and your dad confiding in me about a realtor?"

Colin swivels nervously in Ben's chair. "We can't ignore it."

"Damn right we can't. Fourth, this one is freaking me out a bit. The last day we know of your dad's whereabouts – or his disappearance – is July 2, 1966. Colin, do you remember when Aunt Coleen told us Papa Pete showed up in her home?"

Colin stands so forcefully the chair rolls away. "She spent the morning hanging flags in town...getting ready for the parade on...on..."

"Saturday. The Fourth of July was on a Monday," Colin fires back rapidly. "And she was hanging flags on Saturday, July 2nd," he says excitedly. We asked her if she was sure and...and..."

Katie continues. "and she said, 'the last time I checked a calendar'..."

Together they repeat, "that's a couple days before the Fourth of July."

Katie ask cryptically. So, Colin...coincidence?"

He ignores the murky question. "What do we do now? How do we...connect the dots? My head is spinning."

Katie's calm voice responds, "easy, buddy, easy." Slowly, she flips pages as Colin breathes more cautiously. "Okay, first we need to see if Tracey Honeycutt has any more notes she forgot to turn over. Ben or your mom can help us with that. Second, I need to visit that realtor and try to understand any possible connections. Should be easy enough. Next...not so easy."

Colin acknowledges the problem. "Pittston." And the only solution. "How about Aunt Coleen?"

Katie laughs, "Yeah right. Who's going to do that?"

"Her father," Colin says with conviction.

"Papa Pete?" Katie's tone changes. "Listen to you...you're serious!"

Collin feels emboldened. "Why not? I'm not sure how, but why not? The only person – living or dead – who knows where my dad and Moretti were picking up coal is Aunt Coleen..."

"You're right. She would know who in Pittston was mining that coal."

"Exactly. And the only ones who have a shot at talking with her are you, me, or Papa Pete. I don't know about you, but I vote for our great grandfather."

"In a heartbeat, but who are we kidding? You said we're losing him."

Weakly, a new voice joins the conversation. *"I want to try."*

Colin's neck is tingling.

Startled, Katie says, "you're back...oh, oh Papa Pete. You can't..."

Perplexed, Colin fights the pounding in his chest and asks, "What's going on?"

"He, he looks different Colin. Um, tired...no...he's fading...

like an old photograph. Harder to make out."

"I want to try. I'm ready to see the elephant."

"Excuse me?" Katie asks curiously.

"To break out...see the town...do something a little risky... learning my purpose in all of this."

Papa Pete is standing directly in front of Colin, blocking any limited perspective he has of Katie or the rest of Ben's office. He comes even closer. Colin shuffles clumsily backward, pushing the office chair further away. The chair stiffens as it strikes the credenza behind him. Flecks of mottled light appear as Papa Pete speaks.

"Katie, you said you saw me in that town, um...on the streets of that town..."

"Wallingford?"

"Yes, that's the place. Well, that was miles away from here, correct? So, I can do it. I can travel to Carbondale."

Katie responds softly, "But that was before. You were stronger then. You can't um...look for an elephant now."

"It's not cool when you say it, Katie."

Colin manages a sympathetic snicker. Katie mockingly groans.

"We...you...are getting closer to the truth, and it has given me a purpose. I can't explain it, but I can feel it. I want to try. I want to help. Let me talk to Coleen."

Before Colin can respond, Katie says somberly, "he's gone. And who knows what he'll look like the next time we see him."

Colin adds remorsefully, "or if we'll see him again."

"Okay, don't be so dramatic. I think we have some time but not much." Colin hears Katie shuffling files. "Hey, give me a hand pushing these boxes over to the closet."

As they clear the clutter, Colin probes his cousin. "How much time? The closet door opens, and the sound of boxes being stacked delays her response. Finally, the door shuts and Katie, breathing heavily, grabs Colin's shoulders firmly. "If we're connecting dots then we have to admit that the only date we can connect to Pete's obvious decline and his eventual disappearance is June 28th, the day he died in that mine." She loosens her grip on his shoulders and slides her arms down, tenderly squeezing her cousin's hands.

Colin hears the distinct sound of the front door opening.

In a panic, he asks "what are you saying? What is today?"

"It's June 23rd." she says quickly. "We have five days Colin. Five days before Papa Pete is probably gone and with him any chance of getting to the truth about your father."

Colin stammers to respond. Katie lets go of his hands as the sound of his mother's muffled voice blows in from the kitchen. "Hey, where is everybody? Colin... Ben!"

BEN?

Colin's stomach tightens.

Katie whispers, "They're not together...where the hell is Ben?"

The office door swings open, and Colin's mother enters the room. "There you are. Hey, Katie didn't expect to see your car here. What's up? Where's Ben?"

Katie responds hesitantly. "I think...he went out for a bit..."

"Where?"

"I don't know. I just got here a little while ago."

"Colin?"

Colin barely manages a response. "Not sure, mom."

"Seriously? What's your excuse?"

He taps on his brailler. "I've been working on...some notes from my orientation. You know, just getting organized."

She pats the stack of papers. Her tone is good-natured. "Well, I'd love to know what's on these pages. Looks like you made a lot of progress. Maybe you can read them to me later. In fact, I'll get a reservation at Marra's for dinner, and you can fill me in on your girlfriend."

"Mom, can't we do it tomorrow?"

"No, you've got your freshman picnic and I'm going shopping downtown, remember?"

"Oh, right...well I kind of ate a late lunch. I'm not that

hungry."

"Come on. It's Marra's, your favorite. We'll load you up on ravioli. Katie, want to join us?"

"I really should be going. I've got an early flight tomorrow."

Hannah snaps, "I'm not driving you to the airport,"

"That's cool. I never asked you."

Clearly exasperated, Hannah grumbles, "well, I guess everybody is still ticked off with me for losing my cool this morning. It's obvious nobody wants to be in my company, including my husband. And where the hell is he?"

CHAPTER 26

Betrayed

Tuesday – 4:30 PM

Colin pummels the heavy leather punching bag tethered to the basement's master beam. Each thrust channels the frustration he's feeling over too many loose ends. Thwack. Thwack. Thwack. He steps in, weakly shoves the 70-pound bag, then drops his weary arms. His gloved hands find his hips. Bending forward, he feels sweat dripping freely from his chin. His labored breathing outpaces the slow rhythmic squeaking of the master beam as it bears the weight of the swaying bag. The washing machine lurches into a spin cycle, reminding him that he passed his mom coming up the steps as he was going down. She barely spoke to him, only warning him to watch the laundry basket she left at the bottom of the steps. Colin's solitary thoughts are interrupted by sudden movement upstairs. BEN IS HOME. He steadies the bag and removes his gloves -- dropping them to the floor. Silence returns to the basement until his mother's animated voice rises above the rafters, repeatedly interrupting Ben's fainthearted responses. There's a flurry of footsteps. From the basement door comes the unfamiliar sound of the newly installed latch -- followed by the usual squeak of rusted hinges. The thump-thump-thump of heavy feet on the worn staircase is quickly erased by his mother's shrill voice. "Fine! Go ahead and stay down there. And you can forget dinner. I'm going out. The two of you can fend for yourself!"

Colin retreats to his weight bench and settles. His heart rate does not. Ben's anxious breathing gets closer.

"Where have you been? What happened?"

Ben's labored breaths sound even more agitated.

Colin presses him. "What's the matter? What's going on?"

"Colin, I don't know what to do. I'm sorry but I don't have anyone else I can talk to. It's not fair to you but..." Ben's voice cracks. "Oh, God. Oh God. What am I supposed to do now?"

"Ben, stop. Sit down...tell me what's going on."

"I can't sit."

Colin chooses silence as Ben's blurred form moves briskly past him. He's startled when an unexpected shape fills his line of vision and stops. Colin's skin is tingling.

The punching bag comes alive. Bare hands smash its shell as Ben grunts louder and louder with each blow.

Colin is on his feet, his outstretched arms searching for Ben. "Hey, hey, hey...easy...you're gonna break your wrists. He finds Ben's shoulders. Feels the tension as he pulls him away from the bag. "Ben, it's okay. Talk to me, please. Whatever it is...you can tell me."

His stepfather pulls away and attacks the bag again. Three angry blows, each punctuated by a different word.

Smack. "She."

Smack. "Wasn't."

Smack. "There."

Colin hears Ben slump to the floor. He squats down and asks, "that's what you're upset about? You missed her? Don't beat yourself up, man. It's cool. Just wait until she calms down then talk to her. No big deal."

"I didn't miss her. She lied. She's been lying."

Colin's pulse quickens. "Lying about what?"

Ben's voice no longer sounds agitated. He's sad. "I'm such a fool. I show up at the food bank, introduce myself and ask to see my wife...and...and...the guy tells me she hasn't worked there for six months."

Colin drops to his knees. "That's impossible. Where has she been going all this time?"

Ben doesn't answer. Lost in his own anguish, he continues, "Now what do I do? I went down there to tell her the truth and now I feel betrayed." He manages a wry laugh. "Of course, I get back home, and she's pissed off at me because I wouldn't tell her where I was."

"Hold on. Hold on now. You didn't confront her? She doesn't know?"

"I'm too angry right now. I need to process this...I don't know. I have no idea what I'm saying."

Colin buries his head in his hands and breathes deeply. "There must be an explanation. Something obvious."

"Colin. I'm so sorry. I shouldn't have told you. It's unfair to put you in the middle of this. I just...we just... finally we were being honest with each other."

"Hey...it's okay. You told me the truth. That's what I asked for..."

"No, you didn't ask for this. This is beyond finding out about your dad. This is a whole new shit show. But if we're being honest, I just don't feel comfortable now telling your mom about what you and Katie discussed with me."

Colin reaches toward Ben, finds his chest, and thumps it softly. "I understand. It complicates things for sure."

"That's an understatement. Until I get answers – no matter what they are – I can't even think about sharing the rest of this crap with her." Ben stands and pulls Colin to his feet. "I know that's not fair to you and I'm sorry." He lightly grips Colin's hand.

"Are you sure it's fair to her? Maybe roll the dice and give her a chance to explain."

"Come on, Colin she's been lying for months. What could she possibly tell me that would make all this okay?"

"The truth?"

Ben squeezes Colin's hand harder then let's go. "I'm not a fool Colin. And I don't need another crisis. I need to do this my way, alright?"

"Listen, this is your marriage and it's your business," Colin says respectfully. Then, with a sense of urgency he back pedals. "Of course, I want you to get to the truth, but I can't wait forever. Sooner or later, my mom has to know what we know."

"Fair enough. Just give me a little time, okay?" His voice trails away steadily. "I feel better just knowing we talked." The staircase gently sags under Ben's slow, sad steps. Before the basement door closes, Pete is already pressing Colin.

"Are you okay?"

"No, I'm not okay. I'm confused and sad...for Ben actually. He's trying to do the right thing and now this."

"Are you really going to give him all this space?"

"Absolutely not."

"But you promised. You said you would mind your own business."

"I am going to mind *my* own business...but you're not."

"What does that mean...for me?"

"Tomorrow, my mom is going shopping in the city. I need you to follow her. You said you're ready to see the elephant, right?"

"It's sneaky."

"No, it's necessary. I know you're worried about losing your grip, but I'm really encouraged by your new confidence. Hanging out in Ben's office. Spending time with me down here – another place that used to be off limits."

"Are you taking advantage of me, Colin?"

Colin is dripping with guilt. He says apologetically, "you said we're running out of time."

"That's a bottom fact."

"Well, okay then." Colin retrieves his gloves from the floor and slaps them together, as if shedding his shame. "Hey, you're also the one who said you were ready to help, remember?"

"That was different...visiting my daughter."

We might have to put that on hold just a bit. Instead, it's time to push the boundaries a little more. Really get you out of your comfort zone. Let you wake some snakes."

"You can stop your foolish encouragement. Perhaps I can give

this plan a try…for Ben."

Colin sighs. "Thanks. In the meantime, I'm ready to pull my weight around here…push some boundaries too."

CHAPTER 27

A Brave New Day

Wednesday June 24, 1970 – 7:00 AM

Everything about this morning is awkward. Ben is deliberately avoiding Hannah, staying in his office with the door closed. Colin's mom shuffles silently through the kitchen, barely speaking to him. He sips his coffee near the sink, anchored to his favorite spot by the window. The most welcoming gesture in the room is the sun's brilliance on his face. He allows the warmth to swallow him. The sound of a distant airplane yanks Colin back to this day's daunting reality. Katie is working a puddle jumper to Atlantic City and some other New Jersey airport he can't pronounce. Before she returns home, she'll be taking a detour to visit Honeycutt's widow Tracey. Papa Pete has his assignment. But Colin has a plan too…his far-fetched secret.

His mother's snappish words startle him. "Get moving. I'm dropping you off at Swarthmore."

"It's cool. I'm ready."

"You're going dressed like that?"

"Mom, it's a summer picnic. I'm not playing my first concert. Are you going to take the train from the Swarthmore station?"

"No, I'm driving. I'm not crazy about the summer train schedule, and unlike Ben I'm not afraid to drive on 95 and the Schuylkill Expressway."

"No comment," he says hesitantly.

She moves him aside and dumps coffee into the sink. "Of course, no comment. You boys have to stick together, right?"

He lets her remark pass then moves instinctively to the right and brushes by the humming refrigerator anchoring the edge of the kitchen. Colin feels Pete's presence in the hallway as he moves intuitively toward the garage past Ben's office. He hears his mother's keys jangling as she leaves the kitchen. She pounds loudly on Ben's door. "We're leaving," she shouts. Twenty feet away, Colin stands at the garage door. He wraps his hand around the doorknob, leans in and faintly whispers, "remember what we talked about. You can do this." He opens the door and steps into the garage. He feels wobbly, like none of his body parts are connected.

Very little is said while the Mustang departs the neighborhood and navigates the light summer traffic approaching the campus. Three occupants with very different agendas. Colin tightens his grip on his cane as the car crawls to a stop.

His mother's half-hearted request barely registers. "You want me to walk you up there?"

"I'm fine. I know what to do."

"Fine. Katie will be picking you up around 1:00 so please be..."

"Wait. You're not picking me up?"

"Colin, Katie already said she would do it, so let's just stick with the plan. I have no way of reaching her now anyway."

Colin squeezes his cane even tighter, trying to control his emotions. He mutters questions he immediately wishes he could take back. "Why do you have to go to the city anyway? What's so important about another shopping date?"

He opens the door and swings his feet onto the street. His bare ankles feel the simmering heat. His mother grips his shoulder.

"Hey, what's that supposed to mean? What's going on?"

"Nothing. Forget it."

"No. I'm not going to forget it, Colin," she scolds. You don't get off that easy."

Colin gently removes his mother's hand from his shoulder

but says nothing. Papa Pete's flat voice fills the void.

"Colin we can call this whole thing off."

Papa Pete's comment agitates Colin. His tone is edgy. "Let's just stick with the plan."

He taps the curb with his cane, remaining silent while jumbled messages bombard him.

"I don't know if I can do this Colin."

"Fine honey but we're not finished here."

"What if I get lost?"

"Make sure Katie can find you. Understood?"

He shuts the door and hears one final muffled appeal.

"Let me stay with you."

The car pulls away. Colin stands on the pavement and numbly whispers.

"Just remember what we talked about."

He sweeps his cane back and forth, cautiously advancing toward the campus. The heavy, humid air stifles each step. His Woodstock tee shirt clings to his damp skin while the sun singes the back of his neck. Colin reaches the wide set of concrete stairs that crest a small hill. A cautious climb of six steps and he'll reach the final pathway to the campus. Instead, he stops and waits. Nearby, he hears chatter among some students. Sounds like two girls and a guy. His sweaty palm grips his cane tightly. *HERE GOES.* Ignoring the steps and a path to the picnic, he taps his way toward the group. Their sudden silence tells him they are aware of his presence.

"Hey, sorry to bother you. I could really use your help."

The male voice responds quickly. "Sure man, what's up?"

"Thanks, could you point me in the direction of the train station? I need to be on the platform heading toward the city."

One of the girls says, "you're going by yourself? No one is helping you?"

Colin smiles, and jokes, "I thought you could all come with me."

"Um, well, I have a class in a few minutes..."

Colin laughs and the group joins in, probably relieved that

he's joking.

"Hey, I'm Bob. I can walk you down that way."

"Thanks, Bob. I'm Colin. Just get me going in the right direction and I can take it from there."

Within minutes, they are standing in line at the ticket window. Bob refuses to leave until Colin has paid for his ticket and he's escorted him safely to the platform. Colin assures him he's okay, but Bob insists on hanging around. Colin doesn't resist.

"Man, you are such a badass, you know that? I mean, this is so cool. How many blind guys would jump on a train and ride into Philly? Outta sight, Colin. My new badass friend."

Colin wants to inform Bob that his new badass friend is scared shitless.

"Hey Colin!"

He turns in the direction of a throaty voice. *HER VOICE.*

A soft breeze whisks across the platform. Magically, the odor of creosote-soaked railway ties is gently swept away – replaced by the fragrance of roses.

"Charlie?"

"Oh my God, yes. How did you know?"

"Blind luck?"

Her raspy laugh is interrupted by Bob's cackling.

"Oh, I'm sorry. Charlie, this is…Bob."

"Hey Bob. Sorry, I thought you were lost. I mean…so you're not here for the picnic? I just presumed…oh, never mind. Where are you guys headed?"

"Oh, no…I just met…Bob helped me get my ticket and find the platform…we're just waiting for the train."

"So, you're traveling alone?"

Colin can barely respond. He squeezes out a feeble "uh huh."

"Well, could you use some company?"

Colin squeaks, "sure…I mean, if you don't mind." He feels his face flush with embarrassment.

Bob whistles softly then adds, "looks like my job is done. It was nice to meet you, Charlie. Take care of my friend, here.

Colin, it was a gas hanging out. Good luck man." He shakes Colin's hand vigorously and whispers, "badass."

"Thanks Bob. Very cool of you to help me. Look for me on campus this Fall, okay?"

The clickety-clack of the approaching train smothers Bob's response. Charlie lightly grips Colin's elbow. "Let's go."

"Are you sure you don't mind?"

"Of course not."

He feels the crowd surge toward the train. Charlie guides him through a gaggle of commuters. Her grip on his elbow tightens as the crowd presses him. Now she is pushing. "Sorry Colin. Are you okay?" A booming male voice shouts, "hold on folks. Wait right there please. Let these two through."

"Thank you, sir."

"My pleasure, miss. My name is Carl. You let me know if you need anything once we get moving, okay?"

Colin tilts his head in Carl's direction. "Thanks for your help."

"You are very welcome son. Watch your step there. Okay folks...thanks for your patience. No rush here...not leaving anyone behind."

Charlie leads Colin to a seat. She guides him until he plops down and exhales in relief.

"You okay?"

"Yeah, I really appreciate your help, Charlie. Thanks."

"No problem. It gets crazy out there in the morning."

"You do this every day?"

"Three times a week. I'm taking a summer math class at Temple...need to catch up a bit. So, I get the feeling this is not a regular routine for you."

Colin laughs. "No this is pretty much the first time I tried this by myself." He senses his pulse softening.

"Where are you going?"

"Eventually, Grays Ferry, my old neighborhood. But first I have to get to 30th Street Station."

"And then?"

"I guess I'll take a taxi."

"You guess?"

"Well, yeah…I'll figure it out."

"That's ambitious, Colin. I mean, doing this for the first time. Must be important." They are briefly interrupted by Carl who stops to check tickets and spread some morning cheer.

"It is important. I need to catch up with an old friend and get some answers."

She teasingly asks, "an old girlfriend?"

"God no! I was twelve when we left. Just an old neighbor who I lost touch with. He kind of looked out for me and my mom when my dad wasn't around."

"Does he know you're coming?"

Colin scrunches his face. "No. He doesn't."

The train slows and Carl announces, "Morton. Next stop… Morton."

Charlie's tone is more inquisitive. "What if he's not there?"

"He's not the type who goes anywhere. We kind of hung out together and solved all the world's problems. I'm hoping he can help me solve a new one."

He feels the whoosh of another train passing. The car rocks slightly as it bends through a curve in the track and slides Charlie closer to Colin. She immediately distances herself.

"Anything you want to share?"

"Charlie, you can't imagine how complicated my answer is to that question."

"Try me, Colin. Really. I'm a good listener."

He takes a deep breath. Her scent lingers. "You may regret those words."

Secane – Primos – Clifton Heights.

The stops come and go as Colin shares his childhood memories and his father's struggles.

Lansdowne – Yeadon – Angora.

The train leave the suburbs and rolls toward Philadelphia. He weaves Ben into the tale, surprising himself at how kindly he describes his stepfather to his traveling companion. Colin details his family's exodus to Delaware County and how they shared an apartment with Katie.

"Wait, I know her. Your cousin. I met her at the open house, remember?"

"How could I forget. Sorry about that."

"What are you talking about? I thought she was funny."

"That's not how I would describe her, but that's Katie. Tough outside but a really cool person with a heart of gold. She's like a big sister to me."

"That's so sweet. I hope I get to meet her again. Now, I want to hear the rest. Seriously. What happened after you moved in with Katie?"

Colin sags. Charlie's innocent question pushes him off a cliff. His father is still missing. The crowded train suffocates him.

Kingsessing.

They enter the city as the train slows, giving Colin time to share...just enough. The troubled tale of a young man searching for his father with the aid of his older cousin. While it earns him sympathy from Charlie, there are gaping holes in his version of the facts. Missing details that might send her running as soon as Carl bellows the next available stop. No mention of his great grandfather...Scranton...Aunt Coleen... the Twin Shaft disaster...recording the voice of a spirit...and right now Papa Pete sitting in his mother's car.

I don't know if I can do this Colin.

"This is the big one folks. 30th Street Station...next stop." Carl's deep voice fills the car. It's getting closer. "Gather your belongings and get ready for a brave new day!" He is standing in front of them. His strong voice drops to a soothing whisper. "I know this is your stop, son. You need some help getting off?"

"No, Carl, I'm going with him. I mean...if that's okay with you Colin?"

Colin is blindsided. "What about your class?"

Carl whistles and keeps moving through the car, laughing as

he repeats "30th Street Station…next stop."

"Hey, it's a brave new day, right? I'll be fine…it's just one class. Besides, do you really want to go out there in all that chaos and find a taxi. Let me help…unless you think I should be minding my own business."

Colin doesn't hide his relief. "Are you kidding? Really, I mean it...thank you, Charlie. I hope you don't regret it." He reaches awkwardly as she slides off the seat.

"Better than math class. Let's get this show on the road."

Once on the platform, Colin breaks free from Charlie's grip and gently slides his right hand towards her elbow. "If you don't mind, this is easier for me to follow you."

"Oh geez, I'm sorry. I forgot. You told me at the orientation. Still learning the ropes here."

"No problem. You're doing great for a rookie."

Their shared giggles are interrupted by a male voice.

"Colin? Colin Byrne? Hey partner, it's Gino. Gino Moretti." Charlie stops abruptly. Moretti is animated. "Damn, you've grown. How are you, Colin?"

His odor. The hair tonic. It smothers Colin. He stammers. "Mr. Moretti? Um, wow. This is unexpected. It's been a while. I'm, I'm good. How about you?"

"Better now. Look at you. Hanging out with this lovely thing. Hey, babe."

"Hello." Charlie's tone is dreadfully cold.

"Oh, sorry, this is Charlie...um, Charlene, a friend from school."

"Hello Charlene from school. Can I call you Charlie, too?"

"Whatever."

"I feel like I've seen your face. I get around a lot you know. I never forget a pretty face."

"Nope. Sorry."

So, you're at Swarthmore too?"

"Uh huh."

"Not much of a talker, huh Charlie? Don't worry, I won't bite babe. Colin and I are old buddies from West Philly, right Colin?"

"Yeah, Mr. Moretti is an old neighbor." Colin tries to be matter of fact. "Do you still live on Gerrit Street?"

"Oh yeah. Me and Stiles are the only ones left in the building. I barely spend any time there. It's not the same anymore, ya know? Not since your father was still...ya know...around. Hey, shitty the way things worked out for you and your mom there at the end. But looks like you're doing fine. Better than fine."

Colin tries to be casual, but now his tone is ice-cold. "Where you headed now, Mr. Moretti?"

"Oh, here and there."

"Do you still have your truck?"

"That thing, nah. Got rid of it a few years back. Trying to work steady hours. Less traveling."

"I have fond memories of riding with my dad in that truck."

"Yeah, Tommy and I had some good times too. Real good times."

"Ever get up to Scranton? You and my dad?"

There is a considerable pause. One of those times Colin wishes he could see the expression on someone's face.

"Uh, hell, kid we went a lot of places. Scranton? Yeah probably, I guess." Moretti abruptly shifts the conversation. "So, what brings you two down here anyway?"

Charlie speaks. Her voice still flat. "We're taking a summer class at...Drexel. We're going to be late if we don't keep moving."

"Uh huh. Okay babe. Well, keep moving then. It was good to see you old partner."

"You, too." Colin forces a smile while squeezing Charlie's elbow. She takes off immediately, but Moretti manages to grab hold of Colin's forearm. Charlie doesn't slow down, scampering down the platform with Moretti still attached to Colin.

"Hey, make sure you tell your mom we ran into each other, okay?"

"For sure. Will do."

Moretti releases his grip. His voice trails off. "Don't forget to tell her...don't be a stranger."

"That was creepy, Colin."

"My mom hates him by the way."

"So do I."

Colin manages a laugh. "I think that came through loud and clear. By the way, thanks for the Drexel excuse. Why didn't you just say Temple?"

"Because you wouldn't be getting off at 30th Street Station if you were heading to Temple. Drexel is right down the road. Besides I don't want him stalking me at Temple."

"Sorry. He's the last person I expected to run into today."

Charlie shouts over a loudspeaker announcement, "he freaks me out!"

"Join the club!" Colin bellows in return.

She doesn't respond. The din lessens. It feels awkward.

"Charlie, you okay?"

"What's your deal with him?"

"My deal? Well, right now I just hope he's not heading to Gerrit Street." Colin takes a deep breath and mutters softly, "I didn't think this through."

"The Scranton question. What's that about?"

"Another thing I didn't think through. I should never have asked him that?"

"Well, you certainly got his attention."

Colin grins. "I did, huh?" His smile disappears quickly. "It also means he knows that I'm on to him. That's not good."

"On to him? You know I'm totally confused, right?"

Colin hears the blare of traffic outside the station. "I'm sorry Charlie. It's not too late for you to walk away. Go to your class and I'll grab a taxi. Just show me where to go."

"Shut up Colin. You suck at lying. Follow me."

Colin pulls her arm and stops walking. "Something else is bothering me. How did he know I was going to Swarthmore? I haven't seen him in years. How would he know that?"

CHAPTER 28

Listen

Wednesday – 8:30 AM

With Charlie's help they navigate 30th Street Station and find the taxi stand. Shuffling through the slow-moving line, Colin feels energized as commuters pour back into the city. The harmony of humming traffic is interrupted by shrill whistle bursts. Colin taps Charlie's elbow.

"I wonder what my dad would think if he saw me now...back here in West Philly. Usually, when we were driving around, he would patiently describe everything I couldn't see. It didn't matter to him. He explained it anyway. Including this place... he would describe people waiting for a taxi. And now here I am. It's cool. He would love it."

She urges him forward. "We're next, Colin."

She guides him into the taxi. It's a furnace. Before she slides into the back seat next to him, Colin is already giving the address to the driver, who responds, "got it." The meter clicks.

The taxi moves slowly. Two sharp turns later, it picks up enough speed to allow warm air to circulate through open windows. Colin leans forward and asks, "are you on Market Street?"

"Yes I am."

"Is the post office on my left, or right?"

"Are you serious? You're kidding right? Miss, is he expecting a blow by blow, here?"

"Hey, don't ask me. That's between the two of you." Her voice is dead serious as she elbows Colin in the ribs. "He's paying the fare, not me."

The driver mutters, "on the left...the post office *was* on the left. We passed it now."

"Thanks...what's your name?"

"Joe."

"Thanks Joe. I'm Colin and this is Charlene."

"Uh huh."

"One more question, Joe...I promise."

"Can't wait."

I know this is out of the way a bit...but can you drive past Franklin Field...it's where the Eagles play.

"Jesus Christ, kid...I know where the Eagles play. Hey, it's your dollar."

"Thanks Joe." Colin slides back and leans open palms on the slippery vinyl seat. His fingers find a gash in the material. He senses Charlie keeping her distance.

She asks, "why the interest in Franklin Field?"

"It's one of the places my dad would take me. One time, we were parked there while the Eagles were practicing. He told me that the team had to change in a locker room across the street from the stadium. He rolled the windows down in the truck and told me to listen carefully. I could hear tapping of their metal cleats. He didn't have to do that...but he always did. He made things real for me. No matter where he took me, he always encouraged me to do one thing."

"What was that?"

"Listen. Always listen."

Joe clears his throat and gruffly adds "well, listen to this. The Eagles stink. Four wins last year. Jerry Williams is a bum."

Colin smiles. "My dad would have said the same thing."

Charlie voice softens. "Colin, Joe is driving us through Penn's campus right now. The sidewalk is full of students, but it's not nearly as crowded as it will be in the Fall." A few minutes of silence pass and then she adds, "and coming up on our right is Franklin Field, right Joe?"

The taxi slows. "Yup. This is it. You know this is the last season the Eagles will be playing here."

Charlie asks, "the new stadium is in South Philly, right?"

"A goddam waste of money. Took an extra year to build because of the unions in this town. It's a disgrace. The only good thing is the name..."

"Veterans Stadium."

"Listen to you. Your friend knows her stuff, Colin."

"I'm finding that out, Joe. Hey, are you a veteran?"

"Damn right. Proudly served under Patton. North Africa and Italy."

"My dad was part of the D-Day invasion."

"Well, he's a goddam hero for sure, Colin. You should be proud of him."

Colin hears the taxi's meter shut off. Confused, he hesitates while Charlie asks, "are you stopping here? Letting us out?"

"Nah, I'll get you to Gerrit Street. The rest of the ride is on me. Hold tight, I'm going to kick some ass."

CHAPTER 29

No More Secrets

Wednesday – 10:00 AM

After Joe drops them off at the wrong end of the one-way thoroughfare, Colin's instincts take over. The mailbox is still there, just a few steps away from the deli – although Charlie informs him it's now a self-serve laundromat. He lets his cane guide him easily to the front steps of the apartment building where he spent the first twelve years of his life. He hears the steel glider squeaking on the porch six precise steps above the sidewalk. It stops and so does Colin. Frozen on the pavement, his trembling right hand rests the cane on the first step.

A familiar voice, less gravelly than he remembers, offers, "what are you standing down there for? You're a sight for sore eyes young man. Get up here and give me a proper hello."

Colin reaches the top step, already anticipating the smell of bourbon. It oddly comforts him as much as the bear hug he gets from his old friend. Mr. Stiles digs his fingers into Colin's broad shoulders. "Somebody's been putting meat on these bones." They are so close Colin can feel the stubble on his face. "I missed you son. How's your mom?"

Colin whispers, "not great."

The old man gently pushes him away. "What does that mean, 'not great.' What's the matter? Is she sick?"

"No, no...she's okay. There's a lot going on. It's one of the reasons I'm...we're...oh man I'm sorry. This is Charlie."

"Charlie?"

"Charlene, actually. But it's been Charlie forever. It's so nice to meet you Mr. Stiles. Colin told me all about you."

"I'll bet he did. Well, it's an honor to have you visit me, Charlie."

"You're so sweet. Thank you."

"I don't think I've ever been called sweet before, but I accept the compliment."

An awkward silence follows. Colin rubs the old man's shoulder. "Okay if we sit down?"

"Oh, Jesus...yes...yes. Young lady, here...you sit here."

Colin hears the glider springs gently stretch, followed by a groan as Mr. Stiles plops down next to Charlie. Colin reaches back, finds the railing, and follows it until his hands locate the post that long ago became his backrest whenever more than two people gathered on the porch. He slides onto the floor and leans back. He's no more than three feet away from his old and new friends. Bourbon and roses. The glider creaks slowly, while Colin asks nervously, "hey Mr. Moretti's not around, is he?"

"Not during the day. Never. I rarely see the guy, which is fine with me. Why do you ask?"

Colin exhales in relief. "I'll get to that but first I have some other questions. I hope you can shed some light on things."

"I'll do my best."

"Thanks. Have you and my mom been keeping in touch?"

"Up until a few weeks ago, your mom had been calling me regularly. From the time you left, she'd been real good about keeping in touch -- through the good and the bad. When your dad was doing well. When he went missing..."

"Did she tell you about the letter from my dad?"

The only response is the squeaking glider.

"I need to know...did she tell you?"

"How did you find out about that?"

"So, you do know. She told you?"

"Yes, son. She did. She was struggling to tell you because she didn't want you to think Tommy abandoned you. She wanted to wait, hoping better news would follow. Maybe he would come to his senses."

Colin reaches for the glider and stops it. "Do you think my dad could do that? Abandon me?"

"I don't. I told Hannah the same thing. Told her to be patient. Wait things out. But I guess she decided it was time for you to know."

Colin leans against the post. His fingers play with the blistered paint on the porch floor. "She didn't tell me. Ben did."

"*He* told you? He had no right to do that. That wasn't his decision to make..."

"It's complicated."

"I don't give a shit, Colin. Does your mom know?"

"Not yet. I just found out."

"But I bet Charlene knows, right?"

Charlie responds meekly, "I just found out this morning."

"Well before you leave this porch you need to promise me you *will* tell your mother the truth. Your family doesn't need more secrets."

Mr. Stiles is on his feet. Colin detects the slight limp as he moves away from the glider and stands nearby. He is breathing heavily as he sits on the top step. He touches Colin's arm.

"Promise me."

"I promise, but you need to be honest with me, too. I'm 18 years old, Mr. Stiles. I want to know the truth, whatever it is. What are all these secrets you're talking about? Is this about Mr. Moretti?"

"Is that prick bothering you? Is that why I haven't heard from your mom?"

Colin grunts. "Every time I ask you a question, you ask me two. Do you understand how frustrating that is? I want to help. I want to be treated like an adult. I want to know the truth about my dad, no matter how difficult the truth is. But everyone still treats me like I'm eight years old...still protecting me from the bullies on the street...or the nuns at St. Gabriel."

Mr. Stiles grunts. "I was just looking out for you."

"And now *I* want to look out for my mom. Please let me do that, please..."

"Charlie, what do you think?"

In seconds she is also seated on the porch floor. Squeezed between Colin and the closest thing he has to a grandfather. "Well sir, I can tell you this. I've met a lot of guys Colin's age who see the world a lot less clearly than he does. It sounds like you prepared him well. Maybe you need to let him go now. Start telling him the truth."

Mr. Stiles offers a slow, prolonged whistle.

"How long have you two known each other?"

"Colin responds timidly, "a few days."

"Well, that makes me feel *sooo* much better," he says sarcastically. "Listen, I'm going to tell you everything I know, okay, but..."

Colin replies anxiously, "go ahead, but what?"

"Your mom always calls me. I never call her. So, the next time I hear from her, you better have made good on your promise, because I'm not holding back. She'll know everything we talked about..."

"Fair enough. Now, Moretti. What don't I know?"

"Well, first, you aren't the only one looking for dirt on this guy. There was a private investigator a few years back snooping around too, asking a lot of questions about him."

The mention of a private investigator sharpens Colin's interrogation. "What questions?"

"About his connection to your dad. Their comings and goings. Just a lot of shit that told me he had been doing some digging. Deep digging."

Colin leans forward and wraps his arms around his knees. "What did you tell him?"

"Not a goddam thing, son. Not until I heard from your mom. She called to check in and I told her this guy said he was looking into things on behalf of the family. She had no idea who this guy was. Pleaded with me to ignore him. So, I did. I stopped taking his calls. Then he showed up here again and I told him to piss off."

"When was that? When did he come back?"

"Geez, Colin. You're asking an old man to remember a lot. Let's see..."

"It's important."

"Hold your horses, kid. Um, well I was sitting here on the porch listening to the Eagles. I remember because they tied the Redskins. A tie. That stuck with me. I was bundled up real good sitting out here. It had to be late November or early December I guess."

"What year? It's important."

"Apparently everything is important. You keep saying that."

"Sorry. Just trying to get my timeline straight."

"Hold on." Colin hears the porch creaking and Mr. Stiles' joints popping as he stands up. "I've got the score of every Eagles game written down. Be right back." He shuffles down the steps and Colin hears the gate below scrape against concrete.

"Colin, where is he going?"

"His apartment is in the rear of the building. On the ground floor."

Charlie leans in, whispering, "I'm confused. I thought you said your stepfather and your mom hired the private investigator...why did your mom tell Mr. Stiles she never heard about him?"

"Don't know." He stops talking as the gate opens and closes. Mr. Stiles is muttering as he slowly ascends the steps.

"35 to 35. I told you. A goddam tie." He reaches the top step out of breath. Colin hears the snap of a rubber band as Mr. Stiles shuffles through his papers. "December 3, 1967. That's the day he showed up for the last time."

"Okay, thanks for confirming that. It's..."

"I know, I know. It's *really* important. So back to Moretti, okay?"

"Please."

"One of the reasons your mom wanted to get out of here so badly was that turd. She thought he was a bad influence on your dad. She told me all the time how worried she was about Moretti's connections."

Charlie interrupts, "what kind of connections?"

"Charlene, honey.... you're just an observer. Only Colin asks the questions.

Sheepishly, she whispers, "sorry."

But Stiles still replies to her query.

"To the Philly mob. Two-bit stuff but he was trying to make a name for himself. Move up the ladder. When your dad was drinking and gambling heavily, he got himself into a fix. I know because he came to me for money. I refused. It was tough but I knew unless he was sober, he would eventually be coming back for more. That's just the way it works. So, he turned to Moretti who got him the money...along with all the usual strings attached. Your dad worked his ass off trying to pay it back, but the debt never seemed to budge.

"Is that why he stole from Mrs. Judson."

"I think Moretti framed him for that, but I can't prove it."

"But my mom found all the stuff hidden in our apartment."

"Colin, all it takes is a few bucks to bribe a slimy landlord... and anybody could get into one of these apartments. Like I said, I can't prove it. Just a gut feeling. Doesn't matter. Your mom wanted out of here and I supported her. I missed all of you, but it sounded like things were really working out for your family...except for the debt still hanging over your dad's head. Moretti had a noose around his neck."

Colin grabs the spindles of the railing with both hands and squeezes. "I want to choke him."

"Join the crowd, son. Charlie, close your ears honey 'cause you may not want to hear this, but I've thought about putting one of those Luger bullets right between his eyes."

Colin explains the Luger story to Charlie, who responds, "after everything I've heard I wouldn't mind taking a shot at this guy myself."

"I knew there was something I liked about you Charlie. Colin, hang on to her."

"Hey nobody's shooting anybody, okay. That's the last thing I need."

Charlie nudges him, "you started it. You said you wanted to choke him."

"Did I?"

"Uh, huh."

"Okay, okay you two. That's enough. Listen Colin, I told you I would be honest with you so full disclosure that I saw your dad right before he disappeared. Under very different circumstances."

"Meaning what?"

"He came asking for money again and this time…I listened. First, because he was sober…really had his act together. Second, he told me he thought Moretti was skimming off the top. Whatever your dad was paying him, only part of it was getting to the bosses. He wanted to raise the full amount, go around Moretti and pay the debt directly. Said your mom was getting frustrated…scared…and he wanted to make it right… make a clean start.

"Did you talk to my mom about it?"

"He asked me not to say anything to her until they had a chance to talk. I struggled with that. So, I told him the same thing I just told you. The next time I hear from her, you better have made good on your word, because I'm not holding back. If I'm lending you money, then she needs to know everything. If you're serious about making a clean start, that means no secrets."

"So, what happened?"

"I wanted to do it…help him I mean." Colin feels the blistering anguish in Mr. Stiles' voice. "But the next time I heard from your mom she said he was…gone…missing." Colin's fingernails dig into shards of splintered paint.

"Did she know that my dad wanted to borrow money from you?" His fingers are throbbing.

"She was clueless, Colin. She kept repeating 'why didn't he tell me?' I couldn't console her. She said she would have asked her father for the money."

"That's the last thing on earth my dad would have wanted." Colin wrings his hands and feels warm blood between his fingers. "Do you think Moretti found out. Maybe he threatened my dad and...I don't know...he took off to protect us?"

"Doesn't make sense," interrupts Mr. Stiles. "Doesn't sound like someone making a clean start. Sounds like a coward and Tommy Byrne was no coward."

Twenty minutes later Colin and Charlie are seated in the back seat of a taxi that arrived after Mr. Stiles made a phone call. He escorted them to the curb and shoved a hoagie through the rear window as Colin settled into frayed upholstery. "Sorry it's a day-old but still damn tasty," he growled. Now he delivers emphatic instructions to the driver. "Take them directly home. No stops. No bullshit. This is Tommy Byrne's son."

The driver responds in a thick Irish brogue. "Dahn't wahrry Lenny. I'll be sure to get dem 'ahme. Where to, keds?"

Charlie responds, "Swarthmore College, please." Mr. Stiles pounds on the roof of the taxi as it joins the Gerrit Street traffic.

Colin exhales deeply as Charlie says, "I'm glad I got to meet him...and I'm sorry you're going through all of this."

"Thanks for coming with me."

"Thanks for trusting me. I wish there was more I could do."

Colin laughs. "Like putting a bullet through Moretti's head?"

"Shhhh." She elbows Colin sharply in the ribs. "Quiet."

The driver snorts. "Dahn't wahrry. Yooehr secret is safe wit me. Swear to Gahd."

"She's just joking."

"Sure. Sure. Soehch an innahcent lass."

"You're just joking, right?"

Charlie speaks softly. "Actually, I've fired a Luger...with my dad."

Colin feels every muscle in his face tighten. "Seriously?" The seat vibrates as the taxi rumbles through a strip of cobblestone.

Charlie giggles. “Easy Colin. He’s a cop... detective, actually. In Eddystone.”

“Your dad’s a cop? I didn’t know that.”

“You never asked.”

“God, I’m so sorry. All I’ve been doing is talking about me. Your dad let you fire a Luger?”

“At the shooting range. It’s a very touchy firearm, you know.”

“So, I’ve heard. I hope I never see one again.”

The taxi stops abruptly.

“Ahh jesoehs, we've gaht a cahpper directin traffic oehp 'ere.”

Charlie’s tone changes dramatically. “Hey, Colin. We got out of here just in time.”

He cocks his head toward her. “What?”

“Our friend, Moretti…just crossed the street in front of us… close call, huh?”

Collin leans in. “*Our* friend?”

Charlie snorts and playfully pushes him away. “At this point, I hate him too.”

The taxi starts moving again.

CHAPTER 30

The Footbridge

Wednesday – 1:15 PM

"Charlie, what time is it?"

"Five minutes later than the last time you asked."

Colin hears Charlie's feet land gently on the pavement in front of the four-foot-high brick wall they've been sitting on for the last half-hour. He's anxious to regroup with Katie but grateful he's learned more about Charlie, a young girl with a ton of responsibility.

Charlene Taylor leads a complicated life. She was born and raised in Eddystone; a small Delaware County borough located just south of Philadelphia International Airport. Her home is about four miles from Swarthmore College. Charlie's mom is "pretty beat up." Struggling with ovarian cancer she had been leaning on her daughter as her primary caregiver. Charlie had to take a leave from school until her aunt finally moved in to ease the burden. Now, after nearly two years she's back at school, trying to catch up. Charlie's dad works a second job to help pay for the medical expenses. He's not in the best of health either – an overweight cop with a two-pack-a-day habit. Charlie didn't say how many hours he spends at his other job moonlighting at a scrap yard near the airport, but he's clearly burning the candle at both ends. Today was probably an adventure for her. A chance to escape her weighty commitments.

"I've got my dad's car. Do you want me to drive you home?"

"No. I should wait. I *have* to wait."

"Okay, then you need to chill out. She's been here before. She's not going to abandon you."

Colin feels the campus closing in. He's far from having his act together and it's suffocating. "Sorry. Just a little anxious, that's all. I'm trying to process everything Mr. Stiles threw at me and…it's hard to explain Charlie."

"Listen Colin, I'm grateful you let me join you today. I want to help, but I also know there's a lot you're not sharing with me. And I get that. We barely know each other." She gently jabs his arm. "Let's just get real, okay?" She grabs his right wrist and places his cane in his hand. She tenderly opens the palm of his left hand. He feels the delicate touch of paper on his fingertips – so light it could be a feather. He pinches the tiny sliver she continues to hold.

"What's this?"

"My phone number." She playfully pulls the paper. "Do you want it?"

He pinches harder and pulls it from her grasp. "Sure...yes! Except…tell me your number."

Charlie sounds confused. "I just gave it to you…ahh, you can't read it…sorry."

Colin laughs kindly. "No sweat. I'll memorize it right now."

"And you won't forget?"

"Not so far." He taps his forehead. "All locked in here…even my favorite pizza joint."

"That, my friend, is impressive." She tells him the number.

Colin repeats it back slowly. "Okay, locked in."

"Good. Call me if you need my help or just need to talk, okay?"

"I will. I definitely will."

"Good…now I need to go. My dad will kill me if his car isn't in the driveway by 3:00." Her voice grows distant. "Good luck with Katie."

Colin slides off the wall. He foolishly smells the paper, as if it would hold the lingering scent of Charlie. All that remains is the odor of onions from Mr. Stiles' stale hoagie. He slips the paper into his left pants pocket. He smiles and taps his cane against the wall.

Katie's agitated voice startles him.

"Colin?"

"Hey, Katie...you're late."

She sweeps him away from the wall and moves briskly. He latches on to her elbow. Her breathless voice sounds urgent. "Let's keep moving. I promised your mom I would get you home by 3:30. That gives us less than an hour to talk."

"Why can't we stay here?"

"No, no, no." She pants as she picks up her pace. "Away from this zoo. You wouldn't believe how crowded it is. They're covering every inch of grass around here. We'll talk in the car. That's better."

Colin hears the tat-tat-tat of water sprinklers. A wet mist clings to his face. The grass below his feet feels slippery. He bumps hard into a student who drops whatever she was carrying. He knows better than to stop as the sound of grumbling and scattering objects rumbles from the rear. They are almost trotting now. Colin feels disconnected. He pulls at her arm. "Every time you pick me up here, you're in a hurry. Can we slow down just a little, please." Katie ignores him. He releases his fatigued fingers from her elbow, wondering if she even realizes the caboose is detached from the train.

Her panting voice shows no concern. "Hey, you need to keep up. Let's go."

He drops his hands to his knees, lowers his heads and speaks to the pavement. "I went to see Mr. Stiles."

Her voice is directly above him. "You did what?" She snorts. "on your own...to West Philly?" She hugs him hard. "You're an animal, you know that? How the hell did you pull that off?"

His chin is cradled on her shoulder. He whispers, "I had some help." He pushes his cousin gently away. "It didn't start out that way, but I ran into Charlie, and she helped me..."

Katie squeezes his hand and gently tugs. "Come on, let's go." Off to the races, again. "So, you brought your girlfriend with you? Do you think that was smart?"

"She's not my girlfriend and I don't know what I would have done without her help." A stiff, warm breeze rustles the trees behind them.

"Doesn't matter now Colin...let's just hope we can trust her." Katie's pace slows. Colin's feet sputter along the familiar broken pavement. They're entering the parking lot. Katie's car keys tinkle like wind chimes.

"Here we are." He recoils as she secures his hand against the scalding steel of the chassis. Katie snatches Colin, while guiding him toward the passenger door.

He pours himself into the front seat as a wave of heat escapes. The newness of the interior envelops him. Katie's door opens. Her bag bounces off his left shoulder. She turns the ignition and the 442's engine rumbles. She teases the accelerator and Colin feels the energy course through his legs. The powerful engine stirs him. "So, what happened with Tracey?"

Katie snickers. The transmission chirps as she impatiently launches her car out of the parking lot. "Are you serious? I'm not spilling a thing until you tell me what you learned on your secret adventure. Spare no details, okay?"

Colin's fingers find the window knob. He cranks it slightly. Then, twice more. He settles into his seat. "Well, how's this for starters. I – we – ran into Moretti at the station. Super uncomfortable. He creeped Charlie out."

"Why was he there?"

"I never thought to ask. I just wanted to get far away. I was nervous."

"That's understandable."

"Katie, he knew where I'll be going to school. It's been a long time since I saw him. So how did he know about Swarthmore?"

"Somebody from the old neighborhood? Mr. Stiles, maybe."

Colin squawks loudly. "That's a big fat NO. Trust me. He hates Moretti as much as my mom does." For the next few minutes, Colin revisits their conversation with Mr. Stiles. Katie interrupts to let Colin know they're approaching Little Crum Creek Park. "Change of plans. I'm stopping here. We've still got time and I haven't even told you about Tracey." The car turns sharply left then slows to a crawl as she asks, "why the hell wouldn't Stiles help Uncle Tommy?"

"He said my dad was too deep into the drinking and gambling...still in denial. He wanted to help but he knew it wouldn't have a happy ending.

"But he did get sober. We all saw it, Colin."

"Right, and then my dad went back to Mr. Stiles again and that time he was ready to help. Not just because my dad had his act together but because he learned that Moretti was skimming off the top and that very little of his payoffs were getting to the mob. He wanted to borrow money from Mr. Stiles, settle the debt directly, and walk away from Moretti forever."

"So, did Stiles give Uncle Tommy the money?"

"He never had a chance." Colin barely whispers, "that's when my dad disappeared."

The car stops as Katie asks, "willingly or reluctantly?"

Colin doesn't answer. Neither seems acceptable.

The rumbling engine quits. Katie opens her door and announces, "we're here, but I'm not sitting in this oven...even with the windows down."

"Let's go to the footbridge. It's not that far."

"Yep, I see the sign and the path. Let's go."

As they move toward the footbridge Katie comments, "it's beautiful back here. I should have worn different shoes."

Colin feels a familiar rise as the path pitches upward. "My dad and I used to take our shoes off and wade in the creek."

"Well, that's not going to happen. Even if we had all day..."

Colin interrupts. "He didn't do it. He didn't take my medallion. "

"Well, that came out of nowhere."

"He wouldn't do that. I know he wouldn't take it back."

I DON'T WANT SOMEBODY ELSE TO PUT IT

IN YOUR HANDS AFTER I'M GONE.

"Hey, I believe you Colin."

I WANT TO BE THE ONE TO DO IT.

"He knew how much it meant to me. No way he would do that."

... SOME SMALL CONNECTION TO YOUR PAST THAT COMES DIRECTLY FROM ME.

Katie squeezes the nape of his neck and says nothing. A flurry of birds erupts from the ground. They whistle by Colin's head like bullets. The cousins make their final, gentle ascent from the worn path to the familiar creaking of softening timbers that Colin and his dad crisscrossed just four summers ago.

"We've got twenty minutes tops Colin, so this is far enough."

He moves to the edge, sits down carefully, and dangles his legs over the side. The gently tumbling stream launches cool air towards his face. The back of his head feels warmth from the full afternoon sun that has yet to escape behind the trees. For a moment, he expects to hear his father skipping stones beneath his feet. Instead, Katie's cheerless voice brings him back to a reality far removed from a time when he felt safe and loved.

"So, I've got a curveball for you."

Colin turns upward and feels filtered sunlight kiss his forehead. "I got plenty thrown at me today. I can handle it."

"Colin, I know things are kind of messy with your mom right now. I wish I didn't have to tell you this. I mean, I love her too."

"Just spit it out. Tell me!"

"Okay, be cool." Katie steps closer to Colin and whispers, as if people on the footbridge are eavesdropping. As if they care. "Your mom also went to see Tracey Honeycutt."

Colin swallows hard. "When?"

"This morning. Before I got there. I came down the street, saw her Mustang, and drove past. Five minutes later she came out of the house. She was having an animated conversation with a person I assume was Tracey. I mean, I never met her, so..."

"My mom was supposed to be driving into the city. Papa Pete was with her, remember?"

"Oh yeah." Katie pauses. "I saw *him* too. Trailing behind Hannah and Tracey. He was walking double-time. All the way to her car." She half-chuckles, half-groans. "He even waved at me."

"Glad you think this is so funny." Colin bites his lip. "Well, it looks like Papa Pete got more than he bargained for. Let's hope he has a lot to tell us."

"It just doesn't make sense. Why would Hannah be visiting Tracey Honeycutt?"

Colin wraps his fingers tightly around the edge of the footbridge.

Katie rants. "I thought she was ready to move on. So why the visit? What's she hiding?"

The wooden planks are spongy. Colin's nails probe the mossy texture of the bridge's underbelly. "She's been hiding a lot of things."

"You have more?"

"Well apparently, Honeycutt visited Mr. Stiles too."

"Really?" Katie moves to Colin's side. He feels the vibration as she taps a loose footboard.

"Early December, 1967...a few weeks before he was killed. And the only reason Honeycutt visited Mr. Stiles was to ask about one person. Care to guess?"

"No brainer. Moretti."

"Yup. Unfortunately, he came away with nothing because Mr. Stiles clammed up."

"So, what's your point?"

"Mr. Stiles said that Honeycutt told him he was hired by our family to find my dad."

"Nothing odd about that. Ben told us the same thing."

"Except the next time Mr. Stiles spoke to my mom he mentioned Honeycutt's visit and my mom denied having any knowledge of this guy."

"Oh, boy."

"Yeah, really. Why would she say that? Even Charlie thought it sounded odd." Colin drops his head and braces for Katie's response.

She gasps sarcastically and pokes his shoulder. "Why didn't you tell me that before..."

"Okay you can stop."

"I mean the opinion of a stranger along for a morning joyride...that carries a lot of weight."

"Katie, that's enough."

"Okay, okay. Sorry. I'll admit it *sounds* peculiar but maybe your mom had a perfectly good reason for not fessing up to Stiles about it. Maybe she has a simple explanation for visiting Tracey, too. Besides, we've been at this game for a week now and we haven't exactly been honest with your mom either -- have we?"

"That's the smartest thing you've said all day and I feel like crap about it."

Colin reaches up for Katie's arm. "Little help, here." He slides himself away from the edge of the footbridge while Katie anchors her arms under his shoulders and guides him to his feet. He turns away from the bubbling water and feels the full sun on his face. A faint wind carries soothing laughter of children from somewhere downstream. He takes a deep breath, longing for more innocent times. Katie's fingers barely brush his back. Colin instinctively turns to the right and finds her arm as she gently leads him down the footbridge.

They reach the familiar gravel path that tells Colin they are close to the parking lot. He adds, "So, what's next?"

"I've got to get you home. The last thing we need right now is for me to be in the doghouse with your mom. We also need to hear from Papa Pete."

"Katie, I'm worried about Papa Pete. He was pretty scared this morning."

"Hey, let's just hope he did his job, okay? Maybe you should be worried about *that.*"

"At least I had Charlie to help me. He had nobody."

"At least he has a set of eyes. Let's hope he put them to good use."

Before Colin can respond, wings flap below his feet as more birds launch upward. Their soft drawn-out calls are familiar to Colin who manages a smile while Katie screams, "damn pigeons."

"They're not pigeons. Mourning doves. They're mourning doves. My dad told me about them. They forage for food on the ground. We must have startled them, so they took off."

"Well, they look like pigeons to me, and they just shit all over my car."

Colin laughs. He wonders when he'll laugh again.

CHAPTER 31

Abandonment

Wednesday – 3:30 PM

Colin's stomach tightens. That familiar clunkety-clunk of the manhole at the top of the street tells him Katie's car is seconds away from his house. His mouth is dry. They sidle up to the curb with too many unanswered questions chafing at Colin. He opens the heavy door and feels the added weight of lying to his mother. The smell of freshly mowed grass lingers as he moves tentatively toward the house, waiting for Katie to join him. He freezes, jolted by the sound of shrieking voices pouring from the house. His mother...and Ben. Two mild-mannered adults sounding like wild animals. He picks up his pace but feels Katie brushing by him. He stumbles over a yard rake, managing to blurt out "wait!" before finally spilling face-first onto the dense low-spreading yews. Their berry-like cones press into his cheeks and jab his eyes. He rolls forward – searching for the coarse brick pathway that leads to the house. His fingers dig into loose mortar separating uneven bricks. As he rises to his feet, the crescendo of garbled, squealing voices is disrupted by Katie's plea for silence.

He reaches for the front door but it's already open. He stumbles into his cousin whose shrill shouts are so close he covers his ears. "Shut up!" Katie screams repeatedly as she grabs Colin's hand. She moves briskly, pounds the swinging door, and pulls him into the kitchen. A warm, muggy breeze kisses his face. The window over the sink must be open. There's a break in the bickering. He hears neighborhood kids playing outside. His mother's sobbing comes from the left. Colin feels something warm pooling in his mouth – salty and metallic. He realizes he is bleeding. He swallows hard and listens as the swinging door behind him slowly creaks open and stops. Katie grabs his arm, but she says nothing. Another slight creak and then it stops again.

"I'm here. I made it back," Papa Pete says wearily.

Neither of the combatants acknowledge their arrival. Katie's grip loosens as Ben's fatigued voice echoes from the right – far enough that he's most likely standing in the narrow hallway leading to his office.

"It's a simple question Hannah. Where did you go this morning?"

Hannah's voice remains stern. "Please, can we talk about this later? There's no need to do this in front of my son."

"My son? My son? He's *our* son, Hannah.

"I, I didn't mean it that way."

"It doesn't matter. Just answer..."

"I went shopping in the city...like I always do. Went out of my way to buy you something...like I always do!"

Colin hears crumpling paper.

"Watch out!"

Colin cringes at Papa Pete's warning. An object whizzes in front of him and his field of vision briefly darkens. He hears it plop softly on the counter, followed by the sound of something fragile hitting the floor. Several large fragments carom off Colin's leg. He recoils as Katie yells, "Hannah, please get a grip."

"Shut up Katie. I'm not kidding. Don't say another word."

The closet door opens followed by Ben's voice, now closer, as a broom collects the shattered pieces around Colin's feet. Colin can smell the perspiration and coffee on his stepfather's breath. His slightly panting voice sounds defeated not angry.

"I don't know what to believe anymore Hannah. You lied about the food bank, and still haven't given me an answer for that either."

Colin says, "mom, please just tell us." He senses the

hesitation in Hannah's voice...the realization that her son knows.

"You told him? Without discussing it with me first, you told him?"

"Of course. You weren't just deceiving me. You were deceiving both of us. You get that?"

For the first time, Hannah's voice softens. "I'm trying to do what's best for our family...give me a chance to prove it. That's all I ask."

"Hannah, honey...I don't even know what that means. I thought we had a family. I thought we had the best. But we've been living a lie."

Hannah sobs, "I think I know what happened to Tommy. I'm so close."

Colin is breathless. "Mom!" he gasps. "What are you saying?"

Katie adds, "and why the hell didn't you say something? And don't tell me to shut up Hannah. He's...my uncle. My only uncle." Katie's voice cracks. "Please?"

Colin hears his mother's footsteps coming closer, slowly crunching shattered glass.

"She's crying Colin, wiping tears away."

Hannah hugs him tightly. She won't let go. He can taste her tears.

"You need to trust me. Let me finish what I started." She steps away, still holding his shoulders. I love you, Colin and... Ben...I love you too. I never intended to break up our family. I just wanted to know Tommy was okay, that's all. I just wanted closure for Colin. I thought I could do it on my own. That's the truth."

There's a hard edge to Colin's reply. "Is there anything else you want to tell me?"

Hannah sighs deeply. Her tone is irritated. "I can't play this game Colin. What is it you want me to say? Why don't you and Ben just tell me what you already know."

"He knows about the letter," Ben surrenders.

"Of course, he does." Sarcasm sticks to her words. "What a

shock."

Colin is briefly distracted by the familiar chatter of the Hobson twins close to the house. They always use the backyard as a shortcut to the creek. He battles the jealousy sparked by their innocent giggles. Ben offers, "why don't we go in my office, sit down, and discuss this like adults, okay? Let's get past all the secrets."

Nobody moves.

Hannah's matter-of-fact voice is confident. "You were younger then. That letter basically said your father abandoned you. That was tough news to share. I knew how crushed you'd be."

Colin stutters, "I don't understand."

Ben's one-word explanation is a gut-punch for Colin. "Abandonment."

Suddenly Hannah is on the same page. "The simple explanation honey is that the letter demonstrated that your father was alive and, um...unwilling to...to be a part of your life."

Ben adds, "and legally it gave us a reason to...":

"Stop." Colin's voice is weary. He feels unsteady. "Please just stop. Both of you."

Hannah breathes deeply. Continues forcefully. "No, no...*we* –Ben and I – *we* felt it was the best thing for you. For your stability. And that's what happened. I would do it over again."

"But I deserve the truth."

"And that's what I was working on. I not only wanted to share the letter with you, but I also wanted to tell you more. I wanted you to know where your father was...whether or not he wanted to see you anymore. I didn't want more questions. I wanted closure."

"Don't stop now Colin. You deserve the truth."

Colin suddenly feels fortified. "I'm not finished, mom."

"Okay...what else?"

"When were you going to tell me about the private investigator?"

She softly chuckles. The venom seeps back into her voice. "Ben, you covered all your bases, didn't you?"

Ben is silent so Colin pours it on. "And why did you lie about Mr. Honeycutt when Mr. Stiles told you about his visit. You told him you knew nothing about a private investigator, why?"

"Hold on, hold on. You called Mr. Stiles?"

"No, I went to see him?"

"In Grays Ferry?"

"Yes, in Grays Ferry."

"How the hell did you get there? Ben, you took him..."

Colin interrupts forcefully. "Ben had nothing to do with it."

There's a pause and then Katie exclaims, "hey don't look at me Hannah. Your son did this all on his own."

"Colin, that's brave, but..."

"But what, Mom?"

She grabs his hands and squeezes them gently. "Listen, nobody has been in contact with that old man more than me. I love Mr. Stiles. I owe him so much. But he's slipping. Forgetting. Of course, I told him about Mr. Honeycutt. It's not that complicated. Mr. Stiles just doesn't remember his facts."

"He seemed pretty lucid to us."

"Us? I thought you went by yourself."

Katie whistles. Long and drawn-out.

"My friend Charlene. She came with me."

"You brought a stranger with you to discuss family matters? How much does she know?"

Colin considers the answer. *Moretti. The Luger. The Mob. His father's debt. Charlie knows a lot.* He hesitates. "Nothing."

Hannah's voice sputters in disbelief. "Oh, come on..."

"She doesn't know anything. The Honeycutt thing was brief. Mostly we just talked about old times, the Eagles, stuff like that."

"Colin, just so you know, she's not buying it. She's staring right through you."

Hannah tussles his hair. He feels the fatigue in her fingertips. "Anything else?"

Pete's warning makes Colin pause. There is more he wants to know, but maybe he's gone far enough. Yes, far enough. Except...

"There is, in fact. What about the medal? I want it back."

She squeezes his hands more tightly and pulls him closer. "Honey, I don't have it. It's with my parents' lawyer, along with the letter."

"I want them now mom, before he dies, and some lawyer complicates things."

Her nails dig into his palms. "I didn't realize you knew my father was dying Colin." Her voice is defiant, not remorseful. If Colin could suddenly see the players in this room, he imagines his mother staring at Ben with disdain.

"Look, I'm leaving tomorrow to spend a few days with my parents. I've been putting off a visit...but now is probably a good time to give everyone here some space. I promise I'll get the letter and medallion and bring them back. You have my word."

Colin snickers and pulls his hands away. "Why should I believe you?"

"Because we both want the same thing, Colin. Closure. Listen, I know you want to be treated like an adult. Now let me prove that to you. I am close to the truth about your dad. I can feel it. Let me finish what I started. I promise to get to the bottom of things. And when I come back, I'll have that letter."

"And my medal, Mom."

"Of course. You deserve to have it. Colin, I'm sorry for not sharing things earlier. I thought I was doing the best thing for you. Now I realize I was wrong. I promise to make things right."

Hannah moves away from Colin towards her husband and the room brightens a bit.

"Ben, honey come here."

He hears Ben's plodding steps. Still dragging the broom.

"We've come too far, we'll put all of this behind us, I promise."

"Let me go with you. Your father is dying. I should pay my respects."

"My dad is a prick, Ben. He treated Tommy -- and now you -- like crap. You don't need to subject yourself to that. Plus, Colin has a meeting with his advisor this week about his math placement test, so he needs you right now -- even though he seems to be able to get anywhere on his own.

Colin forces a tortured grin.

"Oh, and Katie, I know you love Colin, but mind your own business. This is between me and my...*our* son. And by the way, just because everyone has been giving me the third degree, don't think I don't have questions of my own. I mean...in a matter of a week, since you and Colin have been hanging around together, our pretty normal life has turned into a shit show. Maybe when I get back you can shed some light on that, okay?"

Colin waits for Katie's response but there is only silence. His heart is still pounding even after Hannah leaves the room and Ben finishes sweeping the floor and retires to his office. Colin knows better than to say anything. Katie taps her nails on the counter, clicking and waiting.

Finally, the one-way conversation begins, from a voice only they can hear. It is profoundly weaker than even this morning.

"Colin and Katie, I don't know how much truth came from Hannah's mouth. It all seems to make sense...it all seems so sincere. But I have been on quite an adventure this afternoon. I have seen things that you'll find troubling."

Katie's weary voice matches the fatigue Colin feels to his core. "Troubling...how?"

"I think she's telling you a thumper."

As Papa Pete's words press Colin to his knees, Katie says flatly, "he's gone. Just faded away."

CHAPTER 32

Unfinished Business

Thursday June 25 – 9:00 AM

Colin sways erratically in the hammock. He rolls his nervous frame sideways and slides his bare feet onto the ground. He senses the inscrutable silence. Not even a trickle from Little Crum Creek. The two-toned whistles of chickadees are conspicuously absent from the morning air. His own small, shallow breaths barely puncture the mysterious stillness. His shoulders move up and down stiffly as he tries unsuccessfully to force air into his lungs.

"I'm here, Colin."

Papa Pete's voice is noticeably hoarse, but Colin doesn't care. His muscles relax. Hopping to his feet he exhales deeply. "I didn't think you were coming back."

"Ever?"

"Yes…never, ever. After yesterday, I wasn't sure what to think. One minute you were dropping a bombshell and then… gone. Please don't do that again."

Another hoarse breath before Papa Pete says, *"I'm sorry. It's out of my control. It's happening more frequently."*

Colin moves instinctively to his left and finds his lawn chair. He eases carefully into the sagging seat and grimaces. "I know. We know. Katie and I think it has something to do with the anniversary of the cave-in. The closer we get to that date, the more we're losing you. You're fading away. That's obvious."

"How long do you think we have?"

Colin answers immediately. "Three days…maybe."

Papa Pete chortles faintly. *"You didn't hesitate."*

"That's all I've been thinking about."

From the top of the yard and closing fast, Katie's energized voice blows in. "I come

bearing gifts. Apple cider doughnuts from Linvilla Orchards. Still warm." She drops the bag on Colin's lap. "Papa Pete, we didn't think you were coming back."

"That topic has been covered."

"Okay, okay…just glad to see you. I mean, you sound like you have a head cold and you look like shit but I'm still happy you're here."

Colin carefully places the bag of doughnuts on the ground. "How *does* he look Katie?"

"Hey, I'm not one to hurt anybody's feelings but if we're honest…worse than before. Fading. Blue eyes look grayer. That beautiful red head is less vibrant. Papa Pete, we think we're running out of time."

"That's also been discussed."

Katie manages a chuckle. "Super…Colin 's already dispatched all the heavy-duty news." She plops herself into a chair next to her cousin. Colin hears the frame scrape the pebbles. Then, tilts his head curiously as Katie asks, "hey, Papa Pete, what's that you're holding?" The spirit responds timidly, *"not now…I'll explain when appropriate."*

"Alright, then let's get down to business. Are we good… where is everybody?"

"My mom is off to her parents' house." Beneath Colin's feet, the donut bag stirs.

Chomping away, Katie mumbles, "and Ben?"

Colin swivels his head toward the house. "Cancelled all his appointments. Said he was going to clean up the basement. Insisted it would be *therapeutic* for him to restore some order down there." Colin pauses, sighs, and adds, "I feel sorry for him. He's just as lost as any of us." A brisk breeze rustles the trees. Colin welcomes the cool air swirling around his head.

Katie is all business. "Feeling sorry for each other can

wait. Papa Pete, you're on a tight leash so let's have it. What happened yesterday?"

"After we left Colin at his college, I was very anxious, so I didn't pay attention to where Hannah was driving. I started to relax and soon was looking forward to my drive to Philadelphia. I had never been to Philadelphia before."

"That's great. I mean we both hoped you would enjoy a day of sightseeing and fun in Philly."

"Katie, knock it off, okay?"

"It's quite alright Colin. I'm used to Katie's sarcasm. I rather enjoy it."

Katie protests. "I just don't want him disappearing in the middle of his story, okay?" Her tone becomes distinctly inquisitive. "So, *did* you go to the city?"

There is a prolonged pause. Colin holds his breath.

"Eventually, but not directly. We went to a home in a serene neighborhood. I felt sneaky."

"Well, that's the whole point," Katie responds. "You were spying on her."

"Please don't say it that way. I followed her. She visited a nice lady's house...but Katie, you already know this. Of course, you remember?"

Colin fidgets nervously.

"Oh, I remember. I saw you *outside*. Tell us what happened *inside* the house. Keep going..."

"The lady's name was Tracey. She met Hannah on the sidewalk, and they embraced for a long time. It was a warm moment..."

"And inside?" Katie presses emphatically. "Forget the small talk and hugs. What happened?"

"Well, Tracey gave her a large envelope. She seemed nervous but Hannah was excited...and relieved. That was obvious to me. Of course...Tracey was equally pleased but very business-like. She said, 'I hope this helps both of us.'"

Together, Colin and Katie ask, "Both of us?"

"Both of us. That's what she said."

Colin slides forward on his chair. It wobbles slightly as the distant sound of kids splashing in the creek invades their conversation. "What else did they talk about?"

"I don't know. I didn't walk out with them."

Pleadingly, Katie says, "what the hell were you doing? The whole point was to ..."

"I stayed in the house. And...and...took this. It's a notebook."

Colin stands and moves away from the chair. "Put it down. Put it here." His curiosity is heightened as Katie's astonished voice asks, "You stole it?"

"I feel so dirty. This is not going to help me. This is a blemish on my soul."

"It's okay," Katie says clumsily. "We'll return it. Why did you...um...*borrow* it?"

"I thought I was helping. Tracey pointed to it during their chat. Said she found it well after she gave Ben the files and thought it would be helpful. But Hannah hesitated. Told her to keep it and patted her bag where she put the envelope and said, 'this is plenty.' Tracey seemed confused by that. She even suggested that Ben might find it helpful. But Hannah changed the subject. I found it odd."

Katie interrupts. "Colin, I need to look at this...right now." He hears a flurry of flipping pages.

"But he isn't finished." Papa Pete...you said yesterday my mom was telling a thumper. You need to tell us why. What else happened?"

"Colin, I must stop now. I'm learning what's best for me.

"You're going to leave?"

"Whether I like it or not, that seems to be happening."

Katie jumps in. "Hey, he's about to disappear on us anyway. Let's dive into this thing."

"Colin calmly asks, "what time is it?"

Katie replies, "It's almost 10:00."

"So, Papa Pete, do you think we could get together again around noon, maybe?"

"I would prefer additional time. Can we speak at 2:00?"

Katie responds first. "That's even better. We'll peek at this notebook, and I'll still have time to hit the realtor's office. Go rest your weary bones, Papa Pete."

Colin cringes. "Was that necessary?"

"Doesn't matter. He's long gone."

"Does he really look as bad as he sounds?"

"Worse...okay let's see if stealing this thing was worth a blemish on his soul."

All Colin can do is listen as Katie describes her findings.

"Well believe me...Honeycutt was a scribbler. There's a lot of stuff in here that makes no sense to me. Probably because it has to do with unrelated cases. But then...."

More turning pages.

"Where is it? Hold on.... here...here it is. It's on a page marked 'unfinished business.' There are two initials 'GM' followed by three items. Two of them are crossed off the list."

"Gino Moretti. That's got to be the 'GM.' What's on the list?"

"Hold your horses. The first is 'Grays Ferry' with a line drawn through it and a notation that says, 'dead end.' I guess that's his visit with Mr. Stiles, right, when the old man blew him off?"

"Has to be. Then what?"

"Ready for this?" Katie reads the second item, almost with glee. "Wallingford Auto – he sold the truck. Follow the trail!"

"Wallingford Auto. Katie, Papa Pete led you there. That goddam truck is for real."

"But it's also crossed off the list. So, Honeycutt must have found something...or he came to a dead end. Not sure."

Colin's neck is tingling when Katie adds, "Oh, it gets even better."

"Tell me!"

Katie responds, pounding the lawn chair emphatically. "Find...the...realtor." She erupts. "Okay, I'm two for two. Papa Pete was staring into that realtor's office. What the hell, Colin? What the bloody hell?"

He can sense his cousin's urgent movement. "Where are you going?"

"Where else? To the one thing that's not crossed off Honeycutt's list...to the realtor. I won't be long, I promise. By the time I get back, Papa Pete will hopefully have his second wind." She stuffs the bag of doughnuts in his chest. The bottom of the bag feels greasy. "In the meantime, finish these off, will you? Before the ants do."

Colin laughs. "All of a sudden, I've got an appetite. Just hurry, okay?"

Katie's footsteps move further away. Her excited breathing marks her ascent up the hill towards the house. Suddenly, her voice – rapid and hushed -- carries back down. "Colin...Colin... come here."

Before he can respond Katie's voice shifts. "Jesus, Ben, what's the matter? You look like you've seen a ghost."

For a moment, Colin is convinced that Ben has seen Papa Pete. The bag rips, dropping its contents to the threadbare grass. Katie beckons Colin again. Her concern intensifies. "Ben, are you okay? Here, give me that...give it to me. Let's go back to the house, okay?"

Colin slowly follows, his toe squishing through warm, congealed dough. His panicked breathing returns. "Somebody want to tell me what's going on?"

CHAPTER 33

Gut Punch

Thursday – 10:30 AM

When Colin reaches the house, Ben and Katie are already seated at the kitchen table. Colin senses the panic in Ben's heavy breathing. "Is he okay?"

Katie slides a chair until it taps Colin's leg. "Sit." Across the table, Ben stifles a sob. To Colin's left, Katie slides an object toward him. She guides his fingertips until they probe the surface. Everything about it is familiar. The quilted padded lid. He moves his fingers to the center of the lid; knowing he'll feel the raised embroidered shamrock on top. He remembers his mom taking his little hand and tracing the soft edges of the embroidery. He flattens his hand and moves his palm to the edge of the box until it finds the detached brittle handle that years ago became useless when Colin dropped his mother's sewing box. He pinches the edge of the lid and wiggles it. Feels those familiar loose hinges scarcely holding the lid in place. He glides his thumb and forefinger until they find a loop of frayed ribbon that used to wrap around a padded button on the front of the box. He pulled that button off one night while his mom was making dinner. Stuck it in his pocket and didn't tell her what happened. Later that night he flushed the evidence down the toilet. Then one day the sewing box was replaced by a hand-me-down from Mrs. Judson. A boring, smelly wooden crate that his mom called her "picnic basket." Colin asked his mom if she tossed her sewing box out. Hugging him tightly, she said, "Never. Now it's my special junk box."

Colin slides his hands away and grips the edge of the table. He pleads, "somebody tell me what's going on, please?"

Ben finally speaks. His voice is shaking. "I was cleaning up, getting things organized...and I decided to use the drawers from some of the old furniture to...you know...store stuff. I found this in one of the drawers...and I opened it... and ..."

Colin leans in. A conspicuous odor greets him as soon as Katie opens the lid. It's Ballistol -- a gun lubricant that smells like black licorice. It reminds him of the same sweet swell that poured from the candy jar in Mrs. Judson's apartment.

Katie gasps. Her bewildered voice explains, there's a gun wrapped in a smelly rag. Oh my God, Colin...it's...it's..."

"Is it a Luger...a German Luger?"

"How did you know that?" Ben stammers.

"Moretti had one. I remember that smell every time he cleaned his gun...but..."

Katie completes his thought. "How the hell did it get into Hannah's sewing box?"

Ben's rapid breathing increases the tension. He whispers, "It gets worse. Look at these."

Colin hears the stiff edges of something being opened...an envelope maybe?

"What's everybody looking at?"

"Polaroids," Katie responds, almost quizzically. "They're... um...pictures of your mom."

"You sound weird. What's the matter?"

Ben explains. "Three of them are photos of Hannah doing innocent stuff. Uh, standing in the street, talking to Stiles on the porch. Walking across the parking lot at a school...Saint Gabriel, I guess. Innocent enough, but..."

"But what?"

Katie blurts, "they were all taken from a distance, like she didn't know she was being photographed."

Ben asks, "why would she be keeping those...and what about this one?"

Katie injects, "Colin, there's a fourth photograph of your

mom standing next to Moretti in front of his truck, but the weird thing is...the picture's been cropped. There's somebody else standing next to your mom, but..."

Ben's deflated voice offers an answer. "It's Tommy. I've seen similar pictures. I don't remember the occasion, but I've seen them before. Your mom and dad and Moretti standing in front of that truck."

Colin chokes back tears. "Why would mom cut dad out of the picture? He whines, "God, what else is in there?"

Katie quickly responds as shuffling papers tease Colin's eardrums. "Okay...an airline ticket...from Las Vegas to Philly and a hotel receipt..."

"From where?" Colin asked.

"It's from Vegas, too," she replies. "All the dates are from February 1968. Any idea what that means?"

Ben's exhausted voice spells it out. "Remember that letter we got from Tommy? It was postmarked Las Vegas...and Hannah received it in March 1968." He grabs Colin's arm and adds compassionately, "but Katie...before Colin gets his hopes up, take a close look at the name on those documents."

There is both sorrow and surprise in Katie's voice. "Moretti's name is everywhere. Did he and Uncle Tommy go to Vegas together?"

"And why is my wife hiding Moretti's gun and his receipts?"

"And what was she doing with this?" Katie takes Colin's hand and slides a hard, cold object onto his fingertips. "It's that missing piece of jewelry Colin. A diamond broach designed in the shape of a..."

"Piano," Colin says sadly. He knows it – even before he feels the long, slender pin on the back of the piece as he squeezes its familiar shape in his palm. He feels anger boiling in his voice. "It's one of the pieces she accused my dad...no *me*...of stealing. How did it find its way here?" Katie and Ben remain silent. Colin feels sweat rolling down his side and tickling his ribs.

Ben's practical voice breaks the silence, "do you think this thing is loaded? I mean should we even be handling it?"

Recalling Mr. Stiles' stern advice about Lugers, Colin says, "they can be super sensitive, so I wouldn't touch it. I'll give Charlie a call. She'll be able to help."

Katie snickers. "Seriously? Now she's a firearms expert?"

Worn to a frazzle, Colin softly says, "relax, her dad's a cop. She's handled one before. Colin pulls his sweaty shirt away from his body, leans back in his chair and offers a suggestion to Ben. "Let me call Charlie and ask her to drive me to my meeting at Swarthmore tomorrow. She'll be happy to do it, really. And while she's here I'll have her check out the gun. Besides, I'm sure this has got to be a gut punch for you. I know it is for me. So, driving to school tomorrow can't be at the top of your list, right?"

"Thanks Colin. I owe you one. Thanks for understanding."

Katie rises from the table. "This is none of my business Ben, but are you going to confront Hannah about this? I mean, nothing is adding up here. She lied to you about the food bank. She's hiding a gun and the rest of this weird stuff in your house. She...she's making secret visits to Tracey Honeycutt's house..."

"What?" The kitchen table shifts abruptly toward Colin as Ben bolts from his chair. "What are you talking about?"

Colin feels the dread in Katie's response. "Oh crap. I'm...I screwed up. I'm so sorry."

Colin, sensing Ben's movement to his right, makes a feeble attempt to intercept him. "Ben, hold on...we can explain."

"Hands off Colin. *We* can explain? Now, you and Katie are hiding something from me? Anybody else in on this little secret?"

Colin drops his hands. "Papa Pete...he knows too."

"This is insane. You're insane. All of you. Shoot me. Take that gun out of the box and just shoot me...please...do me a favor..." He slumps down to the floor behind Colin. Katie moves slowly past her cousin. "Don't touch me, Katie. Stay away. Just leave me alone."

Katie's steps retreat from the kitchen. "Sorry, Colin. I really blew it."

Colin moves to the floor, keeping his distance from his stepfather. "It's okay, Katie. We'll be okay. Go see that realtor. I'll do my best to explain everything to Ben. And when you get back…"

"I can't come back. Not right now."

Ben whimpers emphatically, "not right now." Colin doesn't argue. He hears the front door gently open and close.

CHAPTER 34

Impossible

Thursday – 3:00 PM

Colin paces anxiously inside his bedroom. He's losing them all. His mother. Papa Pete. Now, Katie. Even…he shakes his head grudgingly…even Ben. Moving to the window, he struggles to raise the sash, releasing a loud grunt as the window finally surrenders. He's hoping for a refreshing breeze. Instead, a punch of humidity slams his face. Outside, the only sound comes from a gaggle of critters below his window -- probably scavenging remnants of doughnuts. It's an hour past Papa Pete's promised return.

He's startled by the abrupt opening of his bedroom door followed by Ben's gruff question. "Did you call your friend to pick you up tomorrow?"

The thought of asking his stepfather to knock next time leaves as quickly as it arrived. "Uh, no I didn't. I thought with everything going on, it wasn't that important."

"Well, you thought wrong. Somebody needs to be responsible around here. You're going to that meeting. Because…it is important." Crows cackle outside.

"I could just ask Katie."

Ben's emphatic response is swift. "Not a chance." If you're not going to ask Charlie, then I'll do it. I'd prefer to be here in case your mom gets home but I'll do it."

"No, no…I'll call her."

"Now."

"What?"

Colin hears the Princess phone jingling. "Take it...this is as far as it reaches."

Colin walks toward the middle of the room with his arms outstretched until the phone touches his hands. "Right now?"

"Dial."

Colin clears his mind and easily recalls the number. "You're going to watch me? You don't trust me?"

"There's a long list of people I don't trust right now. Dial."

Colin punches the number and holds his breath. Immediately, Charlie's raspy voice answers.

"Taylor residence."

"Hey Charlie...it's me, Colin." His heart pounds.

"Hey stranger," she says sweetly. "How are you?"

"Good, good. Listen, I'm standing here with my...uh stepfather and we have a favor to ask."

"We? Sounds like you're under a lot of pressure over there."

Colin relaxes a bit and grins tightly. "Just a bit, yeah."

"Message received. What's the request?'

"Well, tomorrow I have meeting with my advisor, and I need a ride. I know you've got your class at Temple so I understand if you can't..."

"What time?"

He grimaces, asking, "is 8:00 too early?"

"Nope. That's better actually. Gives me plenty of time."

I, uh...we really appreciate it."

Curiously, she probes, "doesn't sound like you want to do this."

"It's cool. Thanks."

"Okay, I won't prolong your agony over there. See you at 8:00."

"Wait, wait...I need to give you the address."

"No...no...I have it...you gave it to me."

Colin thinks hard. "I did? I don't remember. Well, I guess we're all set. Oh...come to the back door. Okay?"

"Got it. See you tomorrow morning at 8:00. Back door." The line goes dead.

Colin exhales deeply. His sweaty palms offer the phone to Ben. Waiting for an acknowledgement, he hears the bedroom door shut. He lets the headset drop on the cradle and gently places the phone on the shag carpet. He drops to his knees and then to the floor. If adrenaline could evaporate from his pores, that's what's happening right now. While he needs to hear from Papa Pete and Katie, he needs to rest even more. Rolling to his side in a fetal position, Colin surrenders to sleep.

In his slumber he hears a phone ringing. It rings forever. When he finally answers, Mrs. Judson is screaming at him. "Colin, you're late for your lesson. Please bring my silver back, you little brat. You betrayed me." He never heard her yell like this. He pleads with her to stop. Now she's sobbing. He insists that she stop. He screams at her. He screams louder. The phone rings again, but he keeps screaming at his music teacher. He feels so guilty. His heart is racing.

Another shrill ring and Colin's eyes open wide. He jumps to his feet and scampers to the doorway before remembering the phone is already in the room. He pulls the extended chord towards him, then lifts the handset to his ear. All he hears is static. He jiggles the chord at the base of the handset. Breathlessly, he whispers. ""Hello, hello?"

Katie's irritated voice responds, "Where the hell were you? This is the third time I called."

Colin shakes the cobwebs. "I'm really sorry…I fell asleep." He moves to the door, realizing it's already closed.

"Must be nice, taking a nap while I'm…"

"Katie, I said I'm sorry."

"How's Ben?"

"Don't ask."

"That bad, huh?"

"He's pretty pissed."

"Do you blame the guy?" she asks sympathetically. There's a pause. "Please tell me you heard from Papa Pete."

"Nothing. I'm having a blast over here."

"Colin, he's at least two hours late."

He lowers himself to the floor and sits cross-legged. "You're not exactly on time either. You left hours ago. How did you make out?"

She ignores his question. "Did you call Charlie yet?"

He spares the details. "Yes. She's picking me up in the morning. Last thing I want to do."

"Okay, I'm a little jammed up."

"What's up?" Colin squeezes a tuft of synthetic shag carpet. "Where are you calling from?"

"My apartment. I came from the realtor's office. I hope you're sitting down."

Colin's shoulders sag. He says nothing.

"Hey, you there?"

"Tell me."

"I went there and asked to speak to someone who could help me with some old records for Uncle Tommy. I fibbed that he had relocated unexpectedly a few years back but was returning to the area and was hoping to renew his search. Said I didn't know the name of the original agent but was hoping I could get a head start before he returned."

Colin shrugs and say into the phone, "flimsy."

"Hey, I figured the worst result would be rejection. Turns out I caught a break. The manager found Uncle Tommy's file and said he had been working with one of his agents, Carol McDermott. Turns out Carol is on a leave of absence for health reasons. So, he suggested a new agent might be best moving forward. That's not what I wanted to hear so I thanked him and told him I would be in touch.

Colin scrunches his face and asks, "so where's the bombshell I'm expecting? I mean, seems like there's more work to do with this Carol lady."

Katie sighs. "Oh, there's more. As I was leaving, the guy pointed to Carol's desk and talked about having her back soon. I noticed a picture on her desk. Typical family shot. Husband. Wife." She pauses. "Daughter."

Colin's throat tightens. "So what?"

"Colin. I am 100% sure the daughter in that picture is Charlie."

Colin grips the phone tightly. "No, way Katie. That's impossible." His temples are pounding.

"I wouldn't tell you if I wasn't sure. I am positive. I'm sorry but you needed to know. It kind of makes sense now. Remember what your dad told me? He was meeting with a realtor at a coffee shop near the college..."

Colin overlaps her words. "...she had a kid going there so it was convenient." Wait, wait...you said her name was Carol McDermott, right?"

Katie crushes him again. "Nice try. She used her maiden name for work. Her married name..." Katie's voice drops off.

Colin jiggles the chord. "Hello, you there?" The line is dead. Suspiciously, he slowly draws the hallway chord towards him. It's slack, like a busted fishing line. His pulse quickens as he drops the phone and pulls the chord with two hands. He hears the disconnected end of the line rattle the bottom of the door. It continues under the threshold, finally arriving in his quivering hands. He squeezes the chord and pounds the shag carpet with a closed fist, then instinctively stops, still protecting his precious hand.

Papa Pete's decaying voice asks, *"are you okay?"*

"Not now," Colin pleads.

"I apologize for my tardiness. It's becoming unavoidable."

Colin curls his head into his bended knees.

"We need to talk now. While we still have time. You need to hear what I have to say."

CHAPTER 35

Thunderstruck

Friday June 26, 1970 – 7:15 AM

Colin stands tightly squeezed at the rear of the bathtub. Inches away, scalding water streams from the showerhead. His tears evaporate into the moist mist that covers his body. Sleep evaded him last night. Interrupted first by sorrow, then rage. He screams as loudly as his steam-saturated lungs will allow. It feels so good he does it again. He's made his decision.

Leaving the bathroom, he shuffles down the hallway. At the master bedroom, he stops and pauses. He's telling Ben. He has no choice. Continuing to his bedroom he quickly dresses. There's a lot to do. Charlie will be here soon. On his bed he finds the recorder and rewinds the lethal evidence resting inside. Worried about his own state of mind late yesterday, he decided to record his conversation with Papa Pete. He wanted a firsthand account when he gets the chance to share it... starting with Ben. He promised himself he wasn't going to do this. Listen again. Revisit the anger and profound sadness. He pushes PLAY. A lump the size of his fist forms in his throat as Pete's scrubby words spill out.

Pete: Do you want me to tell you about Philadelphia?

Colin: Do I have a choice? Go ahead.

Pete: She parked near City Hall. I looked straight up and could see William Penn on the top of the building. I heard a tour guide say that no building in Philadelphia can be taller than City Hall. I never knew that…

Colin: We don't have time. Where did she go? Where did you…

Pete: Wanamaker's. She went to Wanamaker's. That's a big store.

Colin: Keep going.

Pete: She made a phone call in the lobby. All she said was "I'm here" and then she went shopping…in the men's department. She bought two shirts, and the salesclerk asked her if she wanted them in separate bags. I think Hannah is a regular there. In fact, everyone seemed to know her, even at the parking lot. And the hotel.

Collin: The hotel?

Pete: Yes. That's where she went next…the hotel. It was about a five-minute walk.

Colin: Do you remember the name?

Pete: Of course. It was the Bellevue Stratford. Rather seedy if you ask me. I'm sure it was once a beautiful place. Well, she went to the ladies' room. It was inappropriate to follow her in there, so I waited. It was very crowded.

Colin: You lost her?

Pete: Almost. I was confused…then I finally saw her getting on the uh, um …

Colin: Elevator?

Pete: That's it. By the time I got there the doors had closed. I don't think I could have gotten on anyway. The thought of stepping into one of those contraptions scares me.

Colin: You worked 400 feet below the earth, how could an elevator scare you?

Pete: Everything changes Colin… after you've been buried alive.

Colin: So, what happened?

Pete: I waited. It took a long time. Maybe thirty minutes. I just stood there, hoping to see her every time the doors opened. And then I finally saw them.

Colin: Them?

Pete: Hannah and a man standing in the elevator. Just the two of them. She, she…

Colin: Spit it out. She what?

Pete: Kissed him. On the cheek. In the elevator. And then she got out.

Colin presses STOP. He feels queasy. Hits REWIND and plays it again, as the same words tear through him. Words that scorch his soul with a judgement of his mother that seems unthinkable: LIAR. The recorder continues to play as he stands and paces aimlessly. He hears his own sad voice and buries his head in his hands.

Colin: Tell me everything you remember. Every detail.

Pete: I will. I will. He was dressed in overalls, not in a fancy suit or anything like that. He had dark hair and an unshaved face. He seemed distracted...and he didn't get off the elevator. Hannah did. The doors closed and the elevator continued down.

Colin: You're sure?

Pete: I am. I was in the lobby and the only floor below was the basement. It most assuredly went to the basement.

Colin: You said he seemed distracted. Why did you say that?

Pete: When she kissed him, he didn't react. He was...inattentive to her.

Colin: Pig. What about the shopping bags?

Pete: Right. She only had one. She went into the hotel with two and she went back to the parking lot with one.

Colin: Ben's token gift. He doesn't deserve this...you said she went to her car, nowhere else?

Pete: No, back to the car and she walked very fast. They had her car ready, and she tipped the man right away.

Colin: Like she had done it many times before?

Pete: I don't know. Perhaps. Colin I'm sorry.

Colin: More lies. I can't keep anything straight in my head...just one more question.

Pete: About what?

Colin: What was my mom like in the car on the drive home? Did she listen to the radio? Did she talk to herself? Did she...

Pete: She cried. She cried all the way home. I found that odd.

Colin: Why odd? What do you mean?

Pete: Because the entire day, from the moment she met Mrs. Honeycutt...all the way though the trip to the hotel, she seemed headstrong. Determined, I'd say...like she was on a mission. And then to see her collapse like that. I found it odd.

Colin feels gutted. On rubbery legs he passes the empty master bedroom and heads downstairs. Inside the kitchen he hears the phone ring briefly in Ben's office followed by his muffled voice. He reaches for the window and grunts as it refuses to open. Instinctively, he walks his fingers up the windowpane until they touch the locked latch. He flips it open and easily pushes the window open, as far as it goes. Ben's office is quiet again. It's now or never. Still, he hesitates.

He moves past the kitchen table and delicately brushes the sewing box, resting in the same spot. He immediately feels Papa Pete's presence. His worn-out voice haunts Colin.

"Are you okay? Did you sleep?"

"No and no," Colin whispers, mindful of Ben in his office. He opens the lid of the basket. "A lot of crap kept me up all night...starting with this. Apprehensive about the Luger, he nervously searches for the envelope with the photos. His heart races. He backs away. "Do me a favor?"

"Of course."

"Be careful, because there's a gun in there."

"I see it."

Papa Pete's composed response settles Colin, who instructs, "okay, well don't touch it. Do you see an envelope with photographs in it?"

Colin hears gentle rustling as Papa Pete responds, *"I have it."*

"There are four pictures. I just need the picture of my mom in front of the truck. See it?"

"Yes."

"Can I have it?"

"She's with a man?"

"Yeah, that's it. That's Moretti."

It's so quiet Colin hears the kitchen faucet dripping. Too quiet.

Papa Pete's voice is energized as the photo touches Colin's fingertips.

"That's him. That's the man."

"What do you mean?" Colin's hand is shaking as he slides the photo into his back pocket. "What man?"

Papa Pete's response is chilling. *"The man in the elevator...at the hotel..."*

Colin is thunderstruck. Breathlessly, he barely responds, "are you sure?"

"I'm sorry."

"You didn't answer me...are you sure?"

"It's him. That's the man in the elevator. Are you angry with me?"

Colin's agitation grows. "What kind of question is that? No... I'm just confused."

From his office, Ben's unintelligible words penetrate Colin's darkness. "He doesn't deserve this. I want to puke."

"I know..."

"Do you...really? Understand, I mean? You have no idea what we're going through."

Papa Pete's deflated voice replies, *"I'll leave you to your thoughts."*

Colin grips the kitchen table. He considers flipping it over, as the basement door opens briefly and closes quietly. On the other side of the door, the sound of Papa Pete's creaky descent is spliced with his anguished apology. *"I really am sorry."*

Colin's grip on the table softens. His stomach churns as he mutters to himself, "I know Papa Pete. I know." He straightens up. "God, he didn't deserve that." Through the open window, the patter of footsteps on the porch announces Charlie's arrival. Colin can't move. "Damn, not now." He forces his trembling legs to the door and clumsily fumbles with the sliding bolt. He presses against the door to release tension on the bolt and slides it to the left. He clutches the doorknob then opens the door. In an instant, rays from the brilliant morning sun are dimmed as a blurred image fills the doorway. He forces a smile. "Hey, you're right on time," he says tepidly.

The porch creaks a bit. Colin cocks his head. Feels his fake smile drain away.

Muffled breathing.

"Charlie?"

Something powerful crushes his nose.

CHAPTER 36

Rotten Eggs

Friday – 8:00 AM

Colin staggers backwards but manages to stay on his feet. He gasps for air, tasting snot and warm blood. His eyes are alive with pain. Two hands grip his left shoulder and toss him aside as wobbly knees discard him to the cold linoleum. He rolls onto his stomach and spits the vile concoction pooling in his mouth. Suddenly, Ben's unsettled voice intensifies the terror. "Hey, put that down!" Colin cringes and crumples closer to the floor. His red-hot skull swivels towards Ben's voice. "Give me that!"

Ben and the intruder are scuffling, close enough to step on Colin's hands. He rolls his fingers into tight fists, like a turtle withdraws into its shell. Colin recoils as something hard rattles the floor. In milliseconds, there is a deafening POP and CRACK as a red-hot object clips his cheek. He yelps and rolls on his side. A piercing pain squeezes his eardrums. The surrounding chaos sounds muffled, as if he's under water. His burning nostrils inhale the aroma of rotten eggs.

His balled fist swipes something large. He spreads his fingers and realizes immediately they're wrapped around a gun. He's held it before. A German Luger. Adrenaline surges through his upper body. He grabs the warm weapon and pulls it under his legs, paralyzed by the fleeting thought that he could blow away his testicles. His free hand searches instinctively for the small object that clipped his cheek. Nestled in his lap is a spent casing that's cool enough for him to handle. He squeezes it tightly. His stomach tenses as he recognizes the sound of blows being struck. He cringes as flesh smacks flesh. The impact of this raw fury is heightened by Ben's whimpering. His assailant is panting.

As the ringing in his ears subsides, he hears the rear kitchen door opening slowly. COME TO THE BACK DOOR.

"Colin…oh my God."

Charlie's rattled voice rouses Colin's dread.

He screams, "run Charlie, run!"

Her legs trip over his body with such force that Colin fears she's being assaulted too. She hits the floor and grunts. Colin shouts through sobs. "Leave her alone!" He raises the gun aimlessly. Tears are tracing his cheeks. "I'll shoot you. I swear. I'll shoot."

Ben stirs and offers a faint, garbled warning. "No Colin. Don't."

His stepfather reacts in agony to another blow, then falls silent.

Colin feels downward pressure on the gun and realizes the assailant is tugging the muzzle. His throat pounds as he strengthens his own grip on the Luger.

A gloved hand squeezes Colin's wrist until he loses grasp of the weapon. The assailant is so close a familiar smell greets Colin. Very familiar. There's no time to process as the basement door opens. The room falls oddly silent. The door shuts forcefully.

"What the hell?" The assailant's voice sounds bewildered. He releases his hold on Colin.

Cabinet doors rapidly fling open. Dinnerware suddenly shatters. A drawer moves above Colin's head. Utensils clatter to the floor. A hand touches Colin and he flinches. Charlie's trembling arms cradle his neck. To his left Colin hears the slow grating of the heavy cast iron skillet that always sits on the stovetop. Seething, Colin whispers, "do it."

The attacker screams.

Charlie gasps in synchrony with a hard thud followed by the

weight of a large body hitting the floor. She digs her fingers into Colin's arm. "Holy shit. Uh, uh...a pan just nailed that asshole. But...there's nobody...nothing." She buries her head in his chest.

Colin whispers, "it's okay. The calvary just arrived." He takes a deep breath and smells *it* again. Something way too familiar and sickening. *MOM, HE SMELLS LIKE A DOCTOR'S OFFICE.* The assailant is close enough that Colin can hear his rapid breathing. Colin fumbles for the gun, but it's gone. The intruder is standing over him again, mumbling as shattered dinnerware crunches beneath unsteady feet. The acrid combination of gun grease and hair tonic finds its way through Colin's swollen nose. He senses that Charlie is also standing. There's no fear in her voice. "Take one more step and I'll blow your balls off."

"You little bitch."

"Take your mask off, you sorry prick." She steps over Colin's legs, her foot barely grazing his calf. "Stay right there. I'm not afraid to use this."

The man's muffled voice moves further away. "It's not loaded babe. The magazine is on the floor...not in the gun." His foot taps something and he giggles weirdly. "See, it's right here."

"Really?" Colin hears a bolt clicking and sliding. Charlie calmly says, "doesn't mean there isn't a bullet in the chamber, right...babe?"

The hairs on Colin's arms stand straight up. He instinctively presses his hands to his ears and waits for the next sound. The swinging kitchen door squeaks, opening grudgingly as Katie announces her arrival, then gasps with fear.

Charlie mutters and spills backward over Colin. Pounding footsteps blend with Katie's shrill scream. Further away, the front door clangs so strongly that Colin is certain it's been ripped from its hinges. The walls shudder. He struggles to his feet. Softly, he pleads, "Katie, call the cops." Charlie -- her soothing voice comforting Ben -- calmly suggests an ambulance too. The cast iron skillet clunks heavily onto the stovetop.

CHAPTER 37

Too Late For Sorry

Friday – 9:30 AM

Colin hangs up the phone and rests his forehead against the kitchen wall, oblivious to the police activity. The only thing resonating is his mother's despondent request, "please tell Ben I love him. I'm on my way." Too late. Ben is already in route to Crozer-Chester Medical Center. Katie insisted on following the ambulance on its ten-minute journey. That leaves Colin, Charlie, and the remaining cops at the crime scene. The now-familiar voice of Sergeant Mooney booms, "five minutes Colin and I'll need to take your statement. Then I'll get you kids to the hospital." Colin slides to the floor and presses an ice bag to his nose.

Charlie is bending over him, her long hair teasing his bruised face. "How's it feel?"

"My face or my ego?"

"Somebody is going to be very black and blue."

Colin swipes at her with the ice bag. "They said I should be fine. Nothing broken."

"We'll let the hospital decide that, okay?"

"How was your father when you called him?"

"Concerned. Angry. Relieved."

"I'm so sorry Charlie. This is my fault."

She tenderly presses the ice bag against his left cheek, then the right. "Bullshit. Wrong place, wrong time. That's what I told my dad. He had a lot to say to Mooney. I think he encouraged him to take Ben to Crozer. Better chance to check out his head trauma…and it's only a few minutes from where I live. So, he'll be meeting us there. Told Mooney he wants to be there when they take my statement."

"Oh, great." Colin pulls the ice bag from her gentle grip and drops it to the floor. Lowering his voice, he says, "what did you tell your dad?"

"I walked in on a robbery. Guy roughed me up. Your cousin saved the day, and he took off."

"That's it…that's all?"

Charlie flatly responds. "You mean did I tell him It was that prick we met at the station?"

Colin feels like he's been punched in the face again. "Wait, you know…. how did?"

Her ho-hum response makes Colin squirm. "He was wearing the same clothes, same shoes…still smelled like a greaseball… and he called me *babe.* What an ass."

Colin pulls his knees up to his chin and delicately leans in. "Charlie, are you going to tell the police? When you make your statement, are you going to identify Moretti?"

"He was wearing a mask. His word against mine. Do you *want* me to say something?"

Colin ignores her. His rapid heartbeat matches the pace of his next question. Still whispering, Colin probes, "and the gun?"

"What gun?"

Colin scrunches his face until pain grips his nose. "I don't understand…why didn't you tell…?"

"I have my reasons *babe.*"

"What kind of reasons? Tell me…"

"Shhhh." She lightly touches his lips. "The cops don't know about the gun because he grabbed it from me before he took off."

Colin lowers his voice. "But it went off. Before you got here."

"And *before* your cousin got here. Plus, I don't think your stepfather is in any shape to remember, right? So, it's just you." She turns the table on Colin. What's holding *you* back?"

Colin squirms. He pulls the metal casing from his pocket. "I have my reasons, too." He opens his palm. "I need to clear some things up with my mom, first. Give her a chance to explain..."

"Explain what?"

He pauses, choosing to deflect the conversation. A hint of dread creeps into his hushed voice. "Would you have done it? Shot him?"

"I guess we'll never know."

Before Colin can reply she squeezes his leg and whispers, "wait."

Mooney gently taps Colin's foot. "Let's get you on your feet, take your statement and then have that face checked out."

Colin starts to rise. Charlie gently helps him to his feet. She hugs him softly and carefully buries her head on his shoulder. "Can we have just a little more time, officer?"

Mooney exhales abruptly. His trailing voice sternly advises, "two minutes tops. Got it?"

Charlie plays up her response. "Thank you so much." Then she whispers sarcastically, "you're doing top-notch police work sarge. My father would freak out the way they're handling this crime scene." More intently she says, "so, you avoided my question. Why do you need to talk to your mom?"

"She was hiding the gun. Here. In our house."

"Are you serious?" She shakes Colin's shoulders. He winces. "You are serious."

"It's complicated Charlie. Confusing and complicated."

"Like those receipts with Moretti's name all over them."

"You have them?"

"No. Katie does. She took that diamond brooch, too. Who would wear something like that?"

"Did anybody see her take them?

"No, she grabbed them off the floor before the cops arrived."

"She didn't tell me."

"Didn't have time. She was all business -- barely looked at me. What are you two hiding?"

Adrenaline escapes Colin's washed-out body. He slumps

against the wall. "I'm so sorry I got you into this mess."

"Too late for sorry, pal. It's time for you to tell me the truth."

Colin hesitates before blurting, "Did your mom ever tell you that she knew my dad?"

"She knows a lot of people Colin. I don't know...maybe. Why are you asking?"

Colin cocks his head in the direction of Mooney's staccato commands. "I don't have time."

"Hey, you brought it up. And when you do have time, how about you start with the slamming doors and flying pans. Don't tell me I'm crazy. I know what I saw."

"No, you're not crazy."

"Colin, are you sure?"

He nods. "I'm sure."

"Sure? About what? Who are you talking to?"

"I'm sure...I want you to know the truth."

Now Charlie is whispering. "Okay, when all that crap was going down you said the 'calvary arrived.' What did you mean by that?"

"You could tell her a thumper. It's not too late."

Colin sighs and smiles. He turns to the warmth he feels on the right side of his body. "No, I'm going to tell her the truth."

"Are you talking to...who are you talking to? Maybe you have a concussion..."

"Can I have a little privacy, Papa Pete?"

"Papa who?" Her tone changes dramatically. The bravado vanishes. "Colin, what's happening?"

The knob on the basement doors turns slowly.

"My great grandfather."

"Um, he's *here*?"

The basement doors creaks. Stops. Opens further. Colin feels cool damp air brush his body. "Yeah, he lives here. He died in a mining accident in 1896."

"But he lives *here*, with *you*?"

"Yeah, for now. He's helping me find my dad..."

Mooney's booming voice startles Colin. "Okay, mister. Let's

get that statement and then we'll roll. Young lady, your dad is anxious to see you. Hey, is she okay? Are you okay?"

The basement door creaks slightly then gently closes.

"I'm fine," Charlie responds cooly. "Just fine. Let's go."

CHAPTER 38

Unraveling

Friday – 11:00 AM

In a tiny room within the hospital's critical care unit, Colin squirms on a hard plastic chair. The room's antiseptic aroma reminds him of Moretti's odor before he pried the gun from his hand. He pinches the bridge of his nose and winces. Another sensation creeps in. The sickening speculation that his mother cheated on his dad…with him. He pulls that telltale photo from his back pocket and crushes it in his right hand. He wants answers…from Charlie too. He hears her – through the thin walls of the adjoining room. Her raspy voice is calm, interrupted frequently by a gruff man who is far more animated than her. Must be her dad. He hopes she's sticking to her story. It was easy for Colin. After all, he couldn't see anything so his account of an intruder with no known reason for breaking into their house was enough. No mention of the gun or Moretti's struggle with Ben for the contents of that basket. For now, it all seems plausible. Until the police talk to Ben. Until he shares a very different version of the chaos in their kitchen. Until they find the bullet. Until.

The door opens and a nurse offers, "honey, you have a visitor."

He turns to the door, expecting to hear Charlie's voice. His jaw tightens when his mother chokes through the words, "thank God you're okay." She squeezes him tightly and begins to sob into his chest.

Colin tries to stand, then pushes her away to regain his

footing. "I'm fine. They said I'm fine."

"You're not fine. Look at you. You could have been killed."

"Ben's the one we should be worried about. They won't tell me anything."

"It's not good Colin. He's in bad shape."

"They told you?"

She gently guides him back to his chair and drags another one close. She plops down hard. Their knees are touching. He tries to slide backward but the wall stops him. She grabs his hand, but he pulls away. She doesn't resist. Her voice is quivering.

"He's in a forced coma."

Colin gasps. "What for?"

"To reduce pressure on his brain. Hopefully for just a few days -- at least that's what they told me. I can't..." She begins sobbing. He struggles to understand her words. "I can't even talk to him...tell...tell him how sorry I am."

Her distress escalates his anger. "Really? Where would you start, mom? There are so many things to be sorry for. Where's Katie? I want to see Katie."

Seconds pass. His mother's deflated voice continues. "She's with Charlie and her father right now. I got to meet them briefly. Thank God that girl is okay. I couldn't live with myself if something happened to her."

Colin leans in. "Did you know your scumbag boyfriend was going to attack us?"

She gasps hard. "What are you saying? Boyfriend, who said I was... I mean I...even if it was him, he's not my boyfriend. Colin."

"Even if it was *him*? Who is *him*, mom?"

Colin extends his right arm and drops the crushed photograph in the direction of his mother. It quietly hits the floor. Breathing deeply, he listens to her retrieve the balled-up evidence.

"Where did you get this, this..."

"Ben found it...another person you've been lying to."

"Please, give me a chance to explain. I *can* explain, sweetheart."

"I'm not your sweetheart." He tries to lean his head back against the wall. His neck is too stiff. He drops his chin to his chest. Daggers stab his cheeks. "By the way, how was your shopping trip on Wednesday?"

"Colin, what's happening? "Her trembling voice emboldens him.

"You lied to me…to Ben. You…"

Another knock on the door then Katie's voice fills the room.

"Hey, just wanted to see if Colin was okay. I'm sorry…I'll come back later."

He simmers through Hannah's suffocating response, "thanks Katie, we need a little time."

"No!"

"Colin, buddy, it's okay. I'll come back."

"No. Katie stays, or this conversation is over."

Hannah complies quickly. "Sure, sure. Whatever you want. I just need you – both of you-- to hear the whole story. Everything."

Katie interrupts. "Well, wherever this conversation is going, I need a little oxygen in here. God, how can the two of you even breathe?" A shade is raised. The afternoon's low sunlight creates unexpected shadows for Colin. His mother's shape invades the space directly in front of him. Fresh air carries Katie's deliberate tone. "Let's play nice, okay?"

"Listen, all I want to do is tell the truth. To Colin and to you, and soon to Ben, I hope. What I said to you at the house -- probably not in the nicest way, I'm sorry – is true. I thought I was on to something. To finding out what happened to Tommy. That's the truth. But I know I've got a lot of explaining to do."

She takes a deep breath while Katie grudgingly admits, "maybe none of us have been truthful, lately."

"I'm glad to hear you say that because I have questions too."

Katie calmly responds. "I'm sure you do Hannah. But let's

stick with the plan. Let's give you a chance to talk. There's plenty of time for us to share our insane adventure."

"Our?"

Katie hesitates and Colin says, "yeah, Katie and me...and Ben sort of."

"Sort of? You're my son and you're confiding in Ben? I've been holding things together for years and now the two of you...and Ben are snooping behind my back?"

Colin's impatience is on full display. "Mom, we're doing it again. Just tell your story."

Hannah's mottled shadow disappears. Her voice is coming from the direction of the open window. Sirens blare below. She waits until the only remaining sounds are from birds outside and muted conversations down the hallway.

"I was always trying to protect you."

"You don't need to protect me anymore. "

"Sweet Jesus, Colin, shut up and let her talk."

"Yeah, well you don't know what I know Katie. Colin grips the edge of his seat. Ready to condemn his mother for what she's about to tell them. "Go ahead mom," he says defiantly.

And she does. Hannah begins to unravel the truth.

Tommy was in trouble. As his drinking got worse, so did the gambling. They were deeply in debt and Hannah had nowhere to turn. She refused to ask her parents for help and too embarrassed to confide in Mr. Stiles. Unwittingly, Hannah found herself drawn into repeated conversations with someone she never anticipated – Gino Moretti. He approached her with concerns about Tommy. Feigning concern, he shared that Tommy was not only gambling he was stealing. Mostly from the families who used him for odd jobs around the neighborhood. Hannah was shocked and frightened. Moretti promised to do anything he could to keep her husband out of trouble, especially when they were on the road together. Relieved, Hannah pleaded that he must never share their conversations with her husband. Moretti agreed. Those private conversations became more frequent and increasingly personal. He would share stories of how he had steered Tommy away from trouble. She would mix gratitude with expressions of doubt about the future of her marriage. Moretti started to help her financially. He would pay the milkman or give her money for Colin's school lunches. Innocent gestures. Nothing big. He was always discreet and respectful. And then it happened.

She started visiting his apartment more frequently. It became intimate and they started having an affair. Tommy was barely around so it wasn't that difficult.

At this moment Katie unleashes her wrath. "This is disgusting. My uncle trusted you."

Colin adds sarcastically, "still okay with chatting, Katie? Ready to shut up and let her talk?"

Katie's voice is dripping with disdain. "Might as well…I want to hear everything. Everything…do you hear me?"

Hannah, sobbing, collects herself and continues. She acknowledges that she knew immediately what a horrible choice she had made. She tried backing away. Then Moretti drove a stake through her heart. He schemed the robbery in Mrs. Judson's apartment. Set the whole thing up without Hannah's knowledge. When she discovered the evidence, still unaware of Moretti's despicable role, Hannah was devastated, thinking her husband was out of control.

Katie interrupts her. "I remember that night…the night you called me. Just so you know, I told Colin about it. He needed to hear the truth from somebody."

"It's okay. I should have done it a long time ago. But remember, when Tommy was confronted, he took the fall."

Colin adds softly, "for me. He was protecting me. Mrs. Judson accused me, right?"

Hannah returns to the empty chair opposite her son. She sits down softly, her knees again touching Colin. This time he doesn't move. "Right, what sickens me is that Moretti always intended for the evidence to point to your dad. When poor Mrs. Judson jumped the gun and accused you, Moretti didn't lift a finger to save you. It was your father – an innocent man – who sadly gave Moretti what he always wanted. Me."

Hannah explains to the cousins how Moretti approached her after Tommy confessed. He was elated and finally revealed what he had done. Now, with Tommy's confession, he believed she had a reason to leave her husband. They could finally be together. Hannah recalls the moment Moretti whispered his plan to her in the hallway outside his apartment; how she shoved past him and vomited before she could reach his bathroom. She was trapped. And truth was the casualty. She couldn't set her husband free from his false confession without telling him about the affair. Mrs. Judson's decision not to press charges was a temporary salve on an open wound. While Tommy wasn't going to jail, Moretti wasn't going away. He became increasingly possessive -- threatening to tell Tommy about the affair.

Hannah's story is interrupted by the piercing wail of the public address system. Colin senses the stampede of doctors and nurses in the hallway racing towards a crisis. When silence returns, Hannah blurts, "What if that's Ben? What if he's in trouble?" The door opens and Katie says, "sit tight. I'll be right back."

In that moment, Hannah gropes for her son's arm. She's trembling. He slides his hand over her wrist until they rest on her knuckles. He squeezes hesitantly. "He'll be okay. He's tough."

"I can't lose him...I can't lose you. I've lied to you both. I'm so sorry."

Colin pulls away. "It's a little too late for that, don't you think?"

"Maybe. Maybe not. I guess time will tell. I'm just relieved that I told you the truth."

The door opens and Katie spreads relief. "Ben's okay. Stable and resting. Everybody can start breathing again."

Colin and Hannah relax their grip on each other. He carefully rubs his face, avoiding his tender nose. "You didn't happen to see Charlie out there, did you?"

"I did in fact. And her dad. Um, he's...rather imposing. He said he would stop by after he wraps up with the cops."

"Oh great, he wants to meet the guy who almost got his daughter killed."

Katie manages a laugh. "Easy, buddy. He's got a right to be upset."

Hannah's tender voice adds, "listen, I hit you with a lot. We can take a break."

Colin squirms in his chair. "Not a chance. Close the door, Katie. Keep going. Moretti threatened to tell dad about your affair, right?"

Hannah inhales deeply and takes Colin's lead.

She explains how she rolled the dice and called Moretti's bluff. She figured he was too afraid to face the consequences of Tommy's unleashed anger. She was right of course. But Moretti wasn't stupid. She knew it was a matter of time before he found another way to subvert their marriage. Unfortunately, it was her husband who unconsciously gave Moretti that path. It started with Tommy's raw confession to Hannah about his mounting gambling debts. She pretended not to know. It was *her* chance to be honest, but she wavered. He desperately revealed more. He was out of options for paying off bookies and calling in favors. These people wanted their money. He was out of time, but Tommy assured her he had a plan – an unsavory one. She asked how and braced herself for the unescapable answer – Moretti. He had already agreed to help. Tommy revealed more, laying bare his soul. Moretti was deep into bootlegging coal and Tommy was breaking the law right along with him. This wasn't a neighborhood operation, he confessed. It was tied to the Philly underworld, and it was profitable. Underworld meant one thing to Hannah – mafia. She had just finished reading *The Godfather* so the notion of her husband connected to the mob freaked her out. Tommy assured her that Moretti was the one taking the risk. The one with the connections. Tommy didn't even know these people.

He was a silent partner and wanted to keep it that way. In exchange, Moretti promised to call off the debtors and work out a payment plan on Tommy's behalf. Then, he would use Tommy's cut of the profits to satisfy the debt. In a few weeks they would be all square and free to walk away from the arrangement. She wanted to tell him, "there's nothing free with Moretti." Fear and guilt held her back.

Hannah describes for Colin and Katie how liberated Tommy sounded. He told her that despite the challenges ahead, he felt relieved that he was finally honest with her. His conscience was free. His burden lifted. He felt like a man again. She felt contaminated. By her own lies. By the suffocating presence of Moretti still in their lives. By the gnawing notion that this may not end well, that it wouldn't be over "in a few weeks."

Still, it seemed to be getting better. Mrs. Judson honored her promise and never pressed charges. They moved to Delaware County for a clean start. Hannah still had Moretti to deal with but at least she didn't live in the same building. When they moved into Katie's place, she rarely saw him – except when he would pick Tommy up for a bootlegging run. Even then, it was from a distance, watching from the apartment as her husband forced himself into that ugly truck.

And her husband? Her sweet, courageous Tommy? He stayed sober. Went to his meetings. Picked up a steady part-time job at a local hardware store. Flourished with Colin. He was happy most of the time. All the time, really – except when Moretti was in the picture. Hannah, impatient with Moretti's continued presence, started pressing her husband. "How long until the debt is paid?" "When will we get our lives back?" "When is the last time we'll have to see him?"

As weeks turned to months, Tommy sounded less and less optimistic. She knew he was worried. When pressed about Moretti's commitment to clean up the debt, Tommy said, "I can't nail him down. This is my fault and I'll fix it Hannah. You've done nothing to deserve this."

If Colin could suddenly see, he imagines his mother would

be unable to look him in the eyes. For just a moment he wants to see the guilt on her face that he already senses in her troubled voice. "It crushed me. He didn't deserve my infidelity. I should have told him. I just couldn't."

Katie surprises Colin with her response. "He would have forgiven you Hannah. I know my uncle...but, um..."

Colin prods his cousin. "But what Katie? Just say it."

"He would have killed Moretti with his bare hands. No question."

Colin responds, "I want to kill him right now."

For the first time since they entered this room, Hannah asserts herself. "Well, that's not going to happen. Nobody's killing anyone."

"Mom, Ben is in a coma. Charlie could have been seriously hurt.... or killed. He's got to pay for all the crap he pulled on you and dad. Look at my face. He just broke into our home."

"That's my fault too."

Katie whistles softly. Colin's head sags. He wants to shake it mightily, but it hurts too much. He feels Katie's palm gently surround his clenched fist.

"It's all my fault..." Before she can continue, the door opens without a knock. "Hey Colin?"

"Hey, Charlie. You okay?"

"My dad. He, uh wants to talk to you."

The gravity in the room is suddenly tenfold. Colin can't lift himself from his chair.

He replies meekly. "Sure, sure. I'll be there in a few minutes. This is kind of important."

She pauses. "He's in the cafeteria. He wants to talk to you right now."

CHAPTER 39

Solar Eclipse

Friday -- Noon

Colin leans nervously into a sticky, narrow table in the hospital cafeteria. Silhouetted by the harsh fluorescent light, the frame of Detective Frank Taylor looms large. Colin's stomach churns with each whiff of the cop's smokey, sweaty odor. His wheezy breathing betrays his cigarette addiction. His voice is deep. Colin imagines he could be a bass singer. He's a man of few words.

"How's the nose?"

"Okay, sir. Not broken."

"Good." His brief cough is broken and full of phlegm. "Whoever did this was pretty violent. The Swarthmore police said your kitchen was a war zone. One look at your kisser tells me that. "Any idea who this guy was?"

Sweat spills from Colin's armpits. "No sir, I couldn't see him."

"You don't need to play the blind card, son. That's not what I asked. Guy just shows up at your back door..."

"I thought it was Charlie. I'm so sorry about this."

"Charlene can take care of herself. She would have kicked his ass. Now, answer the question. Did you know this guy?"

Colin's fingernails dig into his Styrofoam coffee cup. "I explained all of this to the sergeant."

"I'm not looking for an explanation. Did – You – Know -- Him?"

"No."

"Too wishy-washy. Say it like you believe it."

"No, absolutely not."

Detective Taylor slurps his coffee slowly, deliberately. "I don't want you talking to your father until they get his statement."

"My stepfather."

"Whatever. You can't see him until the police talk to him. Hopefully, he comes out of this okay and can shed some light on things. But that could take a few days and I can't keep hanging around here...gotta get back to my other job. Besides, this is out of my jurisdiction so the Swarthmore boys will take it from here. Also, your house is still a crime scene so you can't go home until they finish up." He hacks loosely then says emphatically, "also, no communications with Charlene." He leans closer. Colin flinches. The mixed odors of fresh coffee and rancid cigarettes pack a punch. "Understood?"

"Is she still here?"

He mutters under his rattled breath, "Dimwit."

"I just wanted to say I'm sorry."

"Charlene is *not* here. She's home with her mother."

"Is she in trouble?"

"Should she be?"

"No. It's all *my* fault. She never would have been there if I didn't ask her for a ride to school."

Through wheezy, labored breathing, Detective Taylor repeats, "no communications with my daughter. Are we clear?"

"Clear."

"And there's nothing else you want to tell me? "

Colin thinks about the Luger casing in his pocket. "No sir. Nothing."

He moves away. Colin gratefully gulps fresh air then asks, "um, can I talk to my mom?"

"Jeeezus...what kind of question is that? Yes, you can talk to your mommy."

The next sound is the echo of heavy footsteps bouncing off the cafeteria walls. Colin exhales deeply. His legs are quivering.

"Don't worry, Charlie hasn't betrayed you."

Colin drops his head and whispers, "thank God. He scared the piss out of me."

"He's very large."

"No kidding. When he stood in front of me...now I know what a solar eclipse feels like."

"That's funny, coming from you. You're funny."

Colin keeps his head slumped toward his trembling knees. "I don't feel funny. Hey, was he with Charlie when she gave the police her statement?"

"Yes. She told the sergeant that she came to the house to pick you up and she walked in on the assault. A man wearing a ski mask knocked her to the floor. Katie showed up and he fled.

Colin exhales deeply. "So...no mention of a gun?"

"Not a word. Oh, she did mention a paranormal presence in the house."

"Very funny."

Papa Pete is silent.

"Wait, you are kidding, right? Right?!"

Papa Pete laughs but it sounds like he's gasping for air. *"Oh my...your face right now. Sorry, but that was worth it."*

"I'm glad you had a good laugh. Any other surprises?"

"As a matter of fact, yes...I'm on my way to the morgue." He giggles. *"You have that look on your face again."*

"That's creepy man," Colin says slowly. "What's going on with you?"

"I hope to pay my respects to Patrick Sullivan. He just passed from this life...up on the third floor. Lived a lucky life."

"Who the hell is this Sullivan guy?"

"Please, Colin...show some respect. He was supposed to work the Twin Shafts the day of the cave in, but he broke his leg a week earlier, so he stayed home." Reverently, Papa Pete continues. *"Lost his father and uncle that day. I knew them both. But Patrick got the chance to live a full life."* His voice turns surprisingly animated. *"And he certainly did. He was 94. Ten years younger than me. Good for him. Good, good, good."*

Perplexed, Colin asks, "are you feeling okay?"

"Why do you ask?"

"Well, I don't know if you're looking any better, but your voice has more energy...more..."

"Get-up-and-go?"

Colin nods. "Yeah, that's it."

"I felt it the moment I struck your assailant this morning. I continue to feel it."

Colin feels uneasy. "Have you had that experience before?"

Bullishly, Papa Pete says, *"do you mean feeling exuberant after a vengeful act?"*

Colin presses. "Yeah. Has it happened before?"

"Colin, we have little time remaining. Why are you wasting it on a question to which you already have the answer?"

"So, answer it anyway."

"It upsets me when somebody tries to hurt you."

"So, you hurt *them*...and it makes you feel better."

Papa Pete replies, *"How did you feel when Mr. Moretti got his just reward this morning?"*

Colin points to his face. "So, you know it was Moretti who did this, right? And after talking to my mom, I'm sure he was the guy you saw at the hotel."

"Did she tell you that?"

"We didn't get that far but she said enough. It was him. And of course, we have an eyewitness...you."

"That means you'll have to tell her about me. Just like you told Charlie."

"How do I tell my mom that her missing husband's dead grandfather was a stowaway during her last trip into the city? Or maybe I call Charlie's dad back and explain that it was *you* who tore the kitchen apart in one of your vengeful acts. That should clear it up." Colin's fingers tap the table defiantly.

"While you're at it Colin..." There's an uncomfortable pause, then Papa Pete continues forcefully. *"During this oddly contrived conversation of yours with the detective, why not pose the same question you asked his daughter earlier today?"*

"What are you talking about?"

The spirit's already buoyant tone squeaks higher. *"Would Charlene have shot Mr. Moretti?"*

"What's that supposed to mean?"

"I have nothing further to say."

Colin squirms. He doesn't want to sit...or stand...or be in this place.

"Now, I must gather my strength to visit an old friend."

Colin stands and leans into the table on wobbly elbows, asking, "Now? You're leaving now?" Papa Pete whistles softly. Colin recognizes Katies voice coming closer as the whistling fades.

"I just saw Papa Pete. You should know he looks a little better. He winked at me. Strange. He..."

"...had more get-up-and-go?"

"Well said. He walked by me like he had ants in his pants. Where's he going?"

Colin flops into his chair, bending forward. "Please...let's not go there." His heads sags until his bruised forehead touches the table. Can I just have a few minutes to feel sorry for myself?"

Katie pulls a chair close and settles next to Colin. She tussles his hair and says flatly, "no time for a pity party." Nudging him gently she says "now spill the beans. What did he tell you after spying on Hannah?"

Soon, Katie knows everything about Hannah's rendezvous at the hotel. She's spitting bullets, refueling Colin's rage. Six hours ago, his face collided with Moretti's crushing fist. He's glad Papa Pete sought revenge. Colin wants it too. But Katie has someone else in her crosshairs. She growls, "I'm so pissed at Hannah. At the lies."

Their angst is interrupted by the jarring sound of the PA system and the unexpected announcement for his mother to contact the hospital switchboard. Immediately.

CHAPTER 40

Tracey

Friday – 3:00 PM

As soon as they inquire at the hospital's front desk, Colin and Katie are hit with unsettling news – Ben has been rushed to surgery. Within minutes they've been escorted to a family waiting room where Hannah is waiting. Hushed conversations converge on Colin from every direction. As Katie escorts him further into the room, the melodramatic dialogue of General Hospital dribbles down from above.

"Do you see her?"

"There she is. Over in the corner. She's talking to a woman. Holy crap. That's her..."

"Who, Katie...who do you see?"

"It's Tracey Honeycutt. I'd recognize those blond fluffy curls anywhere. She's looking a lot older and more fragile up close, but that's her for sure." She prods Colin forward. "Your mom sees us. She's waving us over."

Colin slows his pace. "What do we say?"

"How about we let them do the talking?" She squeezes his elbow.

Colin surrenders and moves awkwardly. He's nervous... again. So tired of being nervous. His mother's relieved voice melts him. "He's doing fine. The doctor was already here...he's out of surgery...stable."

Katie is silent. Colin stammers, "what happened?"

"Just a build-up of fluid. God, listen to me. *Just*. He said there was no more bleeding, so I'm trying to be optimistic." She sobs softly.

Colin thrusts his hand out. "Hi, I'm Colin."

Hannah sniffles and says, "I'm so sorry, Tracey this is my son Colin and his cousin...my niece...Oh, God...this is all my fault."

Tracey grabs Colin's outstretched hand. He senses steady shaking. Her slightly slurred speech startles him. "Let me see if I can find an empty room for us," she says flatly.

Colin's aching brain feels like it's being smashed in a vice. His mother is sobbing. Katie is silent, and he has nothing to say. He's washed with relief when Tracey quickly returns. "I got a room where we can talk," she says with little emotion.

The overwhelming odor of the room suffocates Colin. He's led to a rigid plastic seat facing a wobbly round table. As soon as the door closes Katie speaks for the first time in ten minutes. "Can we please keep that open? It smells like an animal died in here and it's hot as hell."

Tracey stumbles through small talk. "It's brand-new carpet. I think that's what you're smelling Katie."

"Uh huh."

"Well, it's nice to meet both you and Colin."

For the first time Colin realizes that Tracey's words seem to trail off the longer she speaks. He squirms. Katie replies harshly. "That's funny, I feel like we've been in each other's company before."

"Oh...that's possible. I don't..."

Hannah's exasperated voice stuns Colin. "Katie, you can cut the crap okay. I know you hate me right now. I know you want to be as far away from here as possible. So, get up and leave this sweatbox if you want. Otherwise, shut up and stop treating my friend like shit."

Katie's chair cuts through the new carpet. She's standing now, leaning into Colin. "You mean the way you treated his father...my uncle...are you really..."

Hannah's resolve thickens. "Then leave. Or stay and hear the truth. Your choice."

Colin's temples are pounding. The seat of his pants are

soaked, sending trickles of sweat down his calves. “Katie, please stay…I can’t do this without you.”

She leaves his side…exhales heavily…and plops down in her chair. “I’m listening.”

Hannah sighs with genuine relief. “Thank you. First, Tracey knows everything. I mean everything…”

Collin feels Katie quiver and he squeezes her arm. Hard. She relents.

Tracey picks up. Her flat voice has a soothing effect. “I know Hannah has more to say but can we at least agree that the common enemy here is Moretti? He murdered my husband. He created chaos in your lives. And all the evidence points to his role in Tommy’s disappearance. So, with the little time we have, let’s make sure we’re all on the same page, okay?”

Katie stutters, “He killed your husband?”

“Yeah, that’s right. Okay if I keep going, Katie?”

“Oh…please do,” she says with wonderment.

“Good, before we start, you need to understand that the police are asking a lot of questions. One of the reasons I jammed us in here is to keep you out of sight, Colin.”

Weakly, Colin whispers, “why?”

The police believe a shot was fired in the house, but they can’t find a bullet or shell casing.

Katie is surprised. “How do they know that? Nobody was in the kitchen to see that.”

“Hear it.”

“Beg your pardon?”

“Nobody saw it Katie, but they heard it. The neighbors. More than one heard a shot.”

Colin deftly slides his hand into his pants pocket and feels the casing. He twirls it in his hand. Over and over. Smooth and cool. Just a few hours ago it was a red-hot reminder of the violence that erupted in his home. He pulls his empty hand out of his pocket. “Mom, what do you want to tell us?”

Katie adds, “just come clean Hannah, please? We promise to listen, okay?”

Hannah takes a deep breath. "Okay, this may sound warped but now that you know the truth about Moretti, I hope what I tell you makes sense. From the start you must understand that hiring Sterling -- Tracey's husband -- was Ben's idea. He suggested it. He paid for it. He was so kind and supportive. But it created problems for me."

Hannah weaves a sobering story, one filled with guilt and deception, driven by her accelerating anxiety that Sterling was good at his job. Really good. As his legwork led more closely to the involvement of Moretti in Tommy's disappearance, Hannah explains that her remorse over the affair intensified. If Sterling should somehow discover her sin, then surely Ben and Colin would find out too.

Moretti remained the other problem. Since Tommy's disappearance he had been visiting the apartment frequently. He kept offering money, but Hannah declined. He also made advances, but Hannah swears she never wavered. "I always stepped outside the apartment to talk to him. Made sure we were in full sight of other people. A couple times he asked to use the bathroom, but I never went in the apartment with him."

Colin interrupts. "Sorry, but back at the house you said Mr. Stiles was confused when Mr. Honeycutt visited him. Was that a lie?"

"Yes, I lied. He's not slipping. What Mr. Stiles told you is true. He called me and said that Sterling was asking questions about Moretti. I panicked and denied knowing anything about a private investigator. So, Mr. Stiles did what I hoped -- he cut Sterling off. I lied to that sweet man but got the result I was looking for. My secret was safe. And then... and then a few weeks later..." Hannah's voice cracks. "Um...Tracey's husband was dead. Shot execution style. Ben and I figured he got mixed up with some bad people and got too close to their business. Never thought for a minute it had anything to do with us. In fact, I'm embarrassed to say that the thing I felt most was... relief? It sounds horrible I know. I'm sorry but I promised you the truth."

"What about dad? Didn't you still want answers?"

"Sure. That's why Ben got Sterling's files from Tracey, who is no slouch."

Tracey's quivering voice interrupts. "Hannah that's not necessary."

"Oh yes, it is. I'm so proud of you Tracey. You were my only confidant when shame and guilt shut me off from the people I loved. This isn't some helpless widow. This woman wanted desperately to get to the truth about her husband's death. She's smart. Real smart. She's helped me so much. Despite everything else she's going through."

Colin is sideswiped when Katie unexpectedly asks, "Is it Parkinson's?"

Tracey replies, without a hint of self-pity. "Noticed the tremors, huh? And my voice of course. Colin, that's why I'm talking funny."

He innocently offers, "I thought you might be a little tipsy."

Laughter lightens the room.

Tracey pulls them back in. "Enough about me. Keep going Hannah."

Tenderly, Hannah thanks her friend and continues. "Well, Ben was so committed to getting answers, he assumed I would be okay with getting Sterling's notes from Tracey. But I wasn't sure what to do next. I didn't know what he would discover in those notes. Maybe something about, about..."

"The affair," Katie says bluntly.

"It's hard to even say it. Yes, my moment of insanity. So, I used the excuse that I wanted to move on for you Colin. Really, I wanted to hide the...affair, from you *and* from Ben. I felt like I was also letting him down, too. He had been so kind to us. Spent his own money to help us find your dad. I just wanted to bury the lie. The holidays were coming so I suggested we just sit on things for a few months. Then, in March the letter arrived from Tommy, and I saw a selfish way out. If I could accept that he abandoned us, there was no need to pursue

Sterling's work. I had my escape.

Colin interrupts. Indignantly, he says, "listen, mom, I just don't understand. If you loved Ben, why wouldn't you tell him the truth?"

"Do you love me, Colin?"

"That's a dumb question. Of course, I do."

"And have you...and Katie...have you been telling me the truth?"

"It's complicated, mom."

"I'm sure it is. Just like *my* life. I'm not looking for your pity, son. But I've felt abandoned since I was potty trained. My parents barely acknowledged me growing up. When I got married, booze and gambling were more important to your father than me...than us. When he disappeared, that letter from him was a dagger to my heart. Proof that I had been abandoned *again*. But it also became a reason to give you a stable life with Ben. I couldn't risk losing that. I did it for you, Colin."

Colin's head sags and his heart sinks. "Dad didn't abandon me. He would never do that to me...to you. Never."

Hannah's voice softens. "It doesn't matter. In hindsight, my decision never made things easier. In fact, it got a lot tougher, because of *him*."

"Moretti." Colin and Katie say his name simultaneously.

"What a creep. I even showed him the letter from Tommy. Just to get him off my back. I told him I was going to find Tommy, track him down and tell him the truth. But Moretti argued with me. He said the letter proved that Tommy didn't want to be found. Instead, he offered a sickening solution -- he could be the father Colin needed."

Colin whispers, "Now I'm gonna puke." He feels his mom's trembling fingers reach across the table and graze his arm. He imagines her heart beating as brutally as his own.

"And then I fell in love with Ben. A kind man who sacrificed so much to find Tommy and to give us stability. When we decided to get married, I figured the hardest part would be the hassles we faced around the court's criteria for abandonment."

"I despise that word," Colin says angrily.

"Not as much as I despise Moretti. Naively, I thought marrying Ben would stop the madness. So, I told Moretti that we were going to get married and give you the kind of stability you deserved…and he flipped his lid."

Hannah described how Moretti made it clear that if he couldn't have a family with her, then he wanted compensation. A lot of it. He crudely leveraged sex as an alternative, but Hannah flatly rejected him. It was the closest she came to considering killing him but losing Colin was too great a risk. Instead, she went to her parents and told them that she needed money for rent -- which was another lie of course because Katie was still supporting her and Colin. As "proof" she reluctantly showed them the letter, with a grudging acknowledgement that Tommy had abandoned them. They agreed to pay her but only if she promised to drop any thoughts of finding him. They also kept the letter and medallion as collateral threatening to cut off support if she told Colin. Desperate to buy time and get Moretti off her back she agreed to their terms. Unwillingly, she also withheld the truth from Ben – and then Moretti raised the stakes.

"Once we got married and moved into Ben's house, it got worse…fast. Moretti set strict ground rules for getting paid. He wanted cash only and demanded to be paid in person. He had taken a job in the boiler room of the Bellevue Stratford Hotel, where he insisted on meeting me once a month to receive his payment. He also suggested that a token gift would go a long way toward keeping our deal private." Hannah recalled the gift arrangement saying, "he even had the balls to pick out something ahead of time in the men's department at Wanamaker's, complaining that my taste was not up to his standards. Still, he wanted me to pick it up, pay for it, and deliver it with his ransom."

At this point, a subtle change begins to creep over Colin.

PAPA PETE WITNESSED THIS.

Slowly, he realizes that his mother's raw revelations are oddly aligned with the secrets and lies he and Katie...and now Papa Pete have stumbled upon. Uncomfortable as they may seem, they resolve conflicts for Colin. They provide a meaningful voice. Like words blending with the music.

To make her forced Philly commute more believable Hannah began using the food bank and shopping sprees as reasons for her trips to the city. After a few months she abandoned the food bank because one of the volunteers kept hitting on her.

THAT'S WHY BEN DIDN'T FIND HER WHEN HE WENT TO VISIT

Finally, she decided to confide in Tracey. She told her everything. Tracey rewarded her with a bombshell. Early on she believed Moretti was involved in Sterling's murder. But Tracey had to move cautiously. She told Hannah that a homicide detective was on the take within the Pennsylvania State Police – linked no doubt to Moretti's mob connections. So, leaning instead on her own reliable sources, she worked back channels to trace details about her husband's execution. It was a slog. At every turn information was conveniently missing or incomplete. The key to her quest was an evasive ballistic report on the weapon used. Tracey assured Hannah that her sources confirmed it was a German Luger. But that wasn't enough. She needed to get her hands on the original report. If it stated a Luger was involved, then she needed Moretti's gun to prove that his weapon fired the bullet that killed her husband. Tracey called it a "ballistic fingerprint." Essential to nailing Moretti, it would also give the burgeoning friends very different closure. For Tracey, Moretti would go to jail. For Hannah, she would be free of Moretti's threats and bribes.

And then came the break that Hannah desperately needed.

On Wednesday, June 17th she met with Tracey at her home. Her friend told her that she would have the ballistic report within a week. It would prove that a German Luger was used. Now, all they needed was Moretti's gun. They hatched a plan that day to get the gun.

THAT'S THE DAY MY MOM SUPPOSEDLY WENT TO THE FOOD BANK TO VOLUNTEER. THE DAY I HEARD KATIE VISITING BEN IN HIS OFFICE. JUST TEN DAYS AGO.

Hannah's next step was to reach out to Mr. Stiles for help. Too embarrassed to admit her affair with Moretti, she kept the request simple. She told him that Moretti was involved in Tommy's disappearance, but she needed to gather more evidence. So, before she went to New York to attend Ben's conference she phoned Mr. Stiles and asked him to break into Moretti's apartment to find anything that might help. She specifically asked him to find the Luger. Her friend quickly agreed. She returned from the conference in the wee hours of Tuesday, June 23rd – coming home early because they were worried about Colin's whereabouts.

WE WERE VISITING AUNT COLEEN

Then, later that day – still admittedly in a huff over Colin's and Katie's shady behavior --she drove to meet with Mr. Stiles.

LYING AGAIN ABOUT THE FOOD BANK.

Mr. Stiles gave her more than she ever imagined – the jewelry, travel documents and photos, all the sickening, incriminating evidence she needed to link Moretti to her husband's disappearance. Then Mr. Stiles presented her with the Luger. She had never seen him so animated. "Let's nail this son of a bitch, Hannah. Whatever you need to do, bury him." Suddenly, she had a way out of her mess with Moretti and possession of the Luger that Tracey desperately wanted. Elated, she returned home only to be confused and agitated by Ben's absence and the cousins' evasive behavior.

UNAWARE THAT BEN HAD JUST BEEN BLINDSIDED BY HIS DISCOVERY THAT SHE NO LONGER WORKED AT THE FOOD BANK.

Under the premise of doing laundry, she hid the evidence in her old sewing box in the basement.

SHE WAS COMING UP THE STAIRS WHEN I WAS GOING DOWN TO WORK OUT. RIGHT BEFORE BEN CAME HOME AND SPILLED HIS GUTS TO ME.

Hannah is emptying her soul, but Tracey interrupts. Her distracted voice fades from the room. "Give me a minute. I'll be right back."

Colin rubs his face and flinches. His jaw is stiff. So is every joint in his body. He hasn't moved in forever. Katie confirms what he's already thinking. "Hannah, this is all making sense now. It's connected. It's still screwed up, but it's still connected."

"To what?"

Katie chuckles lightly. "Oh, I don't know...weird shit you're never going to believe."

"Try me."

Colin interrupts forcefully. "Hold on. Hold on. Katie now is not the time. I need mom to finish. What happened this past Wednesday? After you dropped me off at school. You didn't just go shopping in the city, right?"

Hannah clears her throat. "No, I did not." She doesn't sound contrite. She sounds vindicated...eager to continue. "I went to see Tracey. She had it...the ballistic report...officially identifying the bullet removed from Sterling Honeycutt's skull as a 9x19mm Parabellum, which most likely came from a Luger. I drove to Philadelphia. I wanted that creep to know two things: I had his gun, and now I had the report."

The bruise on Colin's face is stinging from the sweat that drenches him from head to toe.

THIS CONFIRMS EVERYTHING PAPA PETE TOLD ME. BUT WHAT ABOUT THE KISS?

Tracey's breathless voice startles Colin as she returns to the room. "We've got a situation."

Hannah gasps. "Is it Ben?"

"No, no...he's fine." It's the police. They're looking for you, Colin. Your story isn't jiving. Too many neighbors are confirming a gun shot."

Katie responds. “Okay, no big deal. We can figure this out. Let’s just think this through.”

“Yes, it is a big deal,” Colin growls. “Don’t you get it? I lied to the police. Charlie lied…to her father! Oh my God, that guy is going to crush me.” He pulls the casing from his pocket and places it nervously on the table. “I’m going to jail.”

Tracey places her hand on his shoulder. A single finger shakes rhythmically. She reaches over and taps the casing on the table. “Let me hold on to this…now Colin…why did you lie to the police?”

Katie jumps in. There’s urgency in her voice. “Hannah, Ben found the sewing box. When you threatened Moretti, he must have come to the house to get the gun back. It was sitting right there in the kitchen. We didn’t know everything you just told us. We thought that you were hiding Moretti’s stuff *for* him… not *from* him. So…”

“Colin lied for me. You were trying to protect me.” Her voice stiffens. “I’m going to the police. I’m ending this now. “

“Not so fast mom. We need a day…two at the most.”

“To do what?”

Katie and Colin chuckle lightly.

“What’s so funny?”

“We’ve got a plan too,” right Colin?

“We do. With our own secret sources…plus plenty of help from Tracey’s husband.”

“At the end, we could look like fools, or we could still pin this on Moretti and get real closure about Tommy. I know this is asking a lot, but you must trust me…and Colin. Please?”

Tracey weighs in. “Hannah. We’re out of time. Either you go to the police with your story, or I get these two out of here… Hannah?”

“Let’s nail the bastard.”

CHAPTER 41

Unfinished Business

Friday – 5:30 PM

Tracey leads them down a brightly lit corridor overloaded with cool air and the pungent odor of rubbing alcohol. "Wait here," she says calmly.

Colin nudges Katie. "Where's she going?"

"Right around the corner are a bunch of cops. I think I see Charlie's dad."

Colin groans.

Katie gently nudges Colin. "Let's move back a bit. They can still see us." She muses, "Tracey's a tough lady. I really dig her."

"Me, too. No wonder my mom likes her...how did you know she had Parkinson's?"

"All the years I've been flying you learn to pick up on people who might need a little help."

"You help people?"

"Very funny. Here she comes."

The hallway is bustling. Tracey's voice joins the fray. Colin concentrates to decipher her hushed instructions.

"Okay, here's the deal. They haven't found any ballistic evidence at the house. But the police are still there. Your mom is going to get some protection over the weekend...and I'm sure they have instructions to be on the lookout for Colin."

Colin slumps against the wall. "For me?" He feels sick. Frigid air blasts from a nearby vent and he shudders.

Tracey's flat tone never changes. "It's not like they have some massive dragnet out, but the cops do want to talk to you."

"And Charlie?"

"For sure. Her dad's very skeptical."

"'That's comforting," he says sarcastically.

"Easy does it Colin. The wheels of justice don't move super-fast around here, especially with the weekend coming. Still, you don't have a ton of time. Katie, go grab that wheelchair and stay close to this side of the hallway." Colin hears Tracey rummaging through a cart that shifts gently into him. He steadies the cart with his hand. "Here, stuff your hair into this. It's a hair net. Let me help you." As she finishes her task, the rhythmic trembling in her hands feel as if they're massaging his skull.

"Thank you for doing this."

"You're not out of the woods yet." A wheelchair clatters. Something soft presses against his chest. "This is a surgical gown. Katie help him with this...and listen carefully. The only way out of here is past the cops. When we get to the hallway I'm going left. I'll do my best to distract them. They love to bullshit so that won't be a problem. Katie, you go right. Halfway down the hall on the left is a service elevator. Go past it and you'll see a stairwell. Take it down to the basement. From there, you'll see a service corridor that leads to the parking lot. Got it?"

"Every word," Katie says with admiration. "How do you know all this stuff...all these cops?" Tracey gently pushes Colin's straggling locks firmly under the hair net. "I was married to a private investigator for thirty years." She clumsily settles Colin's slender frame into the wheelchair. Her shallow voice sounds suddenly animated. "Hold on. Hold on." Colin hears Tracey rummaging. "I almost forgot. Here, take this." She jams something soft and pliable into Colin's hand and squeezes his fist shut. It feels like leather. Before Colin can react, Tracey urgently whispers to Katie, "Let's go...now!"

Katie's hushed voice repeats Tracey's instructions as the wheelchair starts moving. But Colin isn't listening. Adrenalin surges through his body. He loosens his grip on the leather object and unleashes his fingertips. He feels the zipper. With both hands he brings it to his nose. It smells like his father's toolbox. His skin tingles. OF COURSE...HOW COULD I HAVE FORGOTTEN.

"All good, buddy...almost there." After they enter the stairwell landing, Colin sheds his disguise and the wheelchair. He tries to fold the leather pouch but there's something stiff inside. He jams it into his back pocket. It's eerily quiet as they descend into the bowels of the hospital. Distant voices nibble away at the stillness. Stifling humidity and dank odors greet Colin as Katie explains they've reached a loading dock. Finally, a slight drizzle welcomes them outside as Katie guides her cousin to the parking lot. Colin and Katie pant in synchrony as they ascend a steep ramp then veer sharply right. He hears Katie retrieving her keys. Almost there.

She rushes Colin to the car, her keys jangling against the chassis as she unlocks his door. Katie quickly guides Colin into the front seat and closes his door with vigor. As soon as she settles in her seat the Oldsmobile roars to life. Katie's winded voice finally asks, "what did Tracey give you?"

Unexpectedly, Colin's door opens quickly. Katie gasps as Moretti's menacing voice sends shivers through Colin's weary body. "Hey...where you two going so fast?" Colin gropes the console and leans toward Katie who responds, "Get away from my car, creep."

Moretti laughs mockingly. "Colin, Colin...what's with you, man? Surrounding yourself with all these feisty women to protect you."

Colin's response is tepid. "I know what you did...I know everything," he says shakily. Then, a surge of anger grips him as he spits, "you leave my mom alone."

"Easy, big shot. I'll deal with mommy later. Right now, I need to talk to your girlfriend."

Moretti's odor remains as pungent as this morning. Collin tries to pull the door shut but Moretti's not budging. "She's not my girlfriend...and leave Charlie out of this."

"I'm afraid I can't do that. We have unfinished business."

Katie jams the Oldsmobile into reverse with Colin's door still open. She brakes sharply and Colin – still pulling on the door – feels Moretti's weight release. Quickly, he pulls the door shut and fumbles for the lock. He jams aimlessly with his fist until it clicks. Moretti thumps loudly on Colin's window. His muffled voice sends chills through Colin. "Hey, give Charlene a kiss for me." The car swerves and jerks as Katie burns rubber out of the parking lot.

CHAPTER 42

Into the Abyss

Friday – 7:00 PM

Colin grips the seat tightly as the Oldsmobile veers erratically. "Slow down, the last thing we need is to get picked up by the cops."

"Sorry, sorry." The car finally decelerates. "Can you believe the balls on that guy. What was that all about?"

"He's obviously pissed at Charlie. I need to warn her. About Moretti. About her dad asking questions. I can't believe I got her into all of this." Colin grunts, leans forward and pulls the rigid pencil case from his rear pocket. "And what about this?"

"That's what Tracey gave you?"

"Uh huh. No explanation. There wasn't time." The car slows then turns abruptly to the right, smushing Colin against the car door. "Hey maybe a little heads-up next time?"

"Sorry. Just looking for a place to pull over." The car vibrates to the rapid dah-dah-dah of a jackhammer. Colin winces. "Where are we?"

"How the hell should I know. It's just a residential street. They're doing road work." The car finally stops. Above the hum of heavy machinery, Katie shouts, "you may want to keep your window closed."

Colin can't help laughing. "Is that a tank? You couldn't have picked a quieter neighborhood?" He feels the pencil case slowly leave his gentle grip. His grin disappears. "Is it red, Katie?"

"Sure is. What am I looking at Colin?

"One of the things my dad always did when he borrowed

Moretti's truck was to make sure he filled the tank before returning it. One time, I was sitting in the truck while my dad was talking to the attendant. I heard him asking the guy for a receipt. He opened my door and lifted me down. Told me he needed to get to his secret hiding place. Of course, I asked a million questions, so he took my hand and guided my fingers under the dashboard. I still remember the sensation of rigid wires and the rough edges of metal. But then I touched something soft."

Katie interrupts and taps him with the pencil case. "It was this?"

Colin nods and continues. "It was wedged above the housing for the truck's radio. He told me to pull it out. My hands were dripping with perspiration." He stops and sighs. "I still can feel the sweat trickling down my arm as I wiggled it free. It smelled like my dad's toolbox. Anyway, I gave it to my dad. Like he always did, he described it for me. Told me it was as red as my hair. I heard the zipper open and my dad putting something in or taking something out…I wasn't sure. I asked him why he had a secret hiding place." The staccato sound of a now-distant jackhammer interrupts Colin's story.

"What did he say, Colin? Who was he hiding things from?"

"He said it wasn't important. But he made me swear not to tell. It was our special secret."

Katie smacks him on the shoulder with the pencil case. "Until now. Until Honeycutt discovered it. That's why it was crossed off his list. That's why Tracey gave it to you…to us. She trusts us, Colin. This better be worth it."

Colin takes a deep breath. Quiet returns to the neighborhood. Katie whispers, "okay, this is kind of exciting. Weird but exciting."

"Why are you whispering?"

She ignores Colin. "Alright. Let's see if Uncle Tommy left us any clues."

Colin listens to the zipper open very slowly.

"What, Katie? Tell me?"

"Hold your horses, okay?

Colin hears the crinkling of paper and then a pause. Next the sound of creases being opened. His cousin's deliberate breathing unnerves him. Colin feels the vein in his neck pounding in synchrony with that jackhammer. "Katie, please? What did you find?"

"It's a map Colin. Hand drawn. But very detailed."

Colin leans across the console as if getting closer could help him see what Katie is examining.

"My hands are shaking. I can't keep it still."

Colin reaches out for Katie's arm, but instead brushes a large swath of paper. She grabs his hand and squeezes hard. "There's handwriting. It's not Tommy's. I don't recognize it."

"What does it say?"

"It says a lot." Katie pauses. "Okay, in big letters at the top it says Pittston vein."

"Pittston? Like Papa Pete's Pittston?"

"And where Honeycutt's notes said to go...back to Pittston. But who drew this map and what does it mean? Okay, okay... wait. It also shows the location of this vein..."

"Vein? You keep saying vein."

"Don't you remember? Aunt Coleen told us about these abandoned mine shafts. She called them veins. Papa Pete called them veins too."

"How do you remember that?"

"Oh, I don't know...I guess I was paying attention. You should try it sometime."

"Hey, if Papa Pete was talking about this stuff, then why are you trying to figure it out? Let's show *him* the map."

"Good idea." Katie shifts the unfolded map to Colin's lap. "Careful with that, okay?" She thrusts the keys into the ignition.

Colin grips it tenderly as the engine roars. Unfolded, the map is roughly the size of a 2-page spread of sheet music. He follows the creases and delicately folds them. Then, gently places the map back in the pencil case.

Katie continues. “Our best shot is getting you back to your house. Hopefully, Papa Pete will show up soon…”

“Katie, the cops are there, remember?”

“Damn.” The car slows.

Colin taps the pencil case gently on his thigh. “No. Keep going. We can do this. There’s probably one cop car in front of the house. All you need to do is drop me off at the top of the street and point me in the right direction. I’ll make my way through the backyards and get into my house from the rear.”

“I’ll go with you.”

“Not so fast. No…you’re driving down the street and talking to the police. There can’t be more than a couple of them. They’re not looking for you, remember? You’ve got to keep them busy while I get to the house. Give me 15 minutes tops. That should be easy for you, right? Just bullshit with them. You’re good at that.”

“Well, thank you Colin.”

Colin stirs in his seat. “Listen, tomorrow is the 27th. We have less than 48 hours before we probably lose Papa Pete. So…after you distract the cop, go home, pack a bag, and wait for me to call you.” Excitedly he adds, “and you better fill this gas guzzler up because with or without Papa Pete, we’re going to see Aunt Coleen tomorrow.”

“Good. Listen to you…all pumped up. This is good. I’ll give Doug a call and see if he can fly us. Although the weather’s looking crappy so we might be driving anyway. Okay, we’re turning down your street.” The car slows to a gentle stop. The windshield wipers squeak. He opens his door and Katie helps him to the sidewalk. “You’re right. It looks like one cop car down there.”

“Perfect,” Colin says. “Now, *exactly* where are we?”

Katie explains that they’re standing in the driveway of the property located five houses away from Colin’s home. He remembers this house, bordered on the right by a perfectly shaped boxwood hedge that runs back to a stand of trees.

Colin nods approvingly. He explains that once he reaches those woods, he'll follow the tree line until it brings him to the rear of his home. Katie sighs skeptically. "You sure you can do this?"

"Seriously? Hey, I can do this with my eyes closed."

Katie punches him playfully. "Not funny. Okay, good luck and call me as soon as you know something...anything." She places his left hand on dense oval leaves, already damp with drizzle.

"Katie don't freak out if you don't hear from me right away. First, I need to call Charlie and warn her." Still holding the pencil case he stuffs it carefully into his back pocket. "Then hopefully Papa Pete will make an appearance, so I'll really have something to tell you."

"He better show up," Katie says as she hugs him. "Good luck."

Colin is nearly halfway towards the tree line when he hears Katie's car door open and close. The purring engine disappears, replaced by rustling trees and the slight babble of the distant creek directly ahead. He turns left and slows his pace, remembering that the next property has a fenced in yard. He remembers why. A shrill bark from a dog sends him staggering backward but he maintains his footing. Colin feels for the fence post, careful to protect his fingers from the four-legged sentry. His heart beats rapidly. The dog growls aggressively, matching Colin's movement along the edge of the property. Finally, free from the fence, Colin feels the ground begin to slope downward. The grass is slick as he leans into the hill. Taking smaller steps, he descends cautiously. The pleasantly sweet smell of fresh-cut grass welcomes him to the next yard. The distant, familiar sound of Katie's voice urges him to move faster. Her banter with the police echoes off the trees. He allows himself to relax as his feet sink into the familiar, spongy bed of pine straw unique to the rear of their property. In the home stretch, he quickens his pace...and then he slips, landing hard on his chest and sliding feet first into the woods. Something sharp and spiky pokes his face and arms. Struggling to catch his breath, he crawls quickly on hands and knees out of the brush onto familiar terrain. As he regains his footing, he hears Katie's car driving away. Colin gathers himself and heads up the hill toward the house. He stops to check his rear pocket. He pulls out the pencil case and squeezes it tightly.

Reaching the porch, he quietly jiggles the rear doorknob. He expects it to be locked, and it is. He tiptoes to the far end of the porch and panics when he can't locate the large terra cotta flowerpot that hides the key. He carefully sweeps the small porch surface with his feet. No pot. He hears voices coming from the front of the house. Male voices. Is it neighbors or a couple cops? The voices are stationery but getting louder. Mostly laughter.

The coal chute. He remembers that Mr. Humphrey didn't have time to finish the job. Colin estimates the distance and scurries a few feet to the rear wall of the house. His searching hands discover a plywood panel covering the chute opening. Still holding the pencil case in his right hand, he jiggles the panel with his left. It moves freely. Quietly, he slides the plywood to the side and finds the opening. A thick splinter pierces his palm, and he releases the slab. The plywood wobbles. Colin cringes as it meets the ground with a solid thud. He crouches on the damp wood and waves his left hand through the void in the wall. The odor of wet resins greets him as he squeezes his body through the opening. Immediately, he realizes the absurdity of this desperate act. There is nowhere to brace himself. He tries to back out, but gravity betrays him. He tilts forward and topples immediately into the abyss. He grunts heavily, rolls to his side, and shrinks from the sound of a critter darting past his head. Frantically, he checks his pocket. The map is gone. He was just holding it…up there…outside. Closer now he hears two males approaching the rear of the house. Above his head, the exposed opening invites the inevitable. He retreats deeper into the basement, waiting to be discovered. In the brief silence, the rodent makes repeated rubbing and scraping sounds.

Suddenly, the wailing of a siren startles him. It sounds like it's coming from the front of the house. It's the police car. Somewhere outside, a bewildered voice exclaims, "what the hell?" Colin stands, unsure of what to do, where to go. A damp breeze squeezes through the opening that once carried coal to the basement. Now it carries a message...from Papa Pete. *"Colin, are you down there? Are you okay?"*

Colin scurries to the wall. "I'm here. I'm here." The siren is still wailing.

Papa Pete replies very deliberately. *"That's good news. I think you lost this."* The leather case slaps the concrete and skids between Colin's legs. He snatches it up. "Thank God." The siren stops abruptly while moving plywood forms a sound barrier between him and Papa Pete.

"Let me restore this mess and I'll meet you inside when it's safe."

Colin leans against the damp wall and sucks in cool air. His only companion, safe and content, gnaws innocently somewhere overhead.

CHAPTER 43

Passing Through

Friday – 8:30 PM

Colin drags his aching body up the basement steps. He lumbers into the kitchen without a shred of light to greet him. He's tempted to turn on the bright kitchen light but remembers the cops outside. Each step he takes reminds him of the chaos from this morning. Cutlery and shards of shattered glass pave his way to the kitchen phone. He gently removes the handset and listens for a dial tone. It's alive. He concentrates and carefully punches in Charlie's phone number. WHAT IF HE'S HOME? WHAT IF...

"Taylor residence."

Colin relaxes a bit. It's a woman's voice, but...older, weaker. "Hello, may I speak to Charlie, please?" He holds his breath.

"Is this Colin?" she asks suspiciously.

Unnerved, he sputters, "yes ma'am...yes, it is."

The tender voice whispers, "well, it's nice to hear your voice. This is Charlene's mother."

Colin's brain is working overtime. DID YOU KNOW MY FATHER? DID CHARLENE TELL YOU ABOUT ME? WHO THE HELL ARE YOU? He stutters, "Hello. Mrs. McDermott." Colin cringes as soon as the error leave his lips. I USED HER MAIDEN NAME.

Feebly, she responds, "let me get Charlie for you."

Colin slowly smacks his forehead until Charlie's raspy voice interrupts.

"Colin, how's Ben?"

"He's...he's okay. Can you talk?"

"Of course...why?" She's too composed. It unsettles him.

"The police know we lied. About the gun...going off. Your dad knows. And...I'm worried. Moretti is looking for you. You need to be careful. I'm so sorry."

Coolly, she asks, "Where are you?"

"At my house. I'm hiding at my house."

"Are you alone?" she asks quizzically.

"Sort of...well yes, for now."

Her placid tone continues. "Okay, calm down. I'm fine. My dad will be fine. I'll take care of him. And Moretti? He doesn't scare me."

Colin is incredulous. "Seriously? Do you remember what happened this morning?"

For the first time her tone is teasing. "I remember all of it. I remember all of you. Is that why you're 'sort of' alone?" She giggles. "Is your great grandfather with you?"

Before he responds, she adds, "I'll be fine, okay? Right now, I need to take care of my mom. She needs me. We'll talk soon."

"But..."

"Goodbye Colin."

Colin attempts to replace the handset, missing the cradle a few times before he finds his mark. He's numb. Confused. He swivels his head towards a gentle tapping at the back door. Cautiously he approaches and waits.

"It's me Colin. It's safe."

He unbolts the door and senses Papa Pete's presence. The spirit giggles friskily. *"You're head...it's full of stickers and burrs."*

Colin can't laugh. He picks at his hair. "You still sound happy. Was that you who turned on the police siren?

"Indeed."

"Well, thanks. Your little diversion worked, I guess."

"I enjoyed the adventure immensely. Those boys are very confused right now."

"Sounds like it really put a spring in *your* step. Wish I had some of that energy."

Sadly, I know it won't last. I've had an eventful day. I feel my light dimming. Now, where is that red pouch you left outside?"

Colin steers his way to the kitchen table. "Ahh, yes. Once again you bailed me out. Big time…I hope." He opens the pencil case and retrieves the map placing it on the table. Stepping back, he says, "take a look at this. It's from Pittston. See if it makes any sense to you."

"Pittston? Is that a fact?"

Colin senses the spirit's care examining the document. He asks, "do you need a flashlight?"

"I don't require additional light."

"Of course, you don't. What was I thinking?"

Except for the occasional sound of Papa Pete handling the map, there is total silence.

"This all makes sense. I think I understand."

"Great. Tell me."

"Very soon. But first, allow me to share my experience this afternoon. If you don't mind."

Deflated, Colin responds carefully. "Is this about your visit to the morgue? Maybe we can hold off on that. Just focus on the map right now, okay?"

Papa Pete ignores Colin. *"My encounter with Patrick was fortuitous. We were meant to meet.*

So, you talked to this dead guy…uh Patrick?"

"Oh yes, of course. Now, Patrick's circumstances are quite different. He's just…moving on. 'Passing through,' I believe he said. I hope to get there soon."

Colin gets a lump in his throat. "I hope so too. You deserve peace." He collects himself. "But nobody's going anywhere, okay?"

"We've more work to do, haven't we?

"Right, we should talk about the map."

"Patience Colin. You'll be rewarded. Now…as I said earlier, he was supposed to work on the day of the cave-in. Today, he told me he was so heavy with guilt that he went to the rescue tunnel

every day for a week to help any way he could. He prayed with the families, hoping for any sort of good news...of course that good news never came."

Colin interrupts. "Wait, wait, wait. A rescue tunnel?" There is a stirring inside Colin he hasn't felt during this dreary day.

"That's correct. Inside the Clear Spring Shaft – that's what Patrick told me. It was very close to the Twin Shaft. They abandoned that effort within a week or so. Patrick did not remember all the details, but he was sure of the name and its proximity to where I...we...all of us were...lost."

Papa Pete taps Colin's shoulder with the folded map. Colin gently takes it.

"This map shows the location of the Clear Spring Shaft – the rescue tunnel. I believe it holds the answer to your father's fate."

Again, something stirs, deep within Colin. "Fate? What does that mean...fate?"

"Colin, you're going to need me. We're going to need each other in the short time we have left. So, I must go. I must reserve my remaining strength."

"Please, don't leave me alone here. Not now."

The inevitable silence flattens him.

CHAPTER 44

Alone

Friday – 9:30 PM

Colin sits at his piano, gently rubbing the ivories he mustn't tickle. Outside, he hears the weary chatter of two men he came very close to meeting just a few hours ago. He could meet them now if he chose to play. If he chose to sing. If he turned on the lights. If he surrendered. From the driveway, the invigorated chatter of the cops stirs him. Footsteps trail away. A police radio squawks. Intermittent flashes pierce his darkness. A shrill engine shatters remnants of the silence. They're leaving. A sense of dread creeps in as he shuffles to the front door. He presses the frame, and it wobbles significantly. He remembers that Moretti nearly ripped its hinges off when he fled. The hardware squeaks as he removes his palms and steps back. He listens carefully for any sign of the strangers outside who never knew they were protecting him. They're gone. If this is what he wanted…to be rid of these sentries, well…he was wrong. He's alone and it worries him.

The house creates strange noises he never noticed before. He makes his way up the stairs and feels the relentless sagging of every squeaking step. Down the hallway, his weary legs halt outside the bathroom. The toilet is running -- one of Ben's unfinished projects. Seems so silly now. So removed from the chaos of the last week. From that moment he heard Katie's frantic voice in Ben's office.

Katie. He needs to call her. Three swift steps take him to the end of the hallway and the small phone table. He grabs the handset, leans against the wall, and slides slowly to the bare wood floor. As he dials Katie's number, a distinct scraping sound travels up the stairs. He freezes, chest pounding. Anchored to the floor, his body refuses to move. Creaking door hinges confirm a new arrival. He waits for someone to speak. Instead, the slow crunching of grinding feet on scattered debris leaves him breathless. Panic swallows him whole. He hears the distinct snap of a wall switch being flipped, but his world remains dark. He presses his back stiffly against the wall, willing it to pull him beneath the plaster and paint. He hears a stairstep squeak...then another. Now it's coming from the landing. A fourth step. Starting the final flight. And then it comes.

"Colin, honey...are you here? Are you okay?"

Relief showers him. His saturated shirt peels away from the wall. "I'm up here mom."

CHAPTER 45

One More Question

Friday – 10:15 PM

Colin leans into a long, hot shower, shedding the grime from today. He scrubs so hard with Safeguard his skin tingles. Still, he's oddly overpowered by smells that remain stored in his brain, taunting him. Moretti's essence of hair tonic and grease. The rotten-egg aroma of the discharged Luger. Charlie's dad and his stale tobacco breath. The overpowering antiseptic cloud of the hospital. And then... the fear and dread seeping from his mother's pores when she hugged him fiercely just minutes ago.

She insisted that Colin shower while she tries to restore order to a kitchen dismantled by this morning's struggle and the ensuing investigation. Just like the odors that linger, Colin can't shake the persistent police presence. They followed his mom home and will be checking on the house throughout the night. For now, they think Colin is staying with his cousin. That means they'll be visiting Katie's apartment tomorrow to question him. As for Ben, he continues to improve. That good news has unsettling consequences for Colin. His stepfather may be healthy enough to answer their questions soon – about things he saw and heard.

After quickly dressing, Colin makes a guarded call to Katie from the sanctuary of his bedroom. He speaks quietly into the phone while he monitors the sweeping of broken glass and the clatter of cabinets downstairs. He shares the news about the rescue tunnel and the answer it may hold. Too exhausted to offer more, he deflects her questions and tells her to be at Little Crum Creek Park at 8:00 AM sharp tomorrow. He waits for Katie to hang up. Hesitates. Double clicks the handset and waits for a dial tone. One more call to make and then off to join Hannah.

Colin enters the kitchen and hears pancakes sizzling on the griddle. He smiles when he smells the scented candle. "Cinnamon chewing gum. Where did you find that?"

"Not bad, huh? That's one advantage when you're forced to clean out the cabinets. You find little gems like that. You must be starving."

"I can't even describe it. Although this might be the latest that I've ever eaten breakfast."

She kisses him gently on the forehead. "Are you kidding? Pancakes before bedtime is the best. Your dad and I...." She hesitates. "Come on, sit down." Colin doesn't need a second invitation. As the first plate passes under his nose, his mom sets the ground rules. "Eat first. Talk later." She hands him the syrup. He eats until there's no more batter.

Colin offers to help with clean up, but his mother has other plans. "Chores can wait. God, you look beyond exhausted. You can barely keep your eyes open."

She's right. Even his limbs aren't responding. "It's been a long day, mom...for all of us. I'm really beat. It just hit me. I think I have pancake coma."

"Well, you did just eat a pound of Bisquick."

He grins widely, then slowly drops his head into his chest. "Tomorrow...it's so important. I'm afraid if I fall asleep, I won't be able to wake up."

"And I know if I ask you what's so important about tomorrow, you're never going to finish your answer."

"It's long and complicated" He yawns. "Sorry."

"Don't be sorry. There's been enough apologizing for today. I know you'll be honest with me...soon, right?"

"I swear. No more secrets. I promise."

"Good enough for me." She pushes her chair away from the

table. Colin reaches out and waits until she takes his hand. He stays seated. She gently nudges him. He hesitates. "Can I ask you one question?"

"So, changing the ground rules already. Should I sit down again?"

"Maybe."

He hears the chair come closer so she's sitting directly in front of him. His mom squeezes his hand. "What is it?"

"Mom, with everything we know, do you really think dad sent that letter?"

"Not for a second." She squeezes harder.

"Why?"

"First of all, he would never abandon you. Pure and simple. The man made a lot of mistakes, but he loved you more than anything. So, no way. And secondly -- if you can forgive the affair and the twisted things I did to hide it -- that letter makes no sense to me. It doesn't sound like your father. It's not the way he expresses himself. And..."

"What mom?"

"Well, your dad was a man of few words. But he would still write me notes before he went on the road. Okay, not always. Maybe not when he was in a rut. But a lot of times. And every note, every birthday card, he would always sign it the same way. "You are my forever." That letter was signed, 'love Tommy.' That's nice, maybe. But it's bullshit, Colin. Bullshit."

Colin battles through his fatigue. This is too important. "Mom, we both know who wrote that letter. Dad was *never* in Las Vegas. An envelope with a postmark doesn't prove that. The only one who went there was Moretti. The receipts Mr. Stiles took from his apartment prove it."

"God, I should never have asked Mr. Stiles to do that. I should never have backed Moretti into a corner with the evidence he found. Look where it got us. Ben in the hospital, Charlie roughed up. Your poor face..." She tenderly strokes his cheek. "...and he got what he came for."

"Your leverage...the Luger."

"Which you didn't tell the police about because you were lying to protect me. And now they're watching the house because they want to talk to *you*, while he's still out there."

"That's okay. Without knowing it, the cops are also keeping Moretti away."

"Not for long, Colin. Whatever you and Katie are planning, I'm running out of time. You said you needed a day or two. Fine. But if your plan doesn't work, then I'm going to the police and telling them everything. No matter how embarrassing."

Overwhelmed with exhaustion, Colin feebly responds, "either way, we don't have a choice. We're running out of time, too."

"Just who is *we?*"

"Tomorrow, mom."

CHAPTER 46

Rolling Thunder

Saturday June 27, 1970 – 7:00 AM

Colin sits on the edge of his bed and buries his nose in a freshly laundered shirt. He inhales the lingering residue of Wisk detergent. The long sleeves of his blended cotton jersey feel perfect for a rainy June morning. His fingers easily find the four safety pins at the bottom of the shirt, telling him it's a white Philadelphia Eagles jersey with Kelly green trim. He doesn't know what that looks like, but he doesn't care. His dad would like it and that's enough.

Rolling thunder shakes the roof above his second-floor bedroom. Torrents of water rat-tat-tat the side of the house. He wonders if Katie is still planning on flying to Scranton. He imagines what a boxer must feel like. Battered and bruised, waiting to be sent from his corner for another thrashing. He wrings his hands and leans forward on jittery legs. His edginess is interrupted by a gentle knock on the bedroom door.

"Come in."

"Hey, Colin. You okay?"

He hears his mother's feet softly shuffle through the shag carpet.

"Sure mom. I'm okay."

"Wearing your favorite shirt, I see." She giggles. "You, uh, may want to wear different shorts. They don't exactly go with Kelly green."

He feels Papa Pete's presence on the bed. *"I was going to tell you, but it's better coming from your mother."*

He hears the drawer open...the soft shuffle of clothes. "Here you go. These are better."

He touches slippery fabric, recognizing immediately she wants him to wear one of those weird Sansabelt pants with the elastic waist. "Thanks, but I think I'll just keep these on. They're more comfortable."

She sits down next to him. The bed is getting crowded.

"There's something I want to give you."

He listens to the slight tinkling of metal.

"Bend over. I'm going to put something around your neck."

Colin leans in as his mother gently pulls his hair away from his shoulders. He feels cool metal on his skin. It's a chain. He cradles the slender strand and slides it through his fingertips until they touch something. "Mom, is this..."

"The Order of Saint Barbara Medallion, back where it belongs. I'm sorry it took so long Colin. I put it on this chain for you. I hope that's okay. It's not a girly chain, trust me."

"I never trusted you more." He feels as if a missing limb has been reunited with his body. Tears are running down his cheeks. His mom wipes them gently with trembling hands. "Listen mom I need to explain a few things before I leave. Well, before *we* leave. He moves to the window hoping to harvest more light, but the rain has other plans. He presses his palm against the windowpane. Pounding pellets tickle his fingertips. "Oh...this is crazy."

"Hey, you're talking to the queen of crazy. I think the best thing we can do right now is to be honest with each other. Yesterday was hard for me but it's the only way. Now, it's your turn."

Colin remains at the window, tilting his head toward the bed and the sound of his mother's plea. "Mom, I know the last couple days have been tough."

Hannah responds lightly. "You think so?"

"Yeah, I know so. I also want you to know that I believe everything you told me...told us. I trust you and now I need you to trust me. There's a lot I have to explain. Katie and me, we both owe you that. I promise you'll get all your answers. But..."

"Ahh, here comes the 'but.' I thought you trusted me?"

Colin laughs. "Believe me, it's not about trust. It's about time. I need so...much...time to explain everything. It's complicated. It's not going to seem believable. You'll think I'm crazy."

"Is *he* here?"

"Is *who* here?"

"Pete. Is he in the room...with us?"

A clap of thunder rattles the room, but Colin doesn't flinch. He's breathless.

Papa Pete speaks dully. *"I was going to tell you about this, too."*

"It's okay honey. I don't know everything, but I know enough."

"How?"

"Last night, after you crashed, I pretty much did the same thing. Asleep in seconds. I don't know how long after that, I felt a chill. Both windows were wide open. I was exhausted but not crazy. I didn't open those windows. Then I saw a photograph on the bed. An old photograph of three men in work clothes..."

"Mom..."

"Hey, let me finish. The photo was sitting on your cassette player – next to a neat stack of cassettes, carefully numbered."

Colin manages a grin.

"She deserved to know Colin."

Hannah's voice is remarkably calm. "There was a note too. Written on a sheet of your braille paper. It said, 'My name is Pete. I'm the one in the middle. Please listen to these tapes. And don't ask Colin too many questions.' She pauses. Her voice quivers as she continues. 'He loves you very much.' My first instinct was to wake you up, but something stopped me. Something made me listen."

Colin stutters, "to all of them?"

His mother's voice cracks. "Yes. Then I did the craziest thing. Out loud, I said, 'I want to believe this Pete. Show me you're here.' Very slowly the first window closed. Then the second. It wasn't violent or dramatic. It was...gentle."

Colin feels comforted. He responds calmly. "I'm glad Papa Pete acknowledged you. He can be stubborn at times."

The bedroom window opens. Outside, the rain is amplified. Colin feels swirling drops of rain pepper his mismatched shorts. "And he can hold a grudge."

"I can see that."

The window closes. The muted rain continues to pummel the house.

Hannah goes on. "Still, at the risk of hurting Pete's feelings, I think some of his interpretation of things may have been a little *off*, don't you think?"

"Now, that we got to hear your side of the story, I agree."

"I agree with that."

"So does Pete."

"Good, but I'm not finished. I want to talk about what he saw in the elevator. At the hotel. I can see how Pete might have misunderstood, but I get to set the record straight, okay?"

"Please."

"Pete, wherever you are in this room. I understand what you *saw*, but here's what I *said*...I told him if he stepped one foot out of the elevator, I would kick him in the balls and scream."

Colin whistles. "What do you have to say about that, Papa Pete?"

"But she kissed him. What about the kiss?"

"He wants to know about..."

"A kiss? Oh, no, no." She sounds like she's savoring this moment. "I leaned in as close as I could, blew in his ear, and whispered, 'This is the closest you'll ever get to me again.' Maybe it looked like a kiss but...

Colin cackles, "God, I wish I could have seen his face."

"I told you Colin. I told you she seemed headstrong. Almost defiant. Now it makes sense. It makes me feel so much better."

"Pete's feeling better."

"Well, good for him," she says approvingly.

"Me too Mom."

She quizzes him. "Feeling better or feeling relieved?"

"A little bit of both, I guess. Don't know if that makes sense," Colin ponders.

"Of course, it does. I recall Pete saying on the tape that I cried all the way home. I think what he saw was relief," she explained. "All that anxiety that had been building up inside just gushed out when I realized I might finally be free." She pauses slightly before sadness hangs on every word. "Except I drove home to discover my lies had finally caught up with me. Ben confronted me about his trip to the food bank. Then, you and Katie showed up just in time to pour fuel on the fire. I was gutted. I left for my parents, thinking I had hit rock bottom. And then yesterday you called to tell me about Ben."

"You weren't free at all."

"Not even close. I was exposed. I was trapped. And now it seems we're both running out of time." She claps her hands and says resolutely, "So no more questions. It's time for me to be with Ben. And for you and Katie...and Pete I guess...to do whatever it is you need to do."

The door creaks open slowly. Hannah squeezes her son's hand. He feels her encouragement and trust. She breathes deeply. "Colin, find him. Whatever that means for us, please find him."

A crack of thunder spurs him onward. Towards the unknown.

CHAPTER 47

Carsick

Saturday – 8:00 AM

Hannah pulls the Mustang out of the garage, leaving her car briefly to pull down the door. Unexpectedly, Colin hears her mutter, "crap, its' a cop." She plops back in her seat, shuts the door, and confidently says, "be super quiet. I've got this."

The car slides backward and creeps down the driveway. Before it dips into the street, she brakes softly and waits. Exhaust from the idling car makes Colin queasy.

"Morning ma'am."

"Hello officer. Starting your rounds early?"

"Just checking to see if you're okay. Heading out so soon?"

"Running a few errands and then off to the hospital to see my husband."

"So…you'll be there all day?"

"I suspect, yes."

"Any contact with your son?"

Colin stiffens and holds his breath.

"No, he…he stayed with his cousin last night. Maybe I'll see him at the hospital."

There's prolonged silence.

"Okay, I'm sure we'll be in touch. Have a good day and be careful."

The car is already moving as Hannah responds, "thank you so much, officer."

The Mustang gathers speed and Colin's stomach settles. "You

okay back there?"

"Fine...just a little carsick."

"We won't be long. I promise."

The last time Colin drove with his mom was just two days ago. It feels like two years. Then, he felt helpless. He squeezes the medallion. Now, at least there's hope. His mom deserves that. Perspiration blankets his forehead. Moretti's words from yesterday suddenly haunt him. "EASY BIG SHOT. I'LL DEAL WITH MOMMY LATER."

The disturbing notion that Moretti believed he could marry her and "be the father Colin needed" overtakes him. He scours his memory for any moment that would remind him of Moretti's kindness or interest in Colin's life. Random memories surface but fall short. But then...he remembers the report card. The time he confided in his neighbor that he was afraid to have his father sign it while his mom was off visiting her parents. Moretti offered to forge his signature, saying he had plenty of paperwork that contained his dad's handwriting. Again, Moretti bragged about himself – boasting to Colin that he was good at forgery. He called it a "side job" that kept him busy. At the time Colin's fear of his father's wrath was greater than committing a white lie with the help of his neighbor. So, he agreed, with Moretti's promise that he would never share the misdeed with Colin's parents. Of course, Colin could never judge the man's work since he couldn't see the signed report card, but the nuns bought it and that was the end of it. Or was it? A lump invades his throat. Panic nibbles away as he recalls a rare moment – maybe the only time – that Moretti was in their apartment after they moved to Delaware County. Colin can't remember why his parents weren't around. Moretti showed up claiming he needed to talk to his father about an upcoming haul. He pleaded to use their bathroom. He remembers vividly that he was holding his special Sucrets tin when Moretti entered the apartment. They made small talk and Moretti asked him what he was holding. Colin proudly displayed the contents of the tin – the medal his father recently gave him. Moretti asked to see it and Colin reluctantly shared his keepsake. Moretti mumbled insincerely about his prized possession and dropped it roughly back into the tin. Then he made Colin promise not to tell his parents about the visit. Colin hesitated. Moretti got very close. Colin could smell the hair tonic. Moretti whispered, "you keep quiet, and I won't tell them about forging your dad's signature. Deal?" Colin barely responded. He just nodded. After he thought Moretti had left the apartment, Colin swiftly returned the tin to its special place under his mattress. He remembers hearing the door click. Frozen, he sat on his bed, afraid to move. His stomach ached. He sat there until his dad returned nearly an hour later. He never said a word about the visit.

The familiar churn of gravel brings him back to reality. He's suffocating. His shirt is drenched in sweat. Colin tugs at his medal. HE KNEW. MORETTI KNEW WHERE I HID IT. His knees feel permanently pressed into his chin. He desperately wants to separate himself from the tire iron poking his spine. The prospect of freedom only makes the smell of wasted rubber and oil-soaked rags more unpleasant. He longs for one deep breath that doesn't taste vile. Rain pelts the car and makes the space feel even smaller. A deeper sense of dread swallows him. And then the trunk opens.

The summer rain bathes him. His own unique version of the light offers its greeting. An umbrella snaps open. Katie grunts hello as her firm grip peels him away from the trunk. He stretches his tightly wound frame. "Thank God that's over."

His mother gently rubs his back as pellets of rain pound the umbrella. "Colin, you're soaked. Was it bad?"

"I'll never complain about the back seat again."

As he waits to be led to Katie's car, he senses his mom hugging Katie. Hope returns. It puts a spring in his step. "Let's get this show on the road ladies...and Papa Pete...you with us?"

"Indeed I am."

"By the way Katie, my mom has been introduced to Papa Pete," Colin discloses.

"No shit...you can see him?"

"Nope...I can't hear him, either. Let's just say we've bonded. Another secret shared."

"A sizeable secret indeed. It makes me happy. Gives me energy for our expedition."

By the time they make it to the Oldsmobile, Colin can tell the rain is departing as quickly as it arrived. The pitter-patter of drops on the umbrella disappear. He feels the morning sun heat the gravel below his feet. Water vapor clings to his calves.

Unexpectedly, Hannah asks, "before you leave can I ask Pete one thing?"

"I feel a nervous curiosity."

"You're freaking him out Hannah. Go ahead."

"Katie, I know you went to Tracey's house, saw Pete there..."

Katie murmurs, "you weren't kidding...you know all the secrets."

Hannah laughs. "Enough to be dangerous. Anyway, there's one thing that bothers me...the notebook he took from Tracey's house."

Colin squirms. "It's bugging me too." He imagines a grin on his mother's face as she wisecracks, "very, very soon, Pete is going to make good on his thievery. Isn't that right?"

"She has my word. I need to erase that blemish from my soul."

Colin smiles. "You just got a resounding 'yes'."

"Good enough. It's time for you to go." She guides Colin to the car and opens the door.

"Thanks mom. Now, go be with...your husband. We're all pulling for him."

She hugs him tenderly and gently guides him into the car.

Colin feels her arms stretch across his body and reach for his cousin. Katie leans in so their joined hands gather across his chest. "Katie, go kick some ass." As she pulls away, she kisses her son tenderly on his cheek. "Mom, Moretti will get what's coming to him, I promise."

She sighs deeply. "Maybe so Colin. I'm just scared of what he may have already done."

Colin doesn't respond. The door closes and his mother's gentle hands tap the car.

From the rear, Papa Pete expresses delight that Hannah is going to be at Ben's side. *"He will feel that energy. Trust me. He will know."* There is a profound pause. *"I wonder if I will ever be at her side again?"*

CHAPTER 48

Getting Close
Saturday – 8:45 AM

"Okay. Change of plans," Katie says matter-of-factly as she maneuvers the 442 through local traffic near the park. "Skies are black again. Storms are still popping up." On cue a large thunderclap sends shockwaves through the car. "We are not flying to Scranton."

Colin nods his approval as he rolls the medallion in the palm of his hand. "Thank God. We may actually live to see another day."

"I thought you would be disappointed, Colin."

"Hell no. Keep driving."

"I hoped to experience a plane ride. I'm displeased."

Katie, surprisingly lighthearted, responds, "well, things are different for Colin and me. If we crash, we die. You're already dead, so no offense, but the risk is a little different for us."

"That's a valid observation."

Colin runs his hands through his hair. "Well listen to you. Agreeing with each other. We're off to a good start."

Katie pokes him. "Nice to see you all cleaned up. You looked kind of grungy yesterday."

"Why thank you. Just doing my part to keep your new car smelling clean."

"Aww, that's so sweet. By the way, I love the Eagles jersey. You know your pants don't match, right?"

"Old news." He closes his eyes. Katie is accompanying Karen Carpenter as the radio tenderly plays, *We've Only Just Begun.*

Colin fidgets in his seat.

"You okay?"

"I can't calm myself. My mind is jumping around."

"Colin, I have a strong sense that we are getting close."

"To what?"

"To the reason I'm here. To the truth. To some sort of peace for our family. You must see it. The last few days have been a real lally-cooler."

Katie chirps, "translation please?"

"He means, um success, right...successful?"

"Correct. For example, over the past ten days the Phillies have been a real lally-cooler. That's a bottom fact."

Katie mumbles. "With all that's been going on, you managed to keep track of the Phillies?"

"Well, I don't sleep, remember? Plus, they won seven out of nine games, that's a real..."

"Lally-cooler," Colin says. "I get it, but the things we've been through are a bit more complicated than baseball."

"Perhaps we shouldn't dwell on the <u>things</u>. Instead let's reflect on the <u>people</u>."

Katie sighs. "Here's an idea," she says lightheartedly. "Let's just drive and listen to the radio." She turns up the volume. The Beatle are singing *The Long and Winding Road.* Colin fumbles with the volume knob. He lowers it and calmly guides the conversation. "So, Papa Pete, what have you learned?"

"The lyrics of this song are appealing to me. They are easy to understand, unlike some of the music you listen to."

Colin turns it off. He repeats the question more emphatically. "What have you learned?"

"I have sentiments I'd like to share without commentary from you...Katie. Can you do that?"

"Why are you singling me out? What about Colin? Tell him to shut his trap too!"

Colin grins and flashes a thumbs up sign while Katie continues grumbling.

As the Oldsmobile leaves Philadelphia behind and heads

toward coal country, Papa Pete reflects, *"where shall we start?"*

Colin doesn't hesitate. "My mom," he says affectionately.

"Ah, Hannah…Good choice. Of course, she has made mistakes, but her honesty is courageous. I see a person who loves you very much Colin. Think about how lonely she must have felt for so long. Burdened with guilt. Shackled with the fear of losing you if she told the truth. So, instead she constructed clever lies, convincing herself that each thumper would be her last. Until she reached that breaking point, when she stared down the risk of losing it all for the chance to have you forgive her and love her – the way she has always loved you."

"Wow," Colin says softly. "That's pretty cool."

"I also told you Hannah couldn't be trusted. I misjudged her. I was wrong."

Katie's response, rich with empathy, surprises Colin. "Don't beat yourself up Papa Pete. Colin and I didn't exactly have our facts straight either. We were all jumping to wrong conclusions. We still are."

"Thank you, Katie. I'm not sure how to handle your kind remarks. It's not natural for you."

Katie snorts while Colin gets things back on track. Okay, what about Ben?"

"Of course. Ben. Well, let me begin by saying I am ashamed of the way I made fun of him. Today, I see a person who knows he can never replace your father but is willing to accept the life he has with a woman he loves. He has not been given the chance to prove that, because the truth has been withheld from him. Despite all the unfortunate choices Hannah made, my intuition is that he will forgive them all if given the chance. He deserves that chance."

Remorsefully, Colin says, "I agree with you."

Katie whistles slowly. "My, my, my…somebody has really changed his tune."

"A superlative human gift, don't you think? The ability to change your mind. I'm grateful I did because we are lucky to have Ben in our life. In fact, it's important to note that his decision to hire poor Mr. Honeycutt will prove to be a marvelous reward for

our family. While, in the short run, his tenacity presented a moral dilemma for Hannah, his superb investigation skills will come to bear very soon."

Katie, more animated, asks, "what about his wife Tracey? She fascinates me."

"Well said, Katie. Fascinating indeed. We should not underestimate the role of Tracey Honeycutt. That woman impresses me greatly. She has a trick or two up her sleeve. If I was Mr. Moretti, I would rue the day she became an advocate for her murdered husband."

Colin spits out Moretti's name. "Asshole," Katie adds bitterly.

"Pure evil. He is the root of our family's pain. He is the reason for my presence. I don't know why but my intuition is at its strongest peak when I consider the negative energy this villain poured into the destiny of my grandson."

Colin adds quietly, "my dad."

Katie jumps in. "Yeah, Papa Pete, what about Uncle Tommy?"

"Thomas. Your father, your uncle – my grandson -- like all of us, had demons to conquer. I'm proud of him. I'm grateful for the son he raised and the niece he rescued. I'm thankful you have a lot of good memories, as well. Hold on to them and please be brave, just like him."

Silence follows. Colin speaks first. "Katie, are you crying?"

"Just shut up. Let me drive."

"Do you want me to drive."

She snickers. "That joke is still not funny. No, that would be as dangerous as flying in this weather." She sighs deeply. "Papa Pete, um, that was worth being quiet for. Thank you."

"Thank you for making Katie cry, Papa Pete."

"Thank you for listening. Now, let's hope my daughter can get us closer to the truth."

CHAPTER 49

My, My, My

Saturday – 11:00 AM

"Back in Carbondale," Katie announces. "Look familiar, Papa Pete?"

Colin waits for his answer, but the car is silent.

"He's already on the sidewalk Colin. Strolling back and forth in front of that stubborn gate. There's a For Sale sign leaning up against the porch. I don't remember seeing that last time. But it was almost dark when we got here, so maybe I missed it."

"Katie, that was four days ago. Remember what we promised each other four days ago?"

She groans. "That we would *never* come back here again...."

"And that was *before* we knew she was dead."

She opens her door. "And before Honeycutt's notes told us to 'go back to Pittston.'"

"Yeah, well we're only in Carbondale, 30 miles from Pittston."

"Carbondale brings us to Aunt Coleen. Hopefully Aunt Coleen leads us to Pittston."

"And the Clear Spring Shaft...the rescue tunnel...the answer to my father's fate."

"*If* you believe in Papa Pete...who by the way has decided to bypass the gate and is now floating up to the porch."

The car door slams. Colin is alone. He squeezes the medallion, takes a deep breath, and recalls Aunt Coleen's wheezy voice:

"YOU NEED TO BE PREPARED FOR SOME TOUGH ANSWERS,

HEAR ME BOY?"

Katie's impatient tap on the window brings him back. Colin quickly joins her on the sidewalk. She gently offers her elbow. "Do you want me to get your cane? Remember, there's a lot of tight maneuvering in there."

"I have no intention of straying."

After a few steps, Katie whispers, "looks like we have company...some lady with a fake smile moving in fast." Katie stops.

"Good morning, folks. Is there something I can help you with?"

Katie quickly responds. "Who are you?"

"Oh, oh...I'm Dot Pritchard. I'm a realtor. For this property. You're here for this property, right? One of the neighbors saw you here a few days ago. They called me when you pulled up. I live just a few blocks away, so it's no bother."

Colin smells fruity perfume, or maybe it's cheap wine. He lets Katie do the talking. "Tight-knit neighborhood, huh?"

"Well, we keep an eye on things. You know how that goes." She clears her throat. Continues awkwardly. "You were inside the property, is that right?"

"Maybe," Katie says obtusely.

"Well, my neighbor..."

"Then why are you asking Dot? You already know the answer."

"Right, well it's just that...how did you get the key? The property is all locked up so how did you get in?"

Papa Pete chimes in from the porch. *"My dead daughter let them in."*

Katie's slow groan is barely audible. "The door was open. We went in to check things out."

"You were in there quite a long time."

"Well, he's blind so it's you know...slow going."

"I can see Coleen in there. Let's proceed."

"Dot?"

"Hmmm?"

"Is there a problem?"

"No dear. No, No. You see, the lady who lived here died a few years back and apparently there are no living relatives. So, it seems the house is going to a sheriff's sale." She pauses and whispers, "you can have it for a song."

"We are her relatives", Katie says playfully.

"Oh my. That's confusing. Well, it's not the first time they got this kind of thing wrong."

"She was our great aunt."

Colin finally speaks. "We had a special bond."

"Oh, I'm so sorry for your loss. We can sort this out later. Would you like to go inside? I can open it up for you." Colin hears the jangling of keys as Dot moves away from them and closer to the house. Katie prods him, and they begin moving.

"Coleen is getting impatient."

Colin hears the realtor struggling with the gate, as Katie shouts, "you really need to shake that latch...no...Dot... harder."

Dot is breathless by the time they reach her. Katie rattles the gate violently. It squeaks open.

"Looks like you have some experience with that," Dot says, panting. "Listen, under the circumstances how about I just leave the key with you. I'll come back in an hour or so to answer any questions and lock things up. How does that sound?"

"That works for us. Thanks Dot."

"You're welcome... oh look at me I never even asked your names."

"I'm Katie and this is Colin. Like I said, we're cousins. By the way, that For Sale sign, has it always been there?"

"Funny thing uh, Kitty. I can't seem to keep one in the ground. As fast as I plant one it disappears. I think it's some neighborhood prankster. Other odd things...darn utilities are supposed to be turned off, but neighbors swear lights go on and the phone keeps ringing. Very odd indeed. People around here...they say the place is haunted. Guess I shouldn't be telling you that but considering you're family..."

Colin deadpans, "I don't believe in ghosts."

Katie adds, "yeah, we're not a superstitious family. All that spooky shit...it's stupid."

"Well, to each his own, right Kitty?" I'll see you in about an hour, okay?"

"Perfect. Thanks Dot." Katie guides Colin up the steps. "There is no way that woman wanted to step foot in this house."

Colin giggles, "no way *Kitty*."

"Just keep moving." Katie grabs Colin's hand and drops the keys into his palm. "Here, put these in your pocket. We won't need them. The door's slightly open."

Colin hears the hinges squeak. "Follow me and hold your nose."

The smell is even worse than Colin remembers. Last time it was just a filthy old house. Now, it's a morgue. He tugs his Eagles jersey over his nose. Katie guides him through the logjam. He hears voices. Papa Pete and Aunt Coleen, chatting as if they were sharing Sunday dinner. "Are they talking...about the...Phillies?"

Katie stops. "Apparently so."

"I don't like these West Coast games. They interrupt my schedule."

"But we have the Giants' number. Bunning is pitching today so maybe our luck will continue."

Katie whispers, "she's still wearing that same turtleneck."

Colin prods his cousin. "Why are you whispering? They can hear everything you're saying. Keep moving."

Katie pulls Colin into a familiar space. Pitch scurries under his feet and trills.

"Don't be shy you two. Daddy and I were catching up while you were talking to that moron realtor. So, what brings you back to Carbondale? Still doing your detective work?"

Katie barely speaks before Aunt Coleen sharply interrupts.

"I have no desire to talk to you miss smart-ass. You stole that

private investigator's business card, I know it. So, save your breath – if you know what's good for you. Colin, honey, how are you doing?"

"I'm okay Aunt Coleen. A little confused, but okay."

"Seems we're all a bit higgledy-piggledy these days."

Papa Pete speaks over his daughter. *"Coleen, I want to help you..."*

"Daddy, no disrespect but I'm talking to Colin. You abandoned me, up and left...that's what you did. Now you come back and want to help me. I don't need no help. Not from anybody."

Papa Pete's response is shockingly stern. *"Listen carefully. You are misguided. Let me share the facts and if you choose to ignore me, then I will leave you fester in this Godforsaken house."*

"Daddy, don't be cross."

"Then allow me to explain?"

Her wheezing intensifies. Colin fidgets.

"Go ahead. Explain."

"Thank you, Coleen. When I first arrived in this house, I was lost – like you are now. I didn't understand how I fit – between the living and the dead. Nothing made sense. Now, I found my purpose. Each day, things are becoming clearer."

"Clear for you maybe. I have no clue what you're talking about."

"Coleen, when I came here you were alive. When I left it was not out of abandonment. That's not the way this works."

"What do you mean 'this?' You're losing me real fast daddy."

"Coleen, I spend my days with the living. One day I was no longer with you. Suddenly I was living with Colin because he's alive and you're...well, you...died."

"I am not dead, father. I am living in my home."

"There is a way out Coleen. A path to peace. I know because I'm on that path right now. I'm serving a purpose and when my job is finished, I'll have peace."

"I don't understand."

"Of course, you don't. You're doing this alone, but not anymore. I'm here to help you. We're all here to help you."

"Even the smart-ass?"

"Even her. She has helped me. And she can help you, too."

Colin senses her movement. Her labored breathing passes by. That tiny light by the sofa clicks on. He hears her grunt as she plops down.

"Colin, sit next to me."

Katie quickly guides him to her side, kicking debris aside as she goes. She lowers him down to the sofa. He resists leaning back, teetering instead on the edge of a cushion.

"Do you trust my daddy?"

"Yes, Aunt Coleen. For the past year, I've trusted him."

"Why did he leave me? How did I die?"

Colin struggles to reply, but Papa Pete intervenes.

"Colin can't answer that. It needs to come from you. So, you can move on."

Katie interrupts with a commanding edge to her voice, but it's filled with remarkable compassion. "Okay Aunt Coleen, can I ask some questions?"

"Go ahead."

"When we visited a few days ago, we talked about the private investigator, the one whose card I borrowed."

"You stole it. Don't sugarcoat it or we're done talking."

"Right, I stole it. But it helped a lot. You see that man, Mr. Honeycutt, he was asking you questions because he was looking for information about my Uncle Tommy, who used to visit you along with the uh..."

"...the dago, Gino. The one with the cigarettes."

Colin slides back and stiffens his shoulders. Katie steps in front, closer to Aunt Coleen.

"Right. That's right. Well, Mr. Honeycutt? He thought Moretti, uh Gino -- he did something to my uncle."

"What kind of something?"

"We're not sure but whatever it was, it's not good."

"What does the investigator think?"

Colin is mesmerized by his cousin. She crouches down and leans on his knee for balance.

"Well, that's the thing. You see, the investigator, Mr.

Honeycutt. He's dead."

"Oh my. Oh, my, my."

"And we think...sorry, we *know* Moretti killed him. He was up here in Carbondale asking way too many questions, so Moretti killed him."

"Oh my, oh my, my, my. "

"And we think he was worried that *you* knew too much. Remember all your bootlegging connections? You knew all those places they went, right?"

"I knew he was up to no good. I told you Tommy didn't trust him. But I didn't do anything about it. Those free cigarettes were more important. Oh, my, my, my, my."

"Aunt Coleen, are you okay...is, is she okay?"

Papa Pete finally speaks. *"This is your path to the truth. Go ahead Coleen. Don't be afraid."*

"Tommy hadn't been around. The investigator had stopped coming around too. Then that dago just shows up one day with more cigarettes. Before I had a chance to light one up, he was on me. With a pillow. Pinned me down right there where Colin is sitting. He was so strong. He smelled awful. I heard him grunting and then it was over. And I've been here ever since. Daddy, I'm so sorry. I'm so, so sorry."

Papa Pete's voice is brittle and broken. *"It's okay, it's okay. You don't have to be sorry. Because now you get to be part of the solution, Coleen. Just like me. That's why I ended up with Colin. Because I needed somebody on the other side to help find the truth. Together, we're going to do that. This injustice will be remedied. Then, we'll have peace."*

"What, what about Pitch?"

Katie gasps. "You mean he's not dead?"

"Hell, no darling. He's been on a steady diet of mice and stale cereal."

Colin, still coming to grips with the uneasy fact that he's sitting squarely on the spot where Aunt Coleen was suffocated, inquires, "what about his litter box?"

"Oh, I never worried about that."

Colin slides to the edge of the sofa again.

Papa Pete's steady voice commands the room. *"Pitch will find his way. Just like you. Just like me. And part of that way is to help bring Moretti to justice and to find out what happened to Tommy. Are you ready to help?"*

"Hell, yes. Can Katie help too?"

"I can, if that's what you want?"

"Aww, I always liked you. You're tough as shit."

"Language, Coleen."

"Sorry daddy."

CHAPTER 50

Cold Feet

Saturday -- Noon

Katie asks for the brightest room possible. Aunt Coleen suggests a garden shed attached to the rear of the house. Colin clutches Katie's hand tightly as she clears the path to their destination. Everything is warmer, brighter. Katie explains. "It's a make-shift greenhouse Colin. Pretty cramped and gross but this will work. Use this table, Papa Pete." Colin quickly covers his nose with his sleeve as dust kicks up from the table. His eyes are watering. He pinches his nose to suppress a sneeze but to no avail. The arm of his Eagles Jersey is no longer clean.

"Bless you darling."

"Thanks. Sorry about that."

The map is spread on the small table. Colin feels the paper overlap its edges. Finally, they are ready. Papa Pete leads the conversation.

"Coleen, what do you know about the Clear Spring Shaft?"

"I know it well...and I know this map. That's my printing. I gave this map to those two."

"To my dad and Moretti?"

"That's right. Lots of bootleg mining going on there. So, I suggested they could pick up a load. I knew the fellas doing the digging. It was getting dangerous, so they were pretty much ready to move on. Told Gino it might be their last shot. Gave the map to Tommy. Told him it was my only copy and made him promise to get it back to me after they got their haul. Never saw it again until

now. Where did you get it?"

"My dad hid it for us."

"He did, huh? Why would he do that?"

Katie's answer is brief. "Not sure."

"Coleen, I understand this shaft was used for a rescue tunnel to the Twin Shaft. Is that right?"

"Right, daddy. Is that something you want to talk about?"

"Of course. Tell me. Tell us."

"Well, that was a long time ago, so history has a way of reinventing itself. But I did a lot of reading. Talked to a lot of old souls whose families went through that hell. Kept a lot of clippings I found at the library – stole them actually, but who cares. Nobody took care of that information as good as me. Nobody. Now, let's see where the hell is it?"

Colin hears drawers opening and closing. Catches the ebb and flow of Aunt Coleen's labored breathing as she moves around her cluttered catacomb.

"There you are."

Her voice is right on top of Colin.

"You're gonna have to move precious."

"Oh, sorry Aunt Coleen."

She giggles. *"No, not you honey. The cat. Get him off the table, will you?"*

Colin's not sure who complies but he hears the thump of Pitch landing on the floor.

"Okay, this here is the newspaper article."

She plops it on top of the map. Katie gently elbows Colin aside.

She describes it for her cousin. "Let's see…this…this is from the same paper where I found that front page story, but it's the whole thing, Colin. It's in amazing condition."

"Of course…like everything around here. I stay on top of my cleaning and record keeping."

Colin knows Katie is too absorbed to make a sarcastic comment. He hears her turn the pages gently. "What am I looking for Aunt Coleen?"

"Let's see…keep going. Easy now. There. There it is."

Colin hears gentle tapping on the paper.

"Right, there miss smart-ass." She cackles. *"Read that."*

"There's a lot of information here, what exactly am I reading?"

"Just give it to me."

The paper is lifted at such an angle by Aunt Coleen that it blocks the light from several of the windows surrounding the room. The space darkens as Aunt Coleen begins to read.

"The expert miners who are directing the work of rescue held frequent conversations during the afternoon and evening, the only one new scheme of reaching the men was evolved. That was to cut a tunnel through the 60-foot pillar which separates the Clear Spring and Twin Shaft mines."

She skims and mumbles through several paragraphs, stops, then resumes reading.

"…hope, slim as it is, is virtually dashed to the ground by the report of the men from the Clear Spring shaft who rapped for a full half hour on the pillar yesterday afternoon without getting any response, which they say is a bad sign as it is possible to hear the rapping in the Clear Spring shaft at the point in the Twin shaft where the entombed men are supposed to be."

She drops the paper to the table and sighs.

"There's more but it ain't good. We know the rest, right daddy?"

"I heard them."

"Heard who, daddy?"

"The tapping. It was very, very faint, but I heard it. I was too weak to respond. There was nobody else with me. My feet were so cold. There was a tiny pool of water from an underground spring, but it wasn't enough. I was struggling for air."

Colin discerns a very distinct change in Papa Pete's clipped, monotone delivery. It sounds like he is having trouble breathing.

"I need to go there. We need to go there, right away. There's something else. That's not the end of my story. There's something more. Please, can we go?"

"Daddy, I can't leave here. I'm afraid. Pitch needs me. This is where I belong. I'm sorry."

Colin's heart is pounding. He feels the medallion vibrating on his chest. The comforting sound of Papa Pete's soft delivery returns.

"Don't be sorry Coleen. You did fine. I'm proud of you. Maybe this is as far as you need to go, but I'm not finished. There's more. There's more."

Colin hears the map being pulled from the table. Katie's voice is deliberate as she slowly folds the document, her elbows scraping his in the tight space. "Papa Pete, remember we need to get there too, but we have a slight problem. We have no idea where we're going. None."

Aunt Coleen wheezes slowly.

"Artie."

"Who?"

"He knows every inch of every vein in Pittston. He's your man."

Katie asks, "where do we find this Artie guy?"

"Go to O'Malley's Mining Supplies and wait for him. Warning you...it's not going to be easy."

Colin clears the dust from his throat. "Um, Aunt Coleen, uh no offense now, but..."

"What is it, sweetheart?"

"Well. You said *wait* for him?"

"You heard me right."

"Well, your perspective of time may be a little off, right? I mean it's been a while since you've been out there. So, how do we know if this Artie guy is even alive?"

"Oh, he's not alive darling. He's dead as they come. The spirit of the shafts. The pillar phantom. Artemis Horatio Pilger. He's your man. Like I said, just go there and wait for him."

Katie asks, "can you maybe give us directions to O'Malley's?"

"Sure can. I'll be right back."

Katie waits a few seconds. "What the hell happened to her?"

"Clarity. Purpose. Things are unfolding for Coleen. She's less trapped. She's on a good path now. I'm happy for her. And I'll be

delighted to see Artemis again."

Simultaneously, Katie and Colin ask, "You know him?"

Colin adds, "Since when?"

"Oh, we go way back. I'm remembering. The clarity is coming. For Coleen…and for me."

CHAPTER 51

Artie

Saturday – 1:30 PM

Papa Pete reads directions to Katie from the back seat. Colin listens to their chatter as the 442 tracks Aunt Coleen's course to Moosic, an old mining town south of Scranton. The powder business began very early in Moosic. Aunt Coleen explained that black powder – used for gunpowder – is made from very finely ground coal. He smiles. Wonders if he'll ever see her Aunt Coleen again. His musing is interrupted by Katie.

"So, Papa Pete. How about you put that map down and answer a question you've avoided long enough."

"I'm not sure what you mean. Whatever I have remembered I believe I have shared."

"Really?" Katie's voice is curious. "You sure about that?"

"Katie, what are you doing?"

"Easy Colin. Just helping Papa Pete on his path to peace."

"Aren't we almost at O'Malley's?"

"No fair changing the subject. I just want Papa Pete to answer a question...about his scar?"

"I believe I told you already...I don't recall."

"Bullshit."

Colin nervously taps the dashboard. "He said he doesn't remember."

"Not buying it. Was it one of those times you got yourself into a little mischief with your friends? What did you call it, 'wake snakes,' right?"

"I would prefer not discussing this with you."

"Now, we're getting somewhere. You do remember."

Colin feels nervous...but intrigued.

"A man of unseemly character made an advance on Fannie. I confronted him at a local pub and settled my score, but not before he opened the side of my face with a broken bottle."

Katie gasps. "Oh my God, how did you settle the score...what did you do to him?"

"You asked me how I got my scar. You have your answer. Never bring the subject up again."

Emboldened by Katie's question, Colin digs for more. "When you defend someone who you care about, it makes you feel good, right?"

"Colin, you've pursued this line of questioning before. Please stop."

"Now, what are *you* doing?" Katie says with bewilderment.

"You started it smart-ass," Colin says defiantly. He turns in the direction of the indistinct foggy image. "At the hospital you called your attack on Moretti a vengeful act, remember? You admitted to me that it made you feel better."

Silence. Colin's heart is in his throat. "Katie, is he still there?"

"Uh huh."

"Remember that landscaping kid who was picking on me... he broke his ankle. That wasn't an accident...that was you."

"With the little time that remains, I feel cheated by this impression I've left with you."

Colin grits his teeth and mumbles, "that's not what I meant to do. I'm not judging. It just seems to energize you, that's all. It's fascinating, really."

Papa Pete turns surprisingly gracious. *"Never you mind, Colin. I bear no grudge. And I will continue to do whatever I must to protect the honor of my family...regardless of the impression it may leave..."*

"Well in that case, just one more question. Why didn't you finish Moretti off? I mean, you nailed him pretty good. Why not finish the job?"

Papa Pete sighs with annoyance.

"Care to elaborate?" Colin pesters.

"Charlene was in possession of a firearm. It made me nervous."

"In what way?" Colin asks timidly.

Colin, let me say more emphatically than before that I am done talking about this."

"Great chat, fellas," Katie says dryly. She tries to lighten the mood. "Well, we just turned onto Main Street in Moosic. Just rolls off the tongue, doesn't it? Ladies and gentlemen, welcome to Moosic's Main Street. Home of O'Malley's Mining Supplies."

An awkward silence follows. Finally, Papa Pete's distinctly weaker voice breaks the stillness.

"It will be good to see Artemis Horatio Pilger, the spirt of the shafts...my old friend."

Colin's relief is immediately interrupted by Katie's announcement, "and it's closed. There's not a soul in sight, no pun intended."

Papa Pete giggles softly.

Colin isn't laughing. "Nobody?"

The car slows. "Afraid not. Parking lot is empty. Building looks dark. Yup, it's pretty much closed." The car pulls onto a choppy surface that vibrates Colin's seat. He can tell it's a parking lot desperately in need of repair. Katie stops the car and turns off the ignition. Uncomfortably she asks, "Papa Pete, any suggestions?"

"I will need a moment. Please wait for me."

Papa Pete departs. Katie nudges Colin. "So, welcome to Moosic...and what the hell did he do to the guy in the bar?"

"Not now, please? Where did he go?"

"I don't know. Looking for uh, Artie...what did Aunt Coleen call him?"

"The pillar phantom."

"Right, right...well, that didn't take long." She rolls down her window. "What's up?"

"Drive around the building. There's a detached garage in the

back. Pull up there. Oh, I almost forgot. Colin, I need your medallion."

Colin clenches his keepsake. "What...no way. Not a chance."

"Please, trust me, okay?"

"What for?"

"So, you can communicate with him...Artie."

"I don't understand."

"He wants a connection to you. Remember, you both can communicate with me because we have a blood connection. Now don't believe for a moment that there is a handbook for souls like us who live between two worlds. Each of us finds our way and this is Artie's way. He needs to be wearing something that belongs to you, so he has a link...a bond. So, you can see him. That's how it works...for him."

Katie curiously asks, "So...what's your bond with this phantom guy?"

"We died together."

"Very chummy. Colin, give him the medal."

"And the chain, the whole thing. He needs to wear it."

Colin grunts, "fine." He removes the chain and holds it out. Feels the tug and lets go.

"Now, Katie, please give me your headband."

"I knew it. I knew you were going to rip something off. Here you go, and hey, I want that back too...it's a Woolworth's special."

"Thank you. Okay, please proceed to the garage."

Katie nurses the car over clumps of concrete. Colin feels a steep incline.

"We okay here?"

"Fine, almost there."

"So, how would you describe this place?"

"Uh, abandoned?"

"That's what I figured. Not what you imagined, is it?"

"Nope. It's as battered as Papa Pete's jacket." The brakes squeak. Katie snorts. "Speaking of battered, that must be our new friend Artemis." The car stops, still tilting downward.

"Wow."

"What? Tell me."

"He's very tall. Way taller than you. Um, he's got the strangest looking cap. It's canvas with a leather brim and weird metal brackets on his forehead." She chuckles. "My headband is wrapped around it. Huge smile with a full set of teeth. No jacket, just a set of truly filthy overalls. He's wearing your medallion around his neck and…um just one small detail…he uh…he's missing his right arm…all the way up to his shoulder."

"Good to know, I guess."

"Yeah, so don't try to shake his right-hand cause ya know… you'll come up empty."

"Right. Just how I imagined the spirit of the shafts."

Katie opens her door. "Wait for me. There's a rough patch before we get to the garage."

Minutes later they are on firmer footing. Colin releases his grip from his cousin as she
sweetly says, "well, you must be Artemis. I'm Katie…and this is…"

"Hi, I'm Colin. Can I have my medal back now?"

An incredibly deep voice, soothing and slow, says with a chuckle, *"that's not how it works Colin. But don't worry. No tomfoolery here. It's a beautiful medallion by the way."*

"It belonged to my grandfather. He got it for his artillery service in the First World War."

"Ah, the Great War. The war to end all wars. How foolish huh?"

"Yeah, I guess, but I really need it back."

"You know Colin…and I'm sorry…you too Katie, I apologize for my lack of manners. You know, this medal has special meaning for miners, too."

Colin listens curiously as Katie, asks, "is that so? What's the meaning…Artemis?"

"Well, Saint Barbara is the patron saint of miners. A lot of families of lost souls prayed to her -- that's a fact. I'm sure my family was doing a lot of praying back in June of '96. Must have been extra sad for them."

"Extra sad?"

"Well Katie, my twin baby boys were supposed to be baptized the next day. Bittersweet, wouldn't you say?"

"Oh, I'm sorry. I didn't know."

"Don't be sad now. Just revisiting those memories. That's what I do when I see old friends like Pete again. Looking fine in his O'Malley's jacket…same as he was wearing that day."

"I remember seeing you too, Artie."

"That's right. Pete was down in the number six vein with Sean and Danny. I was there to take a trip of empty cars over to the other side of the shaft for the next day. Where I hitched the mule on to the car the grade was kind of steep. So, as I recall I only took three cars…instead of the usual four you see. At the foot of the shaft, I passed some drivers going in with loaded cars. I don't remember their names. There was a huge rush of air, and somebody yelled, 'look out for the gas.' I pulled off my cap and blew off my light to prevent an explosion. And then a ferocious wind came along. I could hear the coal cracking and tearing and striking against the back of the last car. Those cars were moving down the gangway at a frightful rate of speed. I made the mistake of grabbing on. Lost a limb in the process. The dust was choking and the darkness terrible and that's the last thing I remember."

"Artie, I'm troubled by my memories in a different way."

"Tell me, Pete. It helps to talk about it."

"I remember my shoes being blown off. I remember finding a small opening next to a pillar that had not fully collapsed. Barely breathing, I kept crawling in complete darkness maybe several yards. It wasn't very far...near a trickle of water. I don't know how long I was there. I remember now… for the very first time…I was thinking that each breath I took would be my last. And earlier today, with the help of my Coleen, something else came back to me."

"Go on Pete…keep going."

Colin blurts out, "Papa Pete are you okay? Katie, is he okay?"

"Colin, trust me when I say he has never looked better, alright? Don't interrupt him. If I can shut up, so can you…"

Colin leans against Katie. He buries his head in clenched fists.

"What are you remembering my friend?"

"She reminded us about a rescue attempt from the Clear Spring shaft."

"Many souls have shared their stories of hearing the tapping in that rescue tunnel."

"Well, I heard it too. I was too weak to respond. I took my last breath listening to the tapping. But, but..."

"Keep sharing."

"I'm troubled by another event within Clear Spring that has nothing to do with our demise. I believe it's why I'm here today. I believe it has to do with my grandson. Colin's father. Katie's uncle. I need your help to take us there."

"We are true ghosts, Pete. Living in a place that joins two worlds together. We are trapped in that unexplainable place, stuck between what is spiritual and what is real. I can take you to the physical place but do not surrender to the false impression that I can somehow deliver a satisfactory solution. I cannot – because I'm trapped too."

"Katie, I have no idea what he just said. Do you?"

"Hell, no. But count me in. Let's go."

"Tomorrow. I will meet you back here tomorrow at 8:00 AM."

Katie growls, "now we have to wait?"

"It's for your safety. Too much rain the last couple days. Too unpredictable down there. Not to mention time of day. You need to allow for plenty of time, not just getting in but back out, you see? There's no risk for Pete and me. But you will need daylight to guide Colin and proper equipment of course for the journey. I'll have that ready for you as well."

Colin asks, "How long are we talking?"

"A considerable length of time and distance."

"And you're keeping my medallion, of course."

"Definitely. Yes. It's giving off a lot of positive energy by the way."

"Yeah, well don't get too comfy with it. I don't want you

taking it back to whatever world you're stuck in, okay?"

"Understood Colin. Until tomorrow."

CHAPTER 52

Riddle Solved

Sunday June 28, 1970 – 7:15 AM
74 Years Since the Twin Shafts Collapse

Colin leans against the phone booth outside the motel office, twenty paces from the room where he barely slept. Threadbare evidence, taped conversations, lying to the police. Eyewitness accounts from dead people. All the ingredients he needed for last night's wave of insomnia. He toys with his braille watch, recalling Katie's brief instructions before retiring. "See you at 7:30 tomorrow morning. I want to grab some coffee before the one-armed miner has his way with us. Remember, 7:30 sharp."

Colin flips open the glass cover of his watch. It's 7:15. The ground shakes from nearby truck traffic. He opens the phone booth and rests his hand on the cradled handset...willing it to ring now. The phone is slippery with morning dew. He fumbles with his watch. It's 7:20. He listens for the sound of Katie's door opening. Still quiet. He's tempted to check his watch again, but the call is already late. Too late. He starts counting off the paces back to his room. One. Two. Three. He absentmindedly grabs for his missing medallion. Seven. Eight. Nine. The phone rings. He swivels and slides his hand along the wall as he skips back to the booth. The next ring is interrupted as he answers, "hello."

"Colin?"

"Yes. It's me."

"Okay, you're all set...hey, you still there?"

"I'm here. Thank you."

"Good luck."

Colin returns to his room, closes the door, and exhales slowly. The door of the adjoining room rattles loudly. Katie's groggy voice asks, "hey, you ready to roll? It's 7:30"

"I'm ready! Meet you out front."

They end up grabbing coffee from the motel office. Hot water, Nescafé, and Coffee-Mate. "We serve better crap on the airplane," gripes Katie as they retrace their route to O'Malley's. Within five minutes they are perched again in front of the garage. Katie informs Colin that Papa Pete and Artie are waiting. There's something else. It's Papa Pete's appearance.

Kate explains. "Standing next to Artie, it's so noticeable. I can actually see through Papa Pete. He's not solid. He's disintegrating…falling apart right in front of me. Don't say anything to him, Colin. Don't remind him," she says sadly.

"This is it, Katie. We're almost out of time."

Some equipment is loaded into the car and the group is quickly on its way. Artie informs the group that the Clear Spring shaft is about three miles as the crow flies, maybe a ten-minute drive. He takes the time to prepare Katie and Colin for what to expect.

"Since neither of you have ever been in a mine, I know it can be hard to comprehend, but this is tough terrain even for the most accomplished, so be prepared for some slow going. I need you to understand the vastness of anthracite mining. Now, right here, in Northeastern Pennsylvania you're talking about a coal area that's about 62 miles long and about 5 miles wide. In the deepest part of the basin, a little south of here near Wilkes Barre, the thickness of the coal measures about 2,000 feet. Around these ways it's a little less, but still considerable. Digging these mines, large or small was dangerous work. Cave-ins, explosions, fires, poisonous gas, regular work accidents. A lot of lives were cut short. Pete and I can attest to that. So, stick together, listen to what I say, and wear the equipment I brought. Including boots."

Katie gags. "I have to wear somebody else's shoes? That's

disgusting."

Papa Pete snickers and Artie howls, adding, *"yes ma'am. If you want to save those petite feet of yours. Trust me."*

"Artie is correct. It's best to listen. Now, this mine, Clear Shaft, was run by a different company than owned Twin Shaft. They offered the men and resources to dig the rescue tunnel within their shaft. As we already know their attempt failed."

Artie interrupts.

"Katie, turn off the main road up here and take great care with your automobile. Take it slow and when I tell you to stop, don't go an inch further. Now, all these bootleggers back during the depression did a number on most of these shafts. Mind you, they didn't go into the shafts, cause most of them were still in operation. Instead, they'd sneak their way in from the top or from the side, kind of building their own entrances. Today, now today, the modern bootleggers – and there ain't too many of them – just find themselves an abandoned shaft and take their chances. Okay, stop right here."

Katie breaks immediately.

"Well done. Well done. Everybody out."

Katie opens the trunk and gasps. "What the hell am I supposed to do with all of this. Ropes and lights, and..." She rattles bells. "These, along with the most grotesque boots that are twice my size. Don't worry, Colin...there's a matching set for you. Well, Papa Pete and Artie are way ahead of us having a rather animated conversation. Artie's one arm is flapping rapidly. Oh, he's waving for us, sorry. Grab this stuff and let's go."

By the time the cousins reach Artie and Papa Pete they have moved considerably. Colin is holding fiercely to Katie's oversized jacket. He considers switching with her since he can barely fit into the one that he's wearing. She stops abruptly.

"There it is. Not what I expected. Pretty nondescript. Lots of rocks. Lots of weeds. A small wood-framed opening in a tiny little hill."

"Remember Katie, some of these tunnels are as deep as the Eiffel

Tower is high. Don't be swayed. Follow me and Pete."

With her flashlight on, Katie does her best to describe what she sees inside the opening. It gets wider faster, she tells Colin. There's a bunch of debris, including beer bottles and trash from McDonalds. Big metal buckets are scattered everywhere. Along with a lot of 55-gallon drums. And lines of wheelbarrows. Artie explains.

"Bootleggers get coal up to the entrance any way they can. They don't have cars on rails or sophisticated conveyor systems. They are in and out, moving around and laying low. When people like Pete's grandson show up with a truck, everybody pitches in. These are heavy loads. I'd say one of these 5-gallon buckets probably weighs 35 pounds or so when its filled with anthracite. And lord, those drums, nearly ten times as much, easy. There's a lot of sweat and exchanging of money and everybody is on their way."

"Grateful for the history Artie, but..."

"But that's not why you're here. Sorry, Pete. You're here to get to the rescue tunnel. Okay, here's the plan..."

Artie's instructions are quite simple. Papa Pete will lead the way. There is plenty of rope to get them to the site, which Artie has clearly marked on the map for Papa Pete. One end of the thick rope is anchored to a piling near the entrance of the mine. The other is tethered to a harness Colin is wearing. As the group proceeds the rope will unfurl behind them. At any time, they can use the tethered chord to retrace their steps. Extra batteries are in the pockets of their jackets just in case. One more thing. This is the end of the line for Artie. Pete gently protests. His old friend laughs politely.

"Now, now Pete. You won't get lost. I served my purpose here... delivered you to this place. Mighty proud to do it. Happy to see you and to meet your wonderful kin. I hope you discover your reason for being misplaced...the purpose you served in overlapping two worlds. I hope you find peace...and reach the other side."

Pete does not respond to Artie. He merely offers instruction in the flattest of tones.

"Katie, please turn on your light so you can follow me. Colin,

this shorter piece of rope is connected to your cousin." Colin feels his harness click. *"Just in case you two get separated."*

Right now, Colin's world is void of subtle shadows, muted sunlight, and the unexpected splash of the moon at its fullest. Total darkness withholds all of that. Katie's flashlight serves no purpose. He clings desperately to her. They stumble frequently but maintain a steady pace. At one point the rope unwinding behind him becomes taut.

"Hold on. something snagged the rope." For the first time he let's go of his cousin. His heart races as he leaves her, carefully gripping the rope with every stride. He finds the problem. He frees the rope from a tight crevice and immediately feels it slacken. That panics him even more and he begins tugging himself forward until Katie grabs him.

"Hey, it's okay. You're okay. Just say a prayer to Saint Barbara."

Before her words fully resonate Colin is already ripping the ill-fitting jacket away from his chest. "He has it. The medallion. Artie never returned it to me. We have to go back and get it." He stops talking, knowing how foolish that sounds. Panting deeply, he mutters, "phantom thief." The pace quickens again.

For the first time Colin hears water trickling. It gets louder. His footing changes, a bit sloppier. The ground is wet. His boots settle into some deeper water. Katie advises him to stay to his left. They are approaching a large puddle. She's unsure how deep it is. He presses against the rock, surprised by its warmth. He jiggles the trailing rope and hears it splash behind him.

He guesses they have been walking for at least 45 minutes. He wonders how deep beneath the earth they are. For the first time since they left Artie behind, Papa Pete speaks.

"We're approaching the rescue tunnel. Soon we'll turn left. Stay close now. Don't dilly dally."

Panting, Katie yells, "where else would I go for God's sake?"

Almost immediately she says to Colin, "we're turning. We're here."

Everything slows down. They are still moving but something is holding them back. He tugs Katie. “What’s going on? What’s the holdup?”

“He’s the holdup. Papa Pete. He’s barely moving.”

Suddenly, Colin feels a hard tug of the rope. “Hold up. Hold up. I think we’re out of rope. Katie, can you see it?”

Her arm gently pushes him to the right. “Let me see.”

A dot of light barely registers. “I see it. Yeah, looks like Artie underestimated our little trip. So, what now?”

“We are here.”

“Really, this is it?”

“We’ve gone far enough.”

Colin questions, “Papa Pete, does that mean we’ve arrived or you’re not willing to go any further?”

“A little of both, I suppose. Just a few feet more is where they stopped digging and started tapping. On the other side was where I heard them. My final resting place.”

Katie’s voice is hushed. “They were so close. You could have made it.”

“No. Katie. It was too late. But then...almost 70 years later, something happened on <u>*this*</u> *side of the wall. Something that set in motion the journey I’ve been on for nearly four years. An energy was created here that was out of my control. Beyond my understanding. Until now.”*

Katie begins to softly sob. Colin hugs her from behind. Her whole body is shaking.

“Colin, your lack of vision right now is both a blessing and a curse. I’m not sure which is stronger. There is something here you need to experience, in the only way you know how. Katie, please take his hand and together be the brave people I know you are.”

Katie squeezes Colin’s hand. “You ready?”

Before taking a step, he says, “where is he? I want to touch him.”

Katie shudders and moves forward with Colin. “Oh, no, no, no. My Uncle Tommy. My sweet, sweet friend. He saved me. He saved my life. He didn’t deserve this.”

Colin drops to his knees and carefully reaches forward until...he touches his father's remains. Expecting to feel flesh, he recoils at the sensation of fabric stuck to a wasted frame

Katie sputters through half-breaths. "Bones. Just bones. There's still some red hair. It's him."

Colin gently moves his quivering hand everywhere. Unsure of what he's touching. Afraid to disturb this brittle peace. "Where is his hand, his left hand?"

Katie tenderly guides him. "Here. Right here, Colin."

He finds the wrist. With his index finger he glides over the exposed joints of a hand that held him tightly on the way to get ice cream. He doesn't stop until the tip of his finger finds the wedding ring. He pinches it and reverently spins it between his thumb and index finger. He feels his tears dripping onto his own fleshy hand. He lets go and lets his body slump back into the loving arms of his cousin.

Katie buries her head in his shoulder. Lifts her head briefly and hesitates. "What the hell? What the bloody hell?"

"What is it?"

"Shell casings. There are shell casings on the ground."

Colin gropes the ground.

"No, no. Don't touch. We shouldn't touch. This is a crime scene."

"Katie, I'm going to stay with him a little longer."

"Colin, buddy, we should go. We need to get the police."

"The police are already here."

"What do you mean? I'm not following."

"I promise I'll explain everything real soon. Right now, follow that rope and go as fast as you can to the top. When you get there, I hope to God you find somebody waiting for you who's carrying a badge."

"Okay, okay. Don't move."

"He forces a laugh. Okay, I promise. And Katie?"

"Yeah?"

"Leave a flashlight. Just in case you have a hard time finding me."

"Not funny. Okay, I'm going. I love you, Colin."

"I love you, too. Hurry."

Colin is used to sitting in darkness, but this is different. Aside from the sound of Katie's echoing footsteps, he is isolated like never before. He clicks the flashlight on and playfully shines it towards…nothing. Yet, something moves in front of him. He *sees* it. He actually *sees* it. "Papa Pete?" No answer. His pulse quickens. He gently reaches to his right for the shape of his father's body, but his fingers find nothing. On all fours now he is groping the ground more aggressively still mindful of disturbing the corpse. It's missing. Panic sets in. Katie is gone. Papa Pete is...where the hell is he? A distinct shuffling sound bounces off the chamber walls.

The air is much cooler.

"Hey, Pal."

"Papa Pete?"

"When did Papa Pete ever call you 'pal,' huh? Hey, point that light over here."

Colin fumbles with the flashlight. Shakily, he aims the light and sees him. His father. Not a muddled image. Not a blur. Tommy Byrne. In the flesh.

"Dad, am I cracking up?"

"Probably, but a lot of crazy things are happening right now so let's go with it."

"You look magnificent. I mean…I always imagined how you would look. Aww, hell I don't know what I'm saying."

"Thomas, our time is limited."

"Papa Pete, I can see you too."

"I'm grateful for our time together Colin. Thank you for your patience with me…but I…we…must leave. There's clarity now. You have the truth. You trusted my intuition and now you can get closure, too."

"You can't just leave. It sounds so final. You just found each other."

"No, we found each other the moment Moretti committed murder. That's when I met him."

"You never knew him, but you met him."

"Yes, the riddle is solved. I was on the other side of this pillar the moment my grandson's life was taken. The rest is unexplainable. My path from darkness to the light is illogical. Absurd, really. Now your father needs to move on too. There's no reason for him to be bound here anymore. You have the truth."

"You keep saying that, Papa Pete. What truth do I have?"

"Thomas, perhaps you would care to respond."

"Well, most important, I loved you and your mom. I never abandoned you. Never. Son, I'm sorry you had to discover me this way. But all the hard work that you, and Katie, endured...I think you knew this was the inevitable conclusion."

"I guess. But refusing to believe it gave me hope. A reason to keep going, you know?"

"I understand. But now that you know why, there's nothing more for us to do."

"Can you tell me *how*. What happened down here?"

"Moretti was a curse I couldn't shake. The moment I borrowed money from him, my fate was sealed. Desperate, I threatened him that I was going to go directly to his bosses and tell them he was skimming. I thought that would get his attention. He would be in big trouble if they knew he was taking cash off the top. He was wavering. I really thought I had him. A few days after I gave him the ultimatum, we had just picked up the map from Coleen for this run. We drove his truck here and he was strangely friendly and upbeat all the way. That made me nervous. He went to the shaft to check things out, so I hid Coleen's map. Don't ask me why. I was flying on instinct. We loaded the truck with a decent haul, paid the miners and they took off. We were getting ready to leave and he got all apologetic with me. Said he wanted to settle things fair and square. I was willing to give the guy a break. I mean, I just wanted him off my back. Figured my threat had finally gotten through to him. Then he told me about an extra load of coal sitting in wheelbarrows down here in this tunnel. Easily worth a couple extra hundred bucks that the miners said we could have if we hauled it out on our own. As a peace offering, he promised that I could have

all the dough. No strings attached. So, I agreed. Figured, why not? We got down here and started pulling out the coal. That's when he shot me. Right in the back of the head. Three times. Kind of overkill, don't you think?"

"What happened next, dad? I mean, something had to happen."

Papa Pete politely interrupts.

"I happened Colin. Suddenly I had a purpose. First with Coleen, then with you. Every time you got closer to the truth, I got wiser. My purpose became clearer. It's impossible to explain because it's incomprehensible for somebody with two feet planted in your world. But for me, it was finding peace and the truth. And now... I'm almost there. One step closer to retribution."

Colin stammers, "I don't understand...what do you mean...?" He hears distant voices. His heart races. "They're coming. What do I tell Katie?"

"Just tell her the truth."

"What about mom? She's waiting to hear. How can I tell her I found you like this?"

"You have no choice. You can't fix the truth. But you can give her this."

He reaches out his hand

"You know I can't touch you, son. Open your hand."

Colin extends his palm and his father's wedding rings lands gently on his quivering fingers.

"When you give this to mom, tell her I said, 'you are my forever.' Got it?"

"Yeah, she'll like that. She'll love it. I love you."

"I love you too, pal. Now, you've done all that you can do. Promise me you'll move on."

"I will. I'm not sure how, but I will."

The voices are much closer now. Colin can hear Katie barking directions.

"Papa Pete, thank you. I can't believe this is it. Who's going to clean my room?"

Tell Katie I enjoyed her odd behavior. Forgive your mom. That's what your dad would do. Be nice to Ben, okay? And Charlene, now...she's a wild one. Do you think you can handle her?"

"I want to give it a try, if she'll let me."

Colin hears the clunking of Katie's oversized boots. They are in the rescue tunnel.

Papa Pete's final words, still emotionless to the end, skewer Colin. *"Together we found the truth. But justice may be untouchable."*

"Colin I'm back...we're here...are you okay?"

"I'm okay. It's nice to hear your voice again."

He turns on his flashlight, leans back against the pillar of coal that separated Papa Pete from his grandson. He waves the light slowly while his right hand gropes the ground until it touches the remains of his dad. "We're right here Katie."

CHAPTER 53

Good Enough

Sunday -- Noon

Katie tosses her boots into the trunk of her car. "What the hell are we supposed to do with all this equipment? We can't exactly return the stuff to Artie. Here, let me help you with that." She removes Colin's harness then grabs the sleeve of his jacket. "God this thing is tight, how could you breathe?"

"Wasn't easy, but I took one for the team. Listen, there are some things I need to tell you."

"Colin, my head is spinning. I want to hear it all, but let's wrap things up and get the hell out of here, okay? I'm sure you want to see Hannah too. I know I do. Give me your boots."

Colin leans against the open trunk and kicks off his boots. Katie hands him his sneakers. "Thanks. Never thought I would miss my Chuck Taylors so much." He slides his feet into his high tops and loosely ties the laces. "You ready?"

"I guess Detective Burgoyne needs to give us the okay. So, why did he show up here?"

"I thought you wanted to get the hell out of here?"

Katie hesitates. "Just tell me. What's the connection?"

"I called Tracey last night and told her where we were going and what we thought we might find. She was ready to help. She said she had a very trusted friend high up the chain of command with the Pennsylvania State Police. I gave her the location and the background on the map. The last thing she asked me was 'do you trust your source? Can I make this call with confidence?' I told her I did. She called me this morning and confirmed her friend was coming in an "unofficial" capacity."

"Well, it's official now, trust me."

"I'm sorry I didn't tell you. In case it didn't work out I didn't want you to have to share the blame or lie…we've done enough of that."

Katie hugs him. "Taking another one for the team. I'm sort of bummed that you didn't tell me, but I'm super proud of you too. It took a lot of guts Colin. You can't believe how many uniforms there are around here. Okay, he's walking our way. He's a badass by the way."

A calm, authoritative voice interrupts. "Colin, Katie, I think we have what we need for now. Our detectives will be in touch to follow through on our investigation. Listen, I'm sorry for all you've gone through. I'm sure it's been a tough day. I'll let you go…oh, just curious, where did you get all this equipment? Seems like you actually knew what you were doing down there?"

Colin blurts out, "we borrowed it…from O'Malley's over in Moosic."

"Yeah, I know where it is. They've been closed a bit. Heard they were going to reopen it as a museum. So, who did you borrow it from?"

Katie chimes in. "Well, truth is we kind of took it. I mean… we didn't know it was closed. The garage was open and so we just took what we needed. We're going to return it all, right Colin?"

"Yes sir. Right now. We'll do it right now."

"Uh, huh. Tell you what."

He brushes past Colin.

"Let me take this stuff off your hands. I'll see that it's all returned." Colin can hear the equipment piling up on the ground. "Watch yourself there, Colin."

Colin moves aside. The trunk gently closes.

"Besides, home for you is in the opposite direction, so why

go out of your way, right? You've done enough today. Be careful getting to the main road. Take your time. We'll be in touch."

A few minutes later, Katie's 442 is roaring home. It's silent for a long time.

Colin finally asks, "so do you want to talk?"

"I do, yeah but not now. Let's just drive for a bit. We've got plenty of time to catch up. Oh, by the way, you didn't tell me you got your medallion back."

"What?" He grabs his chest and gets a handful of Saint Barbara. "I don't understand."

"Can't explain it?"

"No, I can't."

"Good enough for me."

CHAPTER 54

Farewell

Thursday July 2, 1970 -- 11:00 AM

Tommy Byrne was buried this morning in the family plot at a Catholic cemetery very close to Carbondale. He received full military honors and rests beside his parents -- just yards away from a memorial stone dedicated to his grandfather who was buried alive in the Twin Shafts disaster. Colin clings to the miraculous image of his dad in the tunnel. His final gesture, the wedding ring, is now linked to a gold necklace on his mother's neck. Katie helped him pick it out.

As Colin sits alone by Papa Pete's memorial stone, he senses Katie's presence.

"You okay, buddy?"

He pulls her down on the cool grass. "Sit here with me."

She eases down and nudges him playfully. "You've got that 'I need to tell you something' tone to your voice."

He smiles and rubs the stone. It feels more like glass. "Sort of. Well, just hear me out, okay? I've had more time to process this?"

Katie's voice turns more serious. "Process what?"

"Read the words on this memorial."

"Okay," she says skeptically.

DEDICATED TO THE LIFE OF PETER BYRNE,
ONE OF 58 SOULS WHO DIED TRAGICALLY IN THE
TWIN SHAFTS MINING DISASTER IN PITTSTON,
PENNSYLVANIA ON JUNE 28, 1896.

MAY THEY ALL REST IN PEACE.

"Papa Pete didn't die on June 28th," Colin declares.

"Not following."

"Since he was fading fast, we figured we would lose him by June 28th, the day of the collapse. That was your 'supernatural shit' theory...I think you called it."

"Probably. Sounds intelligent enough."

"But he didn't die on June 28th.

She sighs heavily. "You need to let go of this."

"Hear me out...please Katie?"

"Okay, okay."

"Papa Pete showed up at Aunt Coleen's house on July 2, 1966. Why? Something happened to trigger his appearance. That something was the murder of my father. Remember, Sterling Honeycutt's notes about the witnesses who saw Moretti without my father on July 2nd? That's the day Moretti shot him in the cave. And a few feet away from that spot...on the other side of the wall...in the rescue chamber was Papa Pete."

Katie's curious voice interrupts and continues. "And Papa Pete told us that he heard the rescue attempt...the tapping on the wall...drinking from a pool of water...waiting. Slowly suffocating. For days. Oh God, how horrible. How many days?"

"Katie, I believe he also died on July 2nd. And then, on the *same* day 70 years later when my father was murdered, Papa Pete was released to...to...find the truth and get peace for our family—that's what he told us."

"Super...supernatural shit," Katie remarks slowly. Then, sullenly, "but what does any of that matter? We got all the answers we're going to get. We can't go to the police with testimony from two ghosts. Moretti got the gun. And if he had a morsel of intelligence, he got rid of it already. So, we got half of Papa Pete's deal. The truth, yes. But peace...not so much."

"Unless he's not finished."

"Maybe you were deprived of oxygen down in those caves."

She grabs him. “Come on…let’s go to the luncheon and have a beer.”

He pulls sharply away. “I’m not finished. In the cave, when we were sharing our goodbyes, Papa Pete said something that has been gnawing at me.” He pauses. “Maybe I am crazy.”

“Really? For Christ’s sake tell me what he said.”

“He said, ‘I’m almost there Colin. One step closer to *retribution*.’ Exact words…I promise.”

“Man, we couldn’t just have a nice funeral. Have you told anyone else your little theory?”

“Of course not. You’re the only unstable one I can talk to.”

She laughs and pulls him away from the stone. This time he doesn’t resist. He’s got nothing left. Katie urges him to rejoin the group. “They’re leaving for the luncheon so get your head back in the game. Plus, look at it this way. Today is July 2nd. One way or another, your little theory will be validated or denied very soon.”

CHAPTER 55

Just One More Thing

Thursday -- 1:00 PM

Tracey Honeycutt embraces Colin. "It's good to see you again."

"Thanks for coming. It means a lot." He wraps his arm around his mom's shoulder. "To both of us." Colin turns toward his mom who pulls him closer. She gently adjusts his necktie. "How much longer is this staying on?"

Colin teases, "three more minutes."

Tracey laughs. "Well, it was a beautiful service. Your dad would be proud, I'm sure. And I'm so happy to see Ben here."

Colin feels the same way. Everyone is encouraged by Ben's presence. He's moving slowly, still forgetting more than he remembers. But the doctors are confident his condition is temporary. They call it post-traumatic amnesia, which is a sign his brain is healing. They could all use some mending.

Beyond that Colin still needs answers -- from Charlie. The ban on phone calls has been lifted by her father, but she warns he's still super protective. "Don't worry," she told Colin. "He'll come around. He's just got a lot to worry about right now." While Colin selfishly needs clarity, he knows Charlie's parents need her more. Her mom's cancer is winning. So, her priority is to be with her family and to give her burned-out dad some relief.

Talking to Mr. Stiles would make him feel better, but he didn't make the funeral either. It was too much to ask him to leave Gerrit Street. Maybe they'll be together soon, sitting on the porch...solving the world's problems. Bottom fact, he could use a stiff dose of his old friend.

After a quiet lunch full of small talk and shared memories, the group moves to the bar for a final toast to Tommy. Hannah slides a shot glass in front of Colin. "It's Jameson's. Your dad approves, especially since it's the last drink you'll have until you graduate college, right?"

He laughs. Holds the glass close to his nose. Places it back on the bar. "Do you mind if I just
have a beer?" Hannah kisses his hand as Katie's voice commands the bar.

"Those we love don't go away. They walk beside us every day, unseen, unheard, but always near, Still loved, still missed and very dear. God bless Tommy Byrne. I love you Uncle Tommy."

Colin whispers softly, "I love you dad." He barely sips his beer.

The small group quickly disperses. Hannah suggests to Colin that they get going. "Ben did great today, but he needs his rest. Katie's ready too, so let's roll."

"Mom, is Tracey still here?"

"Yeah, she's at the end of the bar, talking to Katie, why?"

Well, if it's okay with her, would you mind if we drove back together? I just need to talk through a few things with her. Please?"

"Yeah, honey. I'm sure Tracey would be okay with that. I'll go ask her."

Colin stands up. "Just point me in the right direction. I'll ask her."

Five minutes later, Colin is settled into the thin, contoured front seat of Tracey's 1965 Volkswagen Beetle convertible. The top is down and he's grateful. The gentle humming of the rear air-cooled engine is a perfect accompaniment to the warmish July breeze.

"Sorry for the tight squeeze Colin. I bet you wish you stayed in Katie's car, right?"

"No. This feels great. I hope you don't mind doing this."

"Not at all. I love the company. Just warning you, I do the speed limit. Now, what's up?"

Colin squirms sideways in his cramped seat. "I know it's early. The police are dealing with a lot of stuff."

"The wheels of justice are slow Colin, and sometimes you don't get the result you want."

"TOGETHER WE FOUND THE TRUTH. BUT JUSTICE MAY BE UNTOUCHABLE."

He smiles. "Yeah, I've recently been told that."

"Tough to hear, I know but it's better to be realistic. Listen, nobody wants that bastard nailed more than me. He stole the love of my life. And I know the hell he put your family through. But..."

"Just tell me. Tell me what you think."

It's clear to Colin this is not the first time she's thought about all the possibilities. She lays out the facts quickly.

The number one challenge is the gun that fired the bullets killing her husband and Colin's dad. She's confident the ballistics report will confirm the bullets came from the same gun. That would give them the "fingerprints." Unfortunately, they still don't have the "finger" – the gun. Unless they can connect the Luger to Moretti, their case gets incredibly tougher.

Colin presses her. "But all the evidence. Your husband's detailed notes. The map my dad kept. How he bribed my mom...and swindled my dad. What about the way he set up my dad for the robbery of Mrs. Judson? That poor woman went to the grave thinking my dad stole from her." Colin is all over the place. "The people who saw Moretti in the truck before and after my dad disappeared. What about the bootleg miners? They were the last to see him alive. They could help."

"Colin, take a breather, okay. You asked me what I thought and that's what I'm sharing. All the things you mentioned are shitty, but none of that makes him a murderer. And don't kid yourself. The police are already talking to the bootleg miners. Those guys are not going to admit to anything. Nobody saw anything incriminating, unless you have some surprise witness you haven't told me about."

HE SUFFOCATED AUNT COLEEN. HE SHOT MY DAD THREE TIMES IN THE BACK OF THE HEAD. THEY TOLD ME THEMSELVES.

"Nope. Nothing."

The remainder of the drive is spent on small talk. Ben's recovery. Colin's music scholarship. His plans beyond school. Subtle reminders for Colin that sooner or later, he must move on. He feels the medallion beneath his dress shirt.

"YOU'VE DONE ALL THAT YOU COULD DO.
PROMISE ME YOU'LL MOVE ON."

The Beetle finally creeps through Colin's neighborhood. Tracey tells him that Katie's car is already parked in front of his house. She laughs. "I'm sure she arrived way ahead of us. Oh, here." She hands him his cane. "Do you need help getting to the house?"

He tilts his head and smiles. "Nah, I could do it blindfolded." He opens the door, tilts sideways to exit the car. Tracey suddenly grabs his shoulder.

"Sorry, Colin. Just one more thing. I should have asked you sooner."

"What is it?" He settles back into his seat.

"Did your mom talk to you about my notebook? The one that disappeared from my house?" Colin stiffens. Nervously, he replies, "Um, she may have mentioned it."

"I'll take that as a yes. So, do you have any idea who may have taken it?"

Colin can't think fast enough. He babbles, "Tracey, I can't believe I'm using this expression already, but on my father's grave, I promise you my mom didn't take it."

Her laugh is gentle. "Easy does it," she says soothingly. The odd thing is that I found it yesterday in my hall closet. Completely by accident."

"I NEED TO ERASE THAT BLEMISH FROM MY SOUL."

"I have no idea how it got back in your house. I swear."

"Fair enough. Your mom is innocent. I never doubted that. And how it got back is a mystery to you. I guess I must believe that too."

Colin sighs in relief. "Thank you."

"You're welcome. But you never answered my question. Who *took* it?"

CHAPTER 56

Hushed Tones

Thursday -- 3:00 PM

Colin opens the front door to oddly hushed tones coming from the kitchen. He moves freely to the swinging door, leans in, and pushes firmly. He senses the immediate brightness of the room. Since his time in the mine, he swears that the presence of light, any light, feels oddly different to him. He hears Katie's voice first.

"Hey, Colin."

"Hey, what's up? When did you get back?"

This time it's Ben. "We're glad you're here."

"Mom?"

"I'm here. I'm right here." Her hand softly brushes his arm. Lingers on his shoulder.

"Okay, something's up. What's going on?"

Hannah continues. "Mr. Stiles he uh…"

Colin's heart drops. "What happened? Is he okay?"

Katie quickly responds. "Oh yeah, buddy. He's okay. He's fine. He just called."

Colin's heart is pounding. "Thank God. You had me worried there." He moves toward the refrigerator then abruptly stops and cocks his head back to his family. "Why did he call?"

His mother's voice is vacant. "Gino Moretti is dead. He shot himself. In his apartment."

Colin's question comes immediately. "With what?"

"His German Luger."

CHAPTER 57

Any Way You Look At It

Monday September 7, 1970 (Labor Day)

Colin speaks to the slightly swaying hammock. "Don't you think you should get up there and help Mr. Taylor with your burgers?"

Ben's relaxed reply is interrupted by a gulp of beer. "Nah, looks like Frank has commandeered the barbecue. It's the first time I've seen him out of uniform. Trust me, he looks even more imposing in his Harley t-shirt. I think I'll just hang out here."

"You're doing great Ben. Amazing progress."

"Thanks Colin. I feel better every day. Details of the break-in are still kind of fuzzy, but they said that's the last to come. So, it's all good."

A round of laughter erupts from the house. Colin shakes his head. "Katie must be here."

"So that's everybody, right? Tracey. Charlie and her dad. And your old pal Mr. Stiles, too. That's a nice surprise."

"Yeah, Charlie and her dad went out of their way to pick him up. Sounds like Mr. Taylor quit his night job too, so things are less tense. Charlie's aunt is staying with her mom for a few hours so I'm grateful...you know... spending their free time with us. Our family. That's nice."

"Sure is. So, what about you and Charlie. Anything there?"

"It's hard to say. Today is the first time I've seen her since the hospital. We've hardly talked, really. Besides, we'll see each other in school so plenty of time, right?"

"I think that's wise, Colin. Hey, can you grab me another beer?"

Colin plunges his hand into the ice chest and plucks a bottle from the bottom. He finds the tethered opener and pops the cap, taking a swig before giving it to Ben.

"Feel free to have one."

"No, I'm good."

Katie's loud greeting drifts down from the top of the yard. "Hey boys. Save some beer for me." Colin waves both hands. Ben laughs then says, "I know it's been tough Colin, but this is nice...being together, like this."

"Almost normal. Right?"

"Speaking of normal, How's it feel without a ghost in your house?"

"Ben, you don't have to whisper. Nobody can hear you."

Ben giggles sheepishly. "You're right." Then, thoughtfully he says, "that whole experience for you...It's hard to wrap my head around it."

Colin leans in harder to the topic. "Actually, I had a question for you. Something I didn't feel comfortable talking about when Papa Pete was around."

"Something you didn't want him to hear?"

"Yeah, stuff about his personality that always made me curious."

"Now *I'm* curious." Another beer bottle pops open.

Colin doesn't hold back. "He had a vengeful side. I don't know if that's the right word but that's how I would describe it." It feels meaningful for Colin as he paints a pattern for Ben. When Pete got his scar. When the landscaper "accidentally" broke his ankle. When Moretti met the frying pan. Maybe something else...something more.

"You've certainly given this some thought," Ben replies in a cautionary tone. "But be careful to draw too much into a few events that don't necessarily define the behavior of a person...or a spirit or ghost in your case...who you knew for barely a year. The things you described to me, while vengeful acts, could just be spur of the moment reactions. Defending the honor of his wife. Protecting you from a bully. Punishing Moretti for attacking me."

"You're losing me."

Well, there are overly protective people in our lives...and then there are people seriously affected by a defining moment that causes embitterment.

"What's that?"

"Colin, I'm no expert. Very little research has been done on this..."

"Then just give me your unofficial opinion, okay?"

"Alright, so you get pissed off at somebody. Really angry. But...then it fades. It's transient. You get on with your life, right? Embitterment *doesn't* fade. It flares up every time the person is reminded of the triggering event.

"It festers," Colin suggests.

"That's a good description, Colin. Better than mine. So, as that embitterment against the person who harmed you festers, it could even cause fantasies of revenge that grow stronger and stronger..."

"And more dangerous?"

"They could, I guess. Probably depends on the triggering event. In my opinion it would have to be something that causes a grave insult, humiliation, injustice..."

"Like the murder of your grandson?"

"Okay, that's enough. You're taxing my fragile brain."

"Sorry, I didn't mean for that to get so deep. I should just let it go anyway. Sooner or later, I need to get on with my life."

"Well, it's healthy to talk about..." Ben pauses. Colin hears the hammock release its weight. Ben shuffles past him. "What is this? I'm not sure, but this looks like..."

"What Ben...what's up?"

"In the tree, lodged in the tree up here. It looks like a... a bullet maybe? I mean its smashed up, but the rear of this thing...that's a bullet."

"Are you sure?"

"Maybe I should get Frank down here."

Colin reacts nervously. "No. Um, give him a break, okay? He's off duty, Ben. It's Labor Day."

"Colin, this might be important. The neighbors said they heard shots...and I'm starting to remember things too. I'm pretty sure I heard something."

"Pretty sure?"

"Well, yeah. The doctors say once a memory returns, don't force it. Just let it fill in the blanks naturally. That's what I've been doing."

Colin wipes sweaty palms down his thighs. "That's good. You should keep doing that, but we don't need Mr. Taylor for that."

Ben's invigorated tone catches Colin off guard. "You know what I keep hearing more and more in my head? Moretti's cocky voice confronting Charlie...calling her a 'little bitch.' He taunted her, Colin, saying the magazine was out of the gun. That magazine is what I'm remembering most. It was on the floor, and so was I...staring right at it."

"Could have been anything. I mean, there was a lot of crap on the floor by then."

"Yeah maybe. But I saw Charlie pick it up."

"No, I don't think so. Moretti took the gun, and he picked up the magazine too."

"Moretti was wearing gloves. I should know. He was pummeling my face. No, he didn't pick up the magazine...those were slender hands. A woman's hands."

Colin paces past the hammock. He loses perspective on where Ben is standing. He hears the ice sloshing around in the ice chest. Then, chipping sounds.

"What are you doing?"

"Trying to dig this thing out."

"Hey Ben, slow down okay. We can do this tomorrow. The tree's not going anywhere."

Ben is breathing heavily. "Right, right. I should take it easy." He comes close to Colin and grabs his arm.

Colin feels the opener on his hand and takes it. "Okay, that's better. Now, just chill out." For a moment, just a fleeting few seconds, Colin feels in control.

And then Ben's words wallop him. "She never dropped the gun." Colin's knees tremble as Ben breaks through his fog. "She had it the whole time," he says emphatically.

Colin corrects Ben's absurd revelation...trying to convince himself. "No, no, Moretti grabbed it from her before he took off. That's what...she...said."

"I don't think so, Colin. She tucked it behind her...in her waistband. She raised her shirt and tucked it there. I remember now...she had a huge brush burn on her back. I'm not imagining it. I'm not."

Colin drops the opener to the ground. He rubs his hands through his scalp. "Okay Ben, okay. Let's talk about this later." A burst of laughter drifts down. "Now's not the time."

The next few hours are dreadful for Colin. He feels isolated. Ben is very quiet, but everyone probably attributes his silence to his slow recovery and too many beers. Besides, they're having a good time. Mr. Stiles teases Charlie. Tracey and Hannah share subdued conversations laced with laughter. Their relief is raw and real and comforting to everyone around them. Frank Taylor is the life of the party. Far different from the cantankerous detective who scared the piss out of him in the hospital. He is surrounded by the sounds of happiness and hope. But Colin's world is shrinking.

Katie is the first to leave, announcing that she has an early flight to catch in the morning. She asks Colin to walk her out to the car. "What's going on? You turned into a major party pooper."

"Sorry. I'm a little overwhelmed I guess."

"Colin?"

"Okay, okay. Ben is starting to open up. Starting to remember things about the break-in that I thought he would forget."

"Anything you want to talk about?"

"I don't know where to start. We'll talk when you get back."

She opens her car door. "Sounds like a plan. Take it easy buddy. You've been through a lot. We'll talk soon."

Katie's Oldsmobile rumbles toward the cul-de-sac end of his street. He waits. She comes roaring past, revving her engine, and honking her horn. He waves. His arm feels heavy. He turns to go back to the house and almost collides with Charlie. "Hey, I didn't hear you."

"I didn't want to interrupt. Everything okay? You seemed quiet today."

"Sorry, I have a lot on my mind. Um, do you have time to talk, maybe we can take a walk?" He gently finds her arm and slides his hand down to her elbow. "Come on. Let's walk."

"Okay, but let's stick close to the house. Some nasty storm clouds headed this way."

"We won't go far." He turns instinctively toward the cul-de-sac. "This way."

Out here, away from the tiny creek that skirts his backyard, everything sounds different. The limbs of trees barely move. The gentle meandering of the Little Crum is missing. Backyard festivities are muted. Crumbling asphalt crunches beneath his leaden feet.

Charlie breaks the silence. "Tell me, what's on your mind?"

"You said that Moretti took off with his Luger, right?"

"Uh huh." Colin notices the slightest slip in her gait before she says, "why are you asking?"

"Ben's memory is returning. He's painting a different picture."

"Colin, we've got to get Mr. Stiles home, could you get to the point?"

"Did you take the gun?"

She pulls her elbow away, leaving him isolated. "Why are you doing this?"

"Doing what? It's a simple question."

"Nothing's simple, Colin. You of all people should know that."

He reaches for her but only hears the retreat of shuffling feet. “Charlie, you’re not going to lose me out here. I can find my way back to the house.”

The shuffling stops. “I’m not going anywhere.”

“Then talk to me. Just tell me the truth.”

He feels her coming closer. The subtle scent of roses, ruined quickly by her jarring question, “what was Ben trying to dig out of the tree?”

His jaw tightens. Timidly, he responds, “you saw that?”

“It looked like you were trying to stop him. Why?”

Colin’s shoulders sag. “Because things are better now. Moretti is gone. It’s not perfect but we have justice.”

She gently whispers, “so now *you’re* the judge and jury. You already have the casing, so why not hide the bullet too. Sounds like you can live with that, right?”

“There’s a lot I’m living with Charlie. Things I can’t change.” He senses they’re near the end of the cul-de-sac. “There’s a bench over there, by the path to the creek.”

“I see it.” She offers her hand. It feels clammy. “Let’s sit down.”

The bench is nothing more than a concrete slab on a couple tree stumps. He plops down but she remains standing in front of him. “Colin, there’s something I need to tell you. No matter what I say, it’s not going to come out right...”

He doesn’t respond. The cement is tearing into his thighs.

“The day I met you. The first day...I already knew about Gino Moretti.”

Colin is breathless. He barely utters, “how?”

“Because of my dad.”

“He knew Moretti?”

Charlie exhales forever. “Hear me out, okay?”

“Sure...okay.”

“I love my dad, but he’s a crooked cop. He...just...made some mistakes that he regrets now. Got himself in too deep with the wrong people. The wrong person...”

“Moretti?”

"Of course. It started with small stuff. Looking the other way on petty crimes. Tipping him off when a bust was about to go down. Then it escalated. Tampering with evidence. He started stealing drugs."

"Holy shit, Charlie."

"Yeah, tell me about it. Moretti started demanding money or else he would blow it up. Tell the cops. Even worse, the feds. You know the drill. Extortion, bribery. My father was screwed. Then my mom got sick. He was afraid of losing his medical insurance. Hell, he was scared his whole pension, their retirement, was in jeopardy. He begged Moretti to give him a break. But the prick did the opposite. Demanded more. That's why my dad got the job at the scrap yard. He had to tell my mom the whole shitty story. Now, my mom is a sweet, sweet person. Before she got sick, she was a realtor. A pretty good one. Level-headed, too. She's the one who kept a lid on things in our house. But she became a woman possessed, hell bent on stopping this guy from ruining our lives. Until the cancer stopped her. That's when she told me her plan. Made me promise not to tell my dad. Through her connections she had learned more and more crap about Moretti. Turns out he was screwing a lot of people. A lot. And one of them was this sweet guy out in Swarthmore who was looking for a way out, too."

Colin can't control his quivering legs. "My dad."

"Remember, there were others, too. My mom figured there was strength in numbers."

"To do what?"

"Stop him...but the cancer stopped her."

Colin dismisses a distant rumble of thunder. "So, she *was* the realtor my dad was meeting with. Katie was right."

"Katie knew?"

She said my dad liked her – they had a lot in common."

"Well, we know *that's* true."

"Why didn't you tell me?"

"I didn't even realize the connection until the day we were together on the train."

Colin interrupts, “at 30th Street Station. We ran into Moretti.”

“Right. I was overwhelmed. A man I despised…had never met… standing in front of me.”

Colin tries to stand but Charlie gently nudges him back to the bench, her hands firmly squeeze his shoulders. “Colin, hear me out.”

“You could have told me.”

“Sorry, I wasn’t thinking of you. I was thinking of *my* parents. When I realized you were on to Moretti, I had to see it through for myself…for my mom. This was our chance to…to stop him.”

“So, you used me.”

Her hands slip from his shoulders. “I’m sorry. Things were happening so fast.”

“I could have helped you.”

“Colin, get real. My mom is dying. My father was barely keeping it together. You and Katie were so twisted up trying to find your dad…I was afraid to get in the middle. And then I did exactly that. I walked straight into the middle of a shitstorm, and everything changed.”

Colin leans forward, feels his medal swaying above his knees. He imagines his father sitting next to him. He squeezes the medallion. “Why didn’t you tell your dad?”

She manages an incredulous laugh. “What, tell him that Moretti assaulted me? He would have killed him, ruined his own career, destroyed any chance our family had to get through this. No. I made choices just like you…like your mom. We’re no different.”

Loose twigs and leaves skip along the path behind them as cooler air pours down the street. Deeper rumbles of thunder taunt Colin. Still, he remains on the bench. He grips the pebbled concrete and rocks slightly. “Moretti’s death was too good to be true.”

“Really? For the first time in forever you have closure. Your mom and Tracey were smiling today. Laughing. Hopeful. And my dad? He quit the scrap yard. He's spending more time with my mom, taking care of her for the short time they have together."

"The next Moretti will come along Charlie. Somebody else is waiting in line."

"I'll deal with it. For now, I have a sliver of sanity back in my life. I thought you did too."

Pebbles of rain begin to pelt them.

Colin forces the words from his gut. "Gino Moretti didn't kill himself with his Luger."

"The police report says he did...with the same Luger that killed your dad and Sterling Honeycutt."

"Except...you had the Luger. You had the magazine."

"Says who? Poor Ben with his amnesia?"

"You're scaring me now Charlie. No. No. How would you even begin to stage a suicide? That's crazy. Tell me that's crazy!"

A flash of lightning pops and fades. Darkness returns.

She kneels in front of Colin and lays her head gently on his lap. Her voice is calm and cold.

"Big picture Colin. Our plan worked."

"AND CHARLENE, NOW...SHE'S A WILD ONE.
DO YOU THINK YOU CAN HANDLE HER?"

The rain clips his neck. "What do you mean '*our* plan.' Whose plan? Who helped you?"

Charlie stands and cradles his jaw in the palms of her hands. "Does it matter?"

Colin sweeps her hands away. He squints as red-hot rain stings his empty eyes. "Of course, it matters. The truth matters."

"No Colin. The truth hurts." She leans in and whispers, "any way you look at it...we're all just telling a thumper."

THE END

ABOUT THE AUTHOR

Paul M. Fleming

Paul finally ran out of excuses and published his breakout novel, WHEN COURAGE COMES in 2020. Now, after bidding farewell to his day job (an award-winning ad agency he started in 1987), this restless baby-boomer embraces a career combining his research skills and fondness for history with a passion for startling stories that have never been told. TELLING A THUMPER has now been added to that list. He lives in the Philly suburbs with his wife. They have two grown daughters and four fabulous grandkids who call him "Pop." This ultimate optimist with a wickedly dry sense of humor is already nurturing more unexpected tales -- usually inspired during long walks on the beach at the Jersey shore.

BOOKS BY THIS AUTHOR

When Courage Comes

"...OFFERS READERS AN ARRAY OF INTRIGUING CHARACTERS AND PLENTY OF RICH PERIOD DETAILS. A HISTORICALLY AUTHENTIC WAR TALE..." – Kirkus Reviews

"FLEMING'S RICH PERIOD PIECE IS A SENSITIVE DEPICTION OF ROMANCE AND DIVIDED LOYALTIES DURING WORLD WAR II." -- BookLife Reviews

"A POWERFUL ARGUMENT FOR THE TRIUMPH OF LOVE AND COURAGE OVER THE MOST DEEPLY ROOTED AND THREATENING EVILS."– IndieReader

Made in the USA
Columbia, SC
12 October 2024